# STRANGER THAN KINDNESS

# STRANGER
# THAN KINDNESS

## Mark A Radcliffe

**Bluemoose**

*For Maia and Katie*

Copyright © Mark A Radcliffe 2013

First published in 2013 by
Bluemoose Books Ltd
25 Sackville Street
Hebden Bridge
West Yorkshire
HX7 7DJ

www.bluemoosebooks.com

British Library Cataloguing-in-Publication data
A catalogue record for this book is available from the-British-Library

Paperback  ISBN 978-0-9575497-3-9

Hardback   ISBN 978-0-9575497-4-6

Printed and bound in the UK by Jellyfish Solutions Ltd

# PART 1

23ʳᵈ September 1989

# 1. The Damage Is Done

'I'd love to sit down dear, but I haven't got a body.'

Libby Hoffman was serious, if inaccurate. Of course she had a body. It wasn't a very big one, but it was a body nonetheless: old and thin, she looked like she was made from wire and tissue paper. Still, it was there and it was quite strong given her age: 85, and her occupation: lunatic. On top of this skinny, slightly stooped body sat a crinkled face with an expression set between surprise and contempt. She only smiled at Christmas and that was probably because everyone wore stupid hats, although it is possible that it was also because Christmas reminded her of something funny from before she had become a lunatic, which was a very very long time ago. Or it might have been the sherry.

Adam Sands, who was the nurse in charge, glanced up from his newspaper. The problem with raising his head was that there was more chance of the light getting him. Sure enough here it came, stabbing him through the eyes and scratching around the inside of his skull. Libby had a tea stain on her white cardigan; a student nurse looked primed to talk at her. A patient called Michael Wells was standing in front of the television with a handful of biscuits watching the news. He was wearing a filthy anorak and jeans that were misshapen enough to almost certainly belong to someone else. He was talking to the newsreader—a dour man with a posh accent—comfortable in the knowledge that the newsreader was talking right back.

A Nursing Assistant with hips the size of Belgium was standing over a dazed woman with no hair called Mary Peacock. Belgium was telling her loudly that she needed to open her bowels, preferably into or at least near a toilet. A tiny Irish cleaner was singing show tunes as she mopped the floor outside the nurse's office. Beyond that there wasn't much to see. Adam returned to his paper. He liked to think that by sitting in the day room, by being seen, he lent a sense of safety to the ward. He also thought that his presence would serve to filter out any acts of unkindness or cruelty. The Nursing Assistant, for example, was less likely to lift the confused and obese Mary Peacock up and drop her on to a commode if the charge nurse was sitting nearby. He was not oblivious to the fact that his being there did not stop her from shouting about bowels while the breakfast trolley was still being put away, but Adam believed that if you ask too much of people they will rush to disappoint you.

Adam still read newspapers from the back, starting with the football and leaving the real world until last. Today's outrage was another bomb. This one in Kent on an army barracks, killing eleven people. Adam never looked at the pictures or read beyond the first few lines. A decade of tabloid jingoism and bile about distant colonial wars and 'enemies within' had rendered him immune to the fact that outside of the hospital everyone seemed to hate everyone else. Anyway, he was skim-reading because his head hurt. He was dehydrated from the cheap whisky the night before, and the half-life of last night's diazepam probably didn't help either and if that in itself wasn't enough to numb the brain, Dire bloody Straits were playing on the radio in the background.

This sort of music still made Adam think of Live Aid. He had hated it; thousands of people with bad hair coming together to do some self-congratulatory clapping. When they showed the images of dying, pot-bellied babies overlaid with the carefully chosen soundtrack he cried, of course he did, but unlike his soon-to-depart live-in girlfriend Catherine, who cried very loudly for bloody ages, he wasn't reassured by his tears. He didn't feel they made him a better human being: rather, he just feared he was being manipulated.

He told someone he was in bed with a few weeks later that he was perhaps the only person who didn't give any money to Live Aid.

'I don't know anyone who gave money to it,' she said. 'You can't buy your own conscience.' Which he didn't understand but they had sex anyway.

'There are only two emotions available to us nowadays,' she whispered later. 'You can be either smug or angry. We live in a time where music is for people who don't like music and politics is for people who don't like people.'

That was all he remembered of that night, that and the fact that her soft dark skin had smelled of sweetened coconut. He wished he could remember more; he rather thought he'd like to listen to other things she said.

'Libby, if you haven't got a body how did you get here?' The student was doing some nursing and he was doing it near Adam.

Libby Hoffman ignored the boy. She stood completely still, staring at the blank yellow wall of the day room and hooking her bony thin finger through a hole in her cardigan. Adam had come to know this as her brace position.

'Libby, I am talking to you: how did you get here if you haven't got a body?' He spoke with a see-saw rhythm, too shrill to be warm, too loud to be kind.

'I walked, you silly bugger,' Libby said. Her mouth continued moving after the words as though she was still speaking, or chewing.

Adam almost smiled. He glanced over at the student: he had the thickest hair he had ever seen on a man, a great big bush of mousy brown fleece which stood upright on his head. It had to, there was nowhere for it to settle on the crowded and ungentle head.

'Please don't use that sort of language,' said the boy. 'Come and sit by me,' he instructed, but Libby hadn't wanted to sit beside anyone since the early 1960s. 'Libby. Libby.' The student was getting even louder and Libby Hoffman was moving her weight from one foot to another, like a child who needed the toilet.

The radio was playing *Careless Whisper* by George Michael. 'The bastards,' thought Adam. He looked at Libby and his chest burned a little. He looked beyond her to the office, where he could see one of the new Community Psychiatric Nurses charged with emptying the hospital into the real world, standing at the door, watching. She was unfamiliar and pretty, a slight frame in a long purple skirt and black shirt, jet black hair, bit of a Goth but not so much that you wouldn't take her seriously if she said something about a patient. He closed his eyes, took a deep breath and said surprisingly clearly: 'Libby, you might want to change your cardigan. Student nurse person, please put the kettle on. And will somebody please do something about the radio? Do the people who live on this ward look like George Michael's target audience?' He added more quietly: 'Does George Michael have a target audience? He may be like napalm in that regard. No, I think he probably does and it's not quite the same as ours, so stop it with George Michael someone, thank you.' He felt quite exhausted.

Libby stopped hopping, turned instantly round and walked to her bed area to change her cardigan. Adam heard the Community Nurse say something to Grace in the office. He heard a laugh; the radio station was changed to something less current. Sandie Shaw maybe, or was it Petula Clarke? The student nurse didn't move.

Adam sighed. 'Are you above putting the kettle on?'

'It's not really why I am here.' The student nurse was practicing defiance or assertiveness or belligerence or contempt. Adam thought he appeared to be better at it than he was at talking to patients.

'No, of course, but then why are any of us here? Don't answer that. Have you had any tea today?'

'Yes.' It was definitely contempt.

'Who made it?' Adam was aware of the fact that he sounded patronizing. He knew that probably wouldn't help. He couldn't bring himself to care.

'Pardon?'

'Who made the tea you drank this morning?' Now Adam looked directly at him: he saw a pale face, a jutting jaw, the barrow-load of hair.

'Grace.' The student saw a man in his mid to late twenties wearing a stupid Hawaiian shirt and what was clearly a hangover.

'Well why don't you make her one now? She'd like that.'

'I don't really want any tea,' the student said.

Adam put his paper down and looked at the young man. He tried to read his name badge. He spoke very quietly. He stopped sounding patronizing and he nearly sounded warm. 'Look, William, it is William isn't it?' The student nodded. 'It seems to me that I can take one of three approaches here. The first, not sophisticated, not educational, but emotionally congruent for me at least, involves me telling you that if you ever speak to Libby Hoffman like that again I will remove one of your arms and beat you around your ridiculously hairy head with it until you learn some bloody manners. The second is to spend an inordinate amount of time helping you begin to notice when you sound like an arse. The third involves telling you to make tea. I'm told the first is unprofessional, the second is too tiring, so we are going for number three, OK?'

William's mouth moved but nothing came out. He wasn't sure he had heard right. Was that like a threat, the arm and head thing? Or is that the way these people talk? These ignorant, burnt-out, badly dressed, newspaper-wielding people. He imagined making a complaint to the head of the School of Nursing. 'He said he was going to hit me with my own arm,' he would say and she would look at him with the sort of pitying disdain she tended to wear whenever she noticed him. Two of a kind, he thought. Let it pass but don't look intimidated. He swallowed hard. 'I don't want any tea, thanks.'

'No. No, but you need it. You need tea.' Adam was looking into the young man's eyes and speaking even more softly, so that William found himself leaning forward even though his body wanted to step back.

'I don't.'

'You do. Tea is one of our punctuation marks. Cigarettes are another, writing in the notes another. Let's just work with the tea today, OK? Think of it as a damp comma, actually a full stop and an opportunity to begin a new paragraph. After the nonsense you were just offering you need at least a full stop. It will slow you down, maybe make you think. Stop you from baiting Libby...' William went to speak but Adam raised his finger and continued: 'We act, we stop. When we stop, sometimes we need to think about what we have done and what we may do next and one of the ways of doing that, of pausing between bouts of silliness, is tea. Otherwise you run the risk of not really stopping or thinking, and acting without thinking is what monkeys do and we aren't monkeys are we? That is a rhetorical question. So take a moment to pause and reflect, otherwise you may just carry on in the same vein as your last action and in your case the last one wasn't very good, in fact it was really poor, so tea, don't knock it. No sugar for me, thank you.'

The student paused a moment. He went to speak, then chose instead to use his pause as a sign that he was going to speak but just not immediately. He knew what he needed to say. He needed to say the tea thing was bollocks, not in those words of course, but it was. And that he wasn't baiting Libby, he was doing some nursing: look it up, it's what nurses are meant to do, you badly-dressed drunk. Who the hell wears Hawaiian shirts to an asylum anyway? The patients, maybe, but hell, that's almost a symptom. And who are you to say the patients don't like George Michael? Or tell me to make tea. Everything that is wrong with the world is summed up by you, your stupid shirt and that rubbish about tea. Now how do I say that without getting into trouble? Or hit with my own arm. And the words were coming, slowly, something about trying to build a relationship with the nutty old dear and not really believing the tea thing, when a Community Psychiatric Nurse appeared behind him. Pretty woman, mid twenties, nice breasts.

She smiled a forced smile that didn't reach her eyes, looked straight at him and said:

'He's right about the tea. No sugar for me either, thanks. And hello, my name is Anna.' The last part was directed mainly at Adam.

Anna Newton had spent the best part of the preceding hour in a small room with a lonely, smelly man who had been very heavily sedated for eighteen years and had a swastika tattooed on his forehead. The same man, Michael Wells, who was currently chatting amiably to the television newsreader. She was helping him to prepare for discharge into the community. Twice a week counselling, a new social worker, a new psychiatrist, extra medication and lots of crossed fingers: all pointless, she thought. Mostly he needed a bath and a really big bandanna. She had another patient to see in thirty minutes, a woman who had lived in this hollow old asylum for forty-five years. She hadn't worn shoes since 1954 and her preferred way of showing her displeasure to a world that didn't always do what she required was to take off all her clothes and try to wee on whoever was denying her whatever small pleasure she was pursuing. Anna had a place lined up for her in a nice converted house near Hampstead Heath. She would share the home with five other long-term patients. God help the first shop that doesn't hand over her cigarettes quickly enough. Anna was OK preparing the patients; she sometimes wondered who was preparing the community.

She waited until the student nurse entered the kitchen before turning to Adam and saying: 'I think that probably counts as a teaching session. Have you considered going into education?'

Adam looked down the empty corridor and said distractedly: 'Hasn't he got a lot of hair?'

He looked up and saw a lithe body and sarcastic eyes. She stared at him. He wondered why, before remembering that she had told him her name. 'I'm Adam,' he said. 'So will I get a certificate or something?'

'Excuse me?'

'For the teaching.'

'I think you'll be lucky to get away without him spitting in your tea.'

'Is he the sort?'

Anna shrugged.

'Yeah,' he said, standing up. 'I'll go and see, just in case.' He wandered down the ward, rolling his head and stretching his arms out behind him as he went. He was taller than he had looked when he was sitting down, Anna thought, and when he moved he looked more human.

Adam was reflecting on the good-looking stranger. She had too many bracelets, and bright red lipstick which he liked and she had lovely hair, very straight, very shiny. As he walked to the kitchen he wondered how often she washed it, and then he wondered why he was so preoccupied with the top of other people's heads. By the time he got to the kitchen he had forgotten why he had come, but the kettle hadn't even boiled so he said to the student, just to confuse him, 'Do you want a hand with that at all?'

A few days later there was a house party and Adam had taken two thioridazine—a minor tranquilizer that relaxed him without making him dribble—from the drug trolley before leaving work, and then downed half a bottle of cheap sherry. There were many 'parties' spilling from the hospital. They were not designed to celebrate anything in particular but to provide a gathering point for drinking, gossiping and flirting. This 'party' was hosted by Stephen Moss, the charge nurse of the acute ward where Adam had worked until the previous year.

Temperamentally Stephen and Adam could not be more different: Stephen was flamboyant and camp; he hated being on his own only marginally more than he hated other people. He wore an excessive amount of eye makeup, but only round the house, and he drank cheap champagne and cocktails without ever appearing any more drunk than he did usually, which was actually quite drunk. Adam and Stephen had trained together as very young men a little over five years earlier. They had seen each other shrink in the face of their workplace and slowly change shape as the asylum became the most normal place on earth. And while they grew they shared drink, drugs and an exaggerated disdain for everything from careerists to voyeurs, and from hope to volition.

Stephen had been on duty the day Graham Cochrane, a twenty-eight year old depressed man, had beaten Adam at chess, nodded to him, walked to his room and drunk a litre of industrial bleach. Graham had died spewing his disintegrating throat into Adam's lap and all Adam could do as others turned their heads or pretended to go for help was cradle Graham's head, staring into dying, popping eyes. There were tiny spittle-sized lumps of bloodied Graham soaking through Adam's trousers, leaving baby scars on his thighs, unseen weals that still remained. It had been a while since Adam transferred from that acute ward to the slow rehabilitation ward he managed now. It had been a while since Adam had slept through the night.

When Adam arrived Stephen greeted him with three yellow pills. 'No thanks, I've already eaten,' Adam said. Stephen shrugged, swallowed two of the tablets, looked at the third, shrugged again and swallowed that too.

'Anna's here,' he said, exaggerating a leer.

'Anna who?' Adam deadpanned.

'Anna who indeed.'

Stephen lived in a basement flat about two miles from the hospital. It had a large rectangular living room and a dark blue carpet that somehow absorbed the light. It was true that Anna was cute, but mostly Adam wandered over to speak to her because she was the only person in the house he didn't know. There were about fifteen people milling around the living room, all of whom he knew from the hospital.

Anna was dressed in black jeans and shirt. She was standing beside a table that was full of drinks, spirits mostly, with mixers, some wine, a few cans of beer and some cheap sherry. Anna was pouring herself a whisky and coke. She was slightly built, around five foot four; she looked like a gothic, not quite as pretty, Audrey Hepburn. Adam was nearly a foot taller and looking at the world through a chemical fog. When he tried to talk to her the height difference made him self-conscious. He poured himself a drink, the same as hers, leaned on the wall, felt ridiculous and said: 'I'm not a natural leaner.'

She laughed and pointed at two empty chairs pushed up against the blue wall. They sat down in silence for almost a minute, staring forward. Eventually Adam said 'This is like being on a bus.'

'Rubbish bus,' Anna said. 'Not going anywhere.' A longer silence, comfortable and easy. 'You were not very kind to that student today,' she said tentatively.

He shrugged. 'I was kinder than I might have been. He was being an oaf.'

'Who uses the word oaf anymore? And anyway he is a student, he is here to learn.'

He couldn't tell if she was being sarcastic. 'Righto.'

She sipped her drink. 'Mind you, he does seem to be a bit of a tosser.'

Adam didn't look at her. He was watching Stephen being garish and sweaty near three female staff nurses, one of whom was Grace from his ward. The women were laughing hysterically and Stephen was loving the validation. The more they laughed the more flamboyant, and damp, he became.

'I don't mind him being unskilled,' said Adam impassively. 'I mind him being unkind.' He was a little fuzzy headed: the alcohol was mixing with the tranquilizers he had taken. His voice sounded slightly muffled. It occurred to him that he sounded faintly absurd. Before he could say anything else, Anna turned her head to look at him and said with a gloriously flirtatious smile: 'Poof.'

Adam grinned and stared straight ahead. Stephen had moved into the kitchen and the three women were left surfing on the hysteria he had swamped them with. They were smiling, chatting, pointing at different people in the room. Grace was not conventionally attractive. She was plump, with wide hips and mousy-coloured hair, but she had the prettiest skin and brightest eyes Adam had ever seen, and she always dressed in bold printed skirts that swirled around when she moved. Adam liked her, mostly because he believed she could see the truth but never made a big deal about it. She waved at Adam and said something that made the other two women look over and laugh briefly. Adam nodded and smiled back. Anna sipped her drink again. 'Do you think the student was particularly annoying to you because he was talking to Libby Hoffman, or are you like that all the time?'

'I have known Libby a long time,' Adam said as neutrally as he could.

They had turned their attention to two people dancing in the middle of the room to a Cure song. A young woman—a final year student on the cusp of qualifying who Adam had nearly accidentally slept with the previous Christmas—was shaking her breasts self-mockingly at an even younger man, who was wearing cords and therefore probably a Social Worker. He hopped uncertainly from one foot to another, hoping that either the music would stop soon or other people would start dancing and stop watching him and the breast-shaking woman, who was drunk and looked like she might hurt him.

'I use the office on your ward to do paperwork some evenings,' Anna said without looking at Adam.

'That's nice.'

'Why do you go there?' she asked softly, as if she was interested in the answer. 'I've seen you.'

'It's my job.' Adam felt his chest tighten just a little.

'Why do you go there when you're not working, then? Why do you go to the ward at night?'

Adam looked at her impassively, raised his glass, smiled a half smile, stood up and said: 'Excuse me.'

He found Stephen in the kitchen being exaggeratedly camp and just a little bored. 'Do you have any more of those sweets?' he asked.

'That bad, huh?' Stephen handed him a bottle from the top pocket of his shirt. Adam took two, then a third, nodded and wandered off as Stephen was telling his audience about the time he was mistaken for Princess Grace of Monaco.

Anna and Adam did not speak again for a couple of hours. Adam watched the party from as close to the outside as he could get. He flirted idly with the soon-to-be-qualified dancing woman. He listened to Stephen mock all social workers as if they were Satan's soldiers while desperately trying to get the dancing social worker to like him. And he asked Grace about her mother, who had emphysema, and her boyfriend, who was twenty years older than Grace, married to someone else and extraordinarily dull. Anna meanwhile circumnavigated the room in the opposite direction. Talking to the two staff nurses who had been with Grace earlier, letting herself be chatted up by a chubby, over-confident Occupational Therapist who was wearing a tie and exchanging a raft of double entendres with Stephen. Eventually they found themselves back beside each other.

'You look hot,' she said.

'Thank you,' he smiled.

'Not that kind of hot.'

Adam's head felt as if it was shrinking. His arms were numb, like when he needed them in a dream and they wouldn't work; he looked at his hands to make sure they were still there. Anna's mouth was moving but she wasn't saying anything, or if she was he couldn't hear her. The dancing social worker had begun bobbing up and down next to the breast-wiggling nurse again. The man stopped for a moment, stepped over to the mantelpiece, picked up a bottle and drank from it. As he put the bottle to his lips Adam felt himself fill with a toxic dread. His breathing quickened; his chest was tight now. He tried to speak but nothing came out. He stepped forward towards the man but his legs felt unsure, untrusting of the floor. He felt a hand on his arm. He instinctively went to move his arm away but the hand was soft and it followed him. It wrapped itself around his forearm and gently guided him away from the dancing drinking man. Adam followed his arm out of the living room door.

He was in the hallway, standing against the wall. He was sweating and cold and Anna was standing in front of him. Adam looked down at his body: his shirt was damp and patchily transparent. She let go of his arm and rested her hand on his chest for a moment. His breathing slowed a little, his chest became less tight. 'I need some air,' he said quietly. He walked the few steps down the pale hallway to the front door. It was cool outside and it had been raining lightly. He breathed in deeply and shivered. Anna had followed him. He sat on the front doorstep and she crouched beside him.

'Did you bring a jacket or something?'

He nodded. She paused for a moment before standing up and going back indoors. The moon was quite bright; there were a few thin grey clouds spinning across the sky. Adam pulled himself to his feet and let his head settle. He began to walk. Out of the gate and along the road.

The hospital at night would have been macabre if it weren't for the strip lighting and the echo from the laundry rooms. In the daytime it was a graceless monument to madness; in the dark it visited its past. Emptied of the scuffling patients and the preoccupied workers. The smell of its history lingered always. Stale urine and damp: it would be here for another hundred years. If the hospital became luxury flats or a supermarket or a car park it would be haunted by the stench of urine. When Adam first started here he worked on an elderly ward. He was always the first to do the dirty jobs, always maintaining that he would not be taken seriously unless he was seen by the cynical staff to take the ugliest of tasks and come back for more. That smell used to follow him home. He would bathe every evening and constantly ask Catherine if she could smell anything. She would laugh and say he was deluded and he would smile, but it was there, in his nostrils. After a while he stopped noticing it, but occasionally when he was out in a restaurant or at a gig it would creep into him again, linger a while, invade his senses and his sensibilities. His mood would change slightly. That smell would settle just beneath his skin, draw him back to the hospital and leave him with the feeling that there was something he had left undone.

Adam was walking down the longest corridor in Europe. Some of the lights flickered but you could still see the paint peeling from the ceiling and walls all the way along it. He imagined it was because the paint was either too thin or simply embarrassed by all it had seen. The walls had seen Adam a hundred times, maybe a thousand times, often at night and lately often when he was not on duty. He came here more now, since he had changed wards, since Graham had died. He rarely saw anyone—patients were asleep, wards were locked, the laundry carts wouldn't start until after 5am—but tonight, up ahead, he saw a young man crouching beside one of the windows that looked out onto the grounds. As Adam got closer he thought he would recognize the boy, but he couldn't place him. He expected him to look up but he didn't, although he must have sensed Adam approaching. When Adam drew alongside, the boy spoke with a soothing soft lilt. 'I love this time of morning.' He was a thin, good-looking young man with darkish curly hair and olive skin. Adam could not decide if he was patient or staff.

'Are you supposed to be here?' Adam tried to ask gently but the words still made him sound like a policeman and he closed his eyes in frustration at that.

The boy didn't look up but smiled slightly and said 'Are you?'

Adam laughed. 'Probably not.' He stopped himself from asking what ward he should be on and liked himself a tiny bit more for that. He noticed that the young man was not dressed like a patient. His clothes fitted and matched. They were clean. They looked chosen.

'Sometimes I sit and watch the night and wait for the sun to come up. At this time of year there is a beautiful mist that forms and covers the ground. As it clears you can see the dew glisten through the last bands of haze until all you can see is dampness lightly washing the ground.' He turned to face Adam for the first time and smiled. He had beautiful blue eyes. 'It just looks lovely, and it's hard to see it and not feel hope, you know?'

Adam nodded. 'Have a nice day.'

The boy nodded slightly and turned back to the window 'You could do worse than notice the sunrise, you know, and a lot worse than see the dew on the grass.'

Adam smiled to himself and thought 'hippie' as he walked on.

The ward door was locked. Adam's head felt cleaner now but his body was cold. It was late September; he was wearing a white cotton shirt and thin black trousers. He didn't have any socks on, just plimsolls. And he was just remembering that he had not eaten anything since a banana that morning. He unlocked the ward door and walked straight to the dayroom. In the office, the night nurse rested between two chairs which were draped with a clean sheet. All the night staff sat on clean sheets, just in case they caught madness. The sound of the ward door obviously woke him. On seeing it was Adam he raised his arm.

The night nurse was not particularly surprised to see him. It was two forty-five in the morning; the clock on the wall told him so.

Adam didn't bother to exchange pleasantries with the nurse. In the beginning he used to offer excuses for his visits, but it soon became clear that they weren't necessary once the nurse realized that Adam was not there to check up on him. He was the charge nurse, after all: there was little to be gained in interfering with the things that he did.

Adam walked to the female end of the ward. There he found six beds all in a line. If it were less of a hallway it could almost be a dormitory. In each bed slept a woman, old but still functioning enough to be on a rehabilitation ward instead of the slow death of the overfull elderly units. At the end slept Freda, her head perfectly still in the air, floating six inches above her pillow. Freda never talked, never ever. Except when some new student, zealous and concerned, doing their first set of nights, approached her in the night and suggested she rest her head. Freda slept on a psychological pillow: an invisible imagined head rest that only she could feel. If, and this happened at least once a year, a well meaning student roused her to tell her to rest her head, the presumed mute Freda would bellow: 'Get out of it, you little toe rag.' She said that to Adam once. Maybe a hundred years before. In the bed next to her was Libby. Adam was the only visitor she had ever had, apart from the occasional Christian in December. Adam came often these days. He pulled up a chair and sat beside her. Relief washed over him.

He stared at the old woman. She lay on her back and breathed evenly. Libby remembered how to sleep, as she remembered many things. She was covered by a rough orange bedspread and white sheets, crisp and clean. To Adam's left was a window. Across from there lay the other end of the ward. Offices mainly. Empty now, as most nights, but that would be where Anna worked.

Adam began to rock gently in the chair. He was still cold but he had stopped shivering. 'I thought I saw him again tonight. Looked like him... except he had a throat, the bastard.'

Libby didn't stir, she never did. Adam talked softly. Once it had crossed his mind to climb on to the bed and try to sleep the way she did, but of course he didn't. No matter how screamingly desperate he was for sleep, he was still a professional after all.

Adam leaned forward, resting his head on the bed. 'I'm tired' he murmured, talking into the bedspread now. The cheap fabric was coarse but warm; his eyes were thick, closing. A puddle of saliva gathered at the corner of his mouth. Adam lifted his heavy head and looked at the sleeping old woman. 'I'll just rest here a minute if that's OK.' And then: 'I'm sorry about that student earlier, pet. I hope he didn't upset you...'

# 2. This Woman's Work

The day after the party Anna was doing her job, although increasingly it felt as though she came to work and watched as her job did her.

Maureen Marley was a forty-three year old mother of three who believed herself—with complete and unchallengeable conviction—to be a thirty-eight year old man called George Wimimundu. She did not believe she had children and she certainly did not she believe she had a vagina. The obvious advice brought by students both medical and nursing was to show her the space where her penis should be and ask her to explain where it had gone, but if you are a man and a stranger asks you to prove it by showing them your penis, you will not normally greet that with acquiescence. Whatever Maureen Marley saw when she looked between her legs was her business and she certainly wasn't going to discuss it with anyone else.

Maureen Marley had been in the hospital for nine years. She had been George Wimimundu for nine years and four months. Her children did not visit or write any more. They had been pushed away by the blank looks and low dog-like growl that had greeted the word 'mummy'. The kids were bigger now; they had learnt to dislike her, be ashamed of her, and ultimately to not speak of her. Here in this walled Victorian asylum she was hidden away, and that suited them. It also suited her husband, Benjamin, who now shared his life with a large Jamaican woman called Rita who had five kids of her own and no problems whatsoever in accepting Benjamin's and Maureen's three to her ample bosom, even though the oldest of them was twenty-four now and didn't want to go anywhere near Rita's bosom.

There were two ways of thinking about Maureen Marley and those two ways illustrated the duality of psychiatric care that Anna was employed to bridge. On the one hand Maureen was deluded. She dressed like a saxophone player in a 1950s jazz band: sharp two-piece suit, open necked shirt with a loose tie. She wore black Doc Martens even in the summer and was clean-shaven not because she was a woman but because she shaved every morning. She flirted with the women patients, rolled cigarettes with one hand and joined in with the half-hearted leers that accompanied the Benny Hill show when it wandered on to the television on a Wednesday night.

On the other hand she was, apart from one single and admittedly unusual idea about herself, completely healthy. She was able to help out around the ward and particularly enjoyed the 'proper' work that involved lifting things up and putting them down somewhere else. When the mini tractor that pulled the laundry cart came to pick up the big white sacks of soiled linen, the plump Greek porter didn't even have to get up from his seat at the front. He would exchange betting tips and light a cigarette as Maureen Marley grinned affably and loaded the cart for him. One of the social workers once commented that this seemed wrong, that it somehow exploited her psychosis and that the nurses, in ignoring it, were exposing her vulner-ability. Everyone ignored the social worker. They knew how rarely Maureen grinned.

Maureen enjoyed a fulfilling if limited social life, leaving the ward every day to go to the bookies and maybe nip into the pub for a pint. She could talk about football, television and Margaret Thatcher with the same levels of loudness, flippancy and derision as everybody else. She was effectively a pretty ordinary bloke, for a woman.

She was not a lesbian. That would, by definition, involve being a woman. As far as anyone could tell, she had had no sexual relationships with women and nor had she enjoyed any emotionally binding relationships with anyone since she decided she was a man. Ironically, if she had, for example, checked her genitalia, registered that they were female, noted that this made her unhappy and sustained and articulated that unhappiness for a period of time, aligning it with some sort of argument that conceded that she was in fact a woman but really felt like a man, she might have received affirmative support, counselling or even surgery that would enable her to change her gender. However, she did not mount a case for manhood so much as simply assume it, despite the evidence, and that was an offence against reason. Wanting to be something you are not is aspirational; assuming you are something everyone says you are not is insane.

The hospital was emptying. Community Care was the way forward: radical, modern, liberating. It was going to free the incarcerated and return them to a normal life. It was also going to save lots of money. Progressive and economically advantageous, as an idea it couldn't have been more Eighties if it had dressed like Simon Le Bon and sung in a really whiny voice. Maureen Marley had quite frankly done very well to hold on as long as she had. There were plenty of patients less able to adapt to living in the community—which mostly meant moving to a house with five other alleged lunatics and some low-paid nursing assistants and staying indoors a lot—than Maureen, and there were an awful lot of people still left in the hospital who were going to be much harder to shift. Not least most of the staff.

So Maureen Marley was on the list, which meant seeing Anna every week to discuss and prepare for the transition. Maureen Marley, who gave the impression of being sanguine and self-contained, didn't seem remotely bothered by it. She was a small black woman of medium build; her short-cropped hair augmented her sexlessness. If she didn't speak, most casual observers might consider her male and perhaps this was why she rarely spoke. She almost smiled sometimes though, an Elvis Presley half-smile half-sneer that looked at once shy and sarcastic. When Anna talked to her about the new house Maureen would be living in, its bathroom facilities, its garden, its proximity to the bookies, Maureen would do her smile and sometimes nod, not in an encouraging way but more in a 'who are you kidding' sort of way. After nine years of living on an alleged rehabilitation ward in a crumbling asylum—a ward that she shared with twenty-three other patients, who ranged from a former bus conductor with an Obsessive Compulsive Disorder that demanded he take an hour to choose and put on his socks every morning, to Libby Hoffman who was 85 years old, had been an inpatient for 58 years and had lost her body sometime before they invented Rock and Roll—she really wasn't going to take anyone seriously.

Anna did try to edge toward the idea that one other, perhaps long-term, possibility might involve Maureen Marley maybe seeing her kids too, but Maureen Marley appeared to greet the suggestion that she had kids in the same way that the Pope might.

'Can I ask you: do you have a family?' Anna said once, trying for a different approach.

'Yeah,' said Maureen. 'I have two sisters.'

'No kids?'

Maureen just stared at her as if the question made no sense, or perhaps as if the answer was unutterable.

So Anna had decided to focus on the practical. What did Maureen need to be able to do in order to survive and hopefully thrive? Cooking: that was a problem. For one thing, having lived in the hospital for nine years Maureen had had her food presented to her from a trolley every mealtime. On the odd occasion, when a care plan that sought to extend her capacity to live outside an institution had demanded she re-learn how to prepare her own food, she had mostly stirred whatever pot was put in front of her and laughed to herself before retreating first to her bed and then, on finding that someone would come and get her, out to the bookies. Cooking was women's work; it may even have been one of the reasons that Maureen Marley had resigned from womanhood in the first place.

And there was also grocery shopping to consider. In preparation for discharge Maureen had to buy and prepare her own tea at least twice a week. In her former life Maureen had shopped and cooked for a family of five. Now her rehabilitation programme involved persuading her to prepare to live more independently. And her shopping was the shopping of a single man. It mostly consisted of bread, beans and rolling tobacco. Sometimes a newspaper was involved; gradually, crispy snacks and brightly coloured pot noodles were creeping into the basket. And it was a hand-held basket. Trolleys were also for women.

With three weeks to go until Maureen was to be moved, Anna was trying to arrange a morning when she could visit the house she would be living in and maybe see her room, meet some of the staff and generally get a sense that her proposed discharge wasn't a really bad joke. In Anna's view, seeing the room and meeting the staff were less important than actually reinforcing to Maureen that change was going to happen, the house was real and the hospital was going to close down.

'We could go together Maureen,' she had said. Maureen Marley had shrugged. Impassive, mildly uncomfortable, sitting in a large orange chair in a high-ceilinged yellow interview room that had only one window, which was small and too high to see out of.

'We can have a look round, have a coffee,' Anna had said. 'You can see your room; maybe think about any furniture you might like.'

And so they had. Maureen Marley sat quietly on the bus looking out of the window and walked passively up the garden path to the suburban front door in the suburban well-to-do street near Hampstead Heath. The house smelled of furniture polish and the absence of people. A show home built from pine and scatter cushions.

The 'House Manager,' a tall African woman called Maizie, moved with an elegance that toppled into aloofness. When they arrived she shook hands with Anna and nodded to Maureen Marley; when she led them to the living room she held her hands in front of her, which made Anna feel she was in a religious procession. Maizie offered to show them round the kitchen and managed to get to it before she started reciting the house rules that she had already decided upon. All the residents would eat together at dinnertime and breakfast but lunch would be a free for all. They could have televisions in their rooms, but if they wanted to watch the one in the living room the channel would be decided by consensus. Residents, for that is what they were rather than patients, were expected to help with housework. Maureen looked momentarily confused by that. And then they all went upstairs to look at her room: it smelt of lavender and flat pack furniture. A soft yellow on the walls, plush carpet and a bed with a continental quilt on it that made the bed appear taller than it should be. Everything was new and what it lacked in character it made up for in feminine comfort. It had net curtains, and the quilt cover perfectly matched the pink and yellow floral drapes. It was wholly inappropriate for George Wimimumdu. Maureen Marley laughed her sneery laugh. Maizie ignored her but Anna watched and, after the laugh had passed, she thought she saw something akin to dread. Or humiliation.

After the tour Maureen Marley sat sipping coffee in the kitchen and Anna asked if she could see the garden. 'Maizie, what do you know about Maureen?'

'I know she is a woman who believes she is a man.' Maizie spoke with economy. Her tone was clipped, her accent heavy and her eyes were half closed.

'Right, and that belief is very fixed.' Anna spoke softly, aligning the rhythm of her words to Maizie's, looking for the place where they might meet.

'That is what I have read'

'I think she may find her room a little feminine.'

"Is she not a woman?' Maizie raised her voice on the last word, making it sound like woe-man.

'She is a woman who considers herself not to be a woman. That single belief forms the foundation of the way she chooses to live.'

'Do you think we should collude with her false belief? Do you think we should agree with her that she is a man and in effect lie to her? Do you think that is a way to gain her trust?" Maizie lifted her eyes. They shone with certainty.

'I think if we respect her she will trust us,' Anna said as quietly as she could.

'It is her room,' Maizie said with a dismissive wave of her hand. She has pianist's fingers, thought Anna. 'She can do with it as she wishes. She can put up posters of motorcars or women; she can make it smell of socks and sweat. She can sit up there and watch horse racing if she wants.'

'What if she wants it redecorated?'

'Now you are being silly,' said Maizie, turning away and walking back to the house. 'She will be fine. Indeed, perhaps here she will be better than fine.'

Back in the house Maureen Marley had found some bourbon biscuits, was on her fourth or fifth and had the packet open on the table. Maizie picked the packet up and put them away as she swept by. 'When you live here,' she said without looking at Maureen, 'You will buy your own biscuits and you will be able to eat them as much as you wish.'

On the bus home Anna asked Maureen what she had thought of the house. She just shrugged. She did not speak until the bus drew up at the hospital gates. It was beginning to rain lightly and she had spent the journey watching the raindrops race down the window, placing silent personal bets on which drop would make it to the bottom first. As she walked down the driveway to the main entrance of the hospital, with nothing interesting to distract her, her thoughts turned to her future. 'How many people will be in the house?

'Five, I think,' Anna said.

'All men?'

'I don't know.' A pause as they passed the flagpole and walked up the steps to the large wooden door. And then: 'Would you like me to find out'?

Maureen Marley just nodded. No sneer. No smile.

Later that evening Anna made herself a coffee and two slices of toast in the ward kitchen and retired to a rarely-used doctors' office to write notes, read patient profiles and fill out funding forms to ensure that someone somewhere would pay the rent for Maureen and the others. She preferred doing this at night when the place was quieter. It gave her a different sense of the hospital, a hospital she had never worked in, and a clearer sense of why moving the patients to places with carpets and walls between the beds was a better thing than it sometimes felt. It also meant she could come in late when she wanted. It was a habit she liked. Since she had been working more closely with the asylum she had found herself touched and then almost infected by its routines. Everything here was about entrenched habit. So she took comfort from constructing a little flexibility in her working life.

This evening there were two things she noticed that troubled her slightly. The first was the appearance of Adam Sands after 10.30pm. This was the seventh or eighth time she had worked late in this office and the fourth time she had seen him—and that didn't include the night before, when she was convinced he had come to the hospital when she had gone looking for his non-existent jacket. He wandered down the ward, past the dimly lit but occupied goldfish bowl office and past the small annexed office where she worked under a desk light. He walked straight down to Libby's bed and sat down. Anna could see him from where she sat and she watched, curious and nervous.

She saw him sitting there muttering. He stayed for nearly an hour. When he left he patted the side of Libby's bed. Not her hand, not any part of her that lay still and sleeping under the coarse orange bedspread: he patted the side of the bed for fear of waking her. He got up and walked slowly off the ward.

The second thing she discovered that troubled her was the list of patients being assigned to 12 Wade Avenue, Maureen Marley's new home. They were all women. Indeed, as far as Anna could tell, so were the staff.

Anna's lover was called Black. She didn't believe that was his real name. When they first met, five months previously, she had assumed that he was really called Roger or Bernard but wanted to make himself appear more interesting than he probably was. He worked in advertising and therefore needed all the help he could get.

However, as he plied her with drink and asked her lots of big questions—Why do you do what you do? Do you do what you do because you think it is meaningful or because you need to be needed? What is your favourite TV advert?—he also told her that his parents had been hippies and that they named him Black because when he was born he had a mass of black lanugo hair on his head, shoulders and back that made him look like a shy monkey. 'It could have been worse,' he said in what seemed a pretty rehearsed manner. 'They could have called me Cheetah.'

Anna tended toward relationships that lasted about six months, followed by a period of singleness and the odd one-night stand, followed by another six-month relationship. She felt this allowed her just the right degree of intimacy without any of the associated assumptions, compromise or expectations. Black was ostensibly a standard-issue boyfriend. Sexually pleasing, occasionally charming, well dressed and working in a field that was so removed from hers that it became a helpful distraction. He was also, and this had counted for more than it might have when they first met, quite a good dancer.

For his part he liked the idea of dating a nurse, it being assumed by the people in his office that nurse training contained at least two years study of advanced sexual practice. And anyway, in a bizarre way it made him feel a little closer to righteousness, not that righteousness had ever struck him as a particularly worthwhile place to go.

It would be fair to say there was no love on either part. Some desire, and some pretty vigorous sex—often fuelled by flavoured vodka or cider with a touch of blackcurrant—which was sometimes interspersed with some good-mannered conversation: 'What did you do today?'

'Oh, I counselled a man with a swastika tattooed on his head, who told me he wanted to cut off his fingers because he had used them to touch himself and God had told him, via Angela Rippon on the Nine O'Clock News, that this was dirty and he mustn't do it again. He doubted his ability to avoid his own genitalia in the future so concluded a lack of fingers would please his God.'

'What did you say?' Black noticed that the word genitalia, when spoken by his nurse girlfriend, felt like flirting.

'I asked him how he would roll and light his cigarettes without fingers. Not a conventional counselling intervention, but it's all I had.'

If Anna had asked herself if she liked Black more or less than she had liked any of the other men she had dated over the previous five years she would have shrugged. In fact they sort of blended into one, none more moving than another, none more engaging, some maybe more irritating, although to be fair Anna's abiding memory of all her lovers was of the point where she left, and then she was by definition sick of them. She thought vaguely about this on her way home. Anna knew herself to be easily bored. She had known other nurses who had tended toward emotional recklessness, dating wholly inappropriate men with violent pasts, drug habits or two or three wives, and she was grateful for the fact that she was not moved by such melodrama. She was in fact not moved by very much at all as a rule. Except perhaps, and this idea had crept up on her over the last year or so, the possibility of a baby. Just her and a child. That idea had popped into her head with the last boyfriend but one. His name was Stefan; he was tall, Swedish and a scientist by trade: good genes. It had hung around while she was with Winston, who was a tall black reggae guitarist: also good genes. And she held it still with Black who was not tall, not as discernibly talented as the last two, but pretty and still quite funny and wouldn't be around much longer. The child idea seemed quite constant. Everything and everyone else was transitory. The thought made her smile. When she got home from work she drank hot chocolate and ate breakfast cereal. She went to bed with a book that she didn't open. She listened to comedy on the radio that wasn't funny. She didn't think about work. She didn't think about Black. When she fell asleep she was still smiling.

When she woke up she felt as if a decision had been made. She didn't articulate it, didn't question it. She showered and dressed and ate some more breakfast cereal. Today she would have a word with the doctor about Maureen Marley. She would look in on Michael Wells and count his fingers. She would maybe have a word with Grace about Adam, she would arrange two new assessments and prepare for Friday's ward round and later she would arrange to have sex. Indeed, given the fact that she knew she was ovulating, she would have as much of that as she could fit in from Friday through to Tuesday.

# 3. Stranger Than Kindness

When Adam had begun training to be a nurse nearly seven years earlier, on a whim and with the simple and quite ridiculous idea that he'd like to do something useful, the thing he found most striking, after the smell of piss, was the lack of curiosity. Having spent the previous three years studying philosophy—a degree that had mostly comprised of watching bands and playing guitar, trying to get to know and maybe sleep with as many women from different countries as he could and talking bollocks about consciousness—he had expected this new institution to be full of a less, for him, indulgent enquiry. Polytechnic was a wonderful place to wonder but he had learnt that no matter how earnest the discussion, how intense the search for truth and how seductive the process of meeting people was he had come to feel it didn't really matter. He had reasoned—he was still a young man at the time, so reason remained important to him—that he needed something tangible, something human and authentic and what could be more human and authentic than an asylum? This monument to oddity and difference where enquiry had a purpose. If you are going to ask questions, make them helpful questions: Why did this madness choose you? How do you cope? What might we do?

But in the hospital the enquiry faded quickly. Answers came before questions, usually in the form of a diagnosis. It was an exercise in knowing. It was safer that way. He understood that but he never trusted it.

He had learnt to nurse in the same large Victorian asylum that he worked in still and which stood like a decaying museum in a North London suburb. Surrounded as it was by tidy terraced housing, Indian restaurants and local shops, the asylum hid its incongruity behind high walls and big trees. Throughout the Sixties and Seventies it had doubled as a film set for Hammer Horror, and it still rented out the odd unused corner to TV companies who wanted a backdrop of gothic dread without having to decorate anything. Inside were high curved ceilings with peeling paint, a central corridor that ran for a third of a mile from one end to the other and an intersecting corridor which ran from the main door down into the bowels of the building where the kitchens and other facilities were, a fading mini-industry for laundry and powdered egg.

And the people: lunacy doesn't simply change the minds of people. It changes their physical shape as well, although Adam came to discover it wasn't the lunacy that shaped them so much as the treatment the lunacy was greeted with. Some of the men had eyes that had retreated so far back into their head it was as if their face had turned itself inside out. Thin wiry men, slightly bent in the middle, wearing trousers that never fitted and shoes that had no laces. Men with tongues that rolled around the mouth and flopped out from behind wet loose lips like drunken slugs.

Adam had been a popular nurse. Always calm, usually able to smile. He looked thoughtful when he talked to mad people— thoughtfulness amounting to speaking quietly and listening to whatever was said back—and he thought about what might make things better, within the obvious confines of the large walls, unending collection of drugs and the abandonment of hope that characterized psychiatry. He didn't come up with too much but he wondered nonetheless. Adam Sands was attentive and engaged, and thus he was a charge nurse within two years of qualifying and stealing tranquilizers from the drug trolley twelve months later.

Adam had collected other people's experiences and used them to colour his view of the world. By witnessing dismay he had been infected with it. You don't have to do bad things to be shaped by badness, he had learned, you just have to be close

32

to it long enough and it somehow makes your soul blister and swell as if it had been stung by a large invisible bee. And all the time the smell: there were days when he wondered if he was incontinent. He was twenty-seven. He felt old. Really old, like forty or something.

He had stolen five tablets, minor tranquilizers, a week after Graham had killed himself. He didn't take the good ones: he didn't feel he deserved the good ones. He could have gone for the pink ones that make you feel calm and help you sleep. Or he could have gone for the brown ones that knock you out. Instead he went for the white ones. It was a ridiculous choice. They were useful in managing agitation and anxiety in old and dementing people but rubbish for anything else. If he had thought about it he would have considered his theft self-defeating, even self-harming, rather than tranquilizing, but Adam had always been told that his biggest problem was that he thought too much, so he had stopped. Drinking randomly helped with that sometimes and, since Catherine had left, so did sleeping with people he didn't love. Or know.

And now here he was again. Like he always was. Trying to keep a straight face. Wondering if he was awake. The office was referred to as the goldfish bowl: three sides of reinforced window and one brick wall, designed like someone had circled the wagons. The idea was that nurses could see most of what was going on in the day room while they drank tea or argued with each other about ECT, Phil Collins or Norman Tebbit. There were three large filing cabinets pushed back against the wall; the rest of the office was lined with desks covered with a variety of notes, phones, books and stationery trays. The walls were pale blue, different from the industrial yellow of the rest of the ward, and it was quiet, not just because the mad people were not allowed in but because there was a carpet and the ceiling was lower, so there wasn't the inevitable echo.

Adam glanced up and murmured hello to the smartly-dressed, stick-thin twenty-something woman who had slipped in and was sitting in the middle of the office waiting to speak. He carried on writing. He was placing on record the fact that a patient, Michael Wells, had removed three or maybe four of his own teeth with some slip joint pliers he had borrowed from a porter. The entry in the notes concluded: 'Medication administered. Dental appointment arranged.'

After introducing herself by profession, Trainee Clinical Psychologist, but not by name, the young woman began badly. 'I don't know if you realize it, but actually Maureen Marley's condition is quite rare.'

He was being patronized by a trainee with the social skills of a skip who wanted the opportunity to work with Maureen Marley, to 'understand more' and maybe even 'offer something that may prove a little more substantial than simply drugging her.'

Adam smiled but said nothing. She's as oblivious to her rudeness as she is to her nutritional needs, he thought.

The thin woman continued: 'I just wonder, given the unusual presentation, if filling her full of anti-psychotics that are not making the slightest bit of difference is the best we can do?'

'I wonder that about most of the patients,' Adam said.

'Well, quite.' The psychologist seemed encouraged at the hint of humanity from the charge nurse, who had graying skin and what looked like a hangover. She saw a gatekeeper, a guard in a loud shirt with bloodshot eyes.

'So why Maureen Marley and not, say, Michael?'

'Who is Michael? I'm sorry...'

'Michael Wells is the man in the anorak pacing up and down beside the television pulling rather violently on his ear. He removed some of his teeth last night because he believed that they were responsible in some bizarre dental way for the voices in his head. Having held long and earnest conversations with the BBC news over the last two weeks and become increasingly animated—an energy that has grown exponentially with his approaching discharge into the community—it all became too much and so he borrowed some pliers, went off into the grounds where nobody could see or hear him and wrenched his teeth from his mouth. He thought they were antennas. That's quite a thing isn't it? He talks to himself a lot, looks angry, doesn't wash, has a swastika tattooed on his head.'

'Schizophrenic.'

'That's what they say.'

'Not in itself unusual...'

'I think tattooing a swastika on your head is quite unusual. What do you think that is about?' Adam asked gently, probing, giving the impression at least that he wanted her opinion.

'Pardon?'

'Tattooing a swastika on your head: what might have persuaded him to think that was a bold but alluring fashion statement?'

'Well...' The woman crossed her legs and settled back a little into what Adam assumed was her clinical posture. 'Given his diagnosis and the virulence of his symptoms I assume the voices in his head told him to.'

'Right,' nodded Adam. 'But why?'

'I don't know,' said the psychologist. 'I would have to assess him.'

'You see, I think that might be interesting. I would guess you have to have a lot of self-loathing in you to stick an immovable swastika on your head. I wonder if we could help him with that at all? And Michael is an unfashionable soul. Not the sort of man who attracts the right kind of attention. He might really benefit from some psychology time. Maureen Marley gets a psychologist every time one of you needs to do a case study, but Michael... What do you think?'

The Psychologist looked at him with barely contained irritation. She sighed and uncrossed her legs. 'I didn't come here to talk about Michael.'

Adam smiled. 'No, you didn't.'

'So what about Maureen Marley? If you are uncomfortable I could always just speak to the consultant.'

Adam laughed. 'Frankly, I don't care if you phone Princess Margaret, the answer is no.'

'I'm sorry,' she said, 'but I wonder why you are being obstructive?'

Adam turned towards her, eyebrows raised, offering, he hoped, just a little of the contempt he was feeling. 'Obstructive?' he thought. Obstructive would be ensuring that Maureen Marley is off the ward twenty minutes before you arrive here, when you think you have an appointment to see her. Obstructive is ensuring that all the side rooms are in use when you come to visit anyone at all. Obstructive is keeping the patients' notes locked so that you cannot borrow from them to write your wholly pointless assessments and instead have to go and talk to the patients while they are watching Coronation Street. '"Why are you being so astonishingly arrogant and self serving?" strikes me as the more realistic question,' he said. The young woman reddened and stood up, preparing herself for an exercise in assertiveness. Adam chose not to give her the space and added: 'This is about us having a difference of philosophy. I think clinical decisions should be based on patient need. You think they should be based on whatever you fancy doing.'

The psychologist sneered. 'I look forward to you meeting my boss: he has a way of dealing with people like you.'

She picked up her bag and marched out of the office, slamming the door with Adam's words ringing in her ears: 'You might want to consider a doughnut.'

When Anna got off the bus and began walking down the main drive of the hospital she could see Maureen Marley sitting on the steps outside the main doors. The sun was shining, there was no breeze and as Anna drew closer to the main entrance— which was fronted by a water fountain that didn't work and a flag pole without a flag—she watched Maureen smoking a roll-up and staring at her shoes. Maureen Marley didn't look up once, didn't move except to draw on her cigarette, but didn't seem remotely surprised when Anna approached and sat down on the steps beside her. Maureen may be mad but she wasn't stupid.

'Why they sending me to that house?' she asked, barely moving her lips 'It smells.'

'It did smell, didn't it? Lavender and carpet freshener, I think.'

Maureen let out a snort of fake laughter, just a brisk shrug of the shoulders and an exhalation born of manners rather than glee. 'It's a girl's house.'

'Yeah. I'm working on it,' Anna said softly.

'I'm not moving there. I'll get a flat. Get a job.' Maureen sounded defiant but unconvinced.

'Cool,' Anna said. 'Got anything in mind?'

'Bus driver,' Maureen Marley said.

'Got a licence?' Again Anna tried to sound gentle.

'They teach you,' Maureen said, like a twelve-year-old trying to convince his dad he will be an astronaut regardless of his fear of heights.

'Well yeah, but not from scratch I don't think. You'll need a driving licence first.'

'I could get lessons, pass my test and then do it.'

'Yeah,' said Anna, knowing that she couldn't but not knowing why.

'I've always wanted to drive a bus,' Maureen Marley said quietly. 'Or a train. Do you think you need a driving licence to drive a train?'

'No idea. Don't expect so, it's not like they have a clutch is it?'

Maureen Marley shrugged. She didn't know about clutches. She looked up for a moment and out of the hospital at the cars driving past, drawing on her cigarette. 'These people trying to punish me. They is not God.'

'I don't think they are trying to punish you—' But Maureen Marley turned and glared at her and Anna changed tack. 'Would a different house be OK?'

Maureen turned away, stared at the flagpole and smoked her cigarette. Later she would go to the bookies. Afterwards she might go and look at the trains. Maybe get on a train, see where it went. 'Man needs to be free,' she said quietly. 'Man is free.'

There was a knock on the office door. It was Michael Wells. He still had thin lines of dried blood on his bottom lip and his black beard looked oily, probably because of the soap that Grace had used to try to clean his face up after she had found him in the bathroom with a hand full of teeth and a mouth full of blood. Now, as he stood waiting for the door to be opened for him he looked embarrassed and pale. Adam got up, went to a drawer, took out a packet of John Player Special and removed three cigarettes. He strolled over to the door, opened it and looked at Michael, who said nothing but fixed his stare on the cigarettes in Adam's hand. His skin was yellow and his mouth was swollen. His greasy black hair hung down over his swastika tattoo and he seemed to have retreated into his filthy blue anorak. Adam paused until Michael looked up. His eyes were glazed and wet. After acknowledging that Adam had a face he returned his gaze to the cigarettes.

'How are you feeling?' Adam asked quietly. Michael made a noise and shrugged. 'If it is too hard... if things are too difficult... tell someone, please.'

Michael shuffled from foot to foot, he turned away from Adam and turned back again, he glanced up at the ceiling quickly with a vacant expression and then he looked at the cigarettes. Adam handed them to him and Michael turned and walked quickly back to his dormitory. As he walked he was shaking his head and occasionally hitting himself in the face with the open palm of his hand.

Adam could see Libby over Michael's shoulder. She was in the day room and seemed restless, disturbed even. She was sitting down, standing up again, sitting down, tapping her feet and standing up again. After Michael had left he walked over to her.

'Are you OK, Libby?'

'Of course I'm not OK. I haven't got a body.'

'You seem more agitated than usual,' said Adam quietly.

Libby looked past Adam and into the office from where he had just come. 'What's he looking at?' she said angrily.

Adam turned round but nobody was there. 'Who, Libby?'

'Him. That one in there.'

The office was empty. Tim Leith, the ward doctor, was walking down the corridor toward the office but he wasn't even close to Libby's eye line. 'I can't see anyone Libby,' Adam said softly. Libby tapped both her feet on the floor and pulled at her cardigan. Libby hadn't looked at Adam properly in years but she looked at him now, looked at him like he was a liar, or at least that is what Adam saw. Saw enough to say: 'Really Libby, I can't see anyone.' Libby stood still for a moment; her face stopped twitching as she seemed to mull over the words. She made a low humming noise, very quiet, almost like a growl, and then she walked away.

When Adam returned to the office Tim was waiting for him.

'Have you spoken to Libby lately?' Adam asked.

Tim was a short round-faced man with a foppish fringe and a range of cord suits, today's being a brownish-green colour. He always wore a waistcoat and sounded like the landed gentry. Adam liked him. He worked hard, he listened when someone was speaking and he seemed to like people. Good qualities in a doctor. Not necessarily great for his career though. 'No,' he said. 'Why?'

Before Adam could answer Grace came into the office. Tim blushed. He always blushed when he saw Grace. Grace was kind enough to pretend not to notice.

'What did the skinny psychologist want?' she asked.

'Career advancement. I need to pop out for a minute, are you OK here?'

'Sure. Where are you going?'

Adam smiled at her. 'I'm going to go and be manipulative with the consultant. Won't be long.'

Grace laughed. 'Manipulative about anything in particular?'

'Yes, that skinny psychologist. We need to set a few boundaries before we find ourselves back in the days when the people who couldn't afford the circus used to come in here to look at the mad people at the weekends.'

'Can I come and watch?' Tim asked.

Anna passed the two men in the corridor just as she was approaching the door to the ward. She was wearing a dress, black with a cream trim, the first time she had not worn trousers since she had come here.

'Hello.' Adam spoke without suggesting he was going to stop. 'I was hoping to have a very quick word with you about Maureen Marley later if you are around.'

Anna nodded. 'I'll be here for a couple of hours and I wanted a word too.'

Anna was standing in the large doorway and Adam was past her now.

'I'll be back in twenty minutes,' he said, adding: 'Nice dress.'

'Me too,' Tim said. 'I'll be back then too. And it is a nice dress.'

Grace was still in the office when Anna got there. The day room was empty apart from the singing cleaner, frantically polishing the old wooden coffee table. Grace opened the office door and asked Anna if she wanted a cup of tea.

'Yeah, go on then.' Anna put her bag inside the door and the two women walked down toward the kitchen.

At first sight Grace's name did not suit her. She was measured in her movement. The way she expressed herself came from her eyes rather than her tone of voice or her body. She had that pretty round face and the smoothest of skin. It wasn't until you spent a little time with Grace that you noticed she made you feel calm. Not chemical-cosh calm that made you nervous because you knew your mood did not correspond with the reality it swam around in, but more a herbal-tea-with-Radio-4-in-the-background calm: soothing, at ease.

'I was working late last night,' Anna said quietly, wondering how well Grace knew Adam.

'Make sure you take the time back.' Grace was looking for clean cups. Having found two she went to the fridge to smell the milk.

'I was surprised to see the charge nurse arrive after ten and go and sit with Libby. What's that about? Are they related?'

Grace eyed Anna. 'Don't think so.'

There was a pause as they made tea. Grace poured water; Anna put the milk back in the fridge. Both women moved calmly through the silence, gauging how comfortable they were with each other. Anna may have passed some intuitive test because it was Grace who spoke next. 'Adam has had a funny few months. He worked on this ward when he trained and I remember he said he would never work here again, but after Graham died he couldn't stay on the acute ward. He didn't say anything but it seemed pretty obvious...'

'Graham the suicide with the bleach? I heard about that. Horrible.'

'Yeah, Adam thought he should have seen it coming. He thinks that is the point of being here, to see things. He was playing chess with Graham...'

Anna nodded. If it had been her she would expect to see it too, and it didn't occur to her that she wouldn't have done.

'You know how after something shocking happens you look back to whatever happened before and see it differently? See that there were clues there that if you had been open-minded enough you would have seen? We did that. We all did that. There were no clues. Either Graham decided completely sponta-neously to drink a litre of bleach or he was so at ease with

41

the decision he had made that it lifted some burden from him, because he was so relaxed that day. He chatted to me over breakfast about my holiday. He walked back to the ward from the shops with one of the students and actually told her why he thought she would make a good nurse and then... well... he was with Adam for about twenty five minutes and Adam...'

'Adam didn't notice anything.'

Grace had been leaning against the kitchen worktop looking at the floor but she raised herself now, looking Anna in the eye. 'He'd have seen it if it was seeable.'

'Of course he would.'

'No, I mean it, he would. He had—has—a brilliant eye did Adam, could really see, or sense, what was going on in people. I get that what you see is this shambling, distant... lummox but don't be fooled.'

'Lummox?' Anna laughed.

'Not diagnostically accurate?' Grace smiled.

'No, lummox works.'

'I'm not saying he was Supernurse, he doesn't believe in anything enough to be that, but when I was starting he was the one I went to if I didn't know what to do or couldn't see something. He has a good eye for, well, for people, for nuance.'

'Has?'

'Yeah, well, he's not exactly back to his best but I still trust his judgment above just about anyone else's.'

'And he visits Libby because...?'

Grace shrugged. 'I'm not sure. He doesn't sleep much.'

'He needs help,' Anna said quietly.

'Feel free to let him know.'

Anna sighed. 'Why Libby?'

Grace shrugged again. 'He knew her when he was a student.'

Anna looked at her, just holding her gaze as gently as she could and waited for Grace to speak again.

'I think he... well, the night nurses say... he comes in sometimes and sits and chats to her quietly.'

'Yeah, that was what he seemed to be doing last night.'

'It isn't harmful.' Grace sounded defensive for the first time.

Anna sipped her tea. 'Not normal though, is it?

'What's your point?' And it was the inevitable place in the conversation, the place they knew they had to arrive at sooner or later.

'My point is I noticed it. I don't know the man. I'm pretty new here, so I am asking you rather than anyone else.' Anna smiled again. 'I'm guessing you have known him a while?'

At which point William, the student nurse with too much hair, burst into the kitchen. 'Michael is going doolally with a snooker cue!'

Both women put down their tea and instinctively began to run.

'Did you learn "doolally" in the school of nursing, William?' Grace asked.

'No... it's... well, he's hitting a chair with a snooker cue really hard.'

'Is anyone in the chair?' asked Anna.

'No,' said William.

Both nurses instinctively stopped running and begun to walk purposefully but calmly, letting William jog ahead to the day room where Michael—the near toothless and inarticulate man with schizophrenia, large doses of major tranquilizers in his blood and a swastika on his head—was beating the seat of his chair the way his mother probably beat the living room carpet, or something.

Both women arrived in the day room to find Michael thrashing, dribbling and panting for breath. To be fair, this was the nearest thing to proper exercise Michael had got to in years. He smoked sixty a day, he ate mostly chips and he took toxic, if prescribed, drugs. He was thirty-four but looked fifty, and he was breathing like a man who had given the chair his best but was probably about ready to surrender. One of the reasons for not running: it gave him a few more seconds to pass the peak of exertion and rage.

'What's the matter Michael?' Grace asked quietly.

'Voices...' wheezed Michael.

'From the chair?' Grace sounded as soft as baby milk.

'It's got a transmitter.'

'You said the same about your teeth, Michael,' Anna said gently.

But he had no more reason than he had breath and he slumped to the ground gasping, close to tears. Grace crouched down beside him, placing her hand gently on his shoulder. Michael looked grotesque, his bloody gums visible as he swallowed air and wheezed, snot and sweat gathered around his unkempt black beard. If he were not so full of drugs he would be crying, defeated. Losing a fight to a noise in his head.

'Should I call the doctor?' William asked. Anna shook her head.

'No,' said Grace, 'but you might want to make Michael a cup of tea?' A question directed at Michael, who nodded. Grace put her arm round him as they sat on the floor.

'What are we going to do, Michael? To make it better? Because whatever we are doing right now isn't working, is it?' Michael shook his head and wheezed.

'Tea?' whispered Anna, who was still crouching down in front of him. Michael nodded again. She half turned her head to William. 'Tea for Michael, please William.'

And William walked slowly down to the kitchen muttering 'What is it with these people and bloody tea?'

# 4. In The Wee Small Hours...

Anna lay next to Black, staring at the ceiling of his west London flat and noticing the gentle threading of post coital sweat slipping down her ribs onto his increasingly uncomfortable futon. She could tell he was asleep by his breathing, and she decided to make meaning from the fact that as he drifted off he had slipped from her shoulder—where he had lain heavily after ejaculation, baby-kissing the side of her neck and making her ear itch—then turned on to his back where his breathing grew laboured. Then quite quickly he turned away and faced the wall with his back to her. He was no more interested in her than she was in him. She smiled to herself and wondered if once would be enough, and if she should wake him or wait until the morning. Neither particularly appealed, but then that wasn't really the point. She decided to wait. She didn't want him to feel desired.

She noticed, not for the first time, that when he was asleep he breathed like Darth Vader. His back, which was pale and more expansive than his front suggested it was going to be, had a certain pigskin quality, although that was not how she experienced it the first time she had slept with him. She was curious then. Finding his smell, exploring him and noticing the way he explored her. He had been greedy, which passed as desirous with the right amount of wine. And he had been careful enough to stop to put on a condom. Something she had helped him to ignore tonight.

She didn't feel comfortable in the west of the city. It felt alien: softer than the east but more unsettling somehow. She could walk around in Hackney and feel perfectly safe at any time of the night or day, but here she felt watched rather than seen. She knew rationally that it was just an issue of familiarity, but knowing something didn't change the way you felt. Not unless you wanted it to and frankly she wasn't planning on coming west again for quite a while.

She lay on her back and scanned the room. This was very much a man's flat. One of the walls in the bedroom was even painted black, although it had a big mirror in the middle of it and a Klimt poster, 'The Kiss', in a plastic frame beside the mirror to soften the room and the sense it gave of the man who slept in it. 'I'm fucking a cliché' she thought and sighed. 'Or at least I was.'

*

On the other side of London, at the cheap end of Crouch End that was really Turnpike Lane, getting to sleep hadn't been the problem. Staying asleep was the problem. Adam would wake at 3.12am every night and try to lay still and lure his mind back from the torture that was consciousness. His preoccupations were always simple and mundane at first. Had he ordered the ward medication, had he paid the telephone bill, why was his Yucca plant dying? But as his eyes widened and his brain accelerated his life became a very dark place. He imagined his life through the eyes of his ex-girlfriend because he couldn't imagine a less enthusiastic gaze. Catherine was an upwardly mobile solicitor who changed her accent for career reasons at the age of twenty-four. He didn't like her very much, he didn't find her attractive and he didn't mind remotely that she was sleeping with a fat bloke old enough to be her father, probably also for career reasons. But at 3.25am he looked at himself through her eyes nonetheless, and he looked small and lonely and smelt of other people's piss.

And then, inevitably, he thought of Graham Cochrane. He wondered how dark his night times were and just how invisible and pointless Adam had been to that man. Adam hated Graham Cochrane. How much rage must a man have to drink bleach and keep drinking it? And to do it with other people so near, to do it with other people 'caring' for him just down the hall. Variously he imagined that Graham Cochrane pitied him his unseeing eyes, or held him in contempt for being little more than a warden for the mad, or, such was his struggle with the demons Adam failed to help him wrestle, he simply disregarded him as an irrelevant spectator. Just a part of a system of restraint and pharmacy devoid of softness or warmth, unable to make a meaningful difference. By 3.51 Adam was little more than a concentration camp guard.

But it wasn't the way he labelled his life that troubled him the most. His political failure, his failure of power or purpose or even to prevent harm, was but just a precursor to the full swell of despair that washed in around 4.22. His life, this gift of possibility, was both too precious and too heavy. He was edging toward thirty without a plan, or anything he could put in the space where a plan should go, like some beliefs or love or a purpose or a job that didn't poke him in the liver every day. His body, in which he once invested much time and effort, had once trained almost obsessively, was beginning to bend. He filled it with aimless unhelpful drugs and cheap wine. His mind had stopped reaching outward and instead peered only in. And his heart told him only that it would always be like this. Even noticing his own rumination made him hate himself. He felt clumsy, unwise and self-indulgent.

Because yes, he took silly drugs and hated his failures, but that was hardly tragic was it? He didn't have cancer or schizophrenia. He didn't so much as limp. In theory he could do whatever he wanted but here he lay, psychically throbbing and being crushed by the bloody universe. If he could not control the self-destructive wanderings of his own thoughts, what on earth was he doing taking money from the world to help others? This idea of life, the notion of gathering understanding and using it in some way to produce... produce what? Good? Something helpful? It was a sham. It was all just a nonsense

47

to hide from the existential reality that was his complete and indisputable pointlessness, and now it was 4.27.

If it had been earlier he would have gone to see Libby. Say sorry quietly again for the things that had happened to her that he hadn't prevented, or even been born in time to see. A ritual that made him feel closer to human and somehow less dirty. If it was any later he would get up and soak in the bath but the hot water wasn't on yet and sitting in a cold bath was ridiculous. 5.01 was the worst. Neither one thing nor the other. He put the radio on: something soft and absurd by Foreigner. He retuned: a programme about farming. He retuned: news about banking; disco music; a radio phone-in where everyone was cross about traffic or homosexuality or the fact that it wasn't 1953. He turned the radio off. He turned on to his side and tried to clear his mind of everything. Libby had said once, nearly four years ago, in the single moment of clarity that haunted him still: 'Just because you weren't here it doesn't mean you aren't guilty.' She was talking of a time long before he had even known the hospital existed but the words cut him to the bone. He sat up, picked up one of the books on the table beside him. Some class pantomime by an Amis. He read a few lines. It wasn't funny. He dropped it on the floor. He looked at the next book in the pile: something fraught and emotionally pornographic by an angry woman. Had he stopped liking books? Or had he stopped reading books he liked? Why would someone do that?

He decided not to sleep alone this weekend and he smelt the cover to his duvet, resolving to change it before Friday night. 5.24: if he could just get back to sleep for an hour or so...

*

Anna slept fitfully. She had broken dreams about ovaries and work. They didn't form or even hint at any sort of narrative and by 5.52 she was awake in a way that made her certain she wasn't going to go back to sleep. She toyed with the idea of getting dressed and leaving a note saying 'It's been nice but I'm bored now so don't call. Thanks. Anna.' But she was unconvinced that she would manage to get out of the flat without waking him so she lay staring at the ceiling until 6.24, by which time Black's breathing and occasional movement suggested that he was, if not quite ready to be woken, probably available for arousal. She slid closer and lay close to his back. Her breasts pressed into his back and her breath warmed his ear. That was, she knew, all that it would take.

Later, a little after seven, she sighed and decided to play. 'Tell me a story, Black.'

Black had been stroking her hair distractedly and wondering when she was going to leave. He liked sex in the morning, of course he did, but once it was finished and an appropriate period for post coital good manners had passed he wanted to get on with the day. He was planning what to wear and looking at Anna's right nipple with a detachment that he would have considered unimaginable twenty minutes earlier. A story? He didn't collect stories. He gathered images, sometimes made them into symbols and took money in return, but stories? They tended to confuse the world for him, make it more elaborate than he required. He didn't know any stories. 'I don't know any stories.'

'Of course you do, don't be lazy.'

Black had no time for emotions in the morning, particularly other people's. He had learned, however, that if there were going to be emotions they should be of his choosing. He sighed and he remembered a story someone had told him once, in bed. He had rules of course, rules about not confusing lovers with each other nor letting one body spill over into the next, but those sorts of rules are more like guidelines really, existing mainly to imply that he lived according to a code rather than simply a sex drive. 'OK,' he said, 'but I am not a storyteller.'

Anna rolled on to her back and said neutrally: 'Everyone is a storyteller.'

'Right, OK... Once upon a time...' Black turned to face Anna but she didn't smile. She simply stared at the ceiling waiting for the words. Black sighed, turned on his back, being careful not to let his body brush against hers, and began again.

'There was this woman called Marie. She lived a well-ordered life with a successful husband and two healthy, happy kids. She was a teacher: she taught well-behaved kids in a private school. She also had a lover. His name was Ira.

'Ira and Marie had met as student travellers in the early Seventies. She was already engaged but was travelling alone; her fiancé had gone to Spain with his mates, anxious to have a bit of fun before settling down, before real life began. Marie and Ira met on a Greek ferry and they talked for the whole two-hour crossing. They both booked into the only taverna which rented rooms on the island and that evening, after eating together and drinking together, they slept together. Marie saw in Ira a holiday from what she knew was an already written future. He was idealistic and blonde and his long hair made him appear slightly prettier than he actually was. It should have been a holiday romance, except that it lasted nearly a full month in that first year and perhaps it happened before they were fully set, or maybe they fell a little bit in love... if you can fall just a little bit in love. At the end of the month Ira said to her: "Meet me here one year from now. No matter what, just come. Come as a friend, if you like, or come as a lover, but meet me and we will spend a week together."'

As Black spoke he noticed a sing-song rhythm to his words that almost squeezed any emotion from his voice. He noticed because the word lover sounded clumsy. He paused and looked at Anna. She was still staring at the ceiling, listening, waiting. He sighed and gave up his time to a story that didn't even need to be told.

'She agreed, never imagining for a moment that it would happen, but it did. One year later they both arrived, not expecting the other and unsure as to why they had come. But when they saw each other they remembered, and they spent a week walking and talking, swimming and eating and making love. And so it continued, every year, the same place, the same time. They became constants.

Ira's life was not the adventure he'd planned, but he retained a talent for not being disappointed. He spent time in Central America writing promotional literature for international charities. He felt like an outsider, and he may have been nourished by the fact that once a year he met someone who saw him as an adventurer, or at least as a good and worthy man. When Marie told him of her two daughters, born three years apart, she looked for signs of jealousy or hurt but couldn't see any. When he told her, a few years later, of his new wife and his new job as a production editor for a charities magazine, living in Croydon and commuting into London every day, she felt a pang of sadness but held tight to the vision of Ira as adventurer.'

Anna, to her annoyance, found herself quite liking the story. She remembered why she had chosen Black: he was, despite his protestations, a storyteller. When they first met he told her tales of divas buying attention on the set of TV adverts and he told them neutrally, never to make a point about himself being better or worse than the person in his story. She liked that. She thought it lacked the need to judge. More lately she had come to think that in fact it reflected ambivalence. She knew, of course, that she saw whatever she wanted to see.

Black was still telling his story. 'Only once did they discuss staying together, nearly ten years after they had met. Marie had come away despite having a three-month-old baby at home and was restless and ill at ease. Her husband, who was uncomfortable with the emotions that had accompanied this second pregnancy and birth, had been happy for her to go, secure in the knowledge that the nanny would take care of the children.

"Why did you come?" Ira had asked as tenderly as he could. She had shrugged and looked away. Later Ira had said: "I never felt I could make you happy... and now you have the girls...'''

Black glanced at Anna, who had closed her eyes. 'At the end of that week Marie went home and her husband felt the break had done her good. Ira, unusually, stayed on the island alone for a while.

Twenty-three years after they had first met, Marie arrived at the taverna and waited in all the obvious ways but Ira didn't come. Marie knew that if he could have come he would, and so he was, in all probability, dead. Nobody in his life knew she existed; there would be nobody to tell her. She stayed on the island alone for the week, to remember and to mourn.'

Black glanced at Anna to see if she offered any sign of a reaction. She might, out of politeness, look sad or even say 'Ahh.' She might even tut; deaths in stories can be so convenient, especially if the storyteller is in a hurry. She said nothing. He didn't mind. He remembered the woman who had told him this story a year or two ago, she had built up to a big finish. They had had sex afterwards. Her name was Sarah. He didn't really know what she was doing in his head right now. He took a deep breath.

'At the end of the week Marie sat at the table she and Ira had shared and drank to the end of romance. She asked Elani, the woman who had run the taverna for over thirty years, to join her for a farewell drink. She told her that she believed Ira to be dead and Elani crossed herself and said that she had wondered where he could be. "You two became like the seasons," she said, smiling. "Reminding us that time is passing, but reassuring us that some things stay the same."

Marie realized that this was perhaps the only time she would ever be able to speak of Ira and so she found herself confessing. She said: "I suppose it was love? But it was a funny love. We kidded ourselves that we were an honest corner in the world but I kept a secret from him anyway. He was the father of my younger daughter. My husband doesn't know, or doesn't want to know. I'm not sure which. I never told Ira. I wanted to, but then he got married and time passed and... I did what I thought was best."

Elani poured them both another glass of wine. Then she told of the time many years ago when Ira had stayed on the island alone after Marie had left, and at the end of his stay he had said: "I love her but I cannot have her. I have lied to her and told her about a wife who does not exist. I lie to keep an equal distance between us, to keep a balance and to protect her world." Asked why he did not tell the truth, Ira had replied: "Because if she knew she might not come, and if she did not come what else is there?"

And Elani shrugged and said: "These are the things that people do." Which apparently is true.' Black feigned embarrassment. He expected a hug at least.

Anna nodded and said quietly: 'That is very much a 'you' story.'

'How so?' he asked.

'It's sad and it doesn't mean anything.'

\*

Adam was doing press-ups; it was 7.12. One hundred and fifty of them in sets of fifty. He had already done two hundred sit-ups and eighty tricep presses. He had got up at 5.30, played his guitar very quietly for an hour and then done some old Kung Fu forms in a distracted way for ten minutes. He would cycle to work. This was him fighting back. He began most, if not all, mornings as if preparing for a fight, training himself, knowing that he would crumble the moment he smelt the mix of bleach and piss that was the hospital. He sat cross-legged on the floor and closed his eyes; he tried to empty his mind. It was a ludicrous idea, like emptying a well with a fork. So he tried to think about his body and notice what it was telling him. It was like a gum after a visit to the dentist: numbed by an injection that was wearing off and revealing a throbbing pain that promised to get worse. It started in his chest and worked its way outward. He stopped sitting cross-legged and did some more press-ups. It was 7.18. By 7.29 he was running a bath.

*

'Shall I tell you a story? It seems only fair.'

Black knew that impatience this soon after sex was rude, and rudeness led to time being wasted arguing about manners, so he tentatively said: 'Well, that would be nice, but won't you be late for work?'

'Yes I may be, but I'll make up something dramatic like witnessing a knife fight on the Central Line and it will be forgotten.'

'"I overslept" won't cut it?'

'No, the mundane has no place where I work. If it isn't dramatic people think you are hiding something and that makes them suspicious.' Black stared at her. Anna looked away. 'You wouldn't understand. Would you like a story?'

Black was nervous, unsettled and not equipped to say no. 'Shall I make tea first?'

Anna nodded. 'Yes, tea would be good.'

*

Adam would leave at 8.20. He was dressed and ready at 8.05 and for no good reason had decided he would not leave early. He stood in the middle of his flat staring at his spider plant. His living room was painted a soft grey and characterized by eighteen houseplants located according to their varying needs for light or shade. Two of the leaves on the spider plant were turning brown; he tore the ends off the leaves and felt the soil. It didn't need watering. It was 8.06. He could make a plan, he thought, a plan for the weekend. That was what people did on Wednesday or Thursday or whatever day it was. He picked up a red exercise book from the small table by the window and flicked through it. Louise: he had met her at a hospital party but she wasn't a nurse. She was an art therapist but not too middle class. He picked up the phone and called the number. An Australian woman answered.

'Is Louise there please?'

'It's 8.08,' said the Australian woman.

'Yes it is, but thank you anyway. Did I wake you?'

'No but... oh never mind. Louise!' she shouted.

Adam heard the Australian woman put the phone down and could hear voices mumbling briefly. Louise picked up the phone and said 'Hello.'

'Hello, its Adam Sands, we met—'

Louise laughed. 'I remember who you are. It's nearly ten past eight in the morning.'

'Do you people have a really big clock by the phone?'

Louise laughed again. 'I wasn't sure I would hear from you again.'

'Are you doing anything on Saturday?'

'Dunno, what do you have in mind?'

'A film, pizza, maybe wine. No dancing.'

She laughed again, more flirtatious than joyful but good enough. 'Promise no dancing?'

'Guaranteed. You get to pick the film, nothing too heavy or violent please.'

'Police Academy 3?'

'Or ridiculous.'

'OK, where and what time?

'How about seven, outside Burger King on Piccadilly Circus?'

'OK. I'll check the film listings, you do the same and we can argue about it over pizza.'

'Cool,' Adam said. 'And sorry for calling so early. Work, you know.'

'Yeah, I know. It's fine. See you Saturday.'

It was 8.13. He still had seven minutes to go.

*

Anna was sitting up in bed with the sheet pulled up to cover her breasts and her legs tucked in. She cradled her tea and began her story.

'There was this young girl, seventeen, called Hannah. She lived in Wolverhampton with her younger brother Ian and her parents, Tom and Cora. She was a pretty normal teenager from a pretty normal family but like all normal teenagers she had a 'thing'. Her thing was dancing. She liked any kind of dancing really, and given that this was the Seventies there were less kinds around. She bopped around at discos, she went to tap class; she baulked at that chiffon-waving contemporary dance nonsense because she was working class and not ridiculous, but she took to ballroom dancing, and in 1976, just before Punk reached Wolves, she and her brother came fourth in the All Midlands Ballroom Dancing Contest (Youth Section), and they were up against twenty year olds. Hannah and Ian had a talent. Some people celebrated it, one or two others resented it, but that was the way of things where she was from.

Anyway, one day they were dancing in a competition for their own age group and were frankly head and shoulders above the rest of the couples. They did a wonderful rumba, a glorious bit of swing and, while their tango lacked the sexuality one expects from a dance like that, it was very well executed, or so the judges said.

After they had collected the trophy—a large garish plastic piece of nonsense that they would mock all the way home but miss if it was in anyone else's car—and were getting ready to go, a thin faced middle-aged man, who walked like a dancer and talked like a cross between Quentin Crisp and Noel Coward, approached their parents and introduced himself as Lance Feyeraband: dancer, choreographer and teacher. He managed to be both polite and condescending at the same time, a manner which served to charm Hannah and Ian's parents, while reminding them that they were very working class and they were not in a working class place. Mr Feyeraband—nobody in that family was ever going to call him Lance—talked of the promise he saw in Hannah and Ian, the raw untrained talent, that glimmer of something special and, on the off-chance that their potential was lost on Tom and Cora, he mentioned that they could end up on the television and not ITV either, but BBC2. He felt that they needed, however, a proper coach, someone who knew dance, someone who could loosen Ian's shoulders and lift Hannah's heel that extra half an inch. Someone like Lance Feyeraband. And he wouldn't cost them anything. Just think it over and sign this contract, take it home, read it over, basically it secures a share of prize money and any TV fees that come about as a result of Mr Feyeraband's professionalisation of the talented but naïve couple.'

Anna was talking in a near monotone, almost delivering a speech but with less volume. She paused for a moment to adjust her sheet, pulling it up higher and making sure the whole of her body was covered.

'And so Lance Feyeraband became coach, mentor and agent to Hannah and Ian. He had what can only be described as a very hands-on approach to coaching. Both teenagers were unfamiliar with being touched. They knew they didn't like it but assumed their distaste was born not of a good instinct for broken boundaries but rather a lack of sophistication. Dance was a physical world and was there really a difference between having their shoulders pulled tightly back and held firmly to demonstrate the correct shape of the spine and the casual cupping of a buttock or breast? Ian was always naïve. A very pretty boy, he either didn't notice or didn't process the fact that he was followed home from school every day by small groups of fifteen-year-old girls who would giggle when he turned round and leave cards and chocolates on the doorstep on Valentine's Day, his birthday and most Fridays. Hannah was a bit more knowing. She knew that when Mr Feyeraband stroked her leg as he talked to her about school, dance and the glamorous world of Solihull that it wasn't quite normal, particularly as he edged his hand up and inside her thigh and stretched his fingers clumsily toward the cotton of her knickers. She instinctively pulled her legs away and pushed his hand from her skin and could not, would not, disguise the look of disgust she gave him. But she didn't say anything. She didn't speak.

And neither did Ian, or at least not until he had come home and sat sobbing in the bath for two hours. Then he spoke, hesitantly, shamefully, before he was sick. He spoke about what Mr Feyeraband did, and what Mr Feyeraband made him do. Cora and Tom didn't say anything at first. Hannah began to rage. She expected Tom to beat Mr Feyeraband to a bloody pulp, but only if Cora didn't get to him first. Instead Cora said 'You have the All England Championships coming up, you know.' She said it quietly, something like shame in her voice, but not enough to make the words sound any less revolting to Hannah or her brother. Ian lifted his head to his father and Tom said, without looking at him, 'Are you sure, Ian?'

Later, much later, Hannah screamed at Tom, told him that he had stopped being a father the moment that doubt left his lips, the moment it even crept into his head and Tom said the strangest thing Hannah had ever heard. He said 'Be careful not to cut off your nose to spite your face, you two.' Ian didn't look at his father when he said that, in fact he didn't look at his father ever again but he must have heard him, because months later, after the voices had come and after he had begun to hurt himself in whatever way he could, he got very drunk on Thunderbird and sherry and tried very hard, using his father's razor blades, to cut off his beautiful nose.' Anna fell silent.

Black, uncertain, unable to find a clue in what he should do, looked at the clock, 8.47, and said: 'What happened to them?'

Anna shrugged. 'I don't know. Hannah left home after that. Never went back, changed her name I think.'

'Poor kids,' mumbled Black.

Anna laughed. 'Yeah. Anyway, I like to finish on a story, Black.'

She stood up naked on the bed and stepped over him and began to put on her underwear. 'It's been fun, I liked the sex and it was interesting to meet someone from your world. Weird world, by the way, can't be sure what gets you out of bed in the mornings, it all seems a bit pointless but hey, each to their own.' She put on her black dress very quickly as she talked and began to brush her hair while looking in the mirror. She would do her make-up on the tube, she decided. 'But frankly I am bored now and the sex has peaked, so don't call and good luck and stuff.' She spoke with a cool authority, not rushing, not investing very much in the words and not looking at Black.

'Sorry?" he said.

'Don't be.' She put on her shoes and quickly checked around the room to ensure she had not forgotten anything. 'It was fine but it's done with now. Bye.' And with that she picked up her bag and left.

As she walked towards the tube station she found herself wondering about her body. Ovulation was not an exact science and it would be a pain to have to do this with someone else. She found herself looking at the men she passed on the way to the tube and disliking herself for it. However, if she could improve the odds of success she would be a fool not to. All we can ever do, she thought, is notice when something matters, keep as much control as you can and try to reduce the variables. These were things she believed herself to be good at. By the time she was on the tube, remembering that she had a ward round to go to and noticing that she felt relieved to be heading east, she was smiling to herself. Her instincts told her she was going to be OK and she had come to trust her instinct above just about everything else in the world.

# 5. Parade

Adam hated the ward rounds the way a child hated the dentist. His loathing began as an instinctive distaste that evolved into a physical revulsion. He experienced them as squalid: soulless dances of frailty that aroused the senses of people in ties. A time and place where, essentially, the patients put on a show. He remembered his first, nearly six years earlier:

'How have you been? Yes I know the medication is making you fat and tired but it is making you better isn't it? Isn't it? Hmmm.' And later, after the nervous young man with schizo-phrenia in his head and dribble on his chin had left the arena and the nurse had mentioned that he had told her quietly that he could not get an erection, the doctor had turned to the students and said 'One would like to think he doesn't need such a thing in here.' And, in laughing, they congregated around the belief that he was somehow less than human.

It was the thought of the ward round that had drained him of whatever he imagined his sit-ups had provided. And so he re-armed himself on arriving at work by popping down to the drug room and taking two diazepam and something pink they gave to Mary Peacock for a heart condition. He left the door open as he swallowed them; he always did. If anyone saw him, nobody said anything.

The dayroom was where they held the ward round. It was always a mess: misplaced armchairs faced in random directions; out of date magazines and the odd dressing pack littered the room. It was a cross between a corridor and lounge for twenty-four patients and numerous staff, but it also passed as a dining room, shouting arena and cafe. It was never going to be homely: the chairs smelt of cigarettes and sweat and, if you were stupid enough to sit on the unsprung and ancient piece of sponge that was referred to as the sofa, you would need a winch to get out of it. The last time Adam had seen anyone use it voluntarily was when the when the thirty-four-year-old, 13 stone and 5 foot 2 Karen 'Kazza' Chamberlain—a woman with a diagnosis of manic depression and a penchant for Guinness laced with brandy—had, during *This is your Life*, suggested to four surprised fellow patients that they should have sex with her while the adverts were on. George Wimimundu was one of the 'men' and had laughed at the funny jokey woman with bright red lipstick rubbed into her cheeks and no knickers on. The other three had shrugged and decided to give it a go. The attendant Nursing Assistant had tried to ignore it, hoping in vain that the mad people would come to their senses or lose interest prior to penetration, but in the end the nervous and religious woman had called Adam and Grace for help in disentangling and distracting the patients as well as persuading them to pull up their trousers.

Later, Grace, who was writing in the notes belonging to one of the men, had said to Adam: 'I'm not sure how to phrase the group sex incident? "Colin and two others were invited to have sex with a hyper-manic fellow patient in the day room. He appeared confused but joined in anyway before staff intervened"...?'

Adam had nodded. 'Yeah, that ought to do it. Maybe try "appeared to engage" instead of "joined in anyway"?'

'Thanks,' she said. 'I knew "joined in anyway" made it sound like a craft group.'

In the main people had avoided the sofa since then, but it was nonetheless where the three medical students sat while they waited for the Consultant to arrive.

After breakfast had been cleared away, the nursing assistants tidied the ward with a pace and zeal they applied to nothing else, with the possible exception of feeding patients when the food trolley was late and the end of their shift was drawing near.

They piled up papers, rearranged armchairs, unplugged the TV and radio and chased all the mad people away. They laid out eight chairs in a horseshoe and told the students to get off the sofa. They then covered the sofa with a sheet—they didn't want the Consultant to think it was stained or anything—and retired to the office to eat biscuits.

Next to arrive was the Occupational Therapist, a round-faced young woman in a purple smock and with no discernible chin. Her name was Phoebe. She nodded to the students before sitting down on one of the circling chairs and placing her hands in her lap. She was followed by Tim, laden with patient notes. Tim put the pile of notes on the ground, removed a bleep from his belt, checked it, put it back on his belt and sat down. He pulled his baggy brown corduroy trousers up at the thigh as he sat and immediately stood back up again and checked his bleep before sitting down, turning to Phoebe and nodding hello. Adam sat in the office watching the meeting form and sipping his tea. The last thing he said to Grace before he got up and joined them was: 'If I set fire to a psychologist today it will be your fault.'

When the consultant arrived he was not alone. He had with him a tall plump floppy-haired man wearing a blue blazer, check shirt and—Adam instantly decided—annoying trousers. Walking just behind him, as he laughed at whatever it was the consultant had just said, was the thin blonde psychologist from yesterday.

Dr Walter Peach had been the Consultant Psychiatrist of this and four other wards for over fifteen years. A tall, thin grey haired man with a long nose and an expensive tie, he always arrived last. He had the most authority and therefore his time had the most value. The three fresh-faced medical students sat nervously next to each other, looking at Peach with a youthful mix of awe and terror. Two men and a woman, all young, all white; one of them, a long-faced boy with black hair and a grey crew neck jumper, was playing fretfully with a spot on his chin.

Peach sat down and the man with the blazer sat next to him. 'Adam, good to see you in here. How are you?'

'I'm well, thank you Walter. How are you?' Adam spoke softly, politely.

Peach smiled and nodded. 'I'm well thank you Adam.' And then he paused, glanced at the floor for a moment before looking at Adam and saying: 'I had a letter from Graham's wife yesterday.'

Adam swallowed hard and blinked rapidly three or four times. 'How is she doing?'

'OK I think. She mentioned you. She asked how you were.'

'That is kind of her.'

'Yes.' There was a long silence; the medical students looked uncertain. The dark haired boy picked at his spots more nervously. Tim glanced at Phoebe, who looked blankly back at him. Dr Peach looked around and wondered if he should say any more. 'The child is nearly two now.'

'Really? Adam raised his eyebrows. 'Two already...' He felt a lump in his throat and a burning behind his eyes. Whenever he thought of Graham Cochrane's son he thought of the day, yet to come, when his mother would tell him how his father died. Peach and Adam looked at each other and, for a moment, met in something like sympathy. A pause, long enough for each of them to acknowledge the other, and then they both looked down and away.

Peach lifted his head and looked around, nodded at Phoebe and pointedly ignored the students. 'Do you all know Dr Casells?' He turned his head to the man with the over-ironed trousers. Phoebe shook her head ever so slightly; Adam ignored the question; the students shook their heads vigorously. 'Dr David Casells has recently joined us from The Bethlem. He will be overseeing the Clinical Psychology department, splitting his time between research and clinical work. About half and half David, is that right?

'About 50% research, 50% clinical and 50% supervising other staff,' Dr Casells said loudly, laughing at his own joke to make sure nobody thought he was very poor at sums. Everyone laughed politely except Adam, who yawned.

'And the young lady?' Peach said formally.

'Oh, forgive me,' said Casells. 'This is Carla Tandy, she is a trainee. I was hoping that you might help make good use of her.' He was looking at Adam when he began the sentence but had turned to face Peach by the time he had finished.

'I'm sure we will find something useful for her to do, won't we Adam?' Peach said.

'It's already in hand, Walter.' Adam smiled with a conviviality that was as rare as it was contrived.

'Good. Right, who do we have first?' Peach turned to Tim, but before he could speak the ward door opened and closed quickly and they could all hear the sound of rapid footsteps rushing down the corridor.

Anna appeared, breathless and pink. 'I'm so sorry I am late,' she said. Adam noticed that she directed her apology to the whole room. 'Someone on my bus had a heart attack,' she said, puffing out her cheeks.

'Oh dear,' said Tim.

'He died on the bus, just sitting there in the middle of the top deck. There was nothing we could do.' Everyone was silent for a moment. Anna looked confused. 'I mean I didn't do anything, nobody did, it happened so quickly.'

'Was he a big man?' asked one of the students.

'Pardon?' Everyone looked at the student, a baby-faced blonde boy with near-invisible eyebrows.

'I wondered if he was big: bigger people are more prone to heart attacks.'

Peach frowned. 'Yes, I'm not sure now is the time to be conducting public health research, young man. Our colleague has had a bit of a shock.' The boy reddened and shrank. He might have tried to apologize but no sound came out.

Anna rescued him. 'Someone on the bus, while we waiting for the ambulance, said we should carry him off the bus so the rest of us could get to work. He said the bloke was dead so what was the point of everyone just sitting there staring at him. A woman started crying and called him heartless and the man said if rigor mortis sets in they'll have to cut him out.' Everyone made noises that conveyed outrage. Only Adam's sounded like a laugh. Anna caught his eye and laughed out loud.

'Perfectly natural response,' said Casells. 'To laugh, I mean.'

Anna smiled politely. 'Comes to something when arriving at work feels like I am getting away from the madness. Anyway, I am sorry for being late, Dr Peach.' She turned to Casells. 'I am Anna Newton, Community Psychiatric Nurse.'

Casells stood up, walked over and took her hand. 'David Casells, Specialist Consultant Clinical Psychologist.'

'Well,' said Dr Peach, who may not have forgiven Anna for arriving after he did. 'I am sorry for your awful morning, Ms Newton. We are all glad you are here. Now I think if we may we should press on. Tim? Who is first please?

Tim was momentarily thrown. He was still looking at Anna and appeared deep in thought. 'Right! Sorry!' He swung his whole body round in his chair as if he was unable to turn at either the neck or the hips and as he did so he lifted both legs off the ground. 'Right,' he added as he stopped moving. He picked up a set of notes from the top of his pile. 'First up, Michael Wells, he has had a very difficult week. He became overwhelmed by his voices on Tuesday and in his frustration broke a few things in the day room. I upped his medication but to no avail: two days ago he extracted four of his own teeth with pliers. He felt they were antennae attracting the voices. Yesterday I understand he took a snooker cue to an armchair. He slept OK, I think?'

Tim glanced at Adam, who lifted his hand and moved it from side to side. 'Not well, I don't think,' he said quietly

'Right, well he appears distracted this morning; he says the voices are getting worse. They are telling him he is worthless and is the son of Satan. He says the voices are mocking him. And they are incessant. More recently he says that one of the voices belongs to his father.' Tim glanced at Adam again. 'I am aware that he is at the top of his dosage. I wonder if we might need to rethink his drugs?'

Peach sat quietly, his fingers on his lips. 'What is he on'?

'1200mg of chlorpromazine. 40mg haloperidol. 5mg procyclidine. And last night I gave him some temazepam to help him sleep,' Tim said.

'Drug-resistant psychosis, ladies and gentlemen. What might we try next? Alex?' Peach was looking directly at the spot-twiddling medical student.

'ECT?' the boy suggested.

'Not for psychosis, no,' said Peach dismissively. 'Miss Ray?'

The young lady reddened and stuttered but answered nonetheless. 'A different anti-psychotic perhaps? Er, sulpiride?'

'Good,' Peach said. 'I am not a big believer in sulpiride but we work our way systematically through the treatment options until we find one that works. Tim, start him on sulpiride 200mg three times a day.'

'And cut back on the chlorpromazine?'

'We'll wait a week or so and then look at that, shall we?'

Tim looked at Peach waiting for a rationale. Far too many drugs all trying to do the same thing. It wasn't quite illegal but it was wrong, and unscientific. Peach stared him down.

Tim bit his lip and wrote down the new prescription. Without looking at his boss he said: 'Would you like to see him?'

Peach looked at Adam, who pursed his lips. Adam knew that he possessed a certain goodwill with Walter Peach. In part this was because they had both worked with Graham Cochrane and his death had bound them in shock and in very different ways a sense of failure. In part because, as the charge nurse, Adam was supposed to have some authority and if Dr Peach did not enact that rule he would ultimately be undermining his own status. It was, Adam knew, a pantomime but he had learned that it presented him with tiny flakes of power and that he should use them wisely. Michael Wells would no more benefit from being in here than Adam did.

'No, I think it is OK Tim, thank you. Perhaps you will talk to him later and explain that we think the new drug will help with the voices but that it may take a few days to start working and during that time he might want to use the temazepam to calm him.'

Phoebe spoke up: 'He's making a pot in the craft group.'

Everyone nodded. Peach related an anecdote about a patient he once had. 'I'm sure you remember him.' He was looking at Adam. 'This young man spent the whole time he was here making pots. Some of them were really rather lovely. When he was discharged he opened a little shop called Gone Potty.' Everyone laughed. Adam chose not to tell them that the shop went bust after a few weeks because the mad sod refused to sell any of them.

'Now, who is next?' smiled Peach.

'Forgive me, sir.' Carla Tandy the trainee psychologist glanced at Adam before smiling almost flirtatiously at Dr Peach. 'Can I ask a question please?'

'Of course, my dear.'

'Can I ask the charge nurse: is this the patient you thought I ought to try to do some work with?' she asked with a sarcastic curiosity. 'Or am I mistaken?'

Peach glanced at Adam who pursed his lips and then smiled. 'No, that's right. I'm pleasantly surprised that you remember, as you seemed to suggest that people with a diagnosis like his were not of any interest to you?'

Carla reddened. 'I certainly didn't mean to suggest—'

Adam interrupted. 'You see, I understand that Michael Wells is not unique in his presentation, and of course I understand that therapy tends toward the more articulate and dare I say middle class patients, but my sense is that Michael would benefit from some thoughtful, specialized therapeutic time. I think at the very least distraction helps him and at best a different type of assessment, a psychological ongoing assessment might serve to accompany the medical team's efforts to contain his symptoms. A team approach if you like.'

At no point did Adam look at the woman as he spoke, instead he looked at Casells and smiled. Now he had finished he did not take his eyes off of him. To Casells' credit he held his gaze and did not speak immediately.

Peach, however, did. 'I have to say I think Adam has a point. What do you think, David?'

Casells nodded slowly. 'Well, I wouldn't want to think that someone trains for five years in order to simply distract a patient in distress. We could after all probably do that with a cap gun and some sparklers. However, I do agree that we need to be integrating psychological therapies more routinely into a wider client group than we do currently and it is of course the intention of our team to work with nursing staff. Indeed, as you know, Walter, one of my hopes in coming here is to extend my own research specifically in combined therapy. That is,' he looked around the room, comfortable with the attention, 'designing specific psychological therapies that integrate with the altered mental state created by medication. Why work in parallel with medicine when we could, perhaps with more success, work in unison? What say Miss Tandy does some exploratory work with Mr Wells? Shall we say six weeks? It may be that Michael would prove to be an ideal candidate for our sort of specialist therapy.' Peach looked at Adam.

'How about we review after six weeks, rather than assume it will finish?' Adam said. 'It may be that the process benefits Michael and we certainly wouldn't want to write off that possibility before your trainee even starts, would we?'

Peach nodded and Casells looked away. 'Of course. Who knows, she may cure him,' he said with just a hint of sarcasm, before looking at Adam and saying 'We're delivering a teaching session in the school of nursing next week that outlines the combined therapies programme. You might be interested, Mr Sands?'

'I doubt it,' thought Adam. 'Who knows?' he said with a shrug.

'Good,' said Peach ignoring them both. 'I look forward to hearing your views, Miss Tandy, and thank you, Dr Casells, for your help.'

Adam nodded at Peach but did not look at Tandy. It was, he felt, important that whatever it was she was feeling was accompanied by his contempt.

'Next we have Libby Hoffman,' said Tim.

Adam, who was just beginning to wonder what concession he would have to offer as payment for Peach's support—a support he had negotiated the day before in Peach's office—was to find out more quickly than he had expected. Libby had not been discussed in the ward round for over a year. He raised his eyebrows at Peach.

'My idea, Adam,' the consultant said.

Peach, as he always did on such occasions, offered a history for the students. Adam listened, choosing not to fill in the gaps to a past he had no reason to know so very well.

'Libby, full name Elizabeth Hoffman, is eighty-two or eighty-three?' He looked across the room for confirmation. Adam shrugged petulantly. She was eighty-five.

'Anyway, she is, I'm afraid, something of a product of the hospital. She was admitted in the early 1920s with a diagnosis of melancholia. She was brought in by her parents, who were disturbed to find that she had become tearful and neglectful around the house. It appears that she had developed something of an infatuation with the local post boy, only to discover that he was rather toying with her affections. Libby was treated, when she got here, quite... extensively. A lot of the old notes make no sense and others have been destroyed. However, we can safely assume that she has experienced many things.'

Anna looked at Adam, who avoided her gaze. Peach continued. 'Her present, and I have to say, intractable condition, is a deep-rooted nihilistic delusional state. In short she believes she has no body. She is also a diabetic, the result one suspects, of rather extensive insulin therapy in the forties.'

'Has ECT been considered?' the spot-twiddler asked.

'Do you have shares in the electricity company?' Peach said impatiently. 'She undoubtedly had extensive ECT many years ago. Such treatment now would of course be absurd. There would be unnecessary risk of memory impairment and very little chance that it would have any effect on her ideation. ECT is, as you most certainly should know, a treatment for depression, not psychosis. Indeed, I have to say that I do not feel her beliefs alter her quality of life to such an extent that hospitalization remains necessary. That is why I would like to propose discharge.'

Anna was still looking directly at Adam, which lent him a self-consciousness he could do without at the moment. 'Michael Wells getting a bit of therapy was just a softener for this,' he thought. He raised his eyebrows to exaggerate a show of interest. 'Interesting idea,' he said. 'Do we have any sense yet of where she might go?' Impassive, engaged. He felt his stomach tighten. He chose not to ask himself why.

'There is a new project opening on Delia Road,' Peach said. 'A house for six elderly patients. It is well staffed and well equipped. I've seen the house, indeed I will be the named consultant. I don't imagine funding will be a problem.' Both Anna and Tim shook their heads. 'So you know her best, Adam, before we ask her to come in what do you think?'

Adam nodded slowly, pantomiming thought even though he knew that his thinking wasn't working very well. It could only go so far before it bumped into something: a fog or some chemicals or something. He breathed in slowly and tried to ignore his stomach. He said: 'Well, given the history you outlined, Walter, I certainly think she deserves some comfort in her dotage, don't you?' Peach smiled politely. 'But from a nursing point of view I suppose my concern would be about the impact of change. At her age, consistency and familiarity are important. She has been on this ward for fourteen years. I am not suggesting that that is in itself a good thing, but I am wary of what change might do to her.'

'In assessment she shows no significant deterioration in cognitive functioning,' said Casells. 'Which suggests she is capable of change.' Casells looked from Adam to Peach as he spoke.

'When was she last assessed?' Adam asked.

'I assessed her yesterday at Dr Peach's request. You weren't on shift.'

Adam reddened slightly. Embarrassed and annoyed that something had happened on his ward that he didn't know about. He felt a pang of paranoia too. Someone knew, one of his nurses, and they hadn't told him. He turned to Anna. 'What do you think?' He knew what she would say, what she would have to say, but he preferred the idea of having to concede what would soon become an overwhelming case to a nurse rather than to the pompous sod in the perma-pleat trousers.

'Well, I think you are right about change, obviously. The evidence suggests that significant change for older people accelerates disorientation and physical deterioration.' She directed this at Casells, who nodded and went to speak, but before he could Anna turned to Adam and continued: 'However, I know the Delia Road house and the staff who are setting it up and I think they are good nurses who would be sensitive to that. I also think that we could do some useful work over a reasonable length of time to prepare her for the move. Most importantly, I think that she isn't getting any younger and this ward, even though it is supposed to be a rehabilitation ward, is getting more acute. Michael has been unwell, Kaz, Colin...

I don't believe that is the best environment we can offer an eighty-five year old woman.'

Adam nodded. 'You are right of course.' This was aimed at Anna, with a cursory nod to Peach.

Dr Peach smiled benignly. 'Shall we see her?' he asked rhetorically.

When Tim brought Libby into the room Peach stood up to welcome her but, on noticing that when she saw him she stopped walking and stared at him, he sat back down again.

'Hello Libby, would you like to sit down?'

'I can't sit down.' Libby scanned the room, turning a full circle as she arrived in the middle of the chairs and taking in everyone. 'I haven't got a body.'

There were too many people here, too many strangers. Peach could tell that, and he knew that whatever he wanted to do had to be done quickly.

'Well Libby, how have you been lately? It's been a while since I saw you in here, I think.' Peach was courteous and skilled but Libby wasn't listening. She pointed at Phoebe and said: 'Look at her looking at me.' Phoebe blushed.

'Libby,' Peach said, trying to distract her, but Libby just kept turning in a circle on the spot, looking at everyone.

Adam waited until she was facing him and said quietly: 'Do you want tea, Libby?' Libby stopped for a moment. 'If you could just give us two minutes, Libby, and let Dr Peach talk to you, I will arrange for some tea. OK?'

Libby didn't answer but she did stop circling and Peach took this as acquiescence.

'Libby, we were wondering how you would feel about leaving the hospital, or at least having a look at a lovely new house round the corner that they have built for people like you, older people who have spent a lot of time in the hospital, to live in.' Libby began to chew on her bottom lip. The thumb of her right hand hooked into a button hole on her light blue cardigan. She looked like a wrinkled child who didn't understand what was being said. Adam unconsciously mimicked her lip-biting. 'Libby,' continued Peach, 'do you know Anna here? She will take you on a visit soon. Show you round, see what you think. Is that OK?'

Libby looked at the floor, at her slippers and then up again. 'You can do as you please, it's easier for you, you have bodies. I don't have a body. I don't even have feet.' She stared at her slippers. 'I don't know how those slippers got there. They aren't mine.'

After she had gone Peach turned to the students. 'Observations?'

He was looking most directly at the spot-twiddling ECT fan, who reddened, shuffled in his seat and said: 'She appeared confused, unresponsive, almost mute until the bit at the end. I wonder about depression.'

'Do you?' Peach said without looking at him. 'I wonder where they get medical students from these days. Miss Tandy, might you help them?'

Adam looked at Tandy and saw a bird getting ready to peck at a dead animal. After Libby had left the room Adam had found himself feeling embarrassed. Rationally, what he had said was appropriate, it made some sort of clinical sense and when he conceded the case with a shrug he had done it without petulance. Nor had he shown more emotion than was appropriate, which was the rule in most exchanges but almost cardinal in a so-called clinical setting. However, he felt exposed. Exposed as caring, attached and involved. He felt seen. And he felt the effects of the drugs he had taken before the ward round seeping through his body, bouncing off of the inside of his skin and ricocheting into his liver and the back of his eyes.

And it was the way he felt that dominated him. Thinking was sculpted by the emotions that bubbled up through him. Thoughts that Libby should be left alone, not forced into a community that would mock her and not wrapped in new routines and wallpaper that will make her feel misplaced and unsafe, these were not well-shaped clinical responses to change but rather guardians to the overwhelming and humiliating feeling of loss he experienced when he pictured coming to work and not seeing the eighty-five year old deluded patient, who probably didn't even know his name.

'The nihilistic delusion is interesting,' Tandy said directly to Peach. 'Clearly fixed, clearly fully integrated into the way she both sees the world and functions in it. It is hardly worth saying that not having a body enables her to never actually be anywhere. She certainly managed to not stay here didn't she? Didn't even have to sit down, such was her ability to not stay where she didn't want to be. I suppose it is reasonable to wonder if perhaps she doesn't have a body because she doesn't want to actually be in this place. To her, her body is elsewhere. Waiting, perhaps. Who knows, maybe she will find it in her new house?'

Peach was nodding and Casells looked pleased. Adam and Anna caught each other's eye and shared a moment's contempt. Tim distracted himself by looking at the next set of notes. 'Of course, there might be another possibility.' Adam was surprised by his own voice. 'Perhaps she had her body when she got here and something happened to it. Something unkind. Something she cannot countenance. Perhaps, even, it wasn't just 'something' but a series of things. She has been here a long time and, as you said Walter, experienced many things. Maybe whatever happened to her body means she doesn't want it back?'

'All the more reason for her to spend her last few years away from here and in a place of comfort.' Anna had spoken without thinking and instantly regretted it. She felt disloyal, even though she had no reason to be loyal to Adam.

But Adam nodded. 'Yeah.' He sounded tired. 'But if you don't have a body I imagine the comforts of pine bedframes and soft furnishings are a bit irrelevant.'

There was a moment's silence, just enough to mark a polite pause before moving on. 'Let's see how she gets on with her visits and discuss again in a couple of weeks, OK?' said Peach rhetorically. 'Who's next Tim?'

'Another for discharge, we think.' Tim spoke distractedly as he picked up the notes. 'Maureen Marley, also known—mainly to herself—as George. Should I offer a brief summary?' Tim looked at Peach, who waved his hand and closed his eyes. 'Maureen, in essence, believes herself to be a man. She has had several diagnoses ranging from the current schizophrenia to an initial belief that she had suffered a seizure that had brought about changes in her brain... Anyway, she has a fixed delusional belief and no amount of drugs or indeed therapy—goodness knows, Maureen has been seen by more people than Tottenham Hotspurs—is shifting that belief and so we have been looking at discharge and maybe even some work?'

Anna swallowed and said 'I went with Maureen to visit the house she is currently being considered for, and I have to say I don't think it went very well.' Peach offered a well-mannered surprise. It was less an expression of shock and more a way of establishing that he was going to require some convincing. 'I know of course that Maureen is a woman.' Anna felt she sounded ridiculous. 'And I am not suggesting that we base our care on colluding with her belief that she is not. However...' She looked at Peach who, along with Casells, was impassive and attentive. 'If we are going to discharge Maureen, despite her delusional belief, we are acknowledging that she is not only capable of living with that belief but that it is now part of her reality. Therefore, if we move her into a house that is only for women, we are either contradicting that acknowledgment about her belief and how she chooses to live with it or we are doing something cruel. I think she should be in a mixed house. A house where she can be herself.'

'Interesting point.' Casells nodded approvingly.

'What are your thoughts, Tim?' asked Peach.

Tim was staring at the floor. 'At first I wasn't sure,' he said, 'but I think I agree with Anna. If we are agreeing that hospital treatment is no longer required it is because we cannot 'cure' her. If we cannot cure her, our next responsibility is to help her to live as effectively as possible and I think that is most likely in a mixed house. In fact I think I may have an idea, sir.'

Peach looked unhappy at the prospect of an idea. The house Maureen had been assigned to was a house he needed to fill. 'And what is your idea, Tim?' he asked.

'Well, I believe that you are the consultant for a house on Elm Grove, sir, and I understand that one of the older patients—a Mr Singer, I think—was admitted to the Royal Free following a stroke last week. I spoke with the doctor Mr Singer was under and he does not anticipate Mr Singer being able to return to anything like independent living. In fact, he is far from convinced Mr Singer will be discharged at all, sir. Now forgive me for filling dead men's shoes, so to speak, but as I understand it that is a mixed house in every sense and unless you have someone else in mind for that place...'

Peach thought for a moment. He didn't have anyone else lined up and he would have to make the bed available to another consultant's patient if he did not fill it himself, which had both administrative and financial implications. 'Any thoughts, Adam?'

'I think soft furnishings would drive Maureen up the wall, to be honest.'

Peach smiled. 'I wonder who I could put in that house, though?'

'Well,' offered Anna quickly. 'I was there this week and I don't think they are ready to open just yet. That gives us time to find a suitable person and I have several assessments to do over the coming fortnight. I am sure we can find someone, Dr Peach.'

The room fell silent for a moment.

'OK,' said Peach finally. 'Assuming Mr Singer is unable to return to his home—and I will talk to his consultant later today—then let's place Maureen in there. I don't think there is any reason to see her, do you Tim?'

'Er, no sir, no. I or Anna can talk with her later.'

'Right, thank you.' Peach sounded slightly more abrupt now and to his credit probably noticed. He looked at Adam who had been concentrating mostly on breathing steadily and not thinking about Libby. 'We are emptying this place quicker than I thought we would.'

Adam nodded. 'Yes, but we haven't got to the really tricky ones yet, have we?' He smiled at Peach with something approaching affection.

'No, but it won't be long and then... there'll only be us left.'

Adam smiled genuinely. 'That is who I meant when I referred to the tricky ones, Walter.'

Afterwards, Anna found Adam in the medicine room standing beside the sink staring at the wall. 'You used up a lot of energy in there.'

'Is that how it looked?' Adam was hunched forward, still breathing deeply and feeling like a fool.

'It's in the bag, you know.' Anna sounded more tender than she had expected.

'Yeah, probably.' Adam sighed and turned to face her.

'And actually, for Libby Hoffman, it may be a good thing.'

'Probably,' he nodded.

'So what is the problem, Adam?' Anna had closed the door.

'We decide what is best for people according to what is best for us,' he said, realizing as soon as the words were out that he sounded lazy and naive.

Anna shrugged. 'Yeah, and we call it progress. So what?'

There was a knock on the door. It was Grace. She came in, looked at them both and said: 'What's going on?'

'Libby is being discharged,' Anna said.

'Yeah, she's all better now,' said Adam.

'Good,' Grace snapped, looking at Adam. 'I think she has a lot of bad memories tied up with this place. She probably deserves to finish her days somewhere a little nicer, don't you think?'

Adam let out a single breath that was meant to take the shape of a laugh but sounded a little as if someone had poked him in the stomach. He wasn't railing against what was happening to Libby. His instincts had been OK even if they had made him feel faintly ridiculous: to protect her from change, because in this environment change had always meant some sort of assault. It was the bottom line for a professional carer: to do no harm. He looked at Grace, curled his lips into something suggesting that she was being a pain and nodded.

Another knock at the door. This time Tim came in looking angry, so angry that he forgot to blush.

'Thank you Tim,' Anna said. 'I'm grateful for your support over Maureen.'

'You are very welcome. Any doubts I had about my own judgement have just been removed.'

'How so?' asked Grace, prompting Tim to blush.

'My consultant has just castigated me in front of the medical students. He feels I should not have gone looking so actively for another bed for Maureen and I should have talked to him in private first before giving my opinion in a ward round.'

'I'm sorry...' said Anna.

'No, don't be. He didn't offer any logic, any science, he didn't correct my clinical reasoning. He criticized me for being politically naïve. For not serving the economic imperatives of community care and managing his future income. He made himself look a fool.'

'So why are you so cross?' asked Grace.

'I'm cross for not knowing the right thing to do without you putting it in front of me, Anna. I wonder about my judgement and I'm cross at having give my time and attention to self-serving businessmen rather than medical practitioners and I'm cross that nobody seems to notice that for all the talk we do not appear to be making anybody better.'

'Eh?' Adam said.

'Well that is the point isn't it? Of medicine? To make people better? Not argue about which diagnosis makes us look clever.' Tim paced as he talked, looking at the floor and particularly making a point of not showing his red face and pursed lips to Grace.

'You might need a drink, Tim,' suggested Adam.

'We all might,' said Grace. She reached out and touched Tim's arm gently. 'Five o'clock in The Swan across the road. I'll buy you all a drink.'

Tim blushed again. He looked at Grace with such adoration that even Adam and Anna smiled. 'Thank you,' he said. 'I would like that very much.'

# 6. In My Secret Life

The grounds of the hospital were at their most striking in late September. A thin sparkling mist laced the grass and the only noise that spread across the wide former farmland that surrounded the asylum was the singing of birds and the echo of laundry carts being dragged around the corridors.

If you walked down the long drive from the real world that ended at the large black gates and you had no idea what the imposing brown Victorian façade housed, you would consider both building and setting to be beautiful. You might, however, begin to wonder what it was as you drew nearer to the wooden doors, surrounded by half-hearted graffiti—'*You'd have to be mad to live here*' and '*Jesus already came back: he's inside*'—and the smell of mildew.

The staff didn't notice the grounds or the architecture any more. The building was flavoured by its purpose, not its aesthetic. The greenery, the long majestic building with its intricate tower and rows of thin windows, were lost on the people who saw them the most. There were however some beautiful trees: the largest, a weeping willow, was over a hundred years old and stood behind the east wing that was now empty, rendering the tree unseen. It had boughs you could build a boat from and in the height of summer was shrouded in greenery that cascaded from uncountable branches like a thick sea. Very occasionally a patient would sit beside it smoking, sheltering from the rain or the sun or the nurses, but mainly it went unseen.

One winter a flurry of snow attracted a flurry of photographers to the hospital. A grand Victorian building in a yellowing light with a cover of white: it would be on Christmas cards for years to come. The snow meant there was a bustle of concern over how dangerous the path down the drive was becoming. A catering assistant had fallen and broken a hip, and a handful of nursing auxiliaries threatened to not come to work unless grit was applied—ironically, the last thing anyone ever imagined a nursing auxiliary needing. But the aesthetics were irrelevant.

Leaving the hospital, despite its imposing architecture and muted grace, was the fading of an anaesthetic. The ordinary road at the top of the drive, that stretched along the front of the hospital and into suburbia, was lent character by a bus route and five shops which included a dry cleaners and a bookies. The real world was characterized by engine noise. From the point of passing through the hospital gates to the moment, about three and a half minutes later, that Adam, Anna, Grace and Tim entered 'The Swan' pub, nobody spoke. Instead they adjusted their senses, breathed in the fumes and each made private decisions as to what time they would make their excuses and leave.

The pub had been modernized quite recently, which meant there was a carpet and a series of booths built against a long wall at the back where once there had been round wooden tables. There was a juke box currently playing Phil Collins, and there was even a small non-smoking section that nobody was sitting in because it was a bit embarrassing.

Adam bought everyone a drink. He had whisky with coke, both women had gin and tonic and Tim had a pint of real ale. They sat in a booth and Anna offered Adam a cigarette.

'We are going to have to do something about the music,' Adam said. 'Does anyone have any change?' Tim fumbled for fifty pence. 'That'll do for a start,' Adam said and wandered over to the juke box.

'He is a bit of a fascist when it comes to music,' said Grace. 'He once unplugged a juke box because someone kept playing Meatloaf.'

They talked about pubs. Good ones in Stoke Newington, which had live bands and lock-ins. Bad ones in Wood Green that watered their drinks and wouldn't serve people who 'dressed funny'. Grace talked about Manchester: how much better the music was and how much cheaper the drink. Anna said the same about Birmingham.

'What bloody music has come out of Birmingham?' asked Adam.

'The Specials,' Anna said quickly.

'They're from Coventry.'

'Same sort of area.'

'Oh yeah,' said Adam. 'I bet when Birmingham play Coventry on a Saturday afternoon the fans are pretty ambivalent about who wins, them both coming from the same sort of area.'

'Oh, shut up and put some more money in the jukebox. Did you put this miserablist nonsense on?'

'I may have.' He smiled. 'A little known B side from White and Torch.'

'Who?' said Tim.

And so it continued: music, television, has anyone seen any good films? Identifying a tone and a sense of who was who until they had all had three drinks and shared two packets of dry roasted peanuts.

'My round,' Anna said. 'Same again?'

Tim raised his empty pint glass; Grace and Adam nodded. They all knew by now that they were staying longer than they had each intended.

When Anna returned Tim had removed his silk-lined paisley waistcoat and released his paunch, making space for the real ale that lent him an animation they had not seen before. 'No, no really, it is quite absurd,' he was saying. 'My father assumed I would be a GP like Mother. My mother assumed I would be a surgeon like Father. I, however, may have had some rather grandiose ideas about psychoanalysis or some such thing. When I specialized in psychiatry I thought they were going to disown me. If my sister hadn't come out as a lesbian at around the same time I could have been cast out.'

'But you are excused because she is a lesbian?' asked Grace.

'Well, mostly because she is a lawyer, to be fair, but the lesbian thing was a compounding factor,' he said without blushing. 'So what about you lot? What brought you to the lunatic asylum?'

'I came on the bus,' Anna said, sitting down.

'I hate psychoanalysis,' said Adam. 'Or mostly I probably hate the people who practice it. So bloody evangelical.'

'Yes, yes, yes,' said Tim. 'But maybe you are in denial, Adam. And very good Anna, using distraction and humour to prevent me from finding out about you. But I am trained to see through such strategies.'

'Are you?' smiled Grace 'I thought that mostly you were trained to give labels to people and prescribe them drugs? Aren't we the ones trained in all the people stuff?' Tim blushed and went to speak but stopped and chose instead to relish the fact that the gorgeous Grace was gently mocking him.

*I want to know what love is* by Foreigner came on and Adam shivered theatrically. 'No. I need more change.'

'OK,' said Anna. 'But only if I get to choose with you.'

Adam eyed her suspiciously. 'Do you like this nonsense?'

Anna winced. 'Good God, no.'

'OK,' said Adam. 'But we go together and have to both agree on each song. Deal?' Adam winked at Grace as he left.

The juke box was on the other side of the pub, beside the toilets. It was backed by deep red flocked wallpaper. The nearest person to it was an older thin man in a brown raincoat sitting on his own, smoking a roll-up and drinking Guinness. He looked as though they had modernized around him. He didn't look up when Adam and Anna walked past him.

'You can pick first,' Adam said.

'Are we over here to give Grace and Tim a few moments alone?' asked Anna.

'Mainly we are here to stop Foreigner, but if some other good might emerge from standing outside the toilets looking for tolerable songs, then so be it.'

Anna smiled. She hadn't seen Adam like this before: alive, warm, unsedated. 'The Cure, *In between days*?' offered Anna loudly.

'Oh yes, didn't see that. Bowie, *Heroes*?'

'Of course. There is some rubbish on here...'

'There is,' agreed Adam. 'I have a theory though: I think they keep a check on how many times certain songs are played and when they come to restock the records they keep the ones that have been played the most. Which means we have a responsibility to ensure that the good songs, and the little obscure ones that make people stop and shrug, get played more. If we don't, we condemn future pub goers to Foreigner, Phil Collins and Nick bloody Berry.'

'So essentially we are performing a public service?'

'Everything we do touches the world in some way.' He smiled. 'Ohh, Joy Division? Yes? Bauhaus: no. Your go.'

'That is quite a burden,' Anna said as she surveyed the songs.

'What, not liking Bauhaus?'

'No, believing everything we do touches the world. How about Dionne Warwick? And Otis Redding.'

Adam nodded. 'Good choice and it isn't a matter of belief, it's pretty much a fact isn't it? Whatever we do has consequences, even if they are tiny or seemingly insignificant. We can argue about whether or not that matters very much or if it is a healthy thing to think about, but that doesn't make it any less of a fact.'

Anna looked at him. He was staring intently at the jukebox as he spoke. 'We're out of songs,' she said.

'Just as well. Let's get drinks. I think we've given Tim enough time to get past blushing every time Grace speaks.'

When they got back to the table and put down the drinks Grace was leaning toward Tim conspiratorially. 'Sshhh,' she pantomimed. 'They're back.'

'Aha, there you are,' Tim slurred. 'Don't imagine I have forgotten the question I asked before you chose to take some 'alone' time.' Tim mimed inverted commas in the air when he said alone.

'What question was that?' Adam asked.

'It will come to me in just a moment,' laughed Tim. 'Ah yes. What was it that brought you all into this business. Did you grow up wanting to help the sick but didn't fancy the hats your general colleagues wear?'

'Psychiatric nurses tend to be refugees,' smiled Anna. 'Well, there are probably some who will tell you that they have a fascination with the human psyche and wanted to try to understand what happens to the fried and fragile, but they don't tend to stay very long.'

'Fried and fragile, I like that,' murmured Tim. 'And do we all hate psychoanalysis or is it just Mr Denial over there?'

'It's more self indulgence for the analyst than help for the patient,' said Grace.

'It's for the rich,' added Anna.

'So you prefer drugs?' Tim smiled.

'Two sides of the same coin,' Adam said.

'Polar opposites surely,' countered Tim. 'One is about investing deeply in understanding an individuals psyche and looking to repair it, the other about a generic response to a chemical imbalance: an attempt to crush symptoms and offer solace.' Tim sounded like a doctor, albeit a slightly drunk one.

Adam said: 'They are both industries built on the opportunities presented by other people's madness. They are both about the assumed and largely made-up expertise and self-regard of the saviour, whether he be analyst or doctor. They both lay claim to a science that gave us aversion therapy, lobotomies and treatment by water cannon and have as much real scientific credibility as crystal healing, not that scientific credibility is as important as it thinks it is.'

Grace and Anna both nodded as if Adam were simply stating the time of day.

'But... no, hang on... so what do you believe in, if not psycho-analysis? Other types of therapy? Psychoanalysis isn't the be all and end all, is it? Letting—what was your term, Anna?—the fried and the fragile run unrestrained toward their own destruction? Agonized by misery, hallucinations? We have to act, to help, don't we? What should we do?'

Adam shrugged. 'Dunno,' he said with a smile.

'Oh come now,' said Tim with a flourish. 'You can't abdicate responsibility for what we do like that. Claiming to despise it all, to be above it all, while offering nothing as an alternative.'

'I think you can,' Anna said. 'You can be a critical presence.'

'Or just present,' nodded Adam, adding as if surprising himself: 'Maybe being a witness to it all is the only important thing we do?'

'So if they came to you tomorrow and put you in charge of everything you would stop the drugs, stop the psychoanalysis and do what? Put what in its place?'

Adam shrugged again. 'I don't think they are going to do that.' He smiled warmly. 'So I don't feel the need to prepare.'

'Hypothetically then,' said Tim.

'Tim, I don't know. I don't know because I think not knowing is the best position to take. I think that when you decide to believe in one thing over another in a place like that you become an acolyte, or worse a collaborator. You become part of an interest group and at the risk of being crass and drunk I think that interest groups are insidious. This Thatcherite nonsense means they exist to make money or power or careers for people and that becomes the point of them quite quickly.'

'Vile,' said Anna. 'Lots of blokes jostling for validation.'

'And an increasing number of women mimicking them,' added Grace.

'That's a Thatcher thing,' nodded Anna. 'Act like a man and call it feminism.'

'Confuses uniformity with equality,' offered Adam. 'Easily done.'

'I'm sorry,' said Tim, draining his glass. 'Do you lot all live together in a big house somewhere, where you practice this stuff?'

Anna laughed. 'Actually this is the first time I've sat down with either of them.'

'You're doing very well though,' smiled Adam.

'I'm just agreeing with you 'cos you let me put Dionne Warwick on. Me, I'd love to be a psychoanalyst. Some of them are charging £20 an hour. No, I don't trust any of them, therapists, doctors, half the nurses... Present company excepted, of course.'

'Er... thanks,' said Tim.

'I'm teasing,' said Anna. 'You are no more responsible than the rest of us. You get better paid, of course, and you write the scripts but we draw up the injections, we enforce the rules, we hold the whole thing together.'

'Yes, but you all seem to do things differently, no? Actually, wait, I shall get more drink, unless we are going to eat? Should we eat? I am happy to carry on drinking but some people like food... I like food...'

'Drink is good,' said Anna.

'Food would be good too,' said Grace, 'but not pub food. Curry?'

'Hurrah for curry,' said Tim, standing up and heading toward the bar. 'Should I get a drink while we're deciding anyway?'

When Tim was out of earshot Anna turned to Grace and said: 'Blimey, he likes you doesn't he? He blushes every time you speak.'

'He's quite sweet,' said Adam.

'He is, isn't he?' said Grace. 'If he's for real.'

'I suspect he is thinking the same about you,' smiled Adam.

Tim returned with a flurry, spilling beer on his sleeve as he put all four drinks down on the table. 'So,' he said loudly, 'it occurs to me that you have used your cynicism to distract me from my original question, which was what brought you into this business in the first place?'

'Needed a job,' said Adam.

'I was going to be a singer,' said Grace. 'But so was everyone else, so I found myself doing this instead.'

'Oh,' squealed Anna. 'I was going to be a dancer: dancer, psychiatric nurse, dancer, psychiatric nurse, it could have gone either way really.'

'Speaking of people ending up here,' said Adam. 'That psychologist Peach wheeled in today, what's his angle?'

'Does everyone have to have an angle?' smiled Tim.

'Does everyone have to answer a question with a question?' countered Adam.

'Fair enough,' Tim conceded. 'He's some sort of whiz from The Bethlem apparently. He's probably sleeping with that trainee you upset the other day.'

'That's a given,' said Adam. ''What is he selling, do you think?'

Tim drank his beer and thought for a moment. 'Hope?'

'Oh-oh,' said Adam. 'He'll want a lot for that.'

Tim thought for a moment. 'I know what you mean. There is something a bit sleazy about him, isn't there?'

'Well, yes,' said Adam. 'He's a psychologist, so that too is a given, but I was curious about why now. This place is in its death throes, Peach is old school, coming here is no career move...' He turned to Anna. 'No, really...'

He caught her eye and she smiled and said: 'The recruitment process I was part of talked about exciting and expansive career opportunities, which on the face of it looked silly but it seems there is a lot of research money attached to this move to Community Care. And where there's research money there's a heady mix of psychiatrists, no offence Tim, and psychologists carving it up. Cassells is chasing the money because with money comes careers. Written all over him.'

'Hang on, hang on, hang on,' Tim said, spilling part of his fifth pint down his chin. 'Am I to understand that you are so cynical that you believe research is somehow inherently evil?'

'Yes,' smiled Adam.

'Is evil a bit strong?' Grace looked at Adam, who smiled at her.

'Psychiatry is still in the dark ages. Research is progress, research is hope, a chance to make things better, a chance to lend a bit more thought and sophistication to what we do,' said Tim with a flourish.

'No,' smiled Adam. 'Research is a career opportunity wearing a T-shirt with the words 'New type of legitimacy for the same old shit' written on the front. Research at its best is simply organized curiosity. At its worst it is an exercise in making our squalid little industry appear more respectable than it is. Of course, I may be drunk.'

'That's a big T-shirt' said Anna.

'Yeah, we're going to need fat people,' said Adam. 'Or a snappier slogan.'

'Worked for Wham,' said Anna quietly.

'I'm sorry,' said Tim. 'Are you two flirting or debating?'

'Er, I appear to be flirting with her and debating with you. I don't want to debate with you, although the flirting is nice.'

'You are very cynical,' observed Tim, with shrugging disappointment rather than irritation.

'Yes,' acknowledged Adam. 'But I still draw the wage, so I think it's important to note that even I don't take what I say remotely seriously.'

They were quiet. Adam sipped his whisky and coke.

'Curry? Grace suggested.

'Indeed,' said Adam. 'Enough of this festival of self-loathing. Let's buy food, go to my house, gossip generally and be mean about psychologists.'

'Oh count me in,' said Tim. 'I can't stand them. I don't know if you've noticed but they don't actually know anything.'

As they left the pub Adam said to Anna: 'So tell me your story.'

'What, all of it?'

'Tell me what you don't mind sharing. I'm interested.'

Anna eyed him and grinned. 'No you're not; you're just setting up Tim and Grace.'

Adam laughed. 'I am interested, but I quite like the idea of them hitting it off. She's a good woman is Grace, deserves some attention from someone normal.'

'Did you two...?'

'Us? No. I like her too much.'

It was still early evening, a little past seven; a cool late summer grey hung over North London. People were still going home from work, but the late afternoon drinking had made them slightly immune to the pace and noise of the traffic.

'So what brought you north of the river? Please tell me it wasn't a career move?'

Anna laughed. 'I wanted a change, I was getting a bit bored and probably a bit stale.'

'What's wrong with stale?' said Adam sarcastically.

'Actually, I think I might want something a bit different.' Anna surprised herself a little; she wasn't given to reflecting out loud.

'In what way?'

'Oh I don't know.' She hesitated. 'It probably seems stupid after everything we were saying in there, but I think I want to do something different. Still in psychiatry but something different, something that might change things.'

'Sounds pretty reasonable to me. Not sure about the 'still in psychiatry' bit, but you don't seem as jaded as me.'

They walked in silence. The grey was darkening and there was an orange tinge to the clouds.

'How far to the curry house?'

'Ten minutes,' said Adam.

'So, why do you go to Libby?'

Adam sighed. 'Why do you think?'

'I don't know, that's why I'm asking.'

'I've known her a long time.'

Anna didn't say anything and they walked on. It was cooler now, that turning point that always comes in September where you know the summer is gone and people walk a little faster with their shoulders hunched.

'She spoke to me once,' Adam said suddenly. 'About five years ago, completely out of the blue, weirdest thing that ever happened to me.'

'And you are waiting to see if she does it again?'

Adam laughed. 'No. But that would be the nearest thing to an acceptable answer, wouldn't it? Unless I told you she was my Gran.'

'What did she say?'

'She said: "Just because you weren't here, it doesn't mean you aren't guilty." She said it quietly, looked me straight in the eye.'

'What did you say?'

Adam may have blushed. She saw him swallow and try to smile. 'I said "I'm sorry Libby." She just looked at me and walked away. Weird.'

'Not that weird.'

'No? Felt weird.'

Anna shrugged 'Weird it is then.'

They caught up with Grace and Tim outside the curry house.

'I'm not really very good with women of the opposite sex,' Tim was saying.

'Aren't they men?' said Adam. 'Don't be so hard on yourself. Are we eating here or getting a takeaway and taking it back to my place?'

'Where is your place? Anna asked.

'It's a twenty-minute walk or five-minute minicab. I have gin.'

'Cab it is,' said Anna. Grace shrugged. Tim blushed.

Adam's flat was surprisingly clean. Anna had expected chaos but instead found a Spartan living room, almost square, with grey walls and a darker grey carpet and pink woodwork. There was no television: instead a sleek black record deck and amplifier formed a centrepiece. The walls were lined with records and books. Mostly records. 'Have you not heard of the CD?' asked Anna.

'They don't crackle,' said Adam. 'Gin?'

Grace and Anna spread the tin foil boxes of food on a coffee table while Adam got glasses and ice.

'What are you drinking Tim?'

Tim was looking at the books: philosophy, American fiction, a collection of books by Bruce Lee. 'Who's Montgomery Clift?'

'Actor. 1950s. Very good.'

'Never heard of him.'

'The Clash wrote a song about him.'

'The who?'

'What do you want to drink, Tim?'

'Whose guitar is this?'

'Must be mine.'

'Do you play?'

'Sometimes. Tim: drink?'

'Oh, sorry, gin please.'

They sat on the floor around the coffee table and began spooning bits of sag aloo and chana masala on to their plates.

'We need music,' said Adam.

'Nothing too miserable,' Grace said. Adam got up and put on Sinatra: *Sunday Every Day*. Anna nodded her approval.

'So, Grace, do you still sing now?'

'Not really.'

'She does,' Adam said. 'Not as often as she should, but she does a set at a wine bar over in Fulham once a month and she did something in Islington not long ago.'

'Last year actually,' chided Grace. 'They didn't ask me back.'

'Their loss,' Adam smiled.

'Hold on, hold on, so you perform, on a stage. What sort of songs do you sing?'

'Old standards really,' Grace shrugged.

'She does a lovely *Bewitched, Bothered and Bewildered*,' offered Adam.

'Do you still dance?' asked Grace, uncomfortable with the attention.

'No,' said Anna without looking up.

'Why not?'

'Long story. Anyway it was an unfashionable sort of dancing I was good at: Ballroom. I mean I could do other stuff but I was good at Ballroom and most people think of that as being a bit Terry Wogan. Anyway, not much money in twirling around in a frilly frock. I wish I could sing. Must be lovely to sing.'

They stopped talking for the first time since they had arrived in the pub nearly three and a half hours before. They were as far from the hospital and whatever it was that bound them as they could be, and comfortable enough with the silence to just sit in it chewing chapattis and drinking cheap cocktails. Sinatra stopped singing and Adam got up and quietly turned the LP over, gently placing the stylus on the record and the dust cover down over the deck. 'Good curry,' said Tim. 'Anyone want any of my chicken?'

'So, this psychologist bloke, what's his angle?' Adam was looking at Tim.

'Adam, not now please,' Grace said.

'Sorry. But there is something about him, and I don't just mean the perma-pleat trousers. He watches...'

'That's a good thing, isn't it?' said Anna.

'No, he is looking out for weaknesses, not strengths.'

'I think he is interested in the effectiveness of Community Care,' Tim said grandly.

'We haven't really done it yet, how can we know if it is effective?' Anna said.

'From what little I gleaned when he talked incessantly over lunch at Peach and me, he is charged with exploring ways in which discharge into the community can be done in such a way as to show care in the community is a roaring success. He says that he will get a research grant that will enable him to prove that community care is good for everyone and saves money too. Very good career move if he can pull it off.'

Adam had got up and was flicking through his albums as Tim spoke. 'Billie Holiday?'

'How very late night,' said Grace.

'Yep, and it's only nine o'clock.'

'Well I'm on an early tomorrow, so sadly I shall miss out on Billie,' said Grace. 'And I'm drunk, so I better be heading home.' She glanced at Tim who looked crestfallen. 'That is assuming you are going to escort me, Dr Leith?'

'Yes of course, where are we going? Are we walking?'

'No, we're getting a cab to Hackney.'

'I've never been to Hackney,' Tim said excitedly.

'Of course you haven't,' smiled Grace. 'Adam, I need a cab,' she said loudly and Adam wandered off to the hallway to the phone.

While he was on the phone Grace grinned and whispered to Anna: 'Do you want a lift or are you going to stay a little longer?'

Anna smiled and said 'I can walk from here, and I will... probably.'

Grace put up her hands. 'It would have been rude not to offer.'

Adam came back into the room. 'Cab's on its way, which could mean it's on its way or it could mean they forgot me as soon as I put the phone down. Do you want another drink?' The second part aimed at Anna.

'Are you having another?'

'God, yes.'

'OK, do you have any chocolate? I always want chocolate after a curry.'

The cab came within ten minutes and Tim bumbled his way out of the door in a heady mix of self-consciousness and gin. Grace hugged Anna and kissed Adam on the cheek. After they had gone Anna asked Adam if he thought Grace was going to sleep with Tim.

'I do hope so, but it's possible they may just get a bit angsty for a few hours and sleep near each other wearing vests and fear. I have Maltesers, Fruit and Nut and Fry's Chocolate Cream.'

'Ohh, the last one please! A man with chocolate in the house? Are you sure you live alone?'

They drank more and let the atmosphere change. Quieter now, comfortable but uncertain; sated but alert. They were sitting on the floor leaning against the sofa.

'Tell me about dancing.'

'It made me make sense of myself. I was doing it from the age of about eight. I did it with my brother. I was pretty good, he was better. Then things went a bit wrong and I ended up leaving and moving down here.'

'Wrong?'

'Are you key wording me? Because really it is a bit rude to use basic counselling techniques on another nurse.'

Adam smiled. 'Basic? OK sorry, what sort of wrong?'

Anna shuffled over toward him and sat close enough to be slightly leaning on his shoulder. 'Tell you what...' She spoke more quietly now. 'I'll tell you all about it if you tell me why you go to Libby.'

Adam let his body relax ever so slightly into hers and whispered: 'This is a slightly different counselling technique, right?' And he stared at his record player. The music had stopped but the record was still going round, as it would until he got up and took the stylus off, but he didn't feel like moving and he didn't feel like being evasive. There were dozens of stories that he knew he would never tell for fear of filling the heads of other people with the ghosts that haunted his, but this one?

'OK. Are you sitting comfortably? When I was a student nurse I had every intention of changing the world. For about the first twenty minutes or so it seemed I even thought I could. Believe it or not, I was actually considered to be rather good then. Something of a star student. Mind you, in those days it looked to me as though all you had to do was be able to stand up and chew at the same time and the nursing schools loved you. Anyway, about a year and a half into the course I was stuck on to a rehabilitation unit. You know it quite well. Christ, I hated it. There was I fighting the good fight and there was sod all I could do on this ward. No one wanted saving, the selfish bastards. The place was full of burnt-out schizos, the odd dire poet, a few psychopaths and a handful of old women. Sad and charmless. I had all the energy in the world, the best of intentions, and nowhere to put any of it.

Anyway, in the middle of the placement I had to do a month of nights. I had just moved in here with Catherine, my girlfriend at the time, and I didn't much fancy being away at nightime but it was only for a month. I got to work with one other nurse, he was called Terry and had been working nights on the same ward for about a thousand years. He was like part of the furniture but uglier. At the time, however, I thought he was all right. He'd come out with these crass little soundbites about psychiatry and human suffering and I'd think 'Shit, you can't buy that kind of experience,' which of course you can, quite cheaply, but I was easily impressed.

So I worked nights with Terry and he was really charming. I told him all about Catherine and the new flat. I told him she was nervous about being there on her own and about the amount of work we had to do on the place and he was really sympathetic. He told me I should make sure that I took proper breaks. What he meant was that I could have about a four hour break every night to go off into a sideroom and sleep. He always took a two hour break himself but he always insisted, really insisted, that I take as long as I wanted, even if I didn't want it, if you know what I mean. I never said much, it was my third ward, what the fuck did I know? Anyway, I got the impression that he was trying to be kind but at the same time he was quite happy to have the place to himself.

But one night I'm taking my break, which meant I was reading in the office. I couldn't sleep for some reason. It may have been guilt, I don't know, but it was the office you use now to write up notes and watch me being ridiculous. I looked through the window you look through and saw Terry shining his torch into Libby's face. Libby, like a lot of patients, is a bit closer to sane when she's half asleep and didn't like the torch light in her eyes so she said "Get away, you prat." I heard her. I was impressed: it was an appropriate response. But Terry, quick as a flash, said "Steady Libby, you know what happens to girls who talk like that." And she looked terrified. Lay straight back down and curled up, like a chastised puppy. Terry grinned, he actually grinned and moved on along the line doing his patient checks, which amounted to shining his torch in their faces. I waited until he was back in the office and I went up and sat down and said something about hearing Libby. I thought, and it was a long time ago and I might be wrong, but I thought that he blushed for a moment but he didn't say anything so I asked him outright. I said I heard what you said and I asked him what he meant. At first he said he was making reference to a behavioural programme she used to be on in the Seventies, that she wouldn't be allowed mid-morning tea if she was rude to staff. But Libby didn't have the initiative to be rude. I couldn't imagine that that was ever part of her treatment plan, cutting back on the attitude, so I was pushy. Not in an aggressive way, in a collusive way really: "I bet you have seen some things." I didn't give him the impression I cared, just that I was curious.

Turns out that in the late Fifties and early Sixties the nurses had a card school, and from that they developed their own little therapeutic regime. Patients from the four wards along that corridor, the wards that the nurses came from, were punished for any misbehaviour by having to act as, well, he said helpers and when I said servants he said not exactly. Sometimes it seems they didn't have to help, sometimes they just had to stand there for two or three hours depending on how 'bad' they had been. He said that the threat of that punishment, which was at no point violent, he insisted, improved the behaviour of patients right across the hospital.

So I asked him what he thought about that and he said well it didn't do any harm but I felt he was holding back a bit and I said well I suppose all it amounts to is depriving people of a bit of sleep and getting them to help out a bit and he smiled and said well there was a bit more to it than that and I said what and he said every patient was made to wear an incontinence pad, one of those big yellow ones. And then he smiled and added: "and nothing else..."' Adam paused for a moment and looked at Anna.

'That's sick,' she said quietly.

He nodded. 'Yeah, but you know what? I don't think that was the end of it. Rightly or wrongly I couldn't really stay in the room much beyond that. I had this image in my head, this vile image, and it's still there. I didn't want to hear any more. I didn't want to take the risk that their reality was worse than my imagination. It's like now, I don't want to put that image in your head, nor the idea that people can do that...'

'What did you do?'

'Nothing. Not really. I talked to Libby, when I was back on nights, I told her that I had been told about some things that happened a long time ago and that they may have happened to her and that it was wrong and I was sorry that she had had to tolerate that and that it would never ever happen again but she didn't appear to understand. Although a year later she said what she said.'

'And Terry?'

'He retired a couple of years later. Died within eight months of giving up work. He needed that place more than it needed him.'

They sat quietly, not drinking or speaking until Anna said: 'It's the stories isn't it?'

Adam knew what she meant. Some tales are told and they poison you, others you keep to yourself for fear of poisoning other people. The human decay is contagious, and if we are not careful we can spread it with a reckless self-loathing.

'So why do you go and sit beside her at night?'

Adam turned his head slightly and smelt her hair: he expected it to be clean but it smelt of smoke and long days. 'I don't really know. I think… I think I'm still saying sorry. Not just to Libby. I think it makes me feel closer to human.'

Later, much later, she said to him: 'My mother has a saying, she says people only confess to the sins they can live with or profit from.'

He laughed. 'What a stupid saying. Anyway, you owe me a story.'

'Yes, yes I do and I'll tell you later.'

Anna stayed there that night. As she had planned. They did not discuss it: they kissed over the whisky, they undressed in the living room and had sex on the floor. Later they went to bed. There they made love. They flailed around all night, daring one another to lose themselves in different skin. It wasn't love. It was desperate and generous; it was recurrent and sometimes tender. But it wasn't love. Love was a few floors above them. Adam and Anna were reminding themselves they existed and by a coincidence of nature they both did that by offering service to another. It was, when everything else was stripped away, all that stopped them from spinning off into the Universe.

# 7. Pour A Little Poison

Tim and Adam were sitting in the office discussing the hellish and unhelped existence being lived out by Michael Wells. It had been three weeks since they had got drunk together with Anna and Grace and, while they had never referred to that evening explicitly, they were more relaxed with each other and probably more able to speak freely, which in this case meant with a more open despair.

'He's not sleeping.' Adam had been saying this to Tim for a week.

'He's on enough major tranquillizers to knock out a bull elephant.'

'Not working.'

'Do you want me to prescribe more?'

'If you prescribe more the nation will run out of drugs. They aren't working.'

Tim looked worried. 'Might it be his therapy? Maybe that's throwing things up which are troubling him, keeping him awake.'

Adam scowled. 'The only thing Ms Tandy throws up is her dinner. No, Michael is immune to the drugs. If anything, they seem to make him worse.'

Grace came in with Anna. Tim blushed. So did Grace, a little bit. Anna ignored them both and said to Adam: 'Michael isn't sleeping.'

'I know, that is what we were just discussing.'

Adam nodded at Tim who said: 'I can't give him more drugs, he's on enough to—'

'Yes, I know he's on too many drugs. Maybe that's the problem?'

Tim looked worried. 'I'll call Peach.'

'He'll tell you to give him more drugs,' said Adam.

'Well, he is the consultant,' said Tim primly.

'Yes, he is,' said Adam. 'But if you were the consultant what would you be doing?'

'I thought you didn't do hypothetical questions?'

'Tim!' said Grace sharply. 'What would you be doing?'

Tim blushed. 'My worry is that we have damaged the sleep centres in the brain. There are reports that excessive use of anti-psychotic medication, particularly in high doses, alters the bit of the brain that enables us to go to sleep. It is irreversible. It is torture really: no matter how tired you become you can't sleep, ever, not properly.'

'OK, so how do we help? How do we find out if that is the case?' asked Anna.

'I suppose we need to wean him off the drugs. It's not like they are helping.'

'So do that,' said Grace.

Tim didn't blush, his shoulders slumped and he shook his head.

'What?'

'He can't do that, Grace,' said Adam quietly. 'He can't go to his boss and tell him that one of his patients isn't sleeping and so in order to help him he is reducing the medication that should help him sleep, without seemingly accusing him of excessive prescribing, way over the limit recommended by the drug company, that has led to the prospect of permanent brain damage.'

'No,' murmured Tim. 'But I must.'

A couple of hours later Libby and Anna came to the office. Libby had that 'going to church' look about her. Her thin hair was brushed, and arranged in such a way as to shade if not hide her pink flaking scalp. She had a light brown coat on, which Adam hadn't seen for over a year, and underneath she wore a clean pink cardigan.

'We're going out for tea,' announced Anna. 'And we may look in at a house I have been telling Libby about.'

'Have a nice time, Libby,' said Adam. 'Bring me back some cake.'

'I've nowhere to put cake,' Libby said dismissively. 'It's not like I have a stomach.'

'We'll be a couple of hours,' smiled Anna. 'We'll get something to eat while we are out.'

'Well, OK. But don't let her drag you off dancing.' That was aimed at Anna but for Libby's benefit.

Libby's face filled with contempt. 'Can't go dancing,' she mumbled. 'Don't have any feet.'

Over Anna's shoulder Adam could see the blazered David Cassells and the birdlike Carla Tandy approaching. 'Look out,' he said conspiratorially. 'Psychologists at six o'clock.' Anna turned and Cassells smiled. 'Ms Newton, how lovely to see you. And Ms Hoffman too. Are you two ladies going out?'

Libby started hopping from foot to foot; agitated and uncomfortable with the attention and sheer weight of staff numbers that were surrounding her.

'We are,' said Anna, and then to Adam: 'Play nice now.'

Adam and the psychologists watched them leave and as the ward door closed Cassells smiled and said to Adam: 'Mr Sands, I wonder, do you have a few moments?'

'Of course,' said Adam.

'Is the office OK, or would you prefer a side room where we won't be disturbed?'

'The office is fine. I don't want to keep you.'

Turning to his colleague Cassells said dismissively: 'Carla, would you mind giving us a few minutes alone?' before walking into the office, leaving her outside looking cross.

'Mr Sands, I sensed we got off on the wrong foot, not helped perhaps by my eager, promising but sometimes clumsy trainee trying to undermine you.'

Adam looked at the man in front of him. He was confident, relaxed, good eye contact. And he clearly wanted something. 'How can I help you, Dr Cassells?' he asked gently.

Cassells smiled and put up his hands. 'OK, I'll come straight out and say this and trust that you will treat my... my curiosity with an open-minded professionalism.'

'I'll do my best.'

'Well,' said Cassells, 'while I obviously hold Dr Peach in the utmost regard, and I am grateful that he has helped me settle in, I have some concerns about one or two things I have witnessed, and where I come from if one has concerns one speaks to the charge nurse.'

'What things?' Adam had been expecting something a little more self-serving, like unlimited access to any interesting looking patients or to take Maureen Marley home for the weekend for a DIY project.

'Well, as you will recall, you asked Carla to do some work with Michael Wells. It was a good idea, indeed it is doing her some good and I would like to think it might be of some use to Mr Wells if he wasn't so—'

'Mad?'

'No. So drugged. I checked his drug chart, Mr Sands. You are giving him too many drugs.'

Adam looked at Cassells. The words began to form in his head: 'We administer what is prescribed.' But they didn't come out because he knew they would sound like 'We simply do as we are told.' So he went instead with: 'Yes, I was speaking with the doctor about that very thing this morning.'

'Right,' said Cassells 'So you and, perhaps more importantly, Dr Leith know he is being over-medicated.'

'I think everyone knows, Dr Cassells.'

'Well, what are you going to do about it? Sorry. What are we going to do about it?'

'Tim is going to talk to Dr Peach today. I wonder if Michael's inability to talk to his therapist might also be fed back?'

Cassells nodded. 'I could have a word about that. And what about you, Mr Sands, will you be contributing?'

Adam sensed he was supposed to rise to this, to either align himself to Cassells' crusade for justice or be seen to collude with care that amounted to cruelty. Instead he smiled and shrugged. 'Did you come here to ask if I will side with you in a row with the consultant, Dr Cassells?'

'I wouldn't put it quite like that, Mr Sands, but I suppose I wonder where you might stand, given that you already know the treatment plan you are administering is at best excessive and at worst toxic.'

Adam had the sense that every part of Cassells was a lie, except his words. He was right, the more people who pointed out a concern the more chance it would be heard. He didn't trust the man or his motives but that was not the point. He also felt embarrassed.

'I'll feed back my concerns to Dr Peach. Firstly noting that Michael is struggling to function because of the medication and secondly, noting that in asking my nurses to administer a dosage that is not recommended I am putting them in a very difficult position.'

Cassells nodded. 'Thank you. I don't think you like me, Mr Sands, and I can live with that, but I suspect we might be on the same side.'

Adam shrugged and smiled thinly. 'I wouldn't worry too much about my tastes, Dr Cassells: I don't really like anyone.'

Not long after Cassells had left it was lunchtime. Lunch was brought to the wards in a steel trolley by a grubby kitchen assistant and Adam could tell the time by the arrival of the smell of mashed potato and something that was green and overcooked. But still the patients came, even Michael, sitting when and where he was told and murmuring thanks when his dinner, a gathering of vegetables around some boiled chicken, was put in front of him. Michael liked puddings best. Adam knew that if you wanted to talk to Michael the best time to try was just after pudding, which was treacle pudding and custard. Michael would stay at the table on the off-chance that there were seconds.

When Adam sat down beside him Michael was looking at the trolley hopefully. He had custard on his beard.

'How are the voices Michael?' Adam asked quietly. Michael shrugged. 'Do you want another pudding?' Michael nodded. 'I'll sort that out in a second. Tell me about the voices, please.'

'Bad,' Michael said.

'Are the drugs helping at all?' Michael looked away. 'Michael, are they helping, do you think?'

'Can't tell. Can't sleep. Voices are louder during the day.'

'Well, you have your biggest dose in the morning, Michael, so I'd expect them to be quieter during the day, wouldn't you?' Michael stared at the trolley. Adam turned to the nursing assistant who was dishing out puddings for the remaining patients. 'Can you do an extra one for Michael please?'

'Michael has had one,' she snapped.

'Well, he can have another one,' said Adam without looking round.

'I think you are on too many drugs, Michael, but we need to cut them down slowly so you don't get ill.' He thought he saw Michael laugh. 'But we will cut them down and see, each day, if anything gets better or if anything gets worse. OK?'

Michael seemed to be just staring at the trolley, ignoring Adam until the extra pudding arrived, tossed on to the table in front of him. Before he began to eat he looked at Adam for the first time, held his gaze for a moment and nodded.

Adam went to the room Anna used for counselling her soon-to-be-discharged patients. He closed the door, sat in the large worn armchair that the patients slumped in when being assessed and lit a cigarette. Looking out of the window he watched as the kitchen staff unloaded a van full of processed food. Large boxes of powdered egg and semolina; wooden crates full of tinned beans; big tins of cheap coffee. Originally the hospital had been run as a working farm. Patients had worked the land and grown their own food, selling what they didn't need to the local town. At one time the hospital had been close to self-sufficient; it struggled to make the milk go round the three thousand inpatients but the cows were hardy and waste was frowned upon. They made their own bread. They had a woodwork shop where they made furniture, some of which they sold, which gave them money for cigarettes, fruits which struggled to flourish in North London, and fuel. At harvest time, when the potatoes needed picking on the larger farms further north, then the hospital would provide workers in exchange for potatoes and a less-than-average but better-than-nothing wage.

But, as the idea of what sickness was became more sophis-ticated, the cultural acceptability of the hospital as working farm faded. Sick people, all of them, required treatment and picking potatoes or milking cows was not a treatment. If anything, it smacked of punishment, cheap labour, slavery almost. So they turned the mad into patients and sold the cows to an abattoir in Harlesden. Patients were people you did things to and, as long as you could call them patients, then whatever it was you did was called treatment. The mid-twentieth century was a relatively dark age for madness, and the problem with an asylum when it emerged into the light was that everything looked like progress: insulin therapy, electricity to the head, psychosurgery, drugs. These were the gifts of science and science civilized us, made us modern and better. Especially the drugs.

Adam didn't like Cassells. It wasn't just the power he seemed to have been presented with on arrival. Or the pious manner and annoying student, or the fact that he came into his office and articulated Adam's own concerns as if he had mined them. There was more to it than that: he disliked Cassells more than Peach in the same way that he had always claimed—certainly when drunk—to dislike liberals more than conservatives. Ultimately they do greater harm by vaguely civilizing the damage done by others and they get to feel clean afterwards. 'We can find all sorts of ways to excuse what we do here,' thought Adam. 'We can imagine we reduce pain, police against evil, even do some good, but we can't feel clean. That is simply too much bad faith.'

Adam put out his cigarette and walked back to the office. He picked up the phone and called Tim. 'Have you spoken to Peach yet?'

'No, but I will.' Tim sounded slightly put out that Adam was reminding him.

'I think you should wait, Tim. I think I should speak to him first.'

'Why?'

'Well, for one thing I think it is my job, but I also think he would feel less threatened if it were me, a nurse, asking if we are doing the right thing rather than you, a doctor, reminding him that we are not.'

Tim paused for a moment. 'That doesn't seem terribly fair. You make it sound like a game.'

'Well, we both know it is a game, Tim, and I like to think that we are both more interested in winning this particular part of it than we are in making a stand against the fact that it's a game.'

'Eh?'

'Look, Peach is more likely to listen to me than you.'

'Oh, thank you very much.'

'That's not about you, Tim: it's about me and my shared history with your boss.'

Outside the office the laundry cart had arrived. The driver, a plump bald Greek, got off the cart and lit up a cigarette. He looked around and momentarily appeared to be moving to unload the cart of the clean sheets, nightdresses and towels when Maureen Marley appeared, grinned and set about unloading it for him. The driver said something about a horse race from the day before and Maureen said what seemed to be a full sentence in response. After the cart had been unloaded the driver offered Maureen a cigarette. Maureen took it, put it behind her ear and began loading the dirty laundry on to the cart. She laughed—

not a sustained laugh but a short, genuine laugh—at something he said about the three o'clock at Goodwood. She shook her head and said something and he took out a newspaper from his back pocket, looked at it intently and said something back. They were comparing racing tips, or Maureen was giving them and the driver was taking her seriously. He took a small pen from his shirt pocket and circled something in his paper. Maureen finished the loading and accepted a light for the cigarette. The driver got back on to his cart and drove off the ward shouting: 'See you tomorrow, George.' Maureen was smiling. She was muttering something to herself as well, and smoking, walking back to the day room and nodding, but mostly she was smiling.

Adam picked up the phone and called Walter Peach's secretary. 'Hello Anne, how are you? How are the kids? Five? Already? It's lucky we don't age as quickly as they do, isn't it? No I'm OK thanks, not too bad… Listen, is Walter available at any point today? I need a quick word with him.'

And then he went and found Grace, who was sitting on an armchair with its back against the wall in the day room watching the once-high-as-a-kite Mary Peacock slumped in a chair on the opposite side of the room, wrapped in a grey-skinned misery.

'Grace, I need to go and see Peach now. Will you be OK here?'

'Yeah, we have enough people on the ward to cover.' She didn't look at him as she spoke, and, aware that he would pick up on that, she added: 'Mary is struggling today.'

'So are you. What's the matter?' Grace ignored him and he crouched down beside the chair and said quietly: 'Grace?'

'Not now,' she said quietly. 'It's just man trouble.'

Adam waited a moment. Not now and not here made sense. 'I'll catch up with you later, OK?' and he touched her arm gently before getting up and walking off the ward.

Peach's office was on the other side of the hospital grounds in a newly built annexe about three-quarters of a mile from Adam's ward. He had to walk the full length of the central corridor and out of a side door before crossing what used to be a flower garden but was now a bench with some wasteland around it, followed by a small car park and then the new building which was named after a tree: 'Elm Annexe.' Nobody knew why.

As he came out of the main hospital into the light he saw the young man he'd encountered in the corridor on the night of Stephen's party. He was sitting, quite elegantly, on the wooden bench wearing sunglasses and a cheesecloth shirt, looking up into the branches of a large oak tree. He didn't turn to face Adam when he said: 'Hello again.'

'Hello,' said Adam. 'Have you lost a kite?'

The young man smiled and turned to face him. 'I like trees, what can I say? How goes your day?'

'Oh, so-so. How about yours?'

'Mine's OK, mostly waiting, but I suppose ultimately that's what we are all doing one way or another. I just try to make sure that while I am waiting I am doing something that pleases me.'

'Like looking at trees?'

'Yep.'

The young man never stopped smiling. Definitely a hippie, thought Adam. In the daylight his eyes were even more strikingly blue and, although he was pale, his pallor wasn't that of a patient. Adam wanted to ask if he was a nurse or patient but it felt such a lame question, as though in asking it he would have somehow failed a test.

'This used to be farmland, you know.' The boy smiled. 'And I believe this bit here was a flower garden,' added Adam. 'Not sure what happened, I suppose people just stopped wanting flowers.'

The boy nodded. 'People are strange,' he said.

'Have a nice day,' offered Adam as he walked past him and into the car park.

'You too. And don't forget what I said about the dew.'

'Patient,' Adam thought.

Elm Annexe smelt of pine and carpet freshener and it had a proper receptionist who noticed when someone came in. It housed not only offices for the consultant psychiatrists but also therapy rooms for the clinical psychologists and psychother-apists. This place always made Adam think he should wipe his feet and so he made a point of not doing. It was pristine and modern and he knew he didn't belong. He didn't speak to the receptionist, instead walking through the double doors marked 'staff only' and wandering down the plush carpeted corridor to the door that said 'Dr Peach'. Walter's secretary held up a finger to Adam as he entered, designed to ensure that he wait while she phoned through to her boss to let him know that he had a visitor. Adam would, in other circumstances, have ignored the finger, but today was a day to make friends.

'He can see you now.' The secretary had fair hair and pursed lips. Her large bosom and purple shoulder-padded blouse lent her the sort of severity you'd find in a West End bouncer. Adam nodded but didn't look at her as he entered Peach's office and quietly closed the door.

'This is rare, Adam. Is everything alright?'

'Thank you Walter. Yes, I think things are fine. I just have a bit of a worry and I wanted to talk to you about it in private, if that is OK?'

'Of course.' Peach sat down behind his desk and settled back with his hands in front of him, fingers touching each other like a steeple.

'Well,' said Adam. 'I am a bit worried about one of our patients, Michael Wells: he's not sleeping and he should be. He's on enough meds to knock out Poland but they aren't touching him and now they aren't even sedating him. I'm worried we are doing damage with the drugs and I wanted to talk directly to you about that, Walter.'

'Are you questioning my clinical judgement, Adam?' Not said aggressively but direct and genuinely enquiring.

Adam didn't speak immediately. 'Well, I suppose to be honest, Walter, that depends on what sort of mood you are in. I think what I am doing is being collegiate and open with a consultant I have worked with for a while and expressing some legitimate concerns about a treatment that may be doing more harm than good, but if you are in a place where you experience any discussion or concern as an assault... Well I'm on a loser, then, aren't I? Because we both know you don't have to even entertain me, don't we?'

Peach nodded and half smiled. 'Dr Cassells was in here this morning talking about the same patient Adam.'

Adam reddened. 'Ah, right. Saying the same thing, no doubt? And I suppose that begins to look like a conspiracy.'

'Quite the contrary, Adam. Dr Cassells was saying the opposite, in effect. He was saying that Carla Tandy felt she was making good progress with Michael because of the heavy sedation. Dr Cassells' specialist therapy is designed to work with people who are on high doses of medication. He was saying that he admired me for stepping beyond what he called the arbitrary constraints laid down by the pharmaceutical regulators and putting the patient first.'

'He isn't worried about Michael not sleeping or the fact that the voices are getting worse?' asked Adam.

'He feels we have to keep with the plan.'

Adam looked at Peach, who looked slightly uncomfortable. 'And what do you think, Walter?'

Peach smiled, a genuine smile, and reddened slightly. 'I think I am over-prescribing and I suspect Dr Cassells is being a tad manipulative. However, I am not sure to what end, and I am not sure what to do about it.'

Peach looked older than Adam remembered, more human. Uncertainty does that, thought Adam. 'I think you are right, Walter, about Cassells. And about Michael, for that matter.'

Peach nodded. 'What drug has Michael been on the longest?' he asked.

'Chlorpromazine. Lots of it.'

'How about we start reducing that, easing him off it? Then review where we go from there on Wednesday.'

'We can start with his morning dose, it's not doing much as far as I or Michael can tell,' Adam said.

'I do wonder if I am getting too old for this.'

'I think this makes us all feel old, Walter. Not sure that it's the same thing.'

Peach opened up a drawer in his desk and took out two photographs. He handed them to Adam. 'That,' he said, pointing to Adam's left hand, 'is Graham's little boy. The two in the other picture are my grandchildren. I often wonder what it would be like telling them that their father had killed himself while under my care.'

'Our care, Walter.'

The two men, separated by a large oak desk and around thirty years, sat in silence.

Finally Adam spoke. 'I don't imagine it's any consolation, Walter, but for what it's worth, I feel too old for this too. And—between us?—I wouldn't trust Cassells as far as I could throw him.'

When Adam got back to the ward Maureen Marley was standing outside smoking a roll-up and staring at the floor.

'Hello,' said Adam. Maureen nodded. 'Are you waiting for someone?' Maureen shook her head. 'So.' Adam took a cigarette from his jacket pocket. 'Let's take a moment, if you don't mind?' He held up the cigarette to indicate he was going to stop for a smoke with her. Maureen shook her head to indicate she didn't mind at all. 'Tell me, what is happening about your accommodation?' Maureen shrugged. 'Was the house you went to see any good?'

Maureen laughed. 'Didn't like the smell.'

'Air freshener?' asked Adam.

'Somt'ing like that.' They both leaned on the walls, one on either side of the corridor, dragging on their cigarettes. Maureen looking at the smoke floating towards the arched, pitted ceiling, Adam looking at Maureen.

'You know they can't make you live somewhere you don't want to live, right?'

'Yeah, I know,' laughed Maureen.

'You are not on a section, Maureen, you can leave hospital when you want and you can refuse to go where you are put. They can try and persuade you, they can tell you there is nowhere else to go, but they can't make you go anywhere.' Maureen carried on looking at the smoke. 'Or you can bide your time and wait until you are offered something you like, something nearer the bookies for example?' Maureen smiled. 'If you're not sure and you want to check things out, you can ask me or Anna, you know?' Maureen nodded, or at least Adam thought it looked like a nod, and that felt like the end of the conversation. He stubbed out his cigarette on the concrete window ledge a few feet further down the corridor, nodded to Maureen and went back on to the ward.

Grace was sitting in the office.

'Mary is very low,' she said without looking up when Adam came in. 'Michael seems a wee bit calmer.'

'We're going to reduce his meds. Have you seen Tim, by the way?'

'Good. And no, not today,' said Grace.

'Oh, and Cassells is messing with us, not sure why. Saying one thing to us, another to Peach, testing us or playing around or maybe just undermining everyone,' he explained briefly.

All the time Grace busied herself by putting medical files in the right order in a large grey cabinet in the corner. 'Someone has been in here and not put them back in the right place,' she said.

'So.' Adam sat on the corner of the desk nearest the closed door. 'What's going on with you?'

'Ahh,' said Grace. 'What indeed? Nothing important really, just your normal everyday ridiculousness. I appear to be like flypaper for ludicrous men.'

'Norman? Well, we've known he is ridiculous since day one, Grace. He's never going to leave his family and even if he did...'

Grace's eyes were beginning to blur a little. 'Ahh, but there you go, see Mr Clever Clogs...' Only Grace, thought Adam, could get away with saying Mr Clever Clogs, albeit as a way of slowing down the onset of tears. 'That's where you are wrong, because he is leaving them. For me, it seems.'

'Blimey, what has brought that on and why is it a sad thing? Don't we want Norman any more?'

'Oh Adam, it's bloody ridiculous!' She was crying now, softly, into her hands for fear of being seen. 'You know that night Tim stayed? Well he stayed, you know, it was nice. Next morning Norman phoned, he said he had some time and was coming over. I said no. He guessed someone was there and got all outraged. I got all indignant. You sleep with someone else every bloody night, I said. Yes, but that's my wife, he said, as if that was going to make me feel OK...'

'And where was Tim in all of this?'

'He was sitting on the bed, white as a sheet. I don't think he is used to... things like that...'

'Things like what, pet? Sex? Love triangles? The telephone?'

'Well, sex mostly, but the idea of there being another man surprised him, the fact that he was married with kids shocked him and the fact that he is forty-seven bemused him.'

'Poor Tim.'

'Oh, don't start with the poor Tim. After I got off the phone and I was a bit upset and told him what was going on, he got on his high horse and said to me "Well, I'm afraid I can't take this on." And flounced out like Joan bloody Collins.'

There was a tap on the office door. Anna and Libby were back. Adam opened the door and said: 'Can it wait a moment please?'

'Of course,' Anna nodded. 'I'll make Libby a cup of tea and talk to you in a bit.'

Grace was wiping her nose with a hanky. 'It's fine, it's fine. You shouldn't ask me questions at work, you know that.'

'OK,' said Adam quietly. 'I'll buy you a drink later if you want, but I'm just curious about one thing: why are we crying? Norman wants you, Tim wants you...'

Grace laughed and a bubble came out of her nose. 'If I wanted a marrying man I wouldn't have been sleeping with a forty-seven year old with two kids in the first place, would I?'

Adam found Anna in the kitchen. Libby had gone. 'So how did it go?'

'It went well. She seemed to quite like the house. She even stroked the duvet. Not that she has any hands.'

'Good.' Adam smiled. 'How long?'

'About four weeks, I would think. I'll take her along again next week, and again the weekend after that. There is some money, so she can begin to pick some bits and pieces out for her room. I think she'll be fine. I think she'll be better than fine.'

Adam nodded. 'In other news: we are reducing Michael's meds; we don't know where Tim is, and it has been confirmed that Cassells is either a manipulative bastard or he is conducting some kind of pointless psychological experiment on us all,' he said.

Anna looked cross. 'I think you're overdoing it with Cassells. Maybe you just don't like people who try to shake things up?'

Adam looked at her, nodded and said quietly: 'I think you have the look of someone who wants to be cross.' And he left the room.

Michael was sitting in the day room, pulling at his beard and muttering to himself. Mary hadn't moved a muscle all morning. Libby was standing in the middle of the room staring at nothing on the wall and playing with the button hole on her still-clean, pink cardigan. Adam went into the office and phoned Tim's extension. No answer. He went back to the day room and sat down near Mary. 'Could you drink something, pet?' he asked quietly. She lifted her head and stared at him with the emptiest of eyes. He gazed back softly for as long as he could, but he knew she couldn't see him.

At the end of the shift Adam walked slowly up the drive. He used to go to the gym every day. Now he tended to go two or three times a week, more out of habit than anything else. He'd got through the day without taking any drugs from the medicine trolley and without having an argument with anyone. On the face of it a good day, not that he felt good. He felt agitated, unsettled. He couldn't place why and he was excused from thinking about it by the sound of his name. He turned around and Anna was walking quickly up the drive behind him. He stopped and waited. She was breathing heavily. 'You need to get more exercise,' he said.

'Never off duty eh?' Anna said. 'Actually, I've just run the length of the corridor.'

'Why?'

She looked away, up the drive and out of the hospital. Getting her breath back, fixing her gaze on something outside the gates. 'I wanted to say sorry.' Adam shrugged. 'Hormones,' she deadpanned.

'Bollocks,' he replied in the same tone.

She laughed. 'I'm not sure why I was defending Cassells.'

'Me neither,' said Adam. 'He's playing some silly game, asking Peach to do one thing, me to do another. Divisive, pointless and annoying.'

Anna thought for a moment. 'Right, he's trying to charm me and I'm not sure why. It's not a sex thing, it's something else.'

'What does he want?'

'Not sure. He's being very attentive, lots of active listening. I find it a bit patronizing but I patronize right back.' Adam looked at her. She kept looking up the drive and turning her head back to the hospital.

'What's up?' he asked, looking at the gates.

'Nothing,' she said. 'Look, are you doing anything later?'

'When later?'

'When I finish, about five-thirty?'

'No.'

'Would you mind if I popped over? Just briefly, I promise, I have to be somewhere at seven-thirty. I just wanted to run something past you.'

'OK,' said Adam. 'I can cook you an omelette if you like?'

Anna looked at him and smiled. 'That's nice of you, thank you, but I don't eat eggs. Baked potato with cheese and beans? See you around five-thirty.' And she turned and went back to the hospital.

When Adam reached the gates of the hospital he saw a man standing behind the large concrete pillar staring at him. Adam caught his eye and the man looked away, embarrassed perhaps. When Adam looked back, after he had walked twenty yards down the road, the young man—medium height, expensive leather jacket, black hair—was staring down the drive toward the hospital. He looked like he was afraid to go past the gates for fear of catching madness. He looked like he came from a different sort of world completely.

# 8. Strange Fruit

When Anna emerged from the hospital, Black was waiting. She had seen him at lunchtime as she walked across the front of the hospital toward the canteen, and she had seen him when she had spoken to Adam. In fact, she had wanted to be seen talking to Adam. She hadn't been able to eat her lunch. There was nothing about Black that had intimidated or even unnerved Anna but his presence, here, made her feel anxious now. She rationalized, swallowing down the rising bile of unease by reminding herself that he was nearer to being inadequate than psychotic. He was probably the sort of man—all bottled beer with bits of fruit on top and expensive moisturizer—who wasn't used to being left, certainly not like that. Maybe he wanted a little bit of control back, needed a last word. Or worse, perhaps he had feelings, other, unpredicted feelings, feelings that were about someone other than himself. That would be embarrassing, having to facilitate something earnest or even tearful.

But these imaginings were keeping something bigger at bay. Something that was sitting deep in her stomach and threatening to burn her precious insides out if she did not douse it. What if he knew? What if he had some irrational inkling that she was at the very beginning of a pregnancy that he might have helped with? Not that he could, not that she did, not for absolute sure. She'd done the test and it had turned blue, but she hadn't been to the doctor yet. He couldn't know, it was not possible, but his presence, the fact that he was here, opened up the possibility that if he did know he might care and that was something that, frankly, Anna had not given very much attention to.

'This is a bit out of the way for you isn't it?' She spoke as neutrally as she could, holding a steady gaze, barely stopping as she walked past, sure he would walk with her, which he did.

'I was just passing.'

'You've been there a long time for someone just passing.'

'I wanted a word.'

'It's a bit creepy, to be honest: ex-lover hanging around outside the lunatic asylum I work in for a whole afternoon.'

'Look, can I buy you a coffee? I just want a chat.'

'I have somewhere to be, Black. What is it?' She looked directly into his eyes with a deliberate coldness.

He looked away. 'I haven't come to try to convince you to carry on seeing me.'

'So why have you come?'

'I... I was hoping you might give me some advice.' He looked embarrassed and Anna softened slightly.

'My range of expertise is limited, Black.'

'Yeah... I've been having these... thoughts. My mates say I'm paranoid but...' He looked across the road, almost turning completely away from Anna. As he turned back, in profile, she could see that his eyes were damp: maybe the wind, probably not. 'And a couple of days ago I heard this voice in my head... it told me to come and see you. I didn't want to, not at first, no offence but you were pretty clear when you left that that was it and I'm not stupid, I know that story you told was about you. Mine wasn't about me, by the way, but you know that, I guess. Anyway I didn't want to... you know... but the voice kept saying...'

'OK.' Anna felt herself trying to shift from ex-lover to nurse. 'Have you been smoking?'

'Smoking?'

'Cannabis, Black. Have you been smoking much dope?'

'A bit.'

'More than usual?'

119

'About the same... maybe a bit more. I met this... this person and they like to smoke.'

'Stop it.'

'What? Why? It's harmless...'

'OK, don't stop it and I'll see you in here.' She pointed at the hospital behind her. 'Or one very much like it, in about a week. Bye.'

'No. Hang on, wait. You think it's the dope?'

'Yes, almost definitely. Your age, your symptoms. You're lucky, you can do something to make it better. Most of my patients can't. You need to not smoke any dope. None. You need to actually not be around it. Not inhale it, not even be in the same room as it, OK?'

'OK. Are you sure?'

'Yes, I am. Now listen, for old times' sake you can phone me in a week or so. You can't come here again. You can't come round. We are not having sex. You can check in and we'll see how you are doing OK?' Black nodded and for the first time since she had seen him Anna smiled, a soft, almost warm smile. 'OK. Trust me on this Black, do not smoke any dope. No matter how cute she is, you really really really do not want to end up in here.' She pointed over her shoulder with her thumb.

'She isn't actually all that cute.'

'Good. Find yourself an aerobics instructor. I have to go now.'

Black leaned forward to kiss her and Anna turned her cheek. 'Thank you.'

'You're welcome.'

She didn't look behind her when she walked away but her body was stiff and her breathing more shallow than normal. She noticed herself gathering the fears of other people and packing them into the space between her hips and her breasts. Except it wasn't the fears *of* other people so much as the fears *about* other people that crept under her skin and coloured her thinking, her judgment. She didn't fill herself with what other people felt about the world: she worried instead about what they might do to her, if they were ever given the chance. So she was always careful to ensure that they didn't get the chance.

'Where's my baked potato?' Anna arrived just a little late and, even though she hadn't been in Adam's flat since the one night they had spent together, she was comfortable enough to walk in, put her bag down on the chair and slump on the sofa.

'Takes too long to bake a potato. Especially when I don't have any. Cheese and tomato sandwich. There may be yoghurt after, if you eat your crusts.'

Anna laughed. 'I've had a rubbish day,' she said. 'Yoghurt can only help.'

'Well, I was there for most of it,' said Adam.

Adam brought her a small plate with a sandwich on it and put a glass of orange juice on the table in the middle of the room.

'Thank you. It got worse after you left. Tim showed up in a foul mood, being very snappy with Grace. What's going on there? I told him about Michael's medication and he said that's going to cost us. Next thing I know, I get a phone call from the social worker telling me that Maureen is moving to Wade Avenue, or the House of Pink as we like to call it, and that I need to set up another visit and work towards a discharge date. I told her that that move was on hold and we were working on a different placement and she told me that Peach had told her only today to push through the paperwork. I told Tim, he wasn't surprised. He said that Cassells had been talking about Maureen... Did you know he's been through her notes in real detail? He says she should go to Wade Avenue. Peach agreed. I've not told Maureen. I'm not finished with this yet.'

'Cassells does like to get involved,' said Adam. 'Wonder why? I mean, he can't simply want to spread misery wherever he goes.'

'Maybe it's like you said, he's conducting an experiment? Good sandwich.'

'Divide and rule, I suspect. Or he's a psychopath.'

'Tim was really upset, he said he felt undermined. It was a pride thing I think, but I also thought there was more to it then that. He's not the sort of bloke you imagine being angry, but he was very angry.'

'Did he say where he had been all morning?'

'Headache apparently. Migraine.'

As Anna chewed, Adam thought. He didn't want to, but he did anyway. He could feel a tingling anxiety in the tips of his fingers. Worry? Anger? Fear? It was partly about Maureen. It was the nature of the cruelty that disturbed him. Framed by good intention, rational, spiteful. But there was something about Cassells that made him alarmed, almost made him fearful.

'What would happen if Maureen refused to go?' asked Adam.

Anna shrugged. 'She would be persuaded, I imagine, or put on a section.'

'She isn't sectionable.'

'I'm sure Peach could find a couple of people to say she is.'

'I'll talk to Peach.'

'Hey, I don't mind you making me sandwiches but I don't want you fighting my fights.'

'Not your fight, it's Maureen's. And, in case you hadn't noticed, she is my patient.'

'Mostly mine,' Anna said quietly, mocking.

Adam offered her a cigarette.

'No thanks, I'm giving up,' she said. Anna got up and went to the window.

'You being followed?' asked Adam.

'Yeah, maybe. I didn't come to talk about that though.'

Adam stood behind Anna and looked out of the window. He couldn't see anyone. She was probably being sarcastic.

Adam noticed that he quite liked Anna. He didn't think she made sense and he wasn't sure that he would ever trust her, but he quite liked her. That was, he thought, the advantage of having slept with her. People find it harder to lie when they don't have their clothes on, and anyway it's easier to make sense of someone when they are lying on top of you.

'So, apart from the yoghurt and the surveillance opportunity, what is it you wanted to talk about?'

Anna turned around and smiled, a really big smile, right up to her eyes. 'I'm not sure what order to say this in, so can I just ask you to suspend judgment until I've finished? It won't take long.' Adam shrugged, stepped aside and let her walk past and sit down.

'I liked the sex, it was good sex. I don't want to have a conversation about it meaning anything because we both know it didn't, beyond being good, er... , well done. I may be pregnant; I make it a 50/50 chance it is yours. I sort of wanted to get pregnant, well not sort of, I *did* want to get pregnant. The bloke who may be following me, but probably isn't, was sort of a boyfriend who I split up with. I wanted to get pregnant, so I slept with him and then left him. I didn't and don't want any involvement from whoever the father is, but I thought it might be OK to tell you, rather than make myself really dislike you. Which I could do, in fact I may have begun trying it out in the kitchen earlier, and I have done it with people in the past. Then I thought maybe I didn't have to do that. Erm, sorry.'

Adam looked at her and nodded. It was the sort of nod you offer when you are choosing to demonstrate some sort of acknowledgement that something has been said but you don't really know what you think or feel or should say. He nodded again. He was still nodding when he sat down on the armchair facing the sofa.

'It was only three weeks ago?'

'Yeah, twenty-four days actually. Does that sound obsessive? You might be thinking I'm weird. Actually I am weird, I suppose, but you might be thinking psychopath. Are you thinking psychopath?' Adam half shrugged. 'Look, you know the story I told you about dancing? You get that, right? I left home young and I tend to live a very contained life. I am a serial monogamist,

I haven't ever really fallen in love, not incurably and I want a baby. I don't want the relationship that goes with it, I don't want money or weekend visits. I think I wanted the father thing to be wrapped up in anonymity and it was a nice evening and you're quite cute when you aren't hungover.'

'That's the nicest thing anyone has ever said to me,' said Adam. He pointed to the window. 'And the other guy knows and that is why he is following you around?'

'No, no, he doesn't know. I had no intention of ever seeing him again but he... Well, he thinks he may be having a bit of a breakdown. He isn't, well, I don't think he is, he's just been smoking too much weed. He didn't know what to do and knew that I worked in the industry, so to speak.'

'So you wanted to get pregnant without any complications and chose to sleep with a dopehead beginning a nervous breakdown, and me? Were none of the Muppets available?' Anna laughed. 'The sex was nice,' said Adam.

'It was,' she nodded.

'I'm in no shape to be a dad.'

'I don't want you to be a dad.'

'Why are you telling me again?'

'You'll notice at some point and I don't want to move and I thought if I got it out of the way early you might not... Hell, I don't know. I think I thought you might be OK about it.'

This time Adam laughed. 'I don't know if that says more about you or me.'

Black hadn't followed Anna. He left her with a low-lying sense of relief. It was the drugs that had made him think everyone at work was looking at him oddly. That his idea to dress up some bloke as a bear in a floppy hat to sell beer had made people talk about him behind his back and in the case of Angela and Sheryl laugh in his face, or at least at his trousers. It was the drugs that made him scared on the tube and made him want to eat biscuits more than he wanted to have sex. It was the

124

drugs. Anna would know that sort of thing. Although she had looked at him a bit oddly and she seemed hostile, certainly not pleased to see him. Like she knew something about him. Maybe someone had said something? He wondered about the tall bloke she had been talking to at lunchtime, the guy who had looked at him funny when he was leaving the hospital. Perhaps Anna was sleeping with him? Perhaps Anna had been sleeping with him all the time? He wondered why he cared. He didn't care, but it made him anxious anyway. And as he wandered reluctantly to the tube station to head home he heard a voice in his head that sounded a lot like his father's—as far as he could remember, because he hadn't heard his father's voice since he had died when Black was ten. It said: 'Just because you're paranoid it doesn't mean they aren't out to get you.' And Black noticed a woman walk past him and shoot him an odd look as he nodded to the voice in his head and must have said out loud: 'Ain't that the truth.'

Adam had tried to distract himself with press-ups after Anna had left but it hadn't worked. He put on a record. Otis Redding. It was wrong. Chumbawumba: lively but not subtle. Orange Juice. Nope. The floor was littered with LPs. He tried the radio: it was rubbish. He wanted to phone Grace, who had worked a long shift, and ask her what was going on, but she had just done fourteen hours' work. To call her when she got home to talk about it was too much. Although if he phoned her before she left work that wouldn't be so bad... It was 8.17. She would leave at nine. Anna had left at seven.

Pregnant? She couldn't be sure. Didn't he read that 20% of pregnancies didn't make it past twelve weeks? And if there was only a 50/50 chance he was the dad... What was 80% of a 50/50 chance? 'Don't say 40%' he said out loud to nobody but himself. 'It isn't 40%.'

Isaac Hayes' version of *Walk on by* helped, or at least he didn't take it off after less than a minute as he had with the others. It was 11 minutes 52 seconds long. 'Sod it,' he thought and phoned the ward.

'What's going on?'

'Are you psychic?' asked Grace.

'Anna popped round for a cheese and tomato sandwich.'

'Is that what it's called?'

'No, really. Anyway, what is going on?'

'Tim is behaving like a hormonal twelve year old girl; Maureen is being put in a home for Barbie; Michael is asking for drugs to help him sleep. Mary is still sitting in the same chair you left her in eight hours ago. Norman wants me to marry him, despite his already being married and no, he hasn't told his wife he has proposed to someone else. Oh, and Cassells wants me to do my psychotherapy training. He told me this while he was telling me how outraged he is that Maureen isn't being allowed to live as George. He says I have a naturally calming yet neutral presence, apparently. I think he has a naturally slimy yet wouldn't-trust-him-as-far-as-I-could-throw-him presence, personally.'

Adam didn't say anything for a moment, mostly in case Grace hadn't finished but partly because he didn't know where to start. The polite thing would have been Norman; the thing he wanted to talk about was Maureen.

'You would make a good therapist. I have to say I don't think Cassells is pointing that out for altruistic reasons.'

'He's a psychopath,' she said. 'The psychopath light went off in my head when he was talking to me.'

'Yeah, he is. Out of control too, I fear. He is the one who allegedly persuaded Peach to put Maureen in the home for Barbie.'

'Bastard.'

'Yeah. And Tim?'

'I don't think he's a psychopath... He may be a bastard.'

'No, I meant what is going on there?'

This time Grace paused. 'I'm not sure. There is something he isn't telling me and he's hiding it behind the fact that there was something I didn't tell him.'

Adam waited to see if Grace was going to continue. Relieved that she didn't, he said: 'And Maureen, does she know?'

'No, of course not. She'll be the last to be told.'

'What do you think would happen if we told her?'

'Do you mean what would happen to her? Would she do something stupid? I don't know. I don't think so, but wouldn't bet my life on it. Or do you mean what would happen to us? We'd get called unprofessional, I suppose.'

'Funny idea, really,' mused Adam. 'That keeping a patient informed about their future and the discussions and decisions made about their lives is unprofessional.'

'I think we'd be told that causing undue stress or anxiety is unprofessional, don't you?'

'Oh yeah, definitely,' agreed Adam. 'But that doesn't mean we shouldn't do something.'

'No, of course,' said Grace. There was a pause before she added, 'So what are we going to do?'

Later, Adam was failing to sleep. He had taken two diazepam, drunk three glasses of cheap whisky and smoked a joint. He felt as though his outer layers were ready to sleep but his innards wanted to go dancing. It was 10.53 and he wasn't even going to pretend to try to read. He thought about Anna. He knew, somewhere, that the madness she had brought round earlier was important but he couldn't process it, not through the drugs. His mind kept turning back to Maureen Marley. It wasn't the fact that she was being moved into the wrong home, well it was, that was madness, but it wasn't that that made his liver rage. It was the reasoning behind it or, worse, the way the reasoning had taken place. It was essentially some blokes messing around, playing games, and part of him felt as if perhaps they were inviting him to play. More: demanding that he join in, stand in line with Cassells and Peach and goodness knows who else and see who can piss up the wall the highest. He didn't want to play. He wanted to be seen *not* to play, which was a way of playing. And he didn't want Maureen to live in a doll's house. He sighed, put on his shoes and jacket and decided to go and see Libby.

Anna had not gone home. David Cassells was hosting a lecture by a 'colleague and friend' at what was laughingly called the Academic Centre—a room with a drop-down cine screen, a slide projector and 23 plastic chairs—in the new annexe. The talk began at eight o'clock and was called 'The Therapy of Disdain'. It was by a German called Heinreich Ruber, whose position seemed to be that kindness or even good manners in any therapeutic exchange is less about building a relationship with the patient and more about trying to feel better about oneself as a therapist. Anna wasn't interested in the talk or the wine. She wanted to know why Cassells had gone out of his way to invite her and then follow the invitation up by phoning her in her office to remind her, and tell her how much he was looking forward to seeing her.

She got there at 7.30. There were six people there and Cassells came bounding over to greet her. He offered her wine in a plastic cup; she took orange juice and asked him who else was coming.

'Mostly psychologists and junior doctors, I am afraid. It is so hard to get the nurses engaged in this sort of discussion, that's one of the reasons I am so glad you are here, Anna.' All the time he was smiling.

'Shiftwork.'

'Of course. But you are here. Perhaps you have the sensibilities of a therapist.'

Anna ignored that and asked: 'So how are you settling in?'

'Oh, you know, slowly. You haven't been here yourself very long have you? How did you find it?'

Anna smiled. The game was clearly to get the other person to talk about themself. I can play that, she thought. 'Is it different here to the Bethlem?'

'In some ways, yes. In other ways, not so much.'

'Why did you make the change?'

'You are very direct, Anna.'

'You're a tad evasive, David. I'm curious, why leave there to come here?'

'I felt ready for a change.'

And for the first time it occurred to Anna that David Cassells wasn't coming somewhere new as much as leaving something behind. 'You seem to be settling in quite quickly, and influencing things, too.'

'Well, that's my job.'

'Are you enjoying working with Dr Peach?'

'He's a very experienced doctor and a very welcoming colleague.'

'And the nurses?'

'They are interesting. Your friend Mr Sands is a hard man to read; I rather like him. And Grace is delightful. And you of course, clearly destined for great things, Ms Newton.'

Anna ignored him. 'Am I right in thinking that you think Maureen Marley should be discharged into the all-women's house on Wade Avenue?'

'Really, Anna.' He was still smiling but his lips quivered slightly. He may, she thought, be ready to blush. 'This isn't the time or place is it?'

'Just interested, David, in your opinion, in an academic sense if you like.'

'Well I think...' As he spoke he pulled his shoulders up, shifting from lascivious to professional. 'It's slightly more complicated than it looks.'

'Of course you do,' murmured Anna.

'Now now, you did ask. I think that you are right, and so was Dr Leith eventually, who incidentally I find a little too easily distracted for my tastes, don't you? Not prepared to comment? OK, anyway, if we are not going to cure her—whatever cure means—we need to ensure she lives happily. However, we also need to be careful not to abandon hope that she may recover, and pretending that she is not a woman does that doesn't it?'

'Well, no,' said Anna quickly. 'Moving her into a mixed home lets her be whatever she happens to be.

Cassells reddened slightly. 'A mixed home, you say? I thought it was a men-only house you and Dr Leith were recommending?'

'No, it's a mixed house. Men and women, just like the real world.'

'Ah, I see. Dr Peach told me... Well, never mind. In that case, no, you are right, of course you are right. I will talk to Dr Peach about it first thing tomorrow. Carla, Carla...' He turned and beckoned over Carla Tandy who was holding a handful of crisps in the palm of her hand, as if, thought Anna, that was fooling anybody.

'Carla, did you know that the house where Ms Newton wanted to move that patient you want to do a case study on was a mixed house, not an all-male house?' He exaggerated his surprise.

'Yes David, I did. We did.'

'I certainly didn't!' Cassells raised his voice just enough to get the attention of the three people standing nearest.

'But we talked about it...' Tandy looked embarrassed and then contrite. 'I'm sorry, I thought you knew, David.'

'Well I didn't.'

'Nice dress.' Anna smiled at Carla Tandy in a thin if heartfelt gesture of female solidarity.

'Thanks,' muttered Tandy, who had the look of someone who found her life to be an absolute misery.

Anna stayed for half of the talk, but when there was a break she made her excuses and left. Cassells popped out before her and he hadn't come back when she left. She had no idea what Cassells would say to Peach, if anything. She had no idea what he would do next, or why, and she rather doubted that he did. But she had done all she could do for now. She walked up to the tube station. It was 9.14 and she got half way before changing her mind and going back to the ward. If she wrote up her notes now, even if it meant she didn't get home until midnight, she wouldn't need to come in tomorrow morning; she could pop in to see her doctor instead. And anyway, she hadn't stayed late for a while and she still liked the hospital at night.

When she came on to the ward she was surprised to see Cassells in the nurses' office talking to Tim. Tim had his head in his hands. Tiredness? Tears? Anna guessed he was trying to contain anger. If she were in a room with Cassells that would be what she would have to work on. Cassells was leaning forward in what nurses called the empathy pose: open posture, head tilted, arm ready to reach out and touch in a meaningless way. And so she didn't go any further. She turned around and went home.

For Adam, the walk to the hospital always began quickly. For one thing it was cold. It was after eleven now, and October brought a chill to the air that prevented his body from opening itself to the late evening warmth of a summer month, instead tensing itself slightly and heading off with purpose. Anyway, the hospital was out of sight when he started, so he could fool himself into thinking he was going somewhere else. He liked the cool air. He would lift his chest as he walked, look up at the scattered clouds visible against the near-full moon and try to imagine he was small, or at least smaller than the sense of eternal consequence he carried around with him made him feel.

The streets were relatively empty: a few stragglers staggered home after turning out time; two drunks were trying to do something hilarious with a traffic cone but falling over and laughing loudly on the damp grass verge. They shouted something at him as he walked past on the other side of the road. He felt nothing: no anxiety, no sense of risk. He unconsciously slowed his walk slightly, turning his head slowly and stared evenly at them. One of them shut up. The one on the floor began to shout something about queers, but shouting and standing up proved too much for him and he fell over again, and they both started laughing at themselves or the grass or gravity.

As Adam drew near the hospital he could see three people standing at the top of the main drive, talking; one of them looked familiar. He crossed the road and instantly felt more furtive than he liked to, or had before. He had come here at night many times and he had emboldened himself with a sense of legitimacy, of belonging. This was his place, to come and go as he wanted: a nonsense, but he clung to it anyway. The moonlight showed him the shapes of the three men—no, two men and a woman—but not their faces. He walked down a side street, pausing, turning round and looking round the corner. One of them looked like Cassells: confident stance, expensive-looking coat, floppy hair and talking with his body, moving his shoulders and torso in rhythm to whatever he was saying. That was Cassells, which made the skinny woman Tandy. Adam turned and walked down the side street, dark and residential with muted street lighting and no noise. At the end of the road he turned left, crossed over two more streets and turned left again. This took him back to the main road but further along, near the annexe. He could get into the hospital that way.

He thought about Anna and a baby. Babies existed in another universe. He didn't know anybody with a baby. He and Catherine had never talked about them, beyond musing on how pointless and noisy they appeared to be. He had never imagined himself holding a child, let alone fathering one, but of course this may not be anything to do with him. She wanted him to know but not to care. She wanted him to respond with generosity to her need to tell, but was relying on the fact that he wouldn't be able to muster enough of a sense of responsibility to engage. And she had a fall-back plan just in case he turned out to be more interested than she had hoped: it might not be his. 50/50. Quite clever really.

Or of course she might be less manipulative and controlling than that. She may just be a woman on her own trying to meet her needs without being compromised. She might hold the so-called conventional route to things in the same sort of contempt that he did. She may just want a baby without a husband. Adam's father had left his mother when Adam was four, and died three years later. He hadn't missed what he had never had and his mother had never remarried. She didn't need a man either. 'Drank all the sherry and made the place smell' was her summary. Adam, of all people, should not be quick to judge Anna. But that didn't mean he should be quick to trust either.

There was a side gate that opened on to a pathway to the annexe. Adam went through it and walked round the building. At the side was the small car park he had come through earlier: it was unlit, apart from the half glow of the street lights some fifty yards away, back on the main street. At the end of the car park was another gate, higher than the others, with a stiffer catch, but he slipped through and began walking toward the side entrance of the asylum. As soon as he lifted his head and breathed out an unconscious silent sigh he could see something hanging from the large oak tree in front of him. It didn't occur to him that it could be anything other than a person.

Adam ran forward. All he could hear was his own breathing. He nearly stumbled, caught himself. The body looked familiar. Was it moving or was it swaying slightly? He grabbed it and lifted the weight, heavy. His face pressed against a jacket. It felt like wool; there was no smell, no sweat or pee or cigarettes. He couldn't feel any movement but chose to imagine there might be some. He pushed the body weight up slightly more, taking more weight in his back, relieving the tension in the rope, taking the weight off of the neck. Panting and watching the breath turn to condensation he said: 'Great, what do I do now?' And then, directing his voice upwards: 'Are you conscious? Can you hear me? Can you move?' Nothing. He wondered if there was a twitch in the leg, a gentle kick of acknowledgement. He shifted the weight again and glanced up. Saw the waistcoat under the jacket, the pudgy hands hanging loosely from dropped shoulders. 'Tim. Bollocks, Tim. Can you hear me? Tim? I'm not letting go.' Defiant. Angry. And he wondered: 'How long can I hold a twelve stone man who is dangling from a tree?'

The road was quiet now, no cars. There were always cars. Not that cars were of any use. He looked toward the hospital door he had been heading for. There were no open wards in that wing. The annexe was the nearest place with people in it, maybe fifty or sixty yards away. He tried to focus on his breathing. He closed his eyes and concentrated on pushing his legs into the ground. 'Make a foundation,' he thought, and he muttered those words to himself over and over.

Adam glanced up at the sky. The clouds were moving faster now, wispy and brown, flying across the moon just in his eyeline. 'Someone will come,' he thought, still staring at the sky. 'Someone is bound to come.'

His neck was stiff. He moved it and looked down; the grass was thick and damp, clumped together in tufts. He began to count to himself, three numbers for every inhalation. He got to 140. He thought about his hands: they were gripping Tim's thighs, wasting his energy, he thought. He needed to relax the muscles he wasn't using. His back hurt. He looked at the sky again. The clouds were getting thinner, more pink.

'I'm calling for help,' he said out loud. 'I can't hold you forever.' He heard a noise coming from the hospital door. 'Help! I need help here,' he called, not as loud as he had thought he would. His whole body was hurting and his shoulder was numb where he was leaning into Tim's deadweight body. He called again, louder this time, and he heard a twig. He turned his head, leaning it into Tim's soft stomach.

It was the young man he had seen here earlier, as bright-eyed as before, calm but attentive. He stepped toward Adam. 'Let me'. He wrapped his arms around Tim's other leg and hip and instantly relieved Adam of the weight. Adam exhaled loudly. 'How long have you been holding him?'

'I don't know. You need to get help.'

'No, you have been here a long time.'

'How do you know?' Adam was uncertain. He had no sense of how long he had been standing there, holding Tim up against the world.

'You must have been. It's so late it's early. I'm out here for the dew. I can hold him while you get help.' The young man seemed strong: he was shorter than Adam, slim, athletic. The way he held himself, the way he spread his weight on the grass as he bore more of the load, Adam knew that the young man was taking more of the weight.

'OK. OK,' he said. 'I'll go to the annexe and get help. I'll be straight back, I'll be less than two minutes, I'll bring help.' The young man nodded. 'What's your name?'

'Is now the time for introductions?' he smiled.

'I'm Adam.'

'I know,' the young man said. 'I'm Jonathan.'

'You got him?' asked Adam.

'Yeah. Go.'

Adam eased down the weight he was still holding and Jonathan took it comfortably. Adam hesitated for a moment and then ran toward the annexe.

The door was locked. He pressed every buzzer there was. It was mainly offices but there were two small specialist units, one for eating disorders and one for people with personality disorders who the therapists thought would benefit from intensive work. It seemed to take an age but he kept buzzing.

Finally an angry tired voice said: 'What do you want?'

'I need help. There is a man hanging from a tree out here, a doctor, I need you to call an ambulance and I need some help to get him down.'

'What are you talking about? I will call the police...'

'Yes, call the police and an ambulance. My name is Adam Sands. I am the charge nurse on ward 6. I swear this is the truth. I need help.'

There was a pause and then: 'Wait a minute.'

Two nurses came down to the door, one a middle-aged black man, the other a middle-aged Asian woman. Adam recognized the man and knew that he would recognize him too.

'Have you called the ambulance?'

'Not yet.'

He pointed at the woman. 'You call the ambulance, you come and help me. There is someone holding him.' Adam turned and ran back across the car park toward the tree. He could hear the man trotting along behind him. When Adam got there Tim was still hanging, motionless. Dead. Jonathan was nowhere to be seen. Adam ran forward and grabbed Tim again, looking down at the grass as he did so, noticing the single footprints in the mud and the trail in the dew behind him. The single trail.

'Where is your friend?' And: 'Oh my, that's Dr Leith.' The nurse stepped forward and took some of the weight but not much. Adam held on tightly but now, he knew, it was a different kind of holding.

The ambulance arrived just before the police. They pronounced him dead almost immediately. They cut the rope and eased the body to the ground. And Adam gave a statement.

'How long were you holding him for?'

'I don't know. What time is it now?'

The policeman looked at his watch. '5.20.'

'Really? You sure?'

The policeman nodded. 'Your colleague says you rang the buzzer to his ward at 4.47. How long do you think you held him for?'

'Longer than I thought,' Adam said quietly.

'When did you get here?'

Adam shrugged 'Before midnight.'

'Are you sure?'

Adam nodded and swallowed hard. 'Yeah, a little before twelve, I think. When I let go, when I went to get help, was he already dead?'

The policeman, a thickset man with a big nose and unexpressive eyes nodded once. 'Yes. Ambulance man says six hours or more. Couldn't you tell?'

Adam stared at the ambulance as they put Tim in the back. He looked again at the grass all around the tree. There was no trail coming from the hospital door, no sign of anyone else having been there at all. He turned his head toward the policeman a little, not enough to look him in the eye. His neck hurt, his back hurt. He was cold and waiting for someone to ask what on earth he was doing here at midnight anyway. He shook his head. 'No,' he said quietly. 'I couldn't tell.'

# PART 2

September 17<sup>th</sup> 2013

# PART 2

September 17th 2013

*Adam closed the shop at 4.30pm, secure in the knowledge that he wasn't risking too much prospective business. He looked behind him after locking the door—towards the collection of shops that included an Iceland, a Poundstretcher and somewhere that sold such garish handbags and leather goods that he had always assumed it was a front for drug trafficking—to see if anyone was sprinting toward him waving a book token over their heads, desperate for a late-afternoon browse, but there was nobody. He slipped the shop keys into his pocket and walked in the other direction from the shops, toward the sea. It took less than five minutes to get to the old harbour. He was carrying a small nylon bag and wearing baggy linen trousers and a black cotton jacket; he had a pork pie hat on his head. He was 6 ft 2 and looked mostly downward as he walked.*

*The concrete harbour had a small wooden jetty attached to it. Adam walked along the jetty to his scuffed brown rowing boat. It had the word 'Iris' painted on the side and a flaking picture of a flower beside it. He hadn't named the boat, he'd simply bought it.*

*He threw his bag in and climbed down into the boat. He removed the oars from under a stained and seemingly discarded piece of green canvas and slid them into their oarlocks. He untied the mooring and, with barely a pause, navigated his way from the jetty into the centre of the harbour and began to pull his way outward. An old man in a captain's hat waved to him. Adam nodded and smiled in acknowledgement. He had no idea who the man was. He could have been Captain Birdseye for all he knew, but Adam valued good manners and anyway he knew that someone is meant to notice when you head out to sea, just in case you don't come back and anyone ever asks 'Whatever happened to the bloke who ran that bookshop? The one in the stupid hat.' At least now someone would be able to say dramatically: 'I saw him going out, I never saw him back.' Perhaps followed by: 'Would you like some breaded cod?'*

*When he was out of the harbour he felt himself relax; his rowing became slower, longer. He felt a cool breeze as he left the* shelter and let the boat drift for a few seconds to get a clearer sense of the waves, which were small and half-hearted, and the current, which was coming from the west and not too strong. He turned the boat so that he could see the beach that curled along the seafront and rowed in a straight line away from land.

After about five minutes he stopped. He was far enough away from the beach not to be able to make out discernible shapes, and there were no other boats out. He was alone. He stripped down to his swimming shorts, took some goggles from the nylon bag and put them around his neck. He drew the oars in and took the anchor from the bow of the boat and lowered it into the water. He looked at the land, maybe a mile away, maybe less, and he looked out to sea. No ships on the horizon; nothing but grey chopping channel. All he could hear was the water lapping the side of the boat and his own breathing. He took two weights from the back of the boat and one from the front and moved them all to the side of the rowing boat he was not now sitting on. The boat rocked a little and he took that opportunity to slip into the water. It was cold. It took his breath away. The temperature had dropped since two days ago. It had been a cold summer: the sea had not banked much heat to lose and was quickly giving up what it had. He took a moment to steady his breathing, slipped the goggles on, turned away from the boat, put his face down into the water and began to swim a gentle front crawl. The cold stung his face a little but he knew that would pass. He concentrated on breathing slowly, to the right, turning his body to ensure he was using his back muscles to pull him through the water, stretching his spine as he did so. He thought about his fingers reaching out beyond themselves into the water, trying to find the rhythm of the sea. He tried to glide, letting his stroke complete itself and nearly touching his front hand with his active hand before pulling on the water again. He didn't look behind himself when he breathed, watching only the horizon. The water was cold, he could feel it in his fingers and his feet and so he kicked, which made him move faster and a little higher in the water. The swimming was easy, *he could have gone for miles; on noticing that, he slowed down, glided to a halt and turned on to his back to look behind him. He was maybe 200 metres from the boat. He trod water for a moment, noticed that he wasn't so cold as to be uncomfortable, noticed he was breathing more easily now. He slipped the goggles up and looked around: nothing to see but sea.*

*He pulled the goggles back down, flipped on to his front again and swam. Long languid strokes, pulling his arm through and touching the side of his hip, feeling himself push the water away from him, tasting the thick salt on his lips when he breathed. He didn't stop until he noticed the water had become colder and even then he didn't look behind him. He just rested his head back and felt for the waves. The grey had a denser blue to it now; he knew he was in deeper water. Slowly he turned around; the boat was some way away, maybe a mile, maybe more.*

*He felt the water lap around him. He felt beautifully small. He tried to imagine what could go wrong, what fear would be like here in a fading light as the sea cooled around him. He couldn't think of anything. He felt nothing at all.*

# 9. Who Knows Where The Time Goes

'Could be hormones?' a friend had said over a glass of wine and a takeaway a week or so previously, but Anna didn't really take it seriously. That was the sort of thing people said when they couldn't be bothered to talk. It could be something a bit more existential, Anna had thought: Tom had finished his degree and decided to stay on and do his Masters. To her, that simply put off whether or not he would move back home to London or stay in Manchester, where he had a life, friends, an affordable flat, perhaps a significant other she had never met, but not his mum.

Not that she was a clingy mum, she wasn't. She bordered on obsessive in her non-clinginess, aware that as a lone parent she might be prone to a reliance on his existence that could smother him. She made a point of phoning him only when it was her turn and always after the same amount of time that he had left it since her previous call. She had been able to help him financially, having saved up for his education since he was six, and had been quite proud of his reasoning that Manchester was both a good university and also more affordable than London or Paris or Madrid. She hadn't said that it might have proved cheaper if he had stayed in London and not moved out of their flat in Stoke Newington, because she knew that going to University was about growing up. And anyway, Manchester didn't feel as rejecting as Madrid would have.

But the absent son, the lack of lovers, the quiet she tended to surround herself with when she was not working, felt more telling than any change in her hormones. And her approaching fiftieth birthday felt even more symbolic than irregular periods and a slightly achy hip.

Anna Newton was now a health researcher. She still wanted to giggle when she had to tell people that. In her head, research was done by boffins in white coats, fiddling with Bunsen burners and looking earnestly at 'data', and they never smiled. But she enjoyed being a researcher, she liked going to work and she believed that what she was doing in the world had some form of usefulness, which remained important to her.

Anna had stopped working in practice just before the end of the last millennium. Career progression was limited for experienced nurses. Teaching looked dull, management looked corrupt. In 1999 everyone seemed to be re-training as a landscape gardener or a shiatsu practitioner, or starting their own internet business. When she was asked to be part of a research team looking into what had happened to the patients she had helped move into the community more than a decade earlier, she had become fascinated not just in how they had flourished, or not, but in the process of enquiry itself. She did a part time degree in Social Sciences and when she got the opportunity to turn half of her 'Community Team Leader' post into a Research Nurse, the perk was that they paid for her to do a Masters Degree in Research Methods. She had been working in research full time for more than ten years. She had seen several projects through to completion and was confident in her ability to do what she was paid to do. Her current project was the biggest and most important she had ever been close to, let alone worked on.

On the face of it, the subject of her research, 'Context and Cognition Therapy', was perhaps an inevitable response to the alleged failures of Community Care. It was essentially soft and close to whimsical, and if the health service had not been still riding the wave of post-1997 relief it might not have seen the light of day. As it was, it was not only being taken seriously but it had even attracted money, proper money from Leichter and Wallace Pharmaceuticals, one of the largest drug companies in the world and ironically one of the largest producers of anti-psychotics in the UK. Ironic because 'Context and Cognition Therapy' or CCT, was a treatment that eschewed all drugs. Unlike the fashionable therapies of the time like Cognitive Behavioural Therapy, it was not offered alongside drugs but functioned instead of them.

The idea of CCT was twofold. The first was that context at best contributes to suffering and at worst constructs it. If we take people out of whatever situation their psychosis or depression has developed in, then change becomes inevitable or at least available. Traditionally, over the course of the previous one hundred and fifty years or so, psychiatry has taken people out of their situations and placed them into somewhere often worse. Asylums were at best rule-laden, depersonalizing institutions of containment. At worst they were torturous and abusive. Whenever the idea of hospital as sanctuary reared its head in history someone came and redesigned it, bringing back the chains, the degradation and eventually the electricity and the very sharp knives. CCT happened on small quiet farms with gardens and an obligatory orchard. The farms had music rooms and a library full of books and films. There was fresh food and cookery lessons; woodwork classes; swimming; bread-making and of course more yoga then any body could ever realistically tolerate. When the first CCT centre was established and financed by a Rock Star who had too much money and a diagnosis of depression, and made available for free to fifteen lucky if bemused NHS patients, one of the eager-to-hate tabloids had done an exposé on it, describing it as an 'out-of-time hippie commune for nutters'. Said tabloid had since revised its editorial position.

The second part of CCT involved a talking therapy. However, unlike all the more popular and prescribed therapies available, CCT didn't have a theory of human understanding that defined or branded it. Therapists in CCT essentially chatted; asking questions about random things like enjoyable holidays or favourite shoes and taking note of the fact that sometimes, often even, the 'patient' was increasingly cogent when reflecting on life outside of their alleged madness. Theories were applied to this process and words given to the nature of change that befell some of the patients. However, the small group of people being paid by the Rock Star to do what they did had the good sense to avoid the labelling of what they were doing and instead just did it. Unofficially the recovery rates were rather remarkable and the Rock Star, this time aided by a PR savvy Film Star recovering from the mental health problem that was punching a co-star for not using mouth wash before kissing her on set, opened another CCT centre. By the time the slowly growing collective of OBE-hunting celebrities opened centre number three the NHS felt compelled, mostly for PR reasons, to join in.

The problem for the government was, how should they become involved? On the one hand, the CCT centres were currently not costing them anything and were thus something of a flagship for their 'public/private partnership' motif. On the other, if they weren't involved with them they couldn't really take any credit for them. Beyond having their photograph taken with the Rock Star and friends.

It was also the case that CCT had recently successfully treated the England football captain who had come to believe—perhaps in part due to too many pain killing injections—that one football, somewhere in the UK, would destroy him and had thus become unable to go outside, let alone play for his country, as well as several 'ordinary' but insane patients. People were beginning to wonder if three CCT centres were perhaps insufficient for the mental health needs of the country.

The people in charge, the government people, 'knew' that CCT was a passing fad, a whim with no more evidence underpinning it than crystal healing. However, it was popular, people talked about it and when they did they talked about the mad in a different way—as helpable rather than dangerous—which was a good thing, because the government had been running an anti-stigma campaign for about fifteen years and nobody had noticed. Anyway, the government liked popular things, regardless of the fact that those things might be rubbish; hence the many celebrity photo opportunities.

The problem was one of money. Government cannot throw research money at anything that takes its fancy. It has people in quangoes that do that sort of thing for them and they, by their very nature, take a long time to do anything. They also have people who fix things for them and those sorts of people come in all shapes and sizes and bring all sorts of talents. One such man was was Black Portier.

For Black, CCT was PR heaven. Black had had an unfortunate brush with psychiatric services in the late Eighties. He had smoked too much dope, got a bit paranoid, stopped when he was told to, got bored and started again. As a result he spent 36 hours in an acute psychiatric ward in London and was scared so utterly shitless that he gave up dope, tobacco, beer and, just to be on the safe side, cheese. In what might have felt like a random act of penance, he volunteered to work on the ad campaign for the original anti-stigma campaign, coming up with the slogan 'If you caught madness would it make you less of a person' which was rubbish but somehow encouraged the commis-sioning Department Of Health official to sleep with him. Black noticed that, in career terms at least, one difficult weekend was the making of him and he was, bizarrely, the obvious candidate when the government was hiring spin-doctors by the dozen to sell various messages to a still-relieved population.

By 2004, however, government valued solutions to problems a tiny bit more than slogans. Fortunately, Black Portier had moved with the times and, buoyed by the commitment to public–private partnership, had approached a sceptical Leichter and Wallace Pharmaceuticals with a proposition.

Leichter and Wallace had their own problems. Profits had fallen to £1.48 billion from £1.6 billion the the previous year, and shareholder confidence was not being helped by two lawsuits being taken out against the company: one claiming that its preferred anti-psychotic had caused or contributed to the suicide of fifty-two patients from 1996 to 2000; the other suggesting that a side effect of its popular anticoagulant caused hair to grow inside the mouths of some patients.

Leichter and Wallace, who were represented in their meeting with Black Portier by Nina Sykes, a no-nonsense lawyer from Seattle, had research money to burn. However, who they let burn it was always a distinctly strategic decision. Research funding was speculation money: at worst it was money not wasted on taxes, and at its best it was good public relations that might just lead to a new revenue stream.

'So tell me, Mr Portier, and I must say I have been looking forward to hearing the answer to this all day, why would a drug company put up research money for a project that requires no drugs?'

'Good PR.' Black was trying not to look at her breasts. 'You demonstrate yourself as being committed to patient well-being regardless of where it comes from.'

'And in so doing we concede the possibility that there might be a better way of providing treatment for psychosis than ours? Isn't that rather like a tobacco company assisting in the development of green tea? We have spent the best part of fifty years convincing the world that drugs are good for everything. The merest sign of doubt in that truth would be awful PR.'

Portier smiled. 'But that assumes this CCT nonsense is anything other then hippie drivel that requires something like a proper research base to laugh it out of the water and file it alongside astrology.'

'Spoken like a true Gemini,' she said. 'We're not interested. Unless you are prepared to run a comparison programme. We establish a fourth CCT centre, call it a control group if you like. We do everything they do but we also use drugs. If there is anything good in CCT we'll show it gets better with drugs.' Black had fully expected to offer the control group as part of his pitch: the fact that she had suggested it, and he could make his acquiescence look like her good negotiation skills, was a gift.

'Not that you are presuming the research outcomes or anything...'

'Of course not. And we get to recruit.'

'No,' said Portier. 'You don't. Independent recruitment of all staff, particularly the research team.'

'You can recruit the research team however you wish, Mr Portier, but we recruit the staff to our CCT centre.'

'OK.' Portier shrugged and stood up to offer his hand.

'You haven't said how much?'

Portier shrugged again. '£2 million? Four year project.'

Nina Sykes stared at him for a moment. 'Fine.'

Anna knew she was lucky to get one of the jobs. Not lucky beyond her ability or experience, but lucky in the sense that when 256 people want a job and you get it you have to be a particular sort of idiot not to be grateful. Initially the project was for four years, but it became clear that nobody was sure what recovery was, nor what meaningful results might look like. Was it a measurable reduction of symptoms? Was it to appear less mad to people in the street? Or was it something to do with work, or study, or whatever meaningful activity people valued being as available to patients as it is to non-patients? They also hadn't factored in people getting well, leaving, getting ill again and coming back. How do you measure recurrence? And when do you decide that CCT has failed and another, more conventional treatment should have a go?

The length of the project was also complicated by the Rock Star and his growing band of rich do-gooders—which now included the Film Star, the Former England Football Captain, two comedians, a very well known guitarist and a news reader—who had insisted on opening three more CCT centres. More data became available, more challenges to the research process emerged. And while all this happened CCT passed into the nation's consciousness, regardless of its evidence base. Nina Sykes was concerned. By 2011 she had written to Black Portier to insist that results were released, results that she was sure proved that CCT was little more than a holiday camp that waited for madness to pass of its own accord, whereas medication offered salvation. The problem was, as Portier said in an email he sent to Ms Sykes, there was no evidence to suggest that that was the case.

Anna, not immune to the cynicism that she had gathered around her like an invisible layer of mould, was as surprised as her research colleagues at the collated data. There had been three of them leading the project since its inception eight years before. They had come to like the farms, the workers and the patients. They had become as immune to the on-demand yoga and well stocked libraries as they were to the weekly offers of inducements when visiting the Leichter and Wallace-established farm, which included the overt offer of sexual favours to the research lead, Dr Paul Stern, on more than one occasion. They were not, however, immune to the collated results of eight years' work. To break it down, patients with a psychotic illness have a 1 in 4 chance of a recovery in normal psychiatric service. People in the Leichter and Wallace CCT showed a 1 in 3.3 chance of recovery. People in the drug free CCT services showed a 1 in 2.5 chance. These results were, unless they could be discredited by the methodology or corruption of the research team, sensational. Indeed, they were so annoying and surprising that Portier's bosses told him to make the research team collate them all again. That took five months. The results were the same.

Paul Stern, Anna Newton and the third member of the research team, Meena Ahmed, were taking up a project researching depression management regimes for a large charity. Their work with CCT was done and they simply awaited the call that would tell them when the data would be released and what availability was required from them for the inevitable press rounds. They were satisfied that they had done a good job. They were excited that they had contributed to refining information that might help people. They were happy that their work felt meaningful.

It is possible that Anna would have waited more attentively for the call telling her to prepare to share her work if it had not coincided with the end of Tom's degree. He got a first in English and Music and she was too embarrassed for him to see her cry. She bought him a handmade Gretsch Resonator guitar though, like the one in the picture on his wall. He cried when she gave it to him, and hugged her like he used to hug her when he was eight and had had a bad dream.

While Anna lent most of her conscious attention to her work, all of her unconscious world revolved around her son. Was he doing an MA because he couldn't think of anything else to do? Because he loved his life so much he didn't want anything to change? Because he didn't want to come home? Had he met someone and not felt able to tell her? What if the someone was a man? Tom liked clothes and used moisturizer. He was good at sports but didn't take them seriously. He hadn't had a proper girlfriend before he left home, not proper in the 'can she stay over' sense. And how does Anna make it easy for Tom to tell her he is gay without forcing the issue? Anyway, if he doesn't want to move back to London it might be because she interfered with his life in some way she had failed to anticipate; asking about his sexuality might simply exacerbate the looming presence she had lived in fear of being. Work was a blessed release for Anna. A world of tangibles, of clear lines and hollow belonging that made the fear go away. She was also self-aware enough to know that spending her working life trying to find better ways of looking after people called mad acted as some kind of penance. Not that she had a clear sense of what the penance was for, but she felt something, somewhere, that she knew required acting upon.

The team had two weeks off before starting the new job. Anna had gone to Greece for a week and lay in the sun reading. Paul Stern had spent a week fishing with his son in Scotland.

Meena, being younger than the others, had spent a lot of it dancing. And sleeping.

Four days before they were due to start work Paul had called and left a message. 'It's 11.35. Call please. Bit concerned.' Paul was given to economy in his communication but not anxiety, and he had sounded anxious. Anna had been out running when he called and phoned back as soon as she got the message, but it had gone straight to voicemail. 'Calling back. What's up?' When she hadn't heard from him by the evening she called again and left another message. 'What's going on, Paul?' He didn't phone before she went to bed. Tom did though. He sounded distant and sniffed a lot. He said he had a cold but she wondered, is he on drugs? And then 'how wrong is it to take a urine sample from your son without him knowing?' She closed her eyes and shook her head. Maybe it was hormones after all. Either that or she was becoming a rubbish old woman.

Anna listened to the news on regional radio. Mostly they wheeled out press releases dressed up as events and questioned people without letting them answer, but it was better than anything else available. She might have missed the report of a domestic fire were it not for the word Clapton. Meena lived in Clapton. Indeed, when Anna turned on the TV news and waited for the regional bit in the cheap studio she could see the fire was in Meena's street and eventually her flat. She phoned Meena. No answer. She phoned Paul. No answer. Eventually she phoned the police. Yes, they could confirm there had been a fire: three people were injured, two of them seriously. No, they could not release any names and they could not comment on the cause of the fire until their investigation was complete.

The problem with living alone was that you never had anyone to test your responses against. Was the fear she was feeling, the near certainty that her friend and colleague had been hurt, an appropriate response to the information available to her or was she jumping to conclusions? She decided to walk down to Clapton.

It was a fifteen-minute walk from her flat on Cazenove Road down to Clapton. Anna did it in nine. Most of the road was cordoned off: there were still three fire engines there and several police cars. It was Meena's flat. The house her flat was part of was completely destroyed, as were most of the houses on either side. The building that Meena had lived in was completely gone except for one charred lump of wall and a black smouldering piece of timber. Anna stood and stared at the smoking pile of debris. There was a cluster of people around one of the police cars.

A fireman walked past and Anna said: 'Gas explosion?'

''Fraid not', he mumbled without stopping.

''Fraid not?'

'They were very lucky, neighbours got them out.'

Anna turned around and went home.

On the way she phoned Paul: straight to voicemail again. This time she didn't leave a message. As she turned on to her road she saw two men outside her flat. One was knocking on the door; the other was looking through the living room window with his gloved hands shading his eyes. She was instantly irritated. Who the hell looks through a living room window like that if you don't answer the door? She was about to march up the road and announce her presence with an 'Oi', but something stopped her. They didn't look like salesmen or Jehovah's Witnesses. They could have been policemen coming to tell her about Meena but that didn't make sense, this was a time for family and friends, not work colleagues up the road. And the one knocking on the door didn't look official: he lumbered, almost strutted, and he spat in the road. And the other one: who wore gloves with a three piece suit? In September? Anna slowed. They hadn't seen her but if she simply turned around and walked the way she had come they would notice, so she crossed over and walked down the first side street she came across, Osbaldeston Road. She glanced at the men who were both now standing in the road looking at the flat. She walked fifty yards up Osbaldeston

Road and waited a few moments. Then she walked back to the end of the street and looked round the corner. One of the men had moved his car, a blue Ford Focus, up outside Anna's flat; his companion was still standing looking at the flat. The driver said something and the second man nodded, walked over and got into the car. They drove off. Anna waited a few moments to see if they came back. When they didn't, she walked very quickly to her own front door and went inside.

She had no idea why she did what she did next, but she started packing a bag. Clothes, laptop, flashdrive, address book. She fed the fish. She phoned Tom, who didn't answer, and left a message: 'Hi honey, sorry to bother you, just needed to tell you that we, I, have rats, yeah I know. Having the exterminators in, they are going to fumigate, or whatever the hell it is they do, so I am going away for a few days. I know you weren't planning on coming home this weekend, but if you changed your mind change it back again. The flat is off limits for a little while. I'm going to stay at Grace's. Talk soon. Love you.' Christ, she thought, that came easy. She didn't stop moving as she spoke. She went to the kitchen and threw some bagels, cheese, tomatoes and juice into a carrier bag. 'Pretend it's a picnic,' she said to herself for no reason whatsoever.

Anna drove a blue Citroen Pluriel. In terms of speed it was one step up from a pedal car. Why that mattered to her as she loaded her travel bag, computer and cheese into the back made no sense. Nor did the fleeting thought that if they knew where she lived they would know what she drove. Which she instantly decided was a step too far toward paranoia. She got in, started the car and drove off. When she got to the end of the road the Ford Focus passed her going in the other direction, this time with a third person in the back. 'Good instincts,' she thought, before realising that it did not signal anything good.

Anna drove all the way up to Hampstead Heath. She had no idea why. She didn't particularly like it up there and didn't know it very well, but it felt random, and random felt safe. She parked the car and wandered up Parliament Hill. She took out her phone to call Paul again but she didn't dial. Instead she called Grace.

Grace lived in Muswell Hill. She had been left money by the grandparents of her daughter and she had used it to buy a house which she renovated and sold and used the money to buy another and then another. Grace owned a four-storey townhouse in the heart of London that was worth around one-and-a-half million pounds. She didn't have a mortgage or a job. She lived on the rents of the three other houses she owned and she also supported her daughter, Laura, who was studying medicine at Cambridge. Grace thought the random events that had come to make up her life were funny. Laura and Tom had grown up together.

'Anna,' she said when she answered the phone. 'What a lovely surprise.'

'Grace, I may need a head check but I think I'm on the run.'

'OK,' said Grace slowly. 'I think I am a bit out of practice but I'll give it a go if you like.'

'Meena's flat burnt down, Grace. Did you hear about the fire in East London last night? That was her flat. She was in it. Neighbours rescued them. I asked a fireman if it had been an accident, well actually I asked if it had been a gas explosion. He said no. When I went back to my flat there were two men trying to get in.'

'Trying to get in?'

'Well, banging on the door and looking through the windows. They went away and came back again. In between time I went in and packed a bag. Am I being paranoid?'

Grace didn't say anything for a moment. 'Have you spoken to Paul?'

'I've tried. He left me a message yesterday, asked me to call him, said he was 'concerned'. Concerned for Paul is significant, Grace. Grace? You think I'm being paranoid don't you?'

'I don't know, sweetie. What sort of car were they driving?'

'A blue Ford Focus.'

Grace paused for a moment. 'Well, there is one of those sitting across the road with a man in it reading a paper.' More guarded than dramatic.

'What if it is the same one? Maybe they know you are my best friend and that I would come to you?'

'OK, calm down Anna.'

'What if they have my phone tapped?'

'Can they do that with mobile phones?'

'They can do anything.'

'Can they? How do you know? And hang on, why would they?'

'Oh bugger! Grace, I phoned Tom and told him I was coming to stay with you. If they intercepted that call they would be waiting for me at your house.'

Grace was quiet for a moment. 'OK. You may be being paranoid and goodness knows you've had a shock but...'

'Yes, I know, it could be nothing. But I'm not going to use this phone again, just in case, and I am going away for a few days. Instinct, Grace, my instinct says something bad is happening.' She heard Grace sigh. 'Grace?'

'OK sweetie. Listen to your instincts, but if they start talking too loudly call me. Please.'

Anna cut the connection and something long forgotten to her began to sweep up from her stomach toward her throat. Something like fear, and it concentrated her mind. She walked over to a bench that looked down on London. It was nine in the morning; the autumnal light was trying to break through the smog that hung over the city. It looked a long way away and it felt empty. Her hands were tingling and her stomach was tight. She took her laptop from her bag and opened it up. She logged on to her private email address, hesitated for a moment before typing T into the 'to' box. Tom's address appeared automatically. 'Dear Tom, I've lost my phone! Must be time for a change. Will call you with my new number asap. In other news Grace has suggested we go to Paris for the weekend. How spontaneous am I? Will bring you back an onion. Love mum xx.' She pressed send and turned off the laptop. She wanted to sit and stare down on London for a while but her instinct was to keep moving and so she stood up, almost nodded down at the city in front of her and walked quickly back to her car. It may be, she thought, that actually all my instinct is telling me is that I need a couple of days beside the sea, that I am over-reacting to what are simple coincidences, that I am bored and just trying to shake myself back to life. She raised her eyebrows to the sky and shook her head. 'Listen to your body,' she whispered to herself and unlocked her car door. She got in, locked the door and began to drive in the opposite direction to Manchester.

# 10. A Prisoner Of The Past

Adam Sands was leaving the faintest of marks on the world he found himself in. This was not some sort of ecologically-aware grand design for being. It had simply evolved, the way retreat can.

He lived in Margate and he sold books for a living: some rare, some second hand, some slightly over-priced. He didn't make a lot of money but didn't live a life that required it. He lived quietly; the books helped with that. His small shop was considered quaint by people too polite to call it outdated. It smelt of old paper and salt, and the local community tended to like the idea of having a bookshop rather more than they liked the idea of shopping in it, so it was rarely full. Full would involve about nine people, including Adam. He had been thinking in recent months about modernizing, and by modernizing he meant serving coffee and putting a second-hand sofa next to the History section, but he tended not to make decisions if he could avoid it. Anyway, he got by with the help of online sales, specializing in outdated leftist texts and out-of-print fiction. Niche markets that required as wide an audience as possible. Perhaps the best decision he ever made was getting a website designed and constructed by a bear of a man called 'Freaky Bob'. Adam had paid him for his work by lending him his small boat a few times so Freaky Bob could go fishing, and giving him all three volumes of Leszek Kolakowski's 'Main Currents of Marxism'. These books were received with a reverence that did not correspond with the fact that they were not wanted by anyone else in the country, and had in fact been sitting in the Politics and Philosophy section for the whole of the six years Adam had owned the shop.

Three times a week Adam cycled the nine miles to the sheltered housing, warden-controlled flat his 88 year old mother lived in. He would do her shopping, read to her and sit in silence while she told him about things that didn't make sense, like the internet, mild incontinence, the cost of milk and God. He had ostensibly come to Margate, from Goa via Thailand and four different Greek islands, to be near enough to look after her after a minor stroke. In truth, he had drifted ever since he left nursing and she had managed for the twelve years he had been away from England and he didn't really have anywhere else to settle anyway. She was strong beneath the frailty, and sarcastic. Every time she saw him she asked: 'Are you still persevering with that book business, dear?'

'Yes mum, I thought I'd give it another week, see how it goes.'

And she would sigh and say: 'With your education you should be writing books, not selling them. You do actually sell some don't you?'

'No mum.' Exasperated, tired. 'Mostly I collect them to stop other people from reading.' Later he would cycle home, maybe do some yoga and he would play his guitar very, very quietly.

Today a non-buying customer was lamenting the end of bookshops to Adam and not buying anything as he did so. 'It's the overheads you see,' said the man who didn't own a bookshop to the man who did. 'These big online corporations, your Amazons, they can buy in bulk and they don't have the shop overheads. Have you thought of going digital'? He had well cut hair, an expensive light brown leather jacket, pressed tan trousers and a very red face that hinted at high blood pressure or a tendency toward alcohol. As the man spoke Adam thought that the skin around his face lost interest in holding his head together when it got below his mouth. He could see its point.

Adam said nothing, secure in the fact that the non-buying customer would.

'Not that you would be able to compete of course. It's all about size now. It's just a matter of time I imagine before all shops become a thing of the past...'

'What about the butchers?' Adam said quietly. 'Hard to imagine people buying their meat online, isn't it?'

'Not really, we do our supermarket shop online now. We're almost there already.'

'Right,' said Adam, who didn't eat meat and had no idea why he was wondering about online butchers. 'But you don't know where the meat comes from. Might that not matter to some people?'

'Not really, not when you think about it.'

And both men stood silently pretending to think about it.

Adam had closely cropped grey hair, a tanned well-lined face and a largely passive expression gathered around a tight mouth and blue uncommunicating eyes. His right arm was embroidered with a full sleeve Japanese-style tattoo depicting large waves and floating flowers, clearly displayed under a short-sleeved red and even more floral Hawaiian shirt. Tall and slim, he moved quietly as befits a man in a bookshop and often wore reading spectacles perched on the end of his nose, which softened his appearance enough to attract the random thoughts and occasional feelings of strangers in his shop. A long time ago he made his living by listening to people tell him their troubles, and he rather enjoyed the fact that now he could make his living by barely hearing a word anyone said.

In the corner, carefully looking through second-hand fiction, again, were Grimy Nige and Jim. They were regulars. Adam thought that sometimes they came to simply stroke the books and wondered why they didn't spend more time in the library, or at least he did until he visited the library and found out there weren't very many books in it any more. Adam quite liked Grimy Nige and Jim, in part because they rarely spoke and in part because they were so excited when they bought the latest

James Lee Burke that they argued—they were both probably in their mid twenties—about who was going to carry it.

'What do you do about new books?' asked the man.

'Sell them,' said Adam.

'No, I mean how do you compete with the supermarkets and so forth?'

Who actually said 'so forth'? Adam wondered. The worst thing about working in a shop was that you can't just say 'Well I have to go somewhere else' and walk away. It was his shop, it was a small shop and there was nowhere to walk to. He had to stay there, and the chances of someone coming in and wanting to buy something were slim to nil so he couldn't say 'Excuse me I just need to attend to this less boring person who is actually shopping.' He just had to stand there and be polite. Shops were like prisons in that way, he thought.

'Compete?' mused Adam quietly, ignoring the fact that the man in his shop looked slightly uncomfortable with this. And then something like rescue arrived. Two customers, not apparently together, came in in quick succession. The first was a blonde woman wearing a beige French mac and long brown boots. She smiled confidently at Adam and started looking at the half-heartedly titled 'Psychology and Alternative Therapies' section that formed itself when Adam decided to merge Freud and 'Cognitive Behavioural Therapy for Pets' with Reiki, the I Ching and—just for the hell of it—a book about Astrology.

It was her walk Adam noticed: her stride was short and her shoulders hunched. She moved as though moving was an inconvenience and managed to present a gracelessness which made her appear less attractive than she was. Adam assumed she did this on purpose. He tended to think most people did most things on purpose, even if they didn't always admit it. He wondered why she did that and she instantly became more interesting to him, although he realized, vaguely, that given the man who currently appeared to be trying to move into his shop he would be interested in anyone at the moment. 'Maybe she is clever,' he thought, and women of a certain age who are clever tend to play down their looks for fear they are not taken seriously. 'That would explain the coat,' he thought, which was horrible. 'Or maybe she thinks she is clever but isn't. And has rubbish taste in clothes as well?' Anyway, this was one of the things he did to combat the slowness of the shop when it began to feel oppressive: make stuff up about strangers.

The other customer—who brought the total number of people in the shop to six, and it was neither a Saturday nor the publication date of a Harry Potter book—was a young thin man Adam had not seen before. He looked at Adam and the red-faced man and when they both looked back he turned away and started flicking through the shelves nearest the door, which were 'Cut price—miscellaneous'. If anyone was going to steal anything on their way out let it be something hard to categorize was Adam's reasoning.

'Mind you,' said the man loudly. 'You seem to be bringing in the punters now.' A pointless sentence designed as a precursor to him expanding his boringness outward.

'I was just saying to this gentleman that I imagine it is very hard to compete against the larger bookshops. What is that brings you in here, my dear?'

Adam didn't know whether to cringe or hit him. He didn't need to do either. The pretty blonde woman glanced up and said with the vaguest hint of a sneer: 'I like looking at books.'

'Well that's the problem,' the man said immediately. 'Lots of people like looking at books, not so many of them like buying books from bookshops.'

Adam had had enough now. 'There's a shoe shop down the road, you might want to pop in there later to not buy any flip flops and explain to them the end of footwear is nigh?' As he spoke Adam picked up a handful of books from under the counter and walked round to the fiction section to place them on the shelves. They didn't need to go on the shelves but it left the man at the counter alone, facing outward at a shop full of people who liked books. The man looked confused for a moment. In front of the counter was a small table with large books displayed. They were there because Adam had seen tables like that in other, what he liked to call 'proper' book shops and it offered a place to put books that he didn't really understand but knew it was good to sell on. The odd celebrity biography, some cook books and most recently a book about cake decoration that cost £35. The man stepped forward and picked it up. He didn't open it, he turned it over in his hand seeming to both weigh it and see the price on the back.

'I think the wife would like this,' he said 'Can you gift wrap?'

Adam smiled. 'No.'

'You should think about it,' the man suggested.

Adam walked back to the counter, accepted the man's credit card and put the sale through the till. He put the book into a brown paper bag and said: 'I'll put the receipt in there, shall I?'

The man took the bag and turned round to face the shop, either a triumphant announcement that he had bought something or, more likely Adam thought, an attempt to engage the blonde in conversation. She didn't look up; she appeared too engrossed in a book called 'Psychosexuality and Cultural Impotence.' Adam liked to imagine she was being sarcastic but he conceded she might be an academic.

For a few seconds everyone in the shop was perfectly still, waiting, and Adam had the sense that if the large man with the book about cake decorating didn't leave now they would all be trapped here forever. Fortunately so did the man.

'Best be off, she'll be wondering where I've got to.' Which Adam doubted.

'Bye.' Adam actually lifted his arm in the air and waved. After the man had left there was silence for a few seconds and then Grimy Nige, who was looking over Jim's shoulder at something by Richard Ford, said without turning round: 'He was a tosser wasn't he, Mr Sands?'

The blonde woman smiled to herself and blushed. The unknown thin young man looked up. Adam just nodded. 'Yes Grimy Nige, yes he was. Still bought a big book on cake decorating. What am I going to put on that table now?'

The blonde walked over and put the book she had been intently reading on the counter.

'Can I leave this here while I look around?'

Adam nodded. 'I'm not expecting a rush but yes, of course.'

'Got anything else like that?'

Adam paused for a moment. 'Academic? Psycho-social-sciency stuff?' She raised her head. She was pretty: high cheekbones, no make up, bright eyes, serious expression. Early forties maybe younger, dressed a bit older. She nodded.

'I have a couple of boxes out the back I haven't been through yet. I can bring them through and you are welcome to have a look.'

'Boxes of what?'

'Academic, psycho-social-sciency stuff. That is the technical term, right?'

'Where would you get two boxes...? Sorry, yes please.'

Adam took the three steps required to go 'out the back'. A door beside the counter led to a small room with a kettle, a tiny unused fridge and several boxes of unpriced books. He picked up two medium-sized boxes and brought them back through the door to the counter. 'I have a friend who works for a publisher. They publish magazines about nursing, psychology, social work and stuff, and academic publishers send them books to review. However, they haven't noticed that hardly any of the magazines have reviews pages anymore. He gathers them together and when they are beginning to get in the way or when they want to get a little bit of spare office cash for a jolly he calls me and I buy them from him. It used to be that university students would buy them. I suspect they get most of their materials online now so I don't rush to put them out.'

The blonde woman was nodding while looking through the first box enthusiastically. 'That's brilliant!' she said 'I love it, I want to buy them, well some of them. A few of them, lots of them, maybe three of them. How often do you get them in?'

'It varies: every couple of months, depends...' Adam was wondering how he was going to price up these books that she may buy while she was there without feeling embarrassed.

'I haven't actually had time to price these up yet though,' he said. He may have blushed.

'Well, perhaps I can set aside the ones I want and come back a little later for them when you've worked out how much to charge me'? She smiled. She had a hard to place accent. The walk, he decided, was definitely a trick. 'Take your time.'

'We're not going to have to barter, are we?' he said.

'Excuse me' said the young man who was holding a copy of something by Christopher Brookmyre. 'Are you Adam Sands?'

'Yes, yes I am.' Before the young man spoke again, as Adam looked at him and noticed the nervousness round the lips and the mass of taken-for-granted black, unattended hair, he noted to himself that this was the most social engagement he had had in weeks.

'My name is Tom. Tom Newton. I wonder if I could talk to you for a few minutes? I think you used to know my mum.'

It took Adam a few moments to absorb the name Newton and a few moments more to acknowledge the existence of this young man. And then, and this surprised Adam, he found himself looking at the boy for signs of himself, something round the eyes maybe? And the boy was tall.

The young man looked uncomfortable in the silence Adam presented him with. It wasn't aggressive, it wasn't challenging but it demanded something of him and he wasn't sure what, and so he filled the space. 'Anna? Anna Newton.' And then 'Do you remember her?'

'Yes,' Adam nodded. 'Of course I remember her. How is she?'

'I don't know,' said Tom. 'That's sort of why I'm here. She's gone missing.'

Adam stood very still, as if he was waiting for something and then he began to feel a slight tightening around his chest. He nodded in acknowledgement of the feeling. The nod must have appeared to be an invitation for the young man to carry on talking.

'I know it must seem odd but I wasn't sure what to do and I had to do something. Nobody from her real life knows where she is and it's not like her. The police say that not being in contact for a few days is not technically missing...'

'A few days?'

'Four. Since she emailed me, since she spoke to Grace. Grace was worried but not saying much, which isn't like her. You know Grace, right? She told me where to find you.'

'Yes, I know Grace. I haven't spoken to her in years. I didn't know she and your mum were still in touch. That's nice.' Adam didn't like the feeling in his chest. And now he felt hot as well. 'But I'm sorry, I haven't seen Anna since before you were born.'

The boy looked away and down at the counter. When he had introduced himself he looked about 23. Now he looked about 14.

Adam spoke again. 'Tom? After your grandfather, yes?'

The boy looked at him and shrugged; he reddened. 'I'm sorry,' he whispered and took a pen and piece of paper from his pocket. 'If you hear anything, or perhaps think of anyone who might have any ideas, would you call and let me know please.' He turned and walked to the door. Before leaving he looked back and said: 'I had no idea my grandfather's name was Tom.' He tried to laugh and failed.

Adam had the sense that he needed to slow down the boy's exit. 'What did she say when you last spoke to her?'

'She left a message, told me not to come home because the house was being fumigated. It hasn't been. Emailed me to say she was going away with Grace for a few days but she didn't.

Mum never lies. I phoned Grace, Mum hadn't told her the lie so Grace didn't know what to say. I thought at first that maybe she had met someone, you know, and didn't want to make a big deal about it but nobody has heard anything for four days...'

Adam gazed at Tom as softly as he could. The boy didn't move. The blonde woman continued to look through the books. 'There is something else, Tom?' he said gently.

Tom glanced at the grey cord carpet. 'When I went to the flat there was a man. He wasn't in the flat, he was waiting outside and when I went in he knocked on the door and asked if he could come in. I said no. Mum has one of those chain things and she always made me put it on when I was in the house. He asked where my mum was and I asked who wanted to know. He wasn't the most charming man I have ever met. He said there was a problem at work and they had been trying to get in touch with her but she seemed to have lost her phone. I said her phone was broken and she was getting a new one but she hadn't been in touch with me either. Then I said, no idea why, that I thought she was in France, that she had friends there. He gave me a card and said, and I thought this was odd, he said if she gets in touch call me. Not 'if she gets in touch tell her we need to talk to her', he told me to call them. What's that about?'

The blonde woman had by now stopped pretending to look at the books and was listening to Tom. 'What does your mum do?' she asked. 'Sorry, none of my business...'

'She isn't a spy or anything. She does research, in health stuff, that's all.'

'Why did you come here, Tom?' asked Adam.

Tom shrugged. 'I went round to see Grace. I asked her who mum knew that I didn't know. She said logically only people she knew before I was born. I asked her where you were, I know who you are... I think I know who you might be... I don't care, not right now anyway... She said the last she heard you were running a bookshop in Margate. You weren't hard to find.'

The blonde woman looked at Adam. 'Are you famous?'

'Obviously not,' Adam said without looking at her. 'I haven't seen her, Tom, or heard from her, not in years.'

'I know.' The boy nodded. 'Nice tattoo by the way,' he said distractedly.

'If I hear anything or think of anything I will phone, I promise. Are you staying down here?'

'I booked into a B and B in Margate. Wasn't sure where else to go.'

'OK,' said Adam. Do you want to get a bite to eat later? We could just talk, see if that helps?'

Tom looked embarrassed. 'Thanks, but its OK. I'm with someone; they came down with me...'

'OK.' Adam smiled. 'Perhaps you'll let me know if you hear anything?'

Tom nodded half-heartedly, walked slowly to the door and left.

Two hours later the shop was empty. Grimy Nige and Jim had been the last to leave, having decided to join in the social revelry by buying a second-hand Jake Arnott book. Adam had priced up the books the blonde woman had wanted by halving the listed price and adding 10%. Anything more would have felt rude and Adam was never rude, believing that good manners functioned as a helpful barrier to intimacy.

Today constituted more conversation than Adam had accumulated in the previous three weeks. People were not really the centre of his life. He grew vegetables on a small allotment not far from the shop: it saved him money and gave him outdoor time. He fished from his rowing boat when the weather let him. Often, when it was warm enough and calm, he would head out to sea from the old nearly retired harbour in Margate until land or at least what was on it was out of sight. Then he would put down his anchor, and lay on his back with his head resting over one side and his legs over the other and bob around listening to the lapping of the water and the occasional curiosity of the seagulls. After a while he would slide quietly into the water and swim. Swim until the sea made him feel small. Nothing can shrink you like an ocean.

His contact with the world was half hearted. He exchanged words with a few old friends via email; he occasionally slept with a history teacher from a local girls' school whose name was Lesley, a long-legged olive-skinned woman who wrote poetry and played the drums. She referred to him as 'Sands' and never phoned him. However, when he called her she always told him off for not calling sooner and invited him over. He was currently teaching himself in a distracted way how to make chutney and do yoga, and was playing guitar in a local bar for fun and a few drinks. None of these things demanded his full attention, or if they did he didn't give it and that is perhaps why he did them. He had evolved a life that felt like a visit to the library: quiet, undemanding and pretty much devoid of surprises.

Adam was making himself tea and thinking of closing up when the blonde woman came back in. 'I know you might not have had the chance yet, but I was just passing so I thought...'

'It's fine,' Adam nodded.

'Anyway,' she added, glancing up from beneath her hair and smiling. 'This seems to be a place of intrigue.'

'You caught us on a strange day,' Adam smiled. He pushed the pile of three new books along the counter. 'Have a look and tell me if that seems fair.' He regretted saying that immediately.

The blonde woman looked at them and nodded. 'Yes, that seems fair. How do you work out a price?'

'I work out how much I paid for them and add something for being a bookshop.' He smiled, as he often did, to soften the possibility that he sounded either caustic or defensive.

'Right,' she nodded. 'It's just that, believe it or not, there would be quite a market for these sorts of books at these sorts of prices. I'm not surprised students don't travel to bookshops to actually look at them but, if they were in some way right under their noses, I am sure they would want them. Certainly where I work. Academic books are so ridiculously expensive and I work with research students who don't have much money.'

'Where do you work?'

'Kent University. I'm a psychologist by background.'

'Ahh.' Adam smiled 'Can't stand psychology.'

'Tell me what you think, why don't you?' The blonde woman smiled.

'I think it's important to share all my petty prejudices whenever I am selling books,' Adam said.

'Do you have many?'

Adam paused for a moment. 'I don't know,' he said quietly. 'Most television, Karaoke, people who are earnest about political parties, psychologists obviously, bad poetry, crystal healing...' He looked at her and shrugged. 'Who knew there was so much?'

'And they say books broaden the mind,' she said. 'My name is Alison, by the way.' She put out her hand.

'Adam. And I don't read the books. I simply profit from them.' He gripped her fingers limply because he wasn't sure how to shake hands with a woman. 'So how might I advertise these books in your university, Alison?'

'You could put up some leaflets?' she said, almost demure, mocking them both.

'What is this witchcraft of which you speak?'

'Do you have a website?'

'Yes, I have a website. I think part of me worries that if I advertise them too much the publishers will see and wonder how I got them.'

'But you're not getting them illegally?'

'No but...' Adam trailed off. 'I'm not a natural businessman, I don't think.' Locked now into self-effacement, he noticed he liked this woman's company and he knew that in all probability that would annoy him later.

'So to recap, you don't read them and you are not very good at selling them,' she laughed.

171

'You're right!' exclaimed Adam. 'What the hell am I doing here? Want to get a coffee?'

'Can't,' Alison said. 'Have to be somewhere else fifteen minutes ago. Next time though? I'll even buy. Unless you want cake, in which case you're on your own.'

After she had gone Adam closed the shop and wandered around the shelves rearranging things that had been moved during the day for no other reason than people not knowing how alphabetical order worked. He turned the light out and went upstairs to the one bedroom flat he lived in and distractedly threw some oil and vegetables into a pan. Mixing them with pasta and pesto he ate slowly listening to the news on the radio and watching the sky fill with thick grey cloud.

By seven o'clock the flat had shrunk and he knew he had to get out. He headed, as he always did, toward the sea. Along the cliff tops there stretched wide green lawns that separated the rarely busy coastal road from the thirty-foot drop to the promenade. The lawns were punctuated by flower gardens every 400 yards or so. Sometimes these were hidden by well-kept hedges and one, the one Adam liked the best, was a sunken garden. You had to walk down steps to get into it and once in you were sheltered from the wind, the road and, if you were lucky enough to find it free of cider-drinking teenagers, people. Adam used to work here. Tending the flowers and recovering from more difficult times. The last time he had seen Anna Newton, about twenty-three years ago, he had brought her to this place. She was six or seven months pregnant then. He had wandered down here when he left the hospital and got a job helping tend those gardens. They were kind to each other when she had visited. They had gone for coffee and people had fussed over her in the café and on the train he put her on at the end of the day. She had loved being pregnant. She had winked from the train window. He had blown her a kiss. He had liked her but had not felt anything about not seeing her again.

He had loved working outdoors but it wasn't far enough away, so when he got some money he bought a ticket to Goa, the cheapest place he could think of to live and the furthest place from the hospital he could imagine. He had stayed there for over a year, playing guitar in a covers band twice a week in a large hotel that offered holidays to people who preferred the idea of being in India to actually being in India. He moved on to Thailand and then a Greek Island called Spetse. There he played guitar and sang songs he couldn't stand in a bar most nights, and swam and read a lot. He had also written and sold a few songs, albeit under a made-up name. He had sent the odd postcard to Anna and Grace and Stephen, but always when he was about to leave somewhere. It was nearly ten years before he was back in England; by that time he had assumed everyone had moved on. He didn't actually do anything to find out. And yet, for all the time and space in between then and now, he felt unsettled. It was probably the boy who was creeping under his skin; him and the tiny shame that accompanied his instinct to not try to be more helpful. He hadn't looked at Tom as closely as he had wanted to. It was that that brought the fear, what he might see. Or what he might not. Anna? She was more an echo. Tom was perhaps something else.

He walked home just after eight and poured himself a glass of wine which he didn't drink. He tried to read his book, *Tender is the Night*. He couldn't concentrate, partly because whenever he read that book it made him feel sad. In fact, reading it invited sadness and now he didn't want to feel anything, or at least anything more than he already was. He thought about doing some yoga to still his mind but only got so far as lying on the floor looking upward and out of the corner of his living room window, watching the darkness deepen and the shadows drop. He stayed there and wondered about putting a coffee bar in the shop. Turning the basement into a place with books and coffee and a sofa maybe, although how he could afford the coffee machines or someone to work there was beyond him.

At about 9pm, finally exhausted of distractions, he found the number Tom had left. He picked it and up and put it down. Held it in a closed hand trying not to memorize it and put it in a drawer in the kitchen. At 9.30 he phoned the boy's number. There was no answer; he left a message. 'Hello its Adam, Adam Sands. I was thinking, it's not like Anna and I don't know what she has been doing for the last, god, twenty-odd years, but I'd like to help, if I could. Help you look I mean. Let me know what I can do. Or better still, of course, if she has been in touch, let me know that. Bye.'

When he put the phone down, to his surprise he found himself not thinking about Anna at all, or Tom, but rather of the blonde woman who actually bought books. And so, without a moment's hesitation, he phoned Lesley the history teacher and asked, in a roundabout sort of way, if he could come over if he brought wine and fresh vegetables from his allotment.

'Sands,' she said. 'Get your sorry ass round here now. Where have you been?'

As he left his flat he noticed that the tightening around the chest was still there but it must have lessened slightly because he wasn't so aware of it. Either that or he was getting used to it again.

# 11. Seascape

Anna's instinct had been to go as far from Manchester as she could. If it was the case that she was being followed or was under threat, then her first responsibility was to lead that threat away from her son. In finding herself thinking that, she opened herself up to the realization that if anyone in the world ever wanted to hurt her then the way to do that was through Tom. On the one hand this made her want to call him, warn him, protect him. On the other, her sense of insecurity had become so acute, so tinged with paranoia that her belief, a belief evidenced by the Ford Focus showing up at Grace's house meaning that her phone had been bugged, spread like a stain to consider that maybe her email had been hacked too, and maybe even Tom's phone, and so she couldn't contact him.

Anna had driven to Brighton. She booked into a small hotel on the seafront that was next to a posh fish and chip shop. She hadn't slept that first night. Next morning she got out of bed early, showered and went for a walk along the seafront. She walked into what became Hove and then what became something industrial. Three hours later she was back at her hotel and checking out. She walked toward the pier and up into town. Brighton was always crowded but she was used to seeing it when it was sunny and people were congregating round the seafront or the lanes to celebrate life. Today it was raining and everyone looked cross. It was like being on Oxford Street but with fresher air.

It was Paul she needed to talk to but she didn't have a phone anymore. Anyway, if people were as interested in tracing her as her imagination was leading her to believe, they would perhaps be monitoring the phones of those she was most likely to call, like Paul. She considered her options. She could drive along the coast, say toward Portsmouth, find a public phone booth and call Paul. Yes, they may trace it but she could then drive either on toward Bournemouth or back east toward Eastbourne. Of course that might narrow the search but she knew that at some point she was going to have to take some sort of chance and there was a reasoned voice inside her head telling her that a couple of blokes in a Ford Focus does not constitute MI5, although when she told herself that the image of Meena's smouldering flat and weeping mother crept into her head.

Alternatively she could just buy a phone, new number, no contract. Or do both? Anna went to a cash machine, drew out £300, went back to her car and started driving along the A27 toward Portsmouth. At Chichester roundabout she stopped at a garage and filled up with petrol, paying by debit card. She pulled off the dual carriageway and drove down into Fareham, stopping at the first phone booth she found, which was broken. A mile or so on, she found one that was working. It crossed her mind to wonder who used phone booths any more, to make phone calls in as opposed to urinate. She phoned Paul's number, it rang several times and she was surprised when someone answered it. But it wasn't Paul. 'Hello?'

'Who's this?'

'Simon. Anna?' Simon was Paul's son. A six foot four, rugby-playing chemical engineer who, in the half dozen times Anna had met him, had never shown the slightest glimmer of any emotion, unless you consider affability an emotion.

'Where's your dad Simon? I really need to speak to him.'

'Don't know. No idea.'

'Simon, this is important...'

'I know, it must be. Look, we came back from fishing and there was a message for Dad to call someone at work. He didn't think much of it, he actually said, 'about bloody time,' but when he got off the phone he seemed quiet. I asked him what was wrong and he said he didn't know but he'd left fishing mode and gone into work mode by then, I didn't think much of it. Where are you calling from?'

'Phone booth,' said Anna. 'I got it into my head that my phone might be being tapped. It may be that your dad thought the same about his? That's why he hasn't got it with him?'

'Hang on... phone tapping? Is this something to do with dodgy journalists?'

'No idea' said Anna.

'Dad made a couple of calls and then he packed a bag and took off. Said he'd be back in a few days.'

Anna paused for a moment and imagined the two men in the Ford Focus listening to this conversation, tracing it. Simon hadn't said anything that they couldn't have already known and Simon was a bright enough young man for her to imagine that was intentional.

'OK.' Anna swallowed hard. 'When he gets home, let him know I called, please.'

'Right,' said Simon.

'And let him know that Meena was involved in a fire. She was hurt, I'm not sure how badly.'

There was a pause at the other end of the line. 'I think he already knows, Anna.'

Anna went back to her car. The chances were Paul was doing what she was doing. She immediately imagined him doing it better. She wondered where her confidence had gone. There was a time, a long time, in her life that she lived as though she was just waiting for the world to turn on her, secure in the knowledge that if it did she would be ready for it. As a younger woman she was always in control, indeed she designed a worldview that was wholly suited to the situation she found herself in now, a need for self-sustenance, the emotional equivalent of guerrilla warfare, but something had happened, something like motherhood.

When Tom was young she guarded him the way mothers do but more so. Always watching, always mistrusting. Policing herself to be the quiet focused career woman, yet always present when a parent had the opportunity to see their child. She watched not the sports day or nativity, nor in later years the music, the singing, the piano recitals. She watched the space around him. Was it a happy space, a growing space, a safe space? Tom had a wholly different nature to her. He was so very trusting of the world. Perhaps, she had thought, because he was a boy he expected things to be OK; she expected things to be laced with traps. His casualness, his confidence may have eased down her defences over the years. His ability to gently laugh at her caution, to tease her, had helped her do that, at least up until he was around sixteen or seventeen, when he closed up a little and she began to turn her energies away from keeping guard and toward letting go as gracefully as possible.

Anna drove on to Portsmouth following the signs to the shopping centre called Gun Wharf. There she bought a pay as you go phone, using her credit card. She put £50 worth of credit on it and immediately phoned Grace. 'Hello?'

There was a pause and then Grace's voice said: 'Wait.' And the line went dead.

For thirty seconds or so Anna stared at the phone, at first afraid then terrified and then confused. Until the phone rang. 'Right,' said Grace firmly. 'I'm not taking any chances: this is Laura's phone. Silly child left it here. The local news says that the fire at Meena's might have been started on purpose. Meena and an unnamed man remain in a serious condition. A third person is recovering well. What on earth is going on?'

Anna explained as far as she could. She told her about Paul and what Simon had said.

'So it's about work?' said Grace with surprise.

'Don't know, must be,' said Anna.

'What are you working on Anna? Nuclear weapons?'

'We were just about to start working on this depression project. Can't see anyone needing to kill... Christ, someone tried to kill Meena?'

'We don't know that for sure, Anna.'

'Don't we?'

'We know she is hurt, we don't know it was necessarily an attempt on her life.' Grace paused. 'Having said that...' She decided to change the subject. 'Have you spoken to Tom?'

'Not yet, didn't want to draw any attention to him. I left him a message.'

'OK, that's good. If you call him now, though, he might start worrying.'

Anna thought for a moment. That made sense, in so much as anything made sense, but the thought of not speaking to Tom felt too close to defeat. 'Sooner or later I'm going to have to say something to him.' She felt as if she was almost asking the universe for permission to be illogical.

There was a long pause. 'Let's assume there are some people trying to find you, Anna, and let's assume they had the ability to tap your phone, find out where you live and know that I am your best friend.'

'Right,' said Anna.

'That suggests that they have access to your ordinary life. Your habits, your friends, your... son... that they have information on you, and the same about Paul.'

'Yeah... this isn't actually making me feel any better.'

'No, sorry, but what might exist in your life that they don't know about?'

Anna thought about her life: there wasn't enough in it for there to be parts to not know about. 'Nothing,' she said quietly.

'Your past, Anna. You keep your past under lock and key.'

'My family, you mean?'

'Well, maybe, that's up to you. Or there's Adam?'

'Adam?' Such a long time ago.

Grace didn't speak, sensing that Anna was processing the idea. Eventually Anna said: 'I'll think about it.' And then added, 'What if I am simply going a bit mad?'

It had been her intention to leave a trail along the south coast heading westward and then head back east. Buying the phone was going to be the end of the trail but it occurred to her that up to now she was simply avoiding people unknown and guessing at what was going on. She wasn't learning anything, not anything helpful. So she headed west into Southampton and found a small hotel off the ring road. She booked in using her debit card and told the woman behind the counter that she was going shopping and then on to dinner, but that she was expecting a business acquaintance. She asked the receptionist for the name of a good restaurant, not too close to the hotel as she would like to see a little of Southampton. The receptionist, a pretty plump woman with dark eyes and tired shoulders recommended a small Italian she liked down by the docks. Anna thanked her and gave her her phone number—risky she knew—and asked her to tell her guests that she will be in that restaurant from 8.30 and wondered if the receptionist would be kind enough to phone her to let her know when the men arrived.

'Frankly,' she said conspiratorially, 'I need a bit of preparation before I see them. My little girl needed an operation and I borrowed money from the bank to get it. They say I obtained it illegally. I didn't, and I am paying it back as agreed but they say fraud is fraud...' Anna found herself welling up.

The receptionist lifted her shoulders and breathed in the opportunity to be a force for good rather then just someone who answered the phone and sorted out the bill. 'Bastards' she murmured. Anna smiled and cried a tiny bit at the same time. 'They would say they are just doing their jobs, its just... well if I see them without expecting to see them I get all... flustered.' The receptionist recognized the enemy that was flustered. 'Don't worry Ms Newton' she said. 'I will phone you as soon as they leave.'

'Thank you,' said Anna. 'You are kind.'

'That's why you asked for a restaurant on the other side of the city isn't it? So you will have time to get yourself together?' Anna smiled and nodded. 'Good thinking,' said the receptionist. 'Is there anything else I can do for you?'

Anna shook her head. She thought of tipping her, but somehow tipping someone for an act or even a gesture of kindness seemed cheap. So instead she reached across the reception desk, put her hand on the receptionist's and squeezed. 'I'll bring my bag in later,' Anna said quietly. 'And thank you.'

Anna got back into her car and headed, almost randomly, for Eastbourne.

Anna had never been to Eastbourne before and was struck by its architectural poise. The large regency buildings, the well-ordered sea front. As she wandered along the coast road on her first day there, she felt herself relax slightly, physically at least. She booked into a large Bed and Breakfast on the edge of the town, a four-storey terraced mansion with flaking paint and a yellowing 'Vacancies' sign in the window. It was shabby on the inside and run by a woman who seemed suspicious of anyone who wanted to stay there. Particularly when they were paying cash. Anna spent two days wandering the streets of Eastbourne finding out why the landlady was suspicious. It was a poor town. Laced with street drinkers and angry people in nylon jackets.

The hotel in Southampton never phoned her and Anna noticed that, rather than imagine this meaning that whoever was pursuing her had less all-seeing power than she had imagined, she began to wonder if the receptionist was in on it. That was a step beyond anything resembling logic: that was paranoia. And so she took a chance and phoned Grace on Laura's phone.

'Where are you?' asked Grace and Anna noticed her own paranoia again. Before she could answer, Grace said: 'Don't answer that. Just in case.'

'Have you heard from Tom?' Anna asked.

'Yes he came here. I played dumb really. He was worried about you Anna. He said someone had been to your flat asking for you when he was there.' Anna stopped breathing for a moment.

'Where is he now?'

'Tom? I'm not sure, I think he may be... he may have gone to see Adam.'

'Why the hell would he do that?'

'Because when he asked about any part of your life that he didn't know about, then Adam was all I could think of and I thought, old habits or something, that, well, Adam was nothing if not trustworthy.'

Anna said nothing. All Grace could hear was her own breathing. Finally Anna said:

'Grace, could you do me a favour, do you think? Could you call The Mayfield Hotel in Southampton and find out if anyone came looking for me?'

'Yeah, sure. Anything else?'

'No, I think I'm OK.' Anna laughed. 'Well, under the circumstances.'

'Do you need any money?'

'No. I'll run out of knickers in a few days, but maybe by then I'll have a plan.'

'Have you tried Paul again?'

'No...'

'Shall I?'

Anna thought for a moment. 'Maybe,' she said. 'If you were able to contact his son? Maybe at work or something?'

'Where does his son work?'

'Notts University. Simon Stern. Something to do with chemistry or engineering.'

'Right,' said Grace.

'Thank you,' said Anna.

'Take care, pet.'

'Trying to,' said Anna, who was already imagining what Adam Sands, if he was still alive, was like now.

*

When the sun finally arrived Lesley was in a friendly rush.

'Don't leave it so long next time, Sands,' she said as she emerged from the shower and dressed more self-consciously than she used to in front of him. 'And help yourself to tea and toast if you want.'

'It's OK,' he said softly as he got out of bed and started looking for his underwear 'I'm fine. I'll leave when you do and get the shop open.' It made the following twenty minutes less comfortable than it could have been. If he had stayed in bed he could have pretended to watch her turn herself from post-coital lover to professional woman with an appreciative, flirtatious eye. In truth, while he liked her body very much, her self-consciousness made him feel that watching her was not a tender thing to do. So they dressed awkwardly and quietly and Lesley left the room as soon as she could, to go to the kitchen to make coffee that Adam would not drink.

Before they left her flat, he reached out and touched her hair, still wet from the shower and blacker for the water. 'Are you looking for grey?' she asked defensively.

'No,' he said honestly and added clumsily: 'Do you know you have the best legs I have ever seen on a woman?' Which was true and crass at the same time and he knew it.

'You need to get out more, book boy,' she said, moving round the kitchen table to separate them and check her workbag.

'Maybe,' shrugged Adam.

At the door she turned to kiss him goodbye. They kissed lightly but not on the lips, instead brushing each other's face between the cheek and the mouth and lingering for a moment to formally remember that the night before they had kissed like lovers rather than as members of the same badminton club. 'Call me, Sands,' Lesley said. 'A girl can't be expected to buy her own vegetables you know.'

Lesley got into her car and Adam walked down the street toward the sea. He would walk home. A ridiculous idea as it

183

was four miles to Margate, even longer if he walked it round the coastline, but the buses would be full of people and people were annoying and he needed to be outdoors, even if this was not a particularly familiar bit of outdoors and he would prefer to be nearer home. He stopped at a coffee shop and bought a large peppermint tea and wandered along the cliff top. The breeze was cool, almost cold, and he pulled the collar of his jacket up and his battered pork pie hat down on to his head. He put sunglasses on to stop the wind from making his eyes water. The tide was out and it wasn't raining. It was 8.35; he might be at the shop by ten. He reached the sea. A wide road with an expanse of grass leading to the cliff edge stretched in front of him. He breathed deeply, lifted his head slightly and began to walk home.

As he walked he looked at the sea, imagined being in it and trying to swim home, all along the coast. He knew he could swim the distance and if the current was following him he would enjoy it. He toyed with the idea of stripping down to his pants and doing it, but only momentarily, largely because he would have to jog back to get his clothes. He turned the idea into something less appealing by reminding himself of the many times he had swum against the current, unable to find the rhythm of the water, or at least to fall into step with it. So he settled instead for breathing in the sea air and watching the water move without a plan or pattern, promising himself a swim this evening if the sea looked as though it would let him.

There were a couple of large ships in the distance and a small sailing boat coming from the east; otherwise it was empty. He moved closer to the cliff top. Below was a promenade, and occasionally a dog walker would stride along purposefully. Where he was, on the grass, the view was better but it was less sheltered. There was always a breeze coming off the sea and despite his glasses it made his eyes water, which made him feel old. He took off the glasses and wiped his face. He felt his hat move on his head so he pulled it tighter again and moved away from the edge of the cliff and walked on.

After an hour he was in Margate, having walked along the sea front beneath the old Winter Gardens and Lido on a promenade that would eventually lead to the tiny harbour that lay beyond the bay. It was only ten o'clock. He had walked quickly. He wanted to be later, he didn't know why, so he stopped and sat on a bench and looked down towards the beach. There was a group of people fussing over a small yacht they were wheeling onto the sand; there were a few people walking dogs, and an old couple walking slowly along the cliff top in front of him. And there was a blonde woman walking toward him from the other direction, the woman from yesterday.

'Hello,' she said, smiling through hair that was whipping around her face. 'Shouldn't you be selling books?'

'Shouldn't you be corrupting young minds?'

'Day off? Shopkeepers don't get days off, do they? Or do you have staff?'

Adam smiled. 'No staff, I'm just late. I've been arguing with myself about going for a swim.'

Alison turned to look at the uninviting grey sea. 'In that?' Adam nodded and Alison grimaced. 'So, while you decide, do you have time for that coffee now or will there be a queue forming?'

She was different outdoors, Adam thought, although he wasn't sure how. 'Hell, I'm self-employed and I'm sitting here because I don't want to be there, so coffee would be nice.'

They walked across the lawn to some old stone steps that led to the promenade. Without consulting each other they selected the café nearest the sea and sat outside, both turning their metal chairs to face the beach.

'I like it here,' said Alison after they had ordered drinks.

'There are worse places to be,' he said.

'Do you swim a lot?'

'As often as I can. I have a small boat; sometimes I take it out and swim from it. Feels good.'

'You own a boat? You must be a man of means.'

Adam smiled. 'What do you imagine an owned boat looks like?'

She smiled back. 'I'm thinking yacht, cabins, staff, probably not the same staff that you don't have running your chain of bookshops, but staff nonetheless. Am I wrong?'

Adam laughed: 'So, Kent University? In Canterbury, right? Why are you living round here?'

'I have some family, thought it would be nice to be a bit nearer. Have you always lived here?'

'Good god, no.' Adam noticed his own defensiveness. What would be wrong with always living here? 'No, I've moved around, spent a lot of time in London, lived near Manchester for a while, spent some time abroad. Ended up here more by coincidence really. I suppose I couldn't really live the way I do in many other places.'

'Is that because only people in Kent read?'

'No, there isn't much money in selling books these days and that is probably only going to get worse. Here I can live pretty simply: I grow my own vegetables, I fish, I read. I am old before my time.'

'Sounds good to me,' she said, which Adam didn't believe and so he said nothing.

The people who had been preparing the yacht were finally ready to put to sea: they had removed the boat from the trailer, set it in shallow water, returned the trailer to the promenade, put on their life jackets, tied down ropes and were leading the boat over the small breaking waves to a point where they could all get on and let the wind take them out.

'Is your boat like that?' asked Alison, turning to face him for the first time since they sat down.

'No. So, why psychology?'

'What an unusual question.' The wind caught her hair again and wrapped it round her mouth as she spoke; she had to pull it away. Adam smiled and waited.

'OK, well the superficial answer is I am interested in what it is that makes us human and when I was younger the obvious way to think about that was to study psychology, but I sense you are inviting something a little more authentic by asking me, and I am not by nature superficial. I suppose the fact that my brother was finally diagnosed with schizophrenia when he was fifteen and I had grown up with his, I don't know, weirdness is how I would have experienced it then, difference is how I would think of it now, meant that I either wanted answers or at least greater understanding or I wanted to run away. I opted for the former. Eventually.'

'Eventually?'

'We call that key wording, you know.' She was uncomfortable.

Adam nodded. 'I call it curiosity,' he said.

'I did a degree in French. I fancied myself hanging out in cafés talking about Genet and De Beauvoir, or at least not being in Stoke worrying about why my brother slept under his bed rather than in it. I worked as an interpreter for a while, did other stuff...'

'Stoke?'

'You're doing it again and let's never talk about Stoke'

'Fine by me. Has psychology helped?'

'My brother? Not really, no.'

'I meant you. Has it helped you?'

'I like to think it has helped others a bit and I like the idea of being useful.'

'Good for you.'

'Are you being sarcastic?'

'No.'

'I can't tell.' She was moving around on her chair now.

'I admire anyone who wants to be helpful. Particularly if they can sustain it.'

'But you don't like psychologists.'

'What do I know? I just sell books.'

'Now you're patronizing me.'

The small yacht was slow but it was maybe a hundred metres out now and, even though the sea looked flatter further out, the boat was swinging up and down more than Adam had expected.

'I think there are three sorts of people who try to be helpful. There are the ones who succeed, the ones who fail and the ones who profit from pretending to succeed while failing. You are probably the first, I was the second. Being in the second group means I have to pick on the people in the third group to feel better about not being in the first group.'

'And that is what you think psychologists do? Profit while pretending to be helpful?' Adam shrugged. 'So how do you know I'm not in the third group?' She was not smiling but her eyes were soft.

'I'm trying to learn to think the best of people when I meet them, rather than assuming the worst.'

They sat in silence looking at the bobbing yacht and sipping hot drinks. Finally Adam said: 'I used to be a psychiatric nurse, a long long time ago.' He had imagined it would sound like a confession. Instead it felt like a purging.

Alison didn't say anything; she just glanced over at him and then turned back to the sea. Finally she said: 'Why did you give it up?'

'It made me feel like shit.'

By the time Adam got to the shop it was 11.15. Tom was waiting outside with a young woman: she was around his age, short and thin with mousey brown hair and confident eyes.

'Have I missed much?' Adam asked.

'Those two blokes who were in yesterday came by a couple of times, and a couple of people seemed confused by the fact you were closed but that aside... Do you open at 11.30?'

'Not on purpose,' said Adam. 'But mornings are often slow, or even slower.' He turned to the young woman. 'Hello,' he said.

'Hello,' she replied.

'This is Laura,' said Tom.

'Laura,' nodded Adam and he unlocked the shop door.

Perhaps buoyed by the fact that Adam didn't ask for any further information, Tom said:

'Laura is Grace's daughter.'

Adam stopped in the doorway and turned to look at the young woman. She had Grace's mouth and something around the eyes. He felt his own face tingle. He nodded at the girl again. 'How's your mum?'

'She doesn't know I'm here,' she said flatly

'I can't keep secrets from your mum, I'm afraid.'

'Wouldn't expect you to, Mr Sands.'

'Adam, please.' The three of them stood still just inside the shop, Adam with the sense that there was still something to be said but he at least didn't know what.

'I know who you are,' she said. He looked at her impassively. 'You were the one who tried to save my dad.'

*

Anna had spent a whole day walking round Eastbourne. It occurred to her for the first time that if they did not contact the hotel in Southampton and were not trailing her debit card around the southern coast of England then they might not have the ability to track her movements. They might be a couple of thugs hired by a drug company that has been told their multi-million-pound profit-making medicine is about to be proved to be pointless. They may have just had her address and the address of her best friend. Or it might even have been a different Ford Focus. Would an international pharmaceutical company hire thugs? Surely they could afford something a little more upmarket. Anyway, her fantasies about the mechanics of large corporations were just that. For her they were dull labyrinths of unbridled wealth collection. She had never met anyone who worked in that world.

She and Paul had both felt the need to run when they had heard about Meena. He must have felt threatened, just as she did, and that means it must have something to do with their work. The most significant part of their work was about to reveal that people with psychotic illnesses appeared to recover more fully and more often without being given drugs, at least if they were treated in the right sort of place in the right sort of way. When those results had emerged the three of them had been quite thrilled, but none of them really believed that it would change anything as fundamentally as the evidence itself demanded.

Paul had said that three things would happen. Firstly, the research method would be discredited. It would, he said, only take a professor with a pharmaceutical share option to say the words 'We're talking about a very small sample group' randomly on Radio 4 and doubt would begin to spread. Secondly, there would be counter-research funded by a drug company offering wildly different results or, better still, what the public relations people call a convenient death: a patient, unmedicated, that the drug companies could have saved if those evil Luddites hadn't planted such silly ideas in her pretty if mad young head. And thirdly—and Paul said that this was the one that he both admired and feared the most—there would be a new miracle drug wheeled out, maybe not even a drug, probably not even to do with mental health, but a miracle nonetheless. Something that treated cancer or Alzheimer's or a genetic disorder, that reminded the world just how fantastic medicine is. And that triumph will astonish and reassure. It won't matter that the treatment won't be available for ten years; it will remind everyone that medicine is progress, and all medicines will benefit from that.

Anna had considered Paul to be naturally depressive and eternally cynical. But in truth she didn't feel that she was part of something that was going to revolutionize the management of madness. She had believed that what they had found was important but that it would be subsumed in some way as to ensure everything would stay the same. Where money was concerned that was what always happened. On some level Anna realized that she had always assumed that large corporations had far too much power to ever need to hurt people. They would get their way regardless.

What was obvious to her, however, was that if she got the story out there, if the results to the research were in the public domain, she and Paul would be safe. The thought made her feel nervous, which surprised her. Her first feeling was that they were not her results to release. That there was an issue of manners to observe: Paul was the team leader, he should be the one to release the results. And the fact that he hadn't, and that he would surely have arrived at the same conclusion as her, scared her. And they were Meena's results too. What if she woke up and said the fire had been an accident? What if she was over-reacting to everything?

'You look worried.' A soft voice. She turned to see a pretty young man—high cheekbones, soft if grubby skin, curly shaggy brown hair and the most piercing blue eyes—sitting at a round metal table outside a café, holding a large cup of black tea. His jeans were ripped around the leg revealing a calf and a brown rolled-down sock. He was wearing a light green windcheater that was smeared with dirt or oil. But he had the most beautiful smile.

'Doesn't everyone?' she said.

The young man shrugged. 'Yeah, mostly.'

Anna looked inside the café: there wasn't a queue. The young man followed her gaze.

'Sit a while.' He smiled. 'Talk to a safe if grubby stranger, why don't you?' He spoke rhythmically, knowingly.

'Would you like a sandwich?' Anna asked.

'That's kind of you but no thank you.'

He sounded educated; he had good eye contact; his body posture was relaxed. If it was a mental health problem that

191

kept him on the streets, thought Anna, it was well controlled. Drugs more likely she thought. She pressed: 'Are you sure? I'm going to get something.'

The young man smiled. 'Well, that is nice of you. This may sound strange, but they do these cheese and Marmite buns in there. I wonder if I could have one of those? It isn't my usual fare but I can't help feeling the vitamin B would do me good.'

Anna smiled at him. Usual fare? Vitamin B conscious? He didn't look like a drinker. 'Good thinking,' she said.

She returned with a cheese and Marmite bap for him and a soya latte and avocado wrap for her. 'I'm Anna,' she said.

'JJ. Are you a vegan?' he asked.

'No, why?'

'Soya milk.'

'How can you tell?'

'It smells different.'

'All I can smell is the coffee,' she said.

'Wake up and smell the coffee,' he smiled. He ate more slowly than she did. If he was hungry he didn't show it. 'Why so worried?'

'Oh, work stuff.'

'What is your work?'

She took a deep breath. 'I work in mental health.'

'Oh right, that explains why you didn't run away when I spoke to you and why you offered to buy me food. What were you thinking? Schizophrenia? Drugs? Not drink, surely?'

'I wasn't thinking anything...'

'Really? Are you an OT?'

'No, why do you ask?'

'Well, if you were a psychologist you wouldn't have answered me. If you were a nurse you would have asked me questions by now. OT's are polite, and anyway you're wearing nice shoes.'

Anna looked at her feet. She hadn't changed her shoes for four days. 'I used to be a nurse. Now I work in research.

'What are you researching?'

'We were looking at ways of treating people with psychosis.'

'Drug company stooge?' He said it with a smile.

'I didn't think so,' she said impassively.

'I was diagnosed with a psychotic illness when I was a kid. Pumped full of all sorts of rubbish. Made me fat, made me forever thirsty. Made me smoke dope to take away the tension in my muscles that the drugs put there, and the dope made the voices louder, uglier.'

'Do you still hear the voices?'

'Nope. Not for years. I treated myself.'

'Did you?' Anna felt the top of her spine tingle slightly, aware that she was preparing herself for an encounter with madness.

The young man laughed. 'It's OK, I get how that sounds. You know, if I told you how I treated myself, and how I now help others treat themselves, your registration—you are still on a nursing register aren't you? Yes, of course you are—might mean you felt the need to call someone and report a mad boy in torn trousers in the town centre.'

Anna smiled. 'You don't look to me to be a risk to yourself or others. Beyond that, what you do or think is none of my business.'

The young man nodded. 'That's very... liberal of you.'

'Is it annoying, talking to people like me?' she asked.

The young man looked at her seriously. 'It can be frustrating. In principle you are a force for good, aren't you? You are part of the small minority of people who are interested enough in whatever madness is, and whatever distress it causes, to try to help. But as soon as you sign up you become part of an industry that... well... that doesn't always help very much.'

'Yeah, I can see that,' Anna nodded. 'That's why people like me stop doing it, I think.'

They sat quietly together, drinking their hot drinks and people-watching. Anna noticed that it was the closest she had felt to relaxed in days. The young man may be mad, but he had a presence that appeared contagious.

'Do you mind if I ask,' she said. 'How did you treat yourself?'

'You'll consider me mad,' he said. 'I can see your point. What with the trousers and stuff.' He laughed. 'I choose to live like this. I see it as part of my job, if you like.' He shrugged. 'But OK. When I was in hospital...' He turned and pointed westward. 'A big old hospital over that way, you've probably worked in one like it. Or that one even?' She shook her head. 'When I was in there I was struggling. The voices were bad, getting hateful, and the drugs weren't helping. They mostly just slowed me down. Muffled the voices, which made me strain to hear them. I couldn't think clearly so I couldn't solve my own problems. When your problems begin to belong to other people, that's when you know you are lost. Anyway, I met a bloke while I was in there. Not that much older than me. I don't think he was an inpatient. I met him in the grounds. I thought at first he came to sell drugs to the patients, but he wasn't like that. He said that he could make the voices go away without drugs, any drugs. I was numb with prescribed drugs. I said 'you going to use fairy dust?' and he said sort of. 'What you got to lose?' he said. We went to a park and he started to collect the dew. Really. He just gathered lots of dew from the grass. He made me hold the jars he collected it in. When he had enough he took me back to a bedsit near the hospital. I thought it was going to be a sex thing, but he poured the dew into a small white saucepan and boiled it on a two-ring gas stove. When it was boiled he put a teaspoon of tea in a pot, poured the water in and left it. 'Drink it,' he said. I just looked at him. He said 'What's the worst thing that can happen? You drink some tea without milk. What's the best thing that can happen?' I drank it. Went back to my bed in the hospital. When I woke up the voices had gone. I still felt rubbish, because of the drugs, but the voices had gone. True story.'

Anna didn't look at him. 'And what are you doing with your life now?'

'I do what the other man did for me. He told me that someone had helped him, a long time ago, and that with relief came responsibility. I have helped lots of people, maybe more than you. Drugs are not the answer, or at least not the only answer.'

'Believe it or not, I know that,' she said without thinking.

'Of course you do,' he said, getting up and putting the wrapper from the cheese and Marmite sandwich neatly into his empty cup. 'Question is, what are you going to do about that? Thank you for the sandwich. Take care, Hannah.'

# 12. After Dark

Nina Sykes was no more likely to age than she was to vote. Physical change, like the ordinary affairs of men, was beneath her. She looked as polished and contained now as she had nine years before when Black Portier had first met her. He had put on another seven pounds and wore an even more expensive suit to compensate for that fact. Regardless, he knew it was best not to flirt.

'Mr Portier. What exactly is going on?'

'Well Ms Sykes, as you know the research findings are not what we might have hoped for.'

'Not what one expects to get for what became £3.64 million, Mr Portier, certainly. My boss says to assure your people that we have kept the receipt.' Black wasn't sure what that meant and that may have shown in his face. 'Tax Mr Portier, all in all your government—'

'It's not actually my government, Ms Sykes, I am not politically aligned.'

'Nobody in government is, Mr Portier. I feel I should say that if our money is going to be wasted in this manner we can foresee the need to shift all of our research funding abroad. I understand that the other pharmaceutical companies are watching with interest.'

Black Portier took a deep breath. He knew that she was trying to intimidate him but if he didn't look in her eye it was harder for her to do that.

'Ms Sykes...' Black did the half-mouthed smile he would have been doing if he had been trying to flirt with the clearly frigid and seemingly autistic lawyer. 'My speciality is in the management of information. Let me assure you everything is completely under control.'

Nina Sykes stared at him for what felt like a long time. 'Mr Portier, are you flirting with me?'

'No.'

'Good. I am not sure it will be forgotten, Mr Portier, that you and your government—'

'It's not my gover—'

'You came to us for money, Mr Portier, and we generously—'

'You funded some research that you believed would show the world what you wanted it to see. Namely, that the mad benefited from your drugs more than anything else. I, or rather we, sought to facilitate that and in so doing also demonstrated ourselves to be open minded and enquiring, interested in other emerging treatments.'

'It's not a treatment, it's a spa.'

Black nodded and exhaled through his teeth. 'A particularly expensive spa, Ms Sykes. You need to understand that we have as much to lose as you do, if not more. If it emerged that CCT, which incidentally costs an awful lot of bloody money, was the best way to treat people and we didn't fund it there would be all sorts of difficult questions. Leave it with me Ms Sykes: you'll be laughing about this whole affair by the end of the week.'

Not, Black thought, that she had the look of a woman who ever laughed at anything.

Black Portier had come a long way from being part of the team that advertised microwave chips for almost the very first time. His strength—an ability to appear so shallow people assumed he must be a bit deep—had remained constant, although he had refined it over the years. However, what had changed was the value attached to such a talent. As a young man in the early Eighties he had the advantage of earning a decent wage and not being afraid to stay up late and spend it. The resulting attention lent him a confidence that his clumsy sixteen-year-old self would have considered psychotic. Later, when the real psychosis came, he found out something very important: that at his core, when faced with something flesh-eating and destructive, he scared very easily. This lesson had consequences. Black found that he was quick to save himself, to do anything to be OK and safe, and he knew he would do this regardless of the consequences for anyone else. If the devil had offered him a pact whereby the voices would go if he threw kittens into the river, he would have bought a van to collect kittens in. Madness may change you, but Black Portier knew that before it did that it showed you who you were.

This led quite naturally to Black finding that as he grew older—and of course he knew he was not alone in this—he found himself largely impervious to the lives of others. If you see someone else about to do harm to another person you will, Black believed, respond emotionally in one of two ways. You will either shout out to stop them or you will sit quietly and watch, relieved it is not you, believing subliminally that the universe only has so many stings to dish out and if someone else is getting them you won't. He had, since 1989, been a watcher rather than a shouter.

He kept his brief flirtation with the mental health services a secret for ten years. He felt he was very lucky to keep his job when he effectively went missing for a week without explanation. He was together enough not to phone the office from the psychiatric ward and self preserving enough to later call his boss and plead forgiveness, telling of the surprise death of his father and his midnight drive to Scotland to stop his mother from overdosing on paracetamol. The fact that both his parents were alive and well, and probably only living in Scotland because their eldest son lived in London and he annoyed them in ways parents don't like to be reminded of, simply meant that Black had to remember, should family discussions come up, that his father was dead and his mum a bit fragile. After a while he sort of came to believe it himself and once forgot to write 'dad' on a Christmas card he sent home.

By the late Nineties Black had risen to be a creative director. He was, however, in his late thirties and advertising was for the younger man, so when government got in touch with his company, anxious to use the minds of men who could sell anything from alcopops to Peter Mandelson in order to change the way the nation thought about madness, a tearful confession not only won his company a contract but it also got him a job co-ordinating between government and agency on the development of the campaign to reduce stigma. And got him laid by one of the campaigners.

It was now that his defining quality, 'so shallow he must be deep,' came into its own. Disclosure without either personal reflection or political context was a quality celebrated on countless reality television programmes and—provided it wasn't too shrill—it was an effective means of career advancement in the heady early days of New Labour. The fact that he had once brushed the shoulder of madness and had, from that single thirty-six hour experience, written a hundred stories about himself, lent Black Portier a character that was otherwise hard to see. He was obedient and untroubled by the weight of principle but that didn't mark him out from many others, and of course his history alone wasn't enough to propel him upward. He was good at what he did, persuading people to do things that they might not have otherwise considered, and that was the definition of success in 1999. The fact that he had the ability to extend that skill to controlling not just information but also the very agenda by which information was judged and valued lent him a sense of his own power that reminded one or two older civil servants, who occasionally met him, of one Benito Mussolini.

However such showiness passed over time. Black was now a 54 year old portly spin doctor or 'fixer' as he preferred to see himself, aware, indeed pleased, that in the eyes of those around him he looked like a man whose time had passed. Twenty years ago, the eyes of those around him would have been the most important eyes in his world. Nowadays he had come to realize that power, authority and effectiveness lay some way beyond the judgement of his peers. Black had, in essence, grown up.

At the turn of the millennium Black had been charged with a small spot of housekeeping. A Junior Health Minister had accidentally slept with the winner of the Eurovision Song Contest. No big deal, except for a couple of strange coincidences. The first was that the Junior Minister in question was a leading figure in a Pan-European immunization programme that, once agreed, would ensure all children in the European Union would, if they wanted to be allowed to go to school, be compelled to have a combined vaccination jab. Meanwhile it turned out that the winner of the Eurovision song contest—a flamboyant man with chubby cheeks and a very poor singing voice—was the son of the president of a drug company that made an awful lot of money from the sale of single, non-combined vaccines. A company that had thrown millions at trying to prove their jabs were more effective than the combined vaccine and had failed, and was now throwing the plump popster at a junior minister to the same sort of effect. Black had been charged with ensuring that the story and, more importantly, the accompanying video did not get out until after the agreement had been signed. He had not known of the underpinning intrigue until he was met at Paris airport by a representative of the drug company that made the combined vaccine, who told him everything in the excitable manner of the school snitch.

He made a couple of important decisions during that job. Firstly, he decided not to report the complexities of the problem to his immediate superiors, opting instead to see if he could 'sort it out.' Secondly, he decided that in order to manage a situation like this one you had to decide on what was an acceptable and desirable outcome and aim for that, rather than simply try to do the impossible, which in this case was to save the agreement, which frankly wasn't terribly important anyway, unless you were a child whose life would be at risk without the herd immunity of a widespread vaccination programme, which he wasn't.

The agreement was never signed but nobody minded. Indeed the fact that it was not signed was celebrated as a victory for independent sovereignty in the face of a pushy and demanding Europe. More importantly, the combined vaccine was sold to every single country in the union on separate contracts. The drug company making that vaccine was very pleased with this as it enabled them to negotiate independently with each country to provide the best deal possible. The other drug company was quite happy because, where they would have been wholly neglected by the compulsion to have the combined vaccine, now they could still market directly at the easily distracted parents who had heard that combined vaccines were close to satanic, of which there were many, and turn a nice little profit. Furthermore, as the never-to-be-heard-again Eurovision winner told Black over dinner some weeks later, the whole escapade had brought him and his father closer. And finally the Junior Minister, whose career continues to flourish and who still sends a private Christmas card to Black Portier, was grateful that You Tube hadn't been invented yet.

Black managed that outcome by making each party believe that he was working for them and that he was essentially a conduit for unseen powers far cleverer than himself. When his success seeped back to London it was noted. He had found himself managing several potential embarrassments since then, primarily involving the indiscretions or misjudgments of politicians, civil servants or family members of large corporations; he had developed an instinct for finding solutions to problems which, while not necessarily serving the people who were most anxious or felt most at risk, certainly protected whatever money was involved. Ostensibly, Black Portier appeared to be a middle ranking, slightly-out-of-date spin doctor, who liked fine wines and women who should know better. However, he was also the recipient of a generous bonus scheme each year that was the only acknowledgement in the world that he was both seen and appreciated. It was, in truth, the only acknowledgement he wanted.

*

Anna had gone back to her hotel room. She had sat on the bed propped up by pillows and stared at her feet. Nobody had called her Hannah in over thirty years. Yes, it probably just sounded like Hannah because she was tired and stressed and something about the boy had unnerved her. But then she had been called Anna for a very long time and couldn't remember ever hearing it sound like that before. She should have asked, she should have said 'What did you call me?' But she was so surprised she just froze. She walked away, not far, maybe ten feet and when she realized that she had to ask and turned round he had gone. She had looked around but couldn't see him; her instinctive reaction was not to start to search the immediate area systematically but instead to turn in on herself and wonder why she had not instantly reacted.

Now, sitting on the bed, for the first time since she had seen Meena's smouldering former flat she turned her attention away from her present crisis and instead to her sense of self. She had imagined, absurdly perhaps, that 'Hannah' had been buried so deep as to have become non-existent. She had separated herself from her youth with such ruthless efficiency in her twenties that she never imagined having to address that girl again. Yet she felt hollow, like a cored apple. Maybe, she reasoned, it was not the name but the boy who unbalanced her. She had worked with the so-called mad all of her adult life, she knew psychosis when she heard it and on the face of it his story about the dew was as mad as cheese, but it didn't 'feel' mad. If she thought about it logically, it ranked alongside inducing epileptic fits by electric shocks to the brain to cure psychosis because of the belief that epilepsy and schizophrenia could not inhabit the same brain. Or the magic water nonsense of homeopathy. And those things had been believed, defended, turned into reason and treatments, so why not this?

Because he didn't 'feel' mad? And because she had been taken, perhaps romantically, with the idea of a cure for madness being passed down the generations by a secret circle of kindly former patients? She didn't believe it, but she liked it. But all that was before he called her Hannah, which had made her feel something different: threatened, uncertain, seen? No it was more than that; it had made her feel uncontained, like she was spilling out into the street, into the world. She wasn't the carefully constructed Anna Newton: instead, she was the unformed impetuous Hannah. And maybe because of that she found herself thinking that it would be simple enough to test out the dew thing one day.

It occurred to her for the first time that perhaps she had been on her own for too long. Perhaps she had instinctively realized that when she sat down with the young man. Perhaps the fact that she was drifting eastwards, towards where her son and Adam Sands might be, rather than westward, meant that her unconscious was pulling her toward people, people who might be able to tell if she was making any sense in the world. Although she couldn't remember when she had started to wonder what the hell her so-called unconscious was telling her to do.

She phoned Grace, who answered straight away. 'Anna?'

'Grace, am I going a bit mad?'

'No. I almost wish you were, but no.'

'How do you know? I've just met this young man—'

Grace interrupted without apology. 'Anna have you listened to the news at all today?'

'No, why?'

'They reported earlier that the police are looking for a Dr Paul Stern in connection with allegations concerning a sexual assault on an underage girl.'

'Paul?'

'Yes, Paul. A police spokesman said evidence had come to light following a credit card trail and images found on his computer.'

'Paul hasn't looked at a woman since his wife died.'

'Anna, they aren't talking about women...'

'That's too vile.'

'Coincidence? That this comes out now? Think about it Anna.'

'I can't, I feel sick.'

Anna hung up and went to the tiny en suite bathroom. She stared at herself in the mirror. She looked tired, thick lines had gathered under her eyes. She hadn't washed her hair in four days; her skin was grey and lifeless. She looked as though she had vacuumed up all the fear, uncertainty and ugliness she had come across over the previous few days and stored it just beneath her skin. She looked her age, older even. She closed her eyes and thought of Paul Stern, thought of the sadness he carried with him always. Thought of his son. He was no more a paedophile than she was but once it was said he would be labelled, reviled, discredited forever. And so, of course would his work.

She phoned Grace back. 'I'm sorry,' she said. 'I'm not at my best. I don't believe any of that.'

'Neither do I,' said Grace. 'But now they won't have to kill him, will they? And frankly Anna, they won't have to do anything to you, either. I mean, your work is Paul's work.'

'Did you phone that hotel?'

'Yes I did, they said nobody came for you. Maybe they aren't following you? Maybe they just had your address.'

'And your address,' Anna said.

'Maybe it was a different car,' said Grace. 'What are you going to do?'

'I'd quite like to go home,' said Anna.

'I could drive over there and check it out,' said Grace.

'That might be dangerous.'

'Might it?' said Grace. 'Really?'

Anna paused. 'I don't know,' she said. 'I'm not sure I trust my own judgment. Have you heard from Tom?'

'No, nor my errant daughter, but that's a whole different thing. What is your plan?'

'Not sure,' said Anna. 'I think I'll have a bath, maybe go for a drive. Maybe go home.'

'Give it a day or so, Anna, just to be on the safe side. I'll go over to your flat and I won't go on my own. I'll take a couple of friends. Malcolm, my personal trainer, and his boyfriend, Ben. They look like a couple of heavyweight boxers, both into martial arts, and love me because I helped them design their kitchen. I'll call you tomorrow.'

Anna turned on the radio and ran a bath. She lay in it for half an hour listening to the news programmes until she heard the name Dr Paul Stern. 'Eminent psychiatrist and academic,' they said. Father of one. And then: 'His wife killed herself by overdose several years ago.' And Anna wondered if that information was given as a way of making sense of his moral and personal decay, as if they were giving context to a man's demise. Only later, and it was this that made her stand up and begin to dry herself, did it occur to her that the caveat was perhaps added to suggest something more sinister: that maybe Mrs Stern knew something so horrible she couldn't live with it.

*

Adam had expected to feel the tightening round his chest return when he looked at Laura. Instead he found himself feeling numb, except for his eyes, which burned, and the tips of his fingers, which felt electric and damp. He had gone home after Tim's body had been taken away and he had not been back to the hospital since. He phoned in the following day and said he would be off sick for a couple of days and he had found himself sitting on the floor of his flat for the whole of the next day staring at the wall, expecting to cry but not being able to. Someone had called round twice, maybe three times, but the lights were out and he was silent. They had gone away. The day after, he had gone to see Catherine in her office. She had been very busy and initially reluctant to see him. However he had an offer he knew she would not refuse: sell the flat they had bought together five years earlier, and he had been paying the mortgage on alone for the last three years, and if she took care of the sale he would take a 40% share of the profit, leaving her 60%.

'What's the catch?' she said.

'No catch, I promise,' he replied. 'You draw up a contract now that stipulates that I agree you can take 60% of what is left after the mortgage is settled and all fees are covered, on condition that you manage the sale and forward my 40% to me by cheque. I'll sign it.'

'Come back at 6pm,' she said.

When he did, she gave him the contract to sign and offered to buy him a drink.

'Simon is away,' she said sweetly.

'I have to be somewhere,' he said, avoiding eye contact. 'Take care of yourself.'

That evening he packed everything he wanted into a hire car and drove to his mother's house just outside Margate. He stored his things there and got a job working on the sunken gardens along the coast for four months while he waited for his cheque. He thought the £68,000 he got was obscene. Not as obscene as the £102,000 Catherine pocketed, but obscene nonetheless. He put £45,000 in a savings account, gave his mum £10,000 and went to India with the rest.

Before he went, while he was waiting and digging the flowerbeds less than half a mile from what would many years later become his shop, Anna appeared. He didn't ask her how she had found him and she didn't say. He assumed that Stephen, the only person in the hospital who knew Adam had come from anywhere, might have passed on where his mother lived and she worked it out from there. When he saw her sitting on a bench watching him work he simply nodded. She walked over.

She didn't look pregnant until she got closer, then her perfectly round bump announced itself and she grinned when he looked down at her stomach.

'You OK?' she had said.

'Yeah,' he muttered. 'I think this helps.' He motioned around at the flowers. And that was it. They spoke about her plans for maternity leave and childcare. How her breasts had changed shape and she wanted to eat meat for the first time in a decade. How the flowerbeds looked gorgeous. They didn't mention Tim. They didn't mention Grace. They didn't mention Libby or anyone else. She gave him her address on a piece of paper. She didn't say anything when she gave it to him. He just slipped it into his back pocket. When she left he leaned over, careful to not to brush against her body, and kissed her lightly beside her lips. That was it. He'd sent a couple of postcards, just to tell her, for no good reason, that he was a long way away. But he never heard anything back, perhaps because he had never put a return address on any of them.

Laura looked a bit like a thin Grace. The same confident eyes; she held herself with the same poise. Adam could no more see Tim in her than he could see himself in Tom, but he policed the extent to which he looked.

'Are you two a couple?' asked Adam. Tom blushed, Laura looked away. 'I'm sorry, is that an inappropriate question?'

Tom shrugged. 'Our mums often refer to us as being like brother and sister,' he said.

'We think in part because they both feel a bit guilty about not having any other kids,' said Laura.

'We never thought of each other like that,' Tom said.

'To be honest,' Laura added, 'We never thought of each other much at all.'

'We played together as kids but we went to different schools. We went on a couple of holidays together when we were what? Nine and twelve.'

'We got closer when we were like seventeen, eighteen.'

'And then later, after we had left home, we got closer still,' smiled Tom.

'So,' said Adam, pursing his lips. 'You have been like a couple for how long?'

Laura looked at Tom and blushed. 'Nearly four years?' Tom nodded.

'And neither of your parents know?' asked Adam.

'My mum has secrets,' Tom said defensively.

'And I didn't know anything about my dad until I was like ten,' said Laura. 'Certainly didn't know how he died or that he had cancer.'

'Secrets aren't a big deal,' Tom said.

'So why have them?' Adam said, although the words were automatic. It was the word cancer that was echoing around his skull.

'In our families,' said Tom sarcastically, 'It is de rigueur.'

Grimy Nige and Jim came in and nodded at Adam. Grimy Nige eyed Tom and Laura suspiciously for a moment, then followed his friend to today's area of interest: History, Politics, World Affairs.

Adam was staring at Laura. 'You mentioned cancer?'

'My father had cancer of the brain. Mum didn't know. Grandad told her when she found out she was pregnant. They were scared that mum might terminate because she might think that any child of their son would be predisposed to depression. Mum said it never occurred to her—not the terminate part, that occurred to her—but the depression part. She said that my father was not depressed, she knew that. She also said she didn't believe that you inherited depression. Anyway, Grandad came to see her a few weeks after the funeral and told her he'd had an inoperable tumour.'

Adam stared at her. 'And so he killed himself?'

'Yes.'

'But why like that? That doesn't make sense.'

'That's what mum has always said. She says that Anna saw my dad talking to a psychologist, someone she didn't like.'

'David Cassells?'

'Yeah, that sounds familiar. Not sure what that could have had to do with it but sometimes people latch on to stuff like that, don't they? When the world doesn't make sense.'

Adam nodded. 'I suppose.'

A young couple came into the shop, a little younger than Tom and Laura; they appeared self conscious when everyone looked at them but went to the fiction section anyway.

Tom took the pause in conversation to change the subject. 'Mum said she wasn't sure what happened to you.'

'I'm surprised I came up at all,' Adam said.

'I asked her. Not until I was thirteen, interestingly enough. Until then I think she had created in me a sense that asking about whoever my dad might be would break something unmendable, so I didn't. But when I was thirteen I asked, in as matter-of-fact way as I could, what happened to my dad. She said that he had moved away and that she had encouraged no contact.' Adam raised his eyebrows. 'She implied it was you. Later, when I was fifteen or so, I asked what you were like and she was hesitant. She told me that she wasn't exactly sure who my father was. That it might have been one of two men. You were one of them and you had moved abroad. She was very clear that you were not avoiding any responsibility for me. She said the other bloke was running some government campaign to do with mental health and stigma.'

Adam was struggling to hold on to all the information and he wanted to slow it down, so he went for small talk. 'What do you do Laura?'

'I'm at medical school.'

To Adam's surprise he felt a stinging behind his eyes. 'You are not going to specialize in...?'

'Good God, no,' Laura said. 'Surgery. Like Grandad.'

An older woman, in her late sixties or early seventies, wearing a cravat and brown polyester trousers came in and smiled at Adam.

'Anything?' she asked hopefully. He reached under the counter and brought out a pile of five books.

'Ohh lovely,' she said. They stood at the counter in silence as the woman looked at the books with shaking hands. 'I can't decide between this one or this one.' She held up *The Adventures of Sherlock Holmes* and *Farewell My Lovely*.

'Buy them both?' Tom said gently.

The woman looked at Adam conspiratorially. 'These young people don't understand deferred pleasure do they?'

Adam smiled. 'Or self discipline.'

'I'll take this one please.' She handed Adam the Conan Doyle. 'But I won't call foul if we find Mr Chandler in the next list, Mr Sands.' She handed over £2 and Adam gave her a penny change. After she had gone, Adam took the three books that had not interested her back to the shelves and carefully picked three others: a book of Father Brown mysteries, something by Peter James and *The Return of Sherlock Holmes*.

'This will make her laugh,' he said, forgetting that he was talking to Tom and Laura. They looked at him. 'She comes in three times a week,' he explained. 'I pick out a selection of five books—they have to be crime books, good ones, nothing gratuitous—and she chooses one.' He shrugged.

'You're like her personal shopper,' smiled Laura.

'Not much money in this, I imagine,' Tom said and immediately blushed. Laura looked at him. 'I'm sorry, that sounded rude, it really wasn't meant to. I just noticed, and I hadn't before, that second hand bookshops don't, I imagine, make much money.'

Adam smiled. 'Don't worry, it's just a front for the drug trade I operate from out back.'

'We'll have a pound and a half of your best marriage-wana,' piped up Grimy Nige.

The young couple approached the counter and Adam returned from his book search smiling. 'Can I help?'

'Just these please.' They put five books on the counter. On the top was *The Road*. 'Remarkable book,' said Adam. The couple said nothing, so neither did Adam, until he had put the books in a bag and said 'Fourteen pounds, please.' The young man paid with cash and they left.

Tom, Laura and Adam were silent for a moment.

'My mum says that you and she were good friends,' said Laura. Adam reddened slightly. 'Oh my, you didn't sleep with my mum too, did you?'

Grimy Nige and Jim both stopped staring at *A Short History of the World* and looked up.

'No I didn't,' said Adam quickly. 'I liked her too much.'

'But you didn't like my mum,' smiled Tom.

'That was different. And you two—' looking over at Grimy Nige and Jim, 'Get back to your browsing.'

'Sorry, Mr Sands,' said Jim. 'Still waiting on the marriage-wana, though.'

Adam lowered his voice and his head a little. 'I let your mum down, Laura. After what happened with your dad, I didn't go back. It wasn't just that, if you think about it, and I have—a lot—that wasn't enough on its own to make me leave but I was a mess. I couldn't so much as look back, I don't think, and Grace... well, I think I was ashamed.'

'Because of my father?'

'No, because, well, because we were sort of all in it together. The hospital, the work... and I felt like I was deserting her.'

A middle-aged man came in and headed straight for Military and Engineering. Adam looked at him long enough to offer the man the opportunity to acknowledge him; when he didn't, he turned back to Tom and Laura. 'What do you do Tom?'

'Just finished English and Music at Manchester. Doing Post Grad in Musical Composition.

'Songwriting?'

'Not sure they are songs.'

'Sorry,' said Adam. 'Showing my age.'

'No, we still have songs, people call them tracks for some reason but they are songs.' Tom was smiling. 'I write songs sometimes but I write longer pieces too, modern classical stuff really. Ever heard of Einaudi?' Adam shook his head. 'Not going to make a living out of it...'

'Hey,' said Laura. 'Yes, you are.'

'Not much of a living, so I am staying on at University as long as I can, so I can make as much music as I can before I move into selling insurance.'

Adam considered saying 'I used to write songs,' but didn't. But found himself staring at Tom, unable not to, and the boy noticed and said nothing. Adam wasn't looking for anything, he was just looking, just like Grimy Nige and Jim. And Tom was being kind. He was letting him.

Adam heard the door open but he didn't look round. Neither did Tom. Laura did, and she shook Tom's arm frantically. The young man turned away from Adam and looked at Laura. 'What is it?'

Laura motioned toward the door and smiled. 'Your mum's here.'

# 13. Where Are We Now

'Mum! Where have you been?' Tom was already across the small shop floor and hugging her as he shouted. Even Grimy Nige and Jim looked embarrassed.

'Eastbourne, mostly,' she said, holding her son with her eyes closed, not ready to let go, not ready to take in anything other than his presence.

'I've been worried sick.'

'I'm sorry,' she said quietly. 'So have I.' She opened her eyes and saw Adam. She looked at him for a moment as he stood impassively gazing back at her. 'Nice tattoo,' she said.

'Nice son,' he replied.

Anna nodded and turned to Laura. 'Laura, what are you doing here? Your mum doesn't know you're with Tom.'

'I'm twenty-three, Anna,' she said gently. 'I don't feel the need to report in on all my movements.'

Anna smiled. 'I think she was worried, a bit. Maybe.'

'What's going on, Mum?'

Anna sighed, partly because she didn't have any idea how her story was going to sound to an audience.

Anna told them, quietly, about the research into CCT and the findings that suggested quite strongly that the medicines that helped sustain a billion pound industry were, according to the evidence, quite pointless. She told them about Meena and Paul and her trip round the south coast. She finished by saying: 'I thought I might be being paranoid.'

Tom and Laura both shook their heads. 'Of course not. Why would you think that? Do you know how Meena is? Is she recovering?'

Anna shook her head. 'I don't know. And I think it's because things like this don't happen to nurses doing research. I can't believe a massive international drug company would hire people to... to try to kill someone. Or plant a story like the one they have about Paul.'

'I suppose they have a lot to lose,' said Laura.

Anna looked at her, how close she was standing to Tom, the tops of their arms touching. He must have been so worried to call her, and she found herself wondering how he would have done that, given that Laura had left her phone at her mother's house.

'I suppose so,' she said.

'Sounds like a good bit of research,' Adam said quietly. 'How did it get the funding?'

'What do you mean?'

'Well, I know I'm out of date, but why would anyone fund that sort of research?'

'Apparently one of the drug companies, Leichter and Wallace funded most if it.'

'Why would they do that?' asked Adam quietly.

Anna shrugged. 'I assumed they have a portfolio of research activities that help the profile of the company and they regard that as a better use of money than paying tax.'

'Where did the rest of the money come from?'

'I don't know. There's an organization, a government quango that takes care of all that sort of thing. Gathers together the different funders for a project, oversees it, co-ordinates progress and ensures dissemination. That way everyone gets their money's worth.'

'Unless the results of the research are not what their money requires?'

'Maybe...'

What are they called?' Adam asked. 'This co-ordinating body.'

'CROCK? No, that's not it. Centre for Research, Evidence and the Advancement of Knowledge.'

'CREAK?'

'Yeah, CREAK. They oversaw us. Paul had to report in to them. Leichter and Wallace kept a polite distance.'

'But you assume CREAK must have told the drug company the results and the drug company is out to get you?'

'Yes, I suppose so.'

'Because you assume CREAK—stupid name by the way—wouldn't do anything... bad?'

A couple came into the shop. They were in their early thirties and had been chatting loudly when they opened the door but quietened in the presence of books, even second hand ones. They seemed surprised to see so many people gathered around the counter and Adam remembered that he ran a shop.

'Shall we go and get a coffee?'

'Isn't it bad for business to open late and close after a couple of hours?' asked Tom.

'Yes it probably is, but I wasn't thinking of closing. Jim? Do you and Grimy Nige fancy keeping an eye on the shop for an hour or so?'

'What, like run it?' said Grimy Nige.

'Well, I don't want you making too many major decisions like refusing to sell any books or turning us into a cycle repair shop while I'm out, but broadly, yeah.'

'Cool, thanks Mr Sands. We won't let you down.'

Adam wrote his mobile phone number on a piece of paper and handed it to Jim. 'Any problems, call. I won't be far away.'

'Right.' Jim turned to the new arrivals in the shop and said loudly: 'Can we help you at all?'

'There's a decent little coffee shop not far from here,' Adam said. He handed an old Nokia phone to Anna. 'Here, can you make that work please?'

She took it and turned it on. 'I'd forgotten how much these weigh. You're low on battery. What do you use for stock control, an Etch-a-Sketch?' She handed it back.

Tom hooked his arm through his mother's and they walked ahead of Adam and Laura down the tiny, dated high street, waiting for directions to come from behind them.

'Do you feel safe?' asked Tom, which felt like a grown up question to Anna.

She tried to smile and squeezed his arm with hers. 'I think I do,' she said dreamily. 'But I don't feel very centred.'

'What does that mean?'

'I mean I am off balance, not feeling in control of things, and I like to be in control.'

'Really?' Tom mocked.

'I also think, if I'm honest, that I didn't fully realize how much I still worry about you. I mean I know I worry, and I will until I die, but I thought it had lessened, what with you being six-two, twenty-three and living 203 miles away. But when I got scared, I got scared for you.' Anna was crying now.

Tom couldn't remember having seen her cry before. Shout, yes, throw a plate at a wall once, and kick a door so hard she needed crutches for two weeks, but cry? 'It's alright mum,' he said quietly. 'It's going to be alright now.'

Anna was struck by how young he sounded.

'This one on the left.' Adam was directing them into an orange-fronted coffee shop that looked modern and incongruous.

'Order me an espresso,' Anna said to Tom. 'I have to make a phone call.' Anna stayed outside, pacing up and down talking into her phone. The others sat down at a table in the window watching her.

'So, are you going to tell her?' Adam asked.

'Tell her what?' Tom said.

'Tom!' said Laura.

'If you don't tell her she'll see anyway, if she hasn't already,' said Adam.

'No she won't,' said Tom.

'She will. She can. I did and I don't know you. For all you know she's on the phone to your mum now, Laura, telling her that you two are a couple and to get the hell down here now so they can...' Adam was mocking them gently.

'So they can what?' Laura smiled at him.

'I think we like having a secret,' said Tom.

'There are other secrets. Get a tattoo.'

Anna came in and sat down. The tears were forgotten, the tiredness lifting. She felt efficient. 'I just phoned Simon, Paul's son. It occurred to me that that young man has been through enough and to hear these lies about his dad... Well, I suppose there are two ways to go with something like that, and he has gone for fury. Not at Paul but at whoever is making the story up. He says he and his dad share the only computer in the house and nobody has so much as looked at it let alone seized it. He says the girl that Paul is being accused of assaulting remains unnamed because she is both underage and non-existent. Paul's best friend is a lawyer and Simon has been in touch with him. He was on it anyway. Still no word from Paul but it seems to me it must be time to start taking the fight to them.'

'Whoever they are,' said Adam.

Anna kept glancing at Tom and Laura and then away out of the window. Finally she turned to Adam. 'Hello, by the way. How are you? You look good.'

'I swim a lot. Hello. Did you know Grace was pregnant when you came down that time?' Anna nodded. 'Sorry. She made me promise not to say. She was worried about you...'

Adam blushed, something he had not done for over twenty years as far as he was aware. Anna stared at him for a moment and then looked at Tom and Laura.

'And Tim,' Adam said. 'Did you know about Tim? Having cancer?

'No, no I didn't. I would have told you that, Adam. Grace didn't tell me until later.'

'Did it help Grace?'

'You two don't do small talk, do you?' said Tom.

Later, after they had finished their coffee, Adam decided he should get back to the shop. He hesitated before getting up. 'So, are you heading back to London straight away?' He was suddenly aware that all this activity was about to be stilled and that when it was, when everyone was gone, things would have changed.

'I'd like to get home,' Anna said vaguely.

'Are you sure it's safe?' asked Tom. Anna noticed that Laura edged just a tiny bit closer to Tom when he spoke and it occurred to her that her son might be meeting his dad for the first time.

'Grace said she was going to go round with a couple of friends just to make sure. I'll phone her.' She paused. 'But we don't have to go back today. Maybe we could stay over? Where are you staying Tom?'

'I have a room in a B and B in Margate.'

'Well, maybe I could share it? Just for tonight?' Anna said. Tom was silent.

'I could cook you all something to eat if you like?' said Adam. 'I'm almost certain I could borrow some plates.' Anna was looking at Tom and Laura as Adam was speaking.

'That would be nice, thank you,' she said and without a pause: 'So how long have you two been together?'

'A while,' said Tom with a tinge of the petulance he had employed from the age of fourteen through to seventeen.

'I thought you were gay,' said Anna.

Laura burst out laughing. 'I told you,' she said.

'Why didn't you tell us?' Anna asked.

'You taught me a lot of stuff, mum, but not much about telling.'

*

Malcolm drove a Range Rover. He was built like a bodyguard but was prettier and smelt nicer. A powerful black man who walked gracefully while noticing the people around him who dressed well. Ben was white, taller, thinner, with the build of a

400 metre runner. When Grace was with them she felt a bit like Shirley Bassey, only not as loud. She had explained that she was concerned for a friend and wanted to see if her flat was safe. They were quick to offer to come with her and insisted that they knock on the door and when nobody answered Malcolm used the key Grace had to let them in.

There was no sign of anyone having been in the flat. There was a pile of post, a slightly stale smell that suggested no doors or windows have been open and no suggestion that anyone had touched anything.

'I'll have a look outside,' said Ben.

Grace went to Anna's computer. It wasn't on and there was no way of telling if anyone had touched it. 'I don't think anyone has been here,' she said.

'I'll ask the neighbours,' said Malcolm.

'Is that wise?' said Grace.

'Yes.' And he disappeared outside.

Grace sat down with the mail. Anna's was a basement flat with a large bedroom at the front and an even larger open plan living room with kitchen attached at the back. She was sitting on the sofa where the light from a set of French doors leading to a very small garden was at its brightest. Grace had helped Anna decorate when they were both pregnant. It had been rag-rolled yellow then. It was a neutralizing blue now, tattier somehow. Less cared about, since Tom had gone. The post was mostly pizza leaflets and Digital TV circulars. There were a couple of bank statements, a bill and a letter marked 'Private and Confidential' from CREAK. The postmark was Cheshire. Grace put it on the coffee table in front of her, separated from the other mail, and took out her phone.

Before she could dial Malcolm came back in. 'The woman upstairs says that the blue car didn't come back after Tom had left. She said that she and a couple of other people had been keeping an eye out.'

'Why would they do that?'

'It's what people do round here Grace, keep an eye out. She said that it went away when Tom was here and came back the next day. Waited around for an hour or so, which struck her as a bit half-hearted, and hasn't been back since. I reckon the place is safe, Grace.'

Grace nodded. 'Thank you. I owe you Malcolm.'

Malcolm smiled. 'You're welcome.' He went off to find Ben while Grace called Anna.

'I'm sitting in your living room. I think it needs decorating.'

'Has it been ransacked?' asked Anna.

'No, sorry, I mean it just needs what it needed last week before all this started and I hadn't noticed before. It's fine here, Anna. The neighbours say nobody has been around since the day after Tom was here. You have a letter though...'

'Hang on,' said Anna. 'I have someone here who wants to say hello.' Anna was still in the coffee house and for a moment Adam thought she going to hand him the phone. Instead, she held her arm out straight towards Laura. 'Just let her know where you are?' she said meekly.

Grace was also bracing herself to hear Adam's voice for the first time in at least twenty-three years and it took her a moment to adjust when she heard the words: 'Hi mum.'

'Laura? What are you doing there?'

'I came with Tom, mum. We spoke and I came down with him.'

Grace was surprised by her first feeling, which was of having been left out of something. This was quickly joined by a tiny swelling of pride that her daughter would offer to help her friend and a bit of confusion about why Tom would take Laura with him. Then she added a thin layer of anxiety about the paper that Laura had said she had to write and had prevented her from coming home which was quickly followed by something that looked a little like anger at the possibility that Laura had lied to her about the paper and instead gone to Margate. These feelings arrived like falling leaves and gathered together to form the response: 'Oh.'

There was a silence on the line and Laura said loudly: 'Oh for goodness sake. We have been sleeping together for four years. We love each other. We are a couple. The first time we did it was in—'

'Stop!' said Adam, which surprised everyone. 'Some things are meant to be secret.'

Laura handed the phone back to Anna. Adam mouthed a 'sorry' at Laura, who smiled at him.

'I had no idea until today,' said Anna into the phone.

Adam turned to Tom and said quietly: 'Too many secrets can weigh you down.'

Grace was running through the previous five years looking for clues that she had missed. All that she could come up with was the times when Laura said she couldn't come home because she had something on. She felt distracted and older than she had this morning. She didn't know why. 'There's a letter here for you from CREAK. I've left it on the table.'

'Open it,' said Anna.

'You sure?'

'Yes.'

Grace ripped open the letter and Anna put her phone on speaker.

'Blimey,' said Grace. 'OK. Dear Ms Newton, it has come to our attention that the research project titled 'CCT: a mixed methodology analysis of effectiveness of the CCT provision on psychosis in adults' has been completed. We have become aware of a delay in the release of the findings and, while it may be the case that you find that frustrating, we must remind you that you are contracted to publish all findings on projects overseen by CREAK in conjunction with our media office. We are also mindful that, while the results were of interest, our review panel feel there are some key questions in terms of research protocols that need to be explored. Given the apparent unavailability of the project team leader Dr Paul Stern, we therefore request that you attend a meeting with our Head of Research and his team on September 27th to clarify the protocols you were party to. We look forward to seeing you at Laburnum House, Room 102, at 10am.'

'Where is Laburnum House?' asked Anna.

'Cheshire,' said Grace.

'Posh.'

'What research protocols?' said Anna to nobody in particular.

'Discredit the people, discredit the method, then it won't matter what the results say,' said Laura. 'By the time your results are released there will be so many rumours about your project that nobody will care what it found out.'

'You know what you need?' said Adam, lightly touching Anna on the shoulder. She shook her head. 'You need a plan. And you will need dinner too. I have to go back to the shop. Grimy Nige and Jim haven't ever been in charge of anything bar each other before. I'm surprised we haven't heard fire engines. Come round later, say seven-thirty. We'll eat, we'll talk. OK?'

Anna didn't say anything but Tom nodded. 'I'd like that,' he said.

'Me too,' said Laura.

'Can you even cook?' said Anna.

Adam shrugged. 'I make food safe.' He smiled. 'And I guarantee it will be fresh.'

Adam wandered slowly back to his shop, aware that the others probably needed some time when he, the stranger, wasn't with them. More aware that somehow the stillness of forty-eight hours ago, a stillness he had sculpted quietly over many years, had vanished. Aware also that his past, something he had let wash off him in various seas, was not what he had thought it was. And had left an indelible stain anyway.

When he walked into the shop Jim was behind the counter but there was no sign of Grimy Nige. 'Any problems?'

'Nope,' said Jim. 'Sold four books, too.'

'Cool. Where's Grimy Nige?'

'Downstairs with the woman from yesterday,' he said matter-of-factly.

'Downstairs?'

'The basement,' confirmed Jim, in case there was any confusion about what room might be under the ground floor.

'What are they doing down there?' asked Adam. Jim shrugged.

Grimy Nige and Alison appeared within a minute or so.

'Nice basement,' she said casually.

'Thanks,' Adam said. 'Dare I even ask?'

'Sorry,' she said. 'I came in to tell you that if you wanted to do a stall at the University Freshers reception next week—all sorts of other stalls selling stuff from cakes to dream catchers to journal subscriptions—I have reserved you a slot. And I got talking about the shop and a coffee bar and the boys here said that they thought you had a basement. So we had a snoop around. I'm not sure it's a coffee shop down there, but I think it could be something.'

'I was only gone half an hour.'

'Nearer an hour, actually. You could have gone for longer. We don't mind,' said Jim. 'And we don't want paying. Do we, Grimy Nige?'

'No, of course not,' said Grimy Nige genuinely.

'OK fellers, thank you. Please take a book each of your choosing as thanks.'

'Oh we couldn't,' said Jim in a high-pitched voice.

'I insist,' said Adam.

'We don't have to decide today do we?' said Grimy Nige.

'Take a week if you want,' said Adam. Both young men looked like it was Christmas, which was ridiculous and a little contagious.

'Have you ever thought of using that space downstairs?' asked Alison. Adam shrugged. It occurred to him that he had offered to cook for four tonight and he hated cooking.

'Do you know much about cooking?' he asked.

She laughed. 'I can cook, if that's what you mean.'

'OK,' he said. 'I have had vague ideas about the basement, extending downstairs but then I started worrying about people stealing stuff or me locking up and leaving someone down there all night and coming in the next day to find they have eaten my books. Why are you asking?'

'Why are you asking about cooking?'

'Because I appear to have offered to cook for four people tonight and I don't really know what I am doing.'

'Do you have anything in?'

'I have lots of broad beans in the freezer, I have potatoes, I can pick some sprouting broccoli and maybe a courgette or two, unless they've been eaten by slugs.'

'You grow stuff.'

'I grow stuff.'

'And are you just giving them vegetables?' She was smiling.

'I thought I'd fish, if I can make time.' Both Alison and Adam looked at Grimy Nige and Jim.

'We'll hold the fort, Mr Sands.'

'You sure, fellers?'

'Oh yes, happy to,' said Jim.

'No more taking people into the basement though, please.'

'It was a one-off,' said Grimy Nige.

'She made us,' said Jim.

'Oh I did not!' Alison said loudly.

'She did, Mr Sands,' said Jim seriously. 'I wouldn't be surprised to find she was from the council, checking for damp or, or...'

'Bodies,' said Grimy Nige.

Alison turned to Adam. 'Are there bodies?'

'Feels like it,' said Adam. 'Feels like there are loads of them.'

Alison stared at him and for the first time in a long while he felt self-conscious. When you are young, he thought, and an attractive woman looks at you, you hope she likes what she sees. When you are old you assume she is looking at all the signs of decay in front of her. He thought of the blood-red sun scars around his eyes and nose, his shaven head and grey stubble, and he imagined that she could see that his knees hurt. Whereas she, well, she looked lovely. Washed blonde hair, straight down to her shoulders, and she was wearing a floral print dress that shouldn't have worked unless it was a curtain but she carried it off. And wedges, which probably didn't help with the walk. Really, he thought she had no right to look good dressed like that.

'I'll make a deal with you,' she said.

'Go on.'

'I'll help you with the cooking if you show me how to fish and listen to my absurd idea about your basement without throwing me into the sea.'

'You want to come on my boat?'

'Unless we can fish from here?'

'You're not dressed for it.'

'Fair enough.' She looked awkward.

'I didn't say no, I said you aren't dressed for it.'

'I have some jeans and pumps at my brother's house. I can be back here in twenty minutes.'

'Why not just meet me at the harbour in twenty-five?'

Grimy Nige and Jim were staring at Adam. This was not what normally happened in the bookshop. They looked a little worried. Adam shrugged, which seemed to reassure them and they both nodded in perfect time. Not that anyone saw.

When Alison had gone Adam stood perfectly still in the middle of his shop. He felt surrounded by the events of the day. Anna, Tom, Laura and Grace. Tim's cancer. He had never imagined that he was waiting for his past to visit. He had assumed his past was, if not dead, lying in a coma somewhere a long way from him. He knew that taking the boat out made sense. He had no idea how doing that with someone else was going to work.

He sighed, thanked Grimy Nige and Jim again and went upstairs. He put on swimming shorts, a t-shirt with a fleece over the top and some baggy black trousers. He strolled down to the harbour and sat beside his boat. When Alison appeared she was quieter and he could feel her self-consciousness leaking over him. And it must have seeped in somehow because he felt uncomfortable and he never felt that this close to the water. He wished he was on his own and then he noticed that actually, he was relieved he wasn't.

'We're going to fish for bass,' he said. 'Do you have a problem with worms?' As he rowed round the harbour wall he could see her face change as she faced the open sea.

She sat back slightly, lifting her face to the breeze. 'We have an arrangement,' she said. 'I leave them alone and they leave me alone.'

'Consider this a renegotiation,' he said. 'We need them for bait.' She nodded. She looked behind her; the harbour was fading away already. The boat was rocking on the gentle waves. 'Another five minutes or so and then we'll stop. And fish. And swim.'

'I didn't bring anything to swim in,' she said quickly. 'And it's too far out and it's cold.'

'Me. I meant I will swim. I've had... an unusual day. I need to stretch out in the water.' He rowed on for a few more minutes. The harbour wall was visible in the distance but Alison couldn't make anything out around it. The beach was just a strip of faded yellow. She couldn't see the cars on the road behind it.

'Do you notice the noise?' Adam asked.

'What noise?'

'Well, it's not silent, is it?'

Alison listened to the water as it tapped on the side of the boat. She stared at it as it jumped up the side of the old brown varnished wood and she lifted her head and looked outward at the enormity of the sea. Adam stopped rowing and looked at her. 'How does it make you feel?'

'Not sure,' she said quietly.

'I find it helps me,' Adam said quietly.

Alison nodded. What she felt was like an intruder. Not into Adam's world, she wasn't thinking of him. She felt like an intruder in the water, like the boat was a tiny imposition on an otherwise complete sea. She imagined the waves being mildly irritated to find something in their way.

Adam had put the anchor down and begun baiting two small fishing rods. He threw a few worms into the water. 'Have you fished before?'

'Yes, my father took my brother and me when we were little.'

'Do you remember?'

'Yes, my brother put a hook through his own lip to see how the fish felt.'

'I meant do you remember how to fish?'

'I hold the stick and pull back if something pulls.'

'Pretty much.' Adam cast the line, no more than twenty feet from the boat, and handed her the rod. Then he cast his own line, moved an old stained cushion that he had been sitting on while rowing so it would soften the wood on his back, adjusted his black cotton pork pie hat and settled back.

'Are you cold?' he asked.

'No,' she said. 'I have my thermals on.'

Adam was looking out to sea. There was a tanker miles out on the horizon but nothing else in sight. 'I wondered if it would be misty, it often is, but it's quite clear.' He sounded distracted and kept fidgeting to get comfortable.

'Do you usually do this on your own?'

'I always do this on my own,' he smiled.

'I'm sorry,' she said seriously. 'For invading your space.'

'It's OK, I invited you,' he said, still distractedly. He noticed that she was looking at him. 'Do you say that because I look unsettled? It isn't you being here that is doing that,' he said. She didn't look convinced. 'I want to go swimming,' he said.

'Really? In this?'

'Well... yes.'

'Is it safe?'

'Of course it's safe; we're not that far from the beach.'

'Well, please don't let me stop you.' She was smiling, bemused.

'OK,' he said, taking off his fleece and T shirt at once. 'You're in charge of the boat.' He took off his shoes, socks and trousers and moved on to his knees. He dug around in a small bag and removed a towel and some goggles. 'I won't be long,' he said.

'Er, what about your hat?'

Adam was standing in the boat preparing to jump in. His floral tattoo spread right across his shoulders and down the other side of his back, turning into a black and grey swirling pattern of what Alison assumed was water. She didn't like tattoos. She wondered why anyone would waste time colouring themselves in.

'Wouldn't be the first time,' he said, tossing his hat into the centre of the boat. And he jumped into the water without making a splash.

When he popped back up he shook his head like a dog. 'Bloody ridiculous without a wet suit,' he gasped. He pulled his goggles over his eyes, turned away from Alison and started to swim outward. It was cold. His face was stinging and his breathing uneven. It wasn't usually this cold until November, he thought, and then he wondered if perhaps he just felt it more now: getting older, even thinner-skinned. He turned after about fifteen strokes and noticed his breathing. It wasn't settled. Swimming was like walking for him, usually effortless and easy. He stopped for a moment and looked at the boat. He was breathing at the top of his lungs; he slowed down his breath and felt the water on his skin. He was acclimatizing. He took three breaths and turned his face back into the water and began to swim. His breathing was better. It was cold on his face but he swam faster, stretched his stroke, reaching his arms out until he felt his back and side muscles open. The sea was quite flat; occasionally a wave would lift his head, but not his body. He swam on, not looking back, rolling slightly to pull his stroke for longer, noticing how he was gliding as he did so.

It was only when he noticed that he couldn't feel his toes that he stopped and turned. He had swum a long way, longer than usual. He wondered if that was because there was someone in the boat, because he noticed that he wanted to go farther out.

He stopped and floated for a moment, looking all around him. He shivered and he noticed that as he floated he was moving further from the boat and over toward the west. He swam five or six strokes back against the current and looked up. He didn't seem to have moved; perhaps he had been pulled sideways a little. His fingers were cold. He shook his head and said 'silly sod' to himself quietly. He thought of Tim hanging from a tree and he felt his chest tighten and his shoulders... his shoulders shrink inwards. He found the edges of that feeling and realized that it had never really left him. He looked again at the boat in the distance and then out to sea. He put his face down into the water and began to swim.

# 14. Alone Apart

Anna did not date when Tom was young. She did not sleep with anyone or even flirt, which until she had become pregnant she had done without really noticing. She was mindful of being the single mum and chose not to notice the uneasiness that caused if there was ever a reason for pausing when she dropped him off at nursery. Later, in the playground she became more aware of not being one of the mothers who had had the time to attend the playgroups, the tea parties, the mini music sessions, as they gathered in small groups and she stood alone waiting for Tom to come out. Familiarity eventually overcame suspicion, however, and it was Tom's ability to make friends—not many of them but enough to warrant play dates and parental organization—and later still his ability to play football that enabled her, if not to inhabit the community of mums, at least to sit politely on the periphery.

It wasn't until Tom was seven that she became more conscious, not so much of her singleness as her isolation. She had just turned thirty-three. The last person she had slept with had been Adam, which lent him a significance she had neither anticipated nor was willing to admit. It may have been that realisation that led her to lift her head slightly, to see and let herself be seen, because a nurse called Martin, whom she met while doing a course at the local university, asked her out on a date. He was divorced, a little older than her, with two children of eight and five, both boys. He suggested they take the boys to the park, get coffee while they exhausted themselves in the playground and then go for pizza. She quite liked that date. She found herself having to suppress her distaste for Martin's older boy. He was brash and tubby and began every sentence with 'I'.

At one point she asked Tom, on their way back from the toilets, if the older boy was annoying him. 'No,' said Tom with surprise. 'I like him'. It was just her then.

At pizza Tom was over-excited and she became conscious of the fact that Martin's younger child was behaving better than her son, who had just laughed so much that Coke had come out of his nose. Martin appeared not to judge and she had slept with people for less as a younger woman, but it didn't occur to her to think about having sex with him. When it came time to part they kissed awkwardly on the cheek when the kids weren't watching. He said that they should do it again sometime and she agreed, but they didn't. She found herself relieved by that.

Anna didn't spend a night apart from Tom until he was eleven. She went to a three day conference called 'Qualitative Research and the Evidence Agenda,' in York. Tom stayed with Grace and Laura and had a fantastic time eating crisps and watching *Men in Black* on DVD. She was in bed by ten-thirty. On the second morning she met Martin, who was presenting a paper on 'The Clinical Consequences of the Failure of Nursing Philosophy'. She went to it. She liked it in an easygoing way and they had sex that night. Twice. The next morning over breakfast she said: 'It's been a while.' And 'Thanks.'

'No,' he said. 'Thank *you*.'

She never saw him again.

She didn't feel any different after having had sex and that made her feel a little sad. She told Grace about it. Her first response was a knowing: 'Tell me about it.' Grace, it seemed, had been having occasional sex with the nice-looking man from the delicatessen.

'His mother thinks he's gay,' Grace told her. 'I think he sleeps with me to prove to himself that she's wrong.'

'Is the sex any good?' Anna asked and Grace shrugged.

'I like to feel someone's flesh on mine sometimes. Reminds me that I'm human.'

When Tom was a teenager, Anna had two eighteen-month-long sexual relationships that mimicked being married, she thought, but without having to sleep over. They would meet, sometimes for a meal, sometimes to see a film and then have sex. The first relationship was with a younger man she had met at the university. The second was a married man whose wife felt sex without the potential for reproduction was undignified. She was not upset when both relationships fizzled out, although she was a little put out when the married man told her he was leaving his wife for a younger woman and he thought it best not to begin that relationship while having an affair. Not just because it 'felt wrong,' but because he wasn't sure he was up to it physically.

When Tom was eighteen he asked her why she didn't go on dates. She was surprised and a little annoyed. She assumed she had been annoyed because it was none of his business but in truth it was because she didn't like being seen, by her son, as having needs that were not met. It made her feel less than whole and, while she would always have a sense of herself as being that, she didn't like her son seeing it. She was also annoyed because it heralded some sort of separation, him articulating clearly that he expected her to have an emotional life that didn't involve him and in so doing reminding her that he would be having one himself. Indeed, was already having one.

She dated a researcher after that. A man who was ten years older than her and who didn't make jokes or take his socks off before his trousers. The sex was routine to the point where it felt less like an expression of intimacy or a pursuit of pleasure and more a physical reminder that she was in her forties and that this is what happens in bed at this age. He was good for her mind though, challenging her assumptions and analysing detail in a way that she had not experienced before. And, as a devoted saxophone player, he was good company for Tom, who by that age could play guitar and piano well and had just taken up the oboe because he loved the sound and nobody else played it.

There were a couple more conference liaisons after the saxophonist had faded from the scene, but that aside there had been nothing even resembling romance. Anna had turned alone into normal. She was OK with that but it occurred to her, as she was walking back to the B and B that Tom and Laura were staying in, that alone felt different now.

Bed and Breakfasts in the Margate area are rarely full in August, let alone September, and despite fussing slightly about having to 'air the bed' when Tom phoned from the café to ask if there were any vacancies, the landlady was happy to let the room next door to Tom and Laura's to Anna. Anna would have preferred something down the hall, or in another postcode.

'If you are going to go to CREAK, mum, I'd like to come with you.'

'That's sweet of you Tom, but people don't tend to show up at work meetings with their kids.' Which came out with less warmth than she had intended.

'This isn't just a work meeting though, is it?'

If Tom had heard her coldness he had ignored it. Anna thought for a moment. He sounded more grown up than she remembered but she couldn't tell if that was because Laura was listening to him or because she saw Laura beside him.

'I think,' she said tentatively, 'that they are normalizing everything that has happened. I am not scared that I am going to walk in there and there will be a trap door or an assassin waiting for me. I am worried that I will go and they will have had some for-hire researchers who have sifted through the project and come up with some nonsense that, along with the story about Paul, will turn everything that has happened into... well, nothing.'

'Mum, what if they tried to kill Meena? Or simply knew about it? That makes them capable of bad things.'

'Yes, but what if the fire was an accident? What if I am over-reacting?'

'Anna.' Laura had called her by her first name since she could speak but it sounded different now. 'I take your point, but you are telling the story from their point of view and that makes it look circumstantial. If you tell it from *your* point of view, that three people produced some work that could cost a drug company millions of pounds and potentially embarrass the organization that seems to exist to control information. Then before it is released one is injured in a mysterious house fire, another is discredited and the third is driven from her home and then summoned to be told why work that last week was considered breakthrough social research is now flawed and irrelevant... Well, that's a different story isn't it?'

Anna nodded. 'But it's a conspiracy story, Laura. There are dozens of them out there.'

'It is if that is what you choose to call it,' said Tom.

'Tom, there are whole books written about how drug companies hide research and whole lumps of history written about how corporations, institutions, and organizations control the flow of information. Who is going to listen to me?'

They were back at the B and B now. They had walked just under a mile along the seafront and past the clock tower to a row of houses next to a disused funfair. They stood outside as Anna spoke.

Tom shook his head. 'Christ, mum,' he said quietly. 'When did you become such a defeatist?'

Anna looked at him and almost called him something unforgivable, like naïve. Instead she bit her lip and wondered about the answer. She looked at them together, because it was they who were together, Laura and Tom, with her as an extra, in the room next door and she thought: 'Now. Just this moment I was defeated.' But she didn't say anything.

The landlady, a tiny woman who never showed her teeth and had what sounded like the remains of an East European accent, showed her to her room.

'Shall we walk up to Adam's?' Laura had asked. Anna nodded.

'Leave about seven,' said Tom and before disappearing with Laura he leaned forward and kissed his mum on the cheek. 'Do you want to come in with us and chat? We have tea and coffee making facilities,' he joked.

Anna decided, for no good reason, that he didn't mean it. 'I think I will just lie down for an hour or two, if that's OK?' she said. And she did, listening for her son's voice through the walls and wincing just a little when she heard Laura giggle.

*

Adam kicked as he swam, partly to remind himself that despite the cold his feet were still there and partly to swim against the current. He moved his arms a little quicker, too. Normally he had a long languid stroke: now it was shorter and faster and it made him breathe more heavily; at least, he thought it was the stroke. He knew that he was too strong a swimmer to be overcome by this current; he knew that if he had to he could swim to shore, let alone the boat, and although it was cold it couldn't be less than ten degrees, so he wasn't at risk. Yet he felt something in his chest, that tightening again. 'This would be a bad time to have a heart attack' he thought and then instantly he gave a name to his feeling. He was fearful. Not of drowning, not of being swept out to sea on a cold September tide, not of any specific thing: he was just feeling vulnerable. And he might have smiled to himself, breathing out into the salty water, because why else would he be coming out here every couple of days if it wasn't to feel something?

He looked up and the boat was about fifty yards away. He stopped in the water a moment. Alison was looking at him, still holding the fishing rod. He waved, he didn't know why. She waved back and he put his face down and swam toward her, pulling his arms as far back under water as possible, aware that this was his last bit of swimming for the day and wanting to get as much from it as he could. Alison was sitting at the bow where he had left her, looking at him as he swam past her to the stern where the anchor was. In one movement, with one hand on the anchor rope and the other on the side of the boat, Adam swung a leg over the side and rolled in. The breeze began to cool the droplets of water that rolled down him. He grabbed his towel and wrapped himself in it, looked up at Alison and said: 'It's turned colder.'

'Do you have another towel?'

'I have a shawl thing in that bag,' he said, pointing at a canvas bag under her seat. 'Would you mind?' Alison opened the bag. There was a black hooded towelling shawl on top; she took it out and tossed it over to him. There were also a spare pair of goggles, some strange fingerless gloves that must be for the water and a bottle of red wine. She took it out. 'Do you have a bottle opener?'

'Yeah, somewhere.' Adam was shivering.

'I brought a flask,' she said. 'Your lips are blue.'

'You brought a flask? Clever woman.'

Alison took a fat silver flask from her bag, unscrewed the top, poured tea into the top and handed it over. 'It's cow's milk, I'm afraid,' she said. 'And your lips are actually very blue.'

'Thank you,' he said. 'Could you just hold it for a moment?' Adam took the towel off his shoulders and quickly slipped the towelling shawl over his head. He took the tea, cupped his hands round it and held it close. 'I didn't expect it to be quite as cold as that,' he said. 'That was a bit silly. I should wear a wet suit.'

'You swam a long way out,' she said.

'It probably looks further than it is,' he said quietly, looking at the horizon.

Adam sipped his tea. He didn't feel as cold but was still shivering. 'Forgive me,' he said. 'But I have to get dressed. It normally doesn't matter if I do that inelegantly but...'

'It's OK,' smiled Alison, blushing slightly. 'I'll look away, and if I do catch sight of anything, I'll put it down to the cold.'

Adam laughed. 'Just concentrate on your fishing.'

'OK,' she said. 'But usually I get wine before the man gets undressed.'

Adam took off his shorts under his robe, dried himself as best he could and got dressed quickly and without any grace whatsoever. 'Are you warm enough?' he asked.

'I'm fine, although I may add a very becoming hat to my developing trawler-girl look.'

'Did you bring one?'

'Oh yes.' She took a pale pink beanie hat from her bag and put it on. 'There,' she said self-consciously. 'Glamorous enough?'

Adam put on his pork pie hat and smiled. 'You can get away with it. What else is in that magic bag?'

'Oh nothing really: some distress flares, a taser, some cheese and onion sandwiches I found that were going cheap in M and S on the way down here. Do you get scared?' The change in subject wasn't accompanied by a change in tone; rather she was matter of fact, looking at the end of her fishing line which was somewhere in the descending gloom.

'Not usually, no,' Adam said quietly. 'I did today, just a little bit.'

'Why? What was different?'

'The young man who came into my shop when you were there a few days ago? It is possible he is my son. 50/50 I believe. Not that he came here to discuss that. He hasn't really mentioned it and neither have I. He is looking for his mum.'

'Were you with his mum for a long time?'

'I wasn't with her at all. We sort of worked together, in an asylum, and not for very long either.'

'I visited one of those places once, when I was training. Fascinating.'

'I suppose so.' He shrugged.

'So what part of maybe having a twenty-something year old son you have never met are you scared of?'

Adam looked at what was left of his tea. 'Fancy a glass of wine?'

'Are there glasses?'

'No, there are plastic cups at the bottom of that bag.'

Alison rummaged around at the bottom of the bag while Adam opened the wine.

'It's not the boy, I don't think. Not, yet anyway. I think it was the past. I was involved in some... I witnessed the death of a colleague and I have always felt...' He stopped and looked at her: her nose was red and her eyes were watering. 'I'm sorry, you look cold.'

'I'm fine. Please carry on. You felt what?'

'Are you key-wording me?' he smiled.

'Yes. Yes, I am,' she said.

'Well, it doesn't matter what I felt. It seems that the man who died, who killed himself and I had no idea as to why and I didn't see any sign... apparently he was dying anyway. I found that out today.'

Alison sipped her wine. 'That's a big thing to have to process,' she said quietly and saw him wince slightly at her language. 'I don't normally drink red,' she said. 'Do you have lights on this thing?'

'It is getting dark isn't it? Do you want to head back?' Adam asked.

'Not really,' she said. 'But I don't know what the rules are about rowing boats at sea in a fading light.'

'We can head back, best be on the safe side. It gets misty round here quite quickly sometimes. What time is it?'

She looked at her watch. 'Six fifteen. We haven't caught anything.'

'Vegetable curry it is. And even I can cook that.' He began to row back toward the lights of the harbour.

'They say you can't change the past,' Alison said.

'Who does?' smiled Adam.

'They do, agony aunts, cod philosophers, various songs, but we know it changes all the time, don't we?'

She sounded soft, close to kind, and despite Adam doubting his every instinct he smiled and said: 'Was I wrong about psychologists, too?'

She laughed and shook her head. 'No, I doubt it.'

When they got back to the harbour he threw his swimming bag and the canvas bag from under the seat up on to the jetty and took her hand as she stepped from the boat. Her hand was cold, but he was self-conscious enough to let go the moment she set foot on dry land. 'What was it you wanted to talk about?' he asked.

She hesitated and looked embarrassed. 'Another time. Anyway, that was in return for cooking lessons that you no longer need.'

He looked at her: her eyes were almost as red as her nose and her hair was tangled and dry. 'I'd like to invite you to dinner,' he said. 'But I don't have enough chairs and I think it's going to be an odd dynamic.' As soon as he had spoken he thought that that was a stupid thing to say, but she helped him.

'That's nice of you, really, but I agree. Do you like Tom's mother?'

Adam thought for a moment. He had no idea. He assumed so. 'She's in trouble,' he said.

'Um, about the basement?' Alison blushed slightly. 'I am being a little forward, I suppose.'

'That's OK.'

'I was just wondering... have you ever thought of maybe letting it out?'

*

Anna may have fallen asleep. It was dark outside and a late afternoon gloom hung over her room. The adrenalin of the previous few days had faded. Mostly, she found as she opened her eyes and stared at a grotesque painting of a crying child on the wall opposite her, she felt sad. Her adult life had been an exercise in autonomy. She worked on small projects, in corners

239

of whatever world she found herself in, because there she found some meaning and something like control. It was like swimming in the streams rather than the rivers: less chance of coming across something big enough to eat you and less chance of getting swept along by the current.

In truth, she didn't really imagine the research project would be more than a small-scale investigation into what amounted to the value of kindness in a decent place. She thought the most important thing about it was that someone, somewhere, was prepared to ask those sorts of questions or, more importantly, fund them. In an age where everything had to be measurable, explainable and vaguely scientific, someone had asked about kindness and she had sort of imagined that the next step from asking about it might involve trying to do something that made it more available, both to the people who needed it and the people who offered it.

She or Paul or Meena may have joked at some point about proving that psycho-pharmacology was mostly a placebo, but it was a burlesque joke, born not of excited curiosity but an embodied surety that, no matter what, science and industry win. Deep down, she wasn't surprised their research findings were not going to touch the world in any useful way. She was only surprised by just how unsubtle and brutal the mechanisms that stopped it were. Now, mostly she was tired. For a couple of days she had felt part of something beyond her control. Pursued by people who didn't have normal rules, trying to outwit people who could destroy a man's reputation at will. Now she was a tired old woman in a B and B in Margate, trying not to hear her son having sex. The only thing she was waiting for was dinner with someone she hadn't seen for twenty-four years, followed by a long trek across the country to be told that actually she was rubbish at her job. Tired, but still capable of having a shower, washing her hair and doing something to make her eyes look less like Alice Cooper's.

By the time Tom and Laura were tentatively knocking on her door she was applying lipstick and standing a little straighter than when she had arrived.

'You look good, mum,' said Tom. 'Did you sleep?'

'I may have. Laura you look lovely.' Laura was wearing a black dress with a wild Pollock-esque print over black leggings. She was also wearing make-up. Anna had never seen her in make-up before.

They walked toward Adam's shop along the seafront. The moon was bright enough to silhouette low grey clouds and the smell of the sea was heavy.

'Tom, have you had the chance to talk to Adam much?'

'Not really.'

Anna walked on silently, unsatisfied by the answer. 'I mean have you had the chance to...?'

'I know what you mean, mum, about him. Maybe, who knows, because way back in the Eighties nobody was keeping records, but it is possible that he is my dad.' He had intended to sound lightly sarcastic but it had come out with more irritation than he had intended.

'Since when has it mattered?' Anna snapped.

'Since I met him, actually. It was OK, or at least tolerable, knowing that my father existed in the abstract and had no more chosen to not know me than he had to help me be conceived. I sort of got that. But now he is potentially not in the abstract. Fifty-fifty, mum? Those are rubbish odds.'

'Oh, I'm sorry. Should I have slept with two or three other people that week to make it a bit more of a lottery?'

'Mum, stop it, this is not about you, this is about me.'

'Yes, Tom, it is about you, but it was about me and how I could get you, and that is all I wanted.' She stopped speaking. She was breathing heavily, perhaps through anger, perhaps something else. 'I'm sorry.' She hated apologizing. It was OK if it was a small apology, if you bumped into someone or accidentally took the last Rolo, but for big things? 'Don't take a step backward,' she had told him as a child. 'It encourages people to think they can take advantage.' 'I am sorry, Tom.'

They walked on for another five minutes in silence before Tom took his arm out of his girlfriend's and looped it into his mum's.

Adam had not had three other people in his flat since he moved in. He had enough chairs, although two of them were plastic, and he brought a table up from the shop and covered it with a sheet. Beyond that, he bought a bottle of wine on the way back from the harbour and then went back and bought another, because Alison said one would not be enough. He said goodbye to her outside the shop. She was going to see her brother, she said, and get changed. She would pop by the day after tomorrow to see if he had had the chance to think about her suggestion. In the meantime she gave him her mobile phone number; she suggested he put it straight into his phone. He suggested she write it on a piece of paper, which he put in his pocket.

'So you were after me for my basement,' he said sarcastically.

She didn't say anything. It didn't warrant a reply.

Adam had grown everything he cooked except the rice, which was from a local shop, and the curry powder, which he had bought in bulk in India. Before he started cooking he had considered shaving, chose not to, put Aladdin Sane by David Bowie on his record player, the same record player he had had in London, and had a shower. As he cooked he sang harmonies to *Lady Grinning Soul*, not because of anything he was feeling but because cooking itself was not enough to engage him.

When Anna saw the flat she said: 'It's smaller than the last one.'

The living room and kitchen were part of the same long room. Not a particularly big one, but big enough for a small kitchen at one end and a table for four in the middle of a grey, carpeted one-sofa living space.

'Bloody sight cheaper too.'

'Did you own that flat? I had no idea.'

'I co-owned it. Catherine made a killing thanks to my desire to leave quickly.'

'Do you keep in touch?'

He shook his head. 'She's an MEP, apparently.'

'No!'

'Yeah. Apparently.'

'Blimey, you got off lightly there.'

Adam laughed. 'Yes, yes I did.'

'Who are you talking about?' asked Tom.

'Nobody important,' said Adam. 'Can I get you a drink?'

'We brought wine,' said Laura.

'I love your record player.' Tom was working his way through Adam's albums.

'Pick something to play,' Adam said.

But Tom's attention had strayed to the guitar in the corner. 'That's rather lovely too.'

'Is it?' said Adam who was in the kitchen.

'Don't you know?' said Tom with exaggerated surprise.

Adam smiled and shrugged. 'Do you play?'

'Does he?!' said Laura and Anna in unison.

'Help yourself,' said Adam.

Tom paused. It didn't seem polite and he worried that it might look like showing off. 'Maybe later.'

Laura and Tom busied themselves looking through Adam's LPs while Anna joined him in the kitchen. 'What's for dinner?'

'Vegetable curry.' He didn't look round from the pot he was stirring. 'I tried to catch some fish, got a bit distracted and failed. Sorry.'

'You tried to catch fish? Is that a money saving thing or...'

He turned and looked at her. She looked better than she had when she walked into the shop. Her hair was very black, clearly dyed but it looked good. She had aged well.

'It's the way I live,' he said quietly, looking her in the eye for the first time.

Anna nodded. 'I kind of went the other way I suppose.' She sighed.

'You kind of had a child to support.'

'Did you ever... you know.'

'Have a kid? Who knows?' He nodded at Tom and wrinkled his face.

'Don't you start,' she said, raising her eyebrows.

'Never married or anything. Travelled a fair bit. You?'

'Oh, just on holidays. I went to Australia once.' She smiled and shook her head. 'Nope, never married. Never imagined I would, hence...' She nodded at Tom and wrinkled her face.

'Self-fulfilling prophecy,' Adam said.

'Can I have more wine?' said Anna.

'Help yourself.'

They ate and listened to The Blue Nile. 'Sounds dated now,' Adam said. When it had finished he put on something newer by The National.

'I'm surprised you have this,' smiled Tom.

After they had finished eating, Anna put on Billie Holiday. The conversation was gentle, almost tired. Anna asked Laura about her plans, aware that what a week or so ago would have been the polite enquiry of a supportive near-aunt now felt like she was interviewing her future daughter-in-law to determine her prospects. Tom asked Adam about India, Adam talked more about Greece. Anna checked her phone a lot. Eventually, as they were finishing the second bottle of wine, Tom nodded at the guitar and asked quietly: 'Do you mind if I...?'

'Be my guest,' smiled Adam.

'Is it a good guitar?' asked Anna.

'Oh yes,' said Tom. 'Gibson ES vintage semi, beautiful.' He picked away quietly, tuning it, letting his fingers tap the fretboard, hunching down over the body, smelling the guitar. Whenever Anna saw him with a guitar she thought of him when he had first started learning, gathered around an old battered guitar he had seen in a second hand shop and had asked the music teacher to tune for him.

'He'll be lost to us for the next four hours now,' said Laura; Tom looked up at her and flashed such a grown-up smile at his girlfriend that Anna's eyes stung.

'Is that the same guitar you had...?' Anna asked Adam.

'No, I still have that, it's in the other room. I bought this one when I bought the shop. I'd always wanted one and I kind of knew that that would be the only time I'd ever be able to afford it.'

Tom had finished tuning the guitar and was playing something bluesy.

'Did you come into money?' Anna was embarrassed that she had asked. She was intrigued by the way Adam seemed to live but she was slightly unnerved by it. She couldn't figure out if it was self-contained or just poverty-stricken.

'Yes I did,' said Adam and then he turned to Tom. 'Not bad,' he said.

'He's even better on the piano,' said Anna.

'I always wanted to play piano,' said Adam. 'I've tried a few times but I can't.'

They all stopped speaking and Tom played quietly on.

'Must be hard, him being a long way away,' said Adam.

Anna coloured slightly. Where were these emotions coming from? And she comforted herself by remembering that up to a few hours ago she had been on the run from people she thought were trying to kill her and so emotions were, if not inevitable, certainly forgivable.

'She was pleased to get rid of me,' said Tom jokingly but it was too much for Anna.

'Don't you ever say that,' she snapped. This time Tom blushed. Looking at his mum, she looked teary. And just a little bit smaller.

After that, the conversation grew thinner. Finally, just after eleven-thirty, Tom put the guitar down and said: 'I suppose we should be going. I'm not sure when the B and B lady closes up for the night and we have to sleep on the beach.'

Laura and Adam stood up. 'Thank you,' she said and hugged him.

Anna remained seated. 'You go ahead, Tom. I want a word with Adam if that's OK?' She looked at Adam, who shrugged. Tom hesitated. 'It'll be OK, its not far to walk,' she said.

'I'll walk her back, Tom.' Adam said.

Tom nodded at Adam and turned to his mother. 'More secrets, mum?'

Adam led them down the narrow stairs to the shop. At the door Tom said: 'Do you mind my asking how long you've had that guitar?'

'About ten years I think,' said Adam.

'Where did you get it?'

'A little guitar shop in Doncaster, actually.' There was a pause and, to his own surprise, Adam filled it. 'I wrote some songs that were recorded by and subsequently played live a lot by a—well, over here at least—little-known band called Acme Inc.'

'I've heard of them,' said Tom.

'Yeah, well, they sold pretty well in America and Japan. I think they are based out in California now. I'm not sure, they haven't been in touch. Anyway I got paid and...' He tailed off and shrugged.

'I bet I know the songs,' said Tom enthusiastically.

'I bet you do too,' said Anna, who had followed them down the stairs and was standing behind Adam, looking at her son as though he had said something wrong. Tom returned her gaze, uncertain as to why there was friction but convinced it must be her fault.

He put out his hand and Adam took it. 'It's been nice to meet you. Thanks for the food,' he said.

'My pleasure.'

After they had gone Adam and Anna walked back upstairs. 'Tea?' asked Adam.

'Oh yes please.' Anna sat quietly on the sofa as Adam boiled the kettle.

'Peppermint or builder's?'

'Peppermint, please.'

He brought in the tea and sat in the same chair he had been in before. He picked up his guitar and just held it on his lap, stroking the body.

'Do you still write songs?' Anna asked.

Adam shrugged. 'There seems to be a bit of tension between you and your son,' he said.

Anna sighed. 'I had no idea about Laura. I think I'm cross with him.'

'I think you're furious with him.' Adam laughed. Anna picked up her tea, cupping it in both hands and stared at the carpet in silence. Finally Adam said: 'You OK?' When she looked up she was crying quietly. He thought of putting the guitar down and going the four steps to the sofa, the way a nurse might, but he didn't. He looked at her and said gently, 'What is it, pet?'

She cried a little more, she nodded acknowledgement of his question and he waited.

'Lots of things I suppose,' she said. 'Being fifty. Feeling like I am losing my son, in a way I prepared for it you know, in a good way, but it coming as a surprise nonetheless. Meena, Paul, the pointless stupid fucking job... Running round the coastline like... like a fugitive.' Adam put the guitar back on its stand. He didn't speak. 'And then...' Anna looked up, dabbed her eyes with her fingers. 'Do you have a tissue?' Adam got up and went to his bedroom, returning with a small box of tissues. 'Thanks.'

'And then?'

'It's stupid but... when I was in Eastbourne I met this young man in a café. Looked like, I don't know, like he might be struggling. I bought him a sandwich and we chatted. He sounded bright, clever, engaged.' She hesitated. Adam remained silent. 'He said the strangest thing, well, a couple of strange things really. He told me that he knew how to cure psychosis.

He said his cure had been passed on by patients and he helped people. He said he cured them by making tea using fresh morning dew.' She laughed unconvincingly. 'You see, repeating it, saying it out loud helps. It is mad.' They sat quietly for a few moments, Adam looking at Anna while Anna looked at the floor, the wall, the guitar and the floor again. 'And when I left he called me Hannah.'

Adam raised his eyebrows. 'Wasn't that...?'

'Yeah.'

'Are you sure he said Hannah?'

'Yeah.'

'Might it have been a mistake?'

'Yeah. I don't know...'

Adam sipped his tea and Anna looked at him for the first time. 'It crossed my mind that I was becoming... unwell.' Adam nodded as sympathetically as he could. They were quiet again. Adam listened to a car draw up outside and leave its engine running for longer than one might expect from someone arriving home; its lights stayed on too, just for about twenty seconds. Then the engine and lights went out.

'I don't know why I am going to tell you this,' he said, 'but it's in my head now.' He swallowed hard but before he could speak there was a knock on the door.

'Tom worried about his mum?'

Anna winced. 'Late night visitor?'

'Unlikely,' he said.

'You look worried,' she said. 'That is making me nervous.'

'It's been an unnerving few days,' he said. 'You stay here, OK?'

He went downstairs and Anna noticed that she was holding her breath. This was ridiculous. Her life, her sense of self, was being re-written over the course of a few days by... by whom? A profit-hungry corporation? Some government quango? Over a piece of bloody research? She was hiding above a small bookshop in a town that thought it was 1976. She was afraid. She stretched her shoulders, arching her back slightly and rolled her head. She took a couple of deep breaths and stared at the door. There were two sets of footsteps coming up the stairs and Adam was saying something that she couldn't make out. Anna stood in the middle of the room braced and ready, relaxing instantly when Adam opened the door and stood to one side.

'Grace?"

# 15. You Could Be Forgiven

Black Portier was feeling pleased with himself. He didn't expect any sign of appreciation, but he did believe that they would have noticed the fact that he had managed a potential crisis with his usual quiet deftness.

And so when he found a long white envelope with his name and the words 'Strictly private and confidential' handwritten across it on his desk he opened it with a little uncertainty. What he found was a plane ticket. From Heathrow to Manchester for 7.30am the day after next and a note, also handwritten, saying 'Dear Mr Portier, 10am September 27th, Room 102 CREAK offices, Cheshire. Important.' It was unsigned. There was a distinct lack of respect characterizing the people he was having to work with on this project. Nina Sykes was expecting him in half an hour, essentially because she needed reassurance, and CREAK, who he was bailing out of a crisis, expected him to fly the length of the country for a meeting with someone who can't muster the good manners to sign their name. Who does he ask for at the front desk? How stupid does he look saying: 'I'm here to see someone on the first floor, someone with a nice pen who writes in italics.'

He sighed and shook his head. He deserved better. He was the problem solver, these people were the problem watchers, the worriers; the people, in Leichter and Wallace's case at least, who stood to lose millions off of their share price if it wasn't for him. He should be picking up a cheque from her tomorrow, at least. 'I need to move fully into the private sector,' he said to himself. 'I'd be properly appreciated there.' Not that he was sure where the private sector was any more from where he was sitting.

Nina Sykes looked like a woman who never slept. That is not to say she looked tired: rather, she looked as though she didn't bother with sleep, as if it might use up time and cause her perfect and perpetual French bun to slip out of place. She was wearing the same style of suit she wore the last time they met a few days ago, albeit this one was in black rather than grey. It made her look sexier. Like she was going to a funeral. She looked at him over the top of half-moon reading glasses.

'What news, Mr Portier?'

'One of the researchers remains in a serious condition in hospital, Ms Sykes. Another, you may have heard on the news, is wanted by the police in connection with sexual offences.' Black looked mostly impassive with an incy bit of smug rolled in.

'That is sad. Does it delay the release of the results?'

'Of course, as I told you Ms Sykes, there really was nothing to worry about.'

Nina Sykes eyed him suspiciously. 'You are a strange man Mr Portier. I am never terribly sure what you are talking about and I wonder sometimes if you are. I shall inform my boss that release of the research findings is on hold and will remain so indefinitely. We will not be requesting our funding outlay back at this time, secure in the knowledge that as the major investors in this work we effectively own the knowledge it generates. Therefore you cannot release anything without clearing it with us. Now, officially of course, we are not in the habit of holding back research but let's be clear: we are a business. If the time comes when you plan to release these findings we expect six months notice, full access to the findings and underpinning data and we sign off the publications and press releases.'

Black stared at her.

'If you felt you had the legal right to do that why didn't you say so before? It might have saved me a lot of trouble.'

'It isn't my job to save you trouble Mr Portier. It is my job to protect the corporate interests of this company. You can't imagine that I would leave that in the hands of a government spin doctor?'

'So why am I here?' asked Black.

'Because I keep expecting you to give me a timetable of release, Mr Portier, and instead you give me distracted waffle dressed up as intrigue. I assume there is no timetable?'

'No,' said Black.

'And you do not know when there will be one?'

'I do not believe there will ever be one,' he said evenly.

She looked at him. 'I think under the circumstances we can live with the fact that this project has offered us little in the way of direct return. It is part of what my boss calls a tax avoidance scheme dressed up as a fishing expedition. It does, however, tell us what research to avoid in the future, though, so it's not all bad. Keep me informed of any changes, Mr Portier. Good day.'

Black left without looking at her. She hated him. He hated her, even if he quite fancied her too. Were his efforts entirely without purpose? The arson? The made-up news stories and planted evidence? Really? Or was she just saying all that stuff about contracts in order to make sure that she and her company did not have to say thank you?

Black had begun his career as a fixer by negotiating. He found that in most situations if you address the space between people then the people found themselves moving. However, that type of diplomacy only solved a certain type of problem: namely, a problem that people were willing to solve.

He found that some situations required a more dynamic approach. He crossed what other people would consider a moral line when he was involved in managing a tiny but extremely loud political dissident from a small but politically useful eastern European country entering the EU. She looked like Mia Farrow during her Frank Sinatra period: waif-like and confused. She sounded, however, like Lulu in a shouting competition. Her concerns were to do with human rights. She was articulate, attractive, charming and right. Black arranged for two kilos of cocaine to be found in her kitchen; while that didn't shut her up, it did rather dilute her effect.

He shocked himself when he did that, not because of the immoral nature of the act but the engagement that carried it. He didn't imagine he had either the intuitive imagination to come up with the idea nor the guts to carry it off. He might have been excused for developing a certain arrogance on the back of that, but in truth he didn't. Instead, he went on something of a voyage of discovery. Ever curious to see what he would be capable of in solving the next problem, his method was to simply let go of his conscious thought, in much the same way as he had when he was advertising pizza, and simply let his sense of the world and the problem he was addressing float around until it bumped into something. It didn't have to bump into something that would eliminate the problem, necessarily. But his view was that when something was stuck, if you made it unstuck it would drift toward a better circumstance than the one he found it in. Lulu didn't go away, for example: instead, she became distracted for long enough to enable everyone to stop paying attention to human rights and instead pay attention to a rather marvellous shot putter who represented the more acceptable governmental face of said country. EU admission passed. Lulu later became an MEP. The cocaine was explained away as a misunderstanding, long after it had ceased to matter. Everyone was happy. Black was of the opinion that when he intervened to solve problems in the marketplace it was usual that everyone, even people he had ostensibly done harm to, ended up in a better place. If he ever stopped to reflect on the ethics of his actions, it would be this that stood out.

Since then he had, among other things, blackmailed a large shareholder in an energy firm who was considering voting yes to something ridiculous to do with wind farms. Paid someone to run over a nun, yes he had to pay extra, no she wasn't killed, yes there were bruises and a fractured hip and she was unable to sustain her touching and very press friendly campaign against 'Free Schools' but she did get her own radio show. And he had co-ordinated an outstanding smear campaign which, by coincidence, was against a leading research scientist who now taught chemistry at a comprehensive in Burnley and was happy doing so, who claimed he had developed a cure for psychosis that had something to do with tea and would have made no money for anybody. He had liaised with a completely different drug company for that job. One that sent champagne afterwards. It's those little gestures that make all the difference.

*

Grace was sitting with peppermint tea, looking slightly flushed. It may have been the stairs. She was heavier than she had been twenty-four years ago and she was self conscious about it. 'I've swollen,' she said to Adam.

He shrugged and said: 'Haven't we all? I used to have hair you know.' She smiled. 'It's good to see you, Grace.'

'You too.'

'And you have a lovely daughter I didn't know about.' He said it gently, without rancour.

Grace shrugged. 'What to say, when to say it? I didn't know if you would want to hear from me. I thought you might come back.'

Adam nodded. 'Do you need something to eat?'

Grace paused long enough to encourage Adam to insist on heating up a little vegetable curry. 'I've been driving a while and forgot to eat,' she said.

While he was in the kitchen he listened as the women he felt as though he had introduced talked about their children.

'I'm hurt,' said Grace. 'Not that they are together but that they didn't say anything.'

'I know,' said Anna. 'And for so long.'

Adam took his time, turning the reheating of vegetables into a slightly more complex task than growing them had been. When the exchange between the women had slowed, he turned

254

out the kitchen light and came back with food, sat down and poured himself and Grace a glass of wine. Anna was reading the letter that Grace had brought with her.

'Are you going?' Grace asked.

'I think so, yes,' said Anna.

They were quiet. It may have been that there was too much to say, thought Adam, about too many things. He took a deep breath, breathing out through his mouth, closing his eyes as he did so; at the top of his lungs he could feel that thin edge of fearfulness he remembered from the asylum. He took another deep breath and said, surprising himself as he did so,: 'I was just about to tell Anna something about my last night at the hospital, and about finding Tim. I wonder, is that OK?'

Grace smiled. 'Yes,' she said. 'Of course. Look, I know this may sound insensitive, I liked Tim, he was nice, but in many ways I didn't get to know him until after he was dead. Did you know he had cancer?'

'I found out earlier today.'

Grace looked at the floor then spoke quietly: 'We slept together once. It probably had something to do with how angry I was with Norman, with myself. I don't know.' She hesitated. 'I'm sorry.'

'What for?'

'For not trying to find you. For not seeing how you were.'

The end of the living room where they were sitting was darker now without the light from the kitchen. There was no music playing, no sound from the streets. They were three old friends above a bookshop who didn't really know each other and didn't really mind.

'When I found Tim, I suspect he was already dead.'

Grace nodded. 'The coroner's report said he had been dead for quite a while.'

Adam nodded. 'Yes, but I held him for quite a while, Grace. By my reckoning, a really long time.'

'How long?'

Adam shrugged. 'I couldn't really work it out.' He swallowed deeply and felt the fear spread right across his chest, down his arms, to his fingers. Why did it always swell in the tips of his fingers? 'It might have been four or five hours...'

'That isn't possible.' Anna said. 'Not physically possible.'

Adam nodded. 'I know, but I got to the hospital before midnight, I saw Cassells and that skinny girl chatting outside.'

'They had been at a presentation,' said Anna. 'I'd been there myself but I left early. I went to the ward and I saw Cassells there talking to Tim, who seemed upset. I didn't want to talk to them so I went home. I've gone over that a million times... If I had stopped, spoken to Tim...'

Grace touched Anna's arm. 'Yes and if I had not ignored his sulking, or smiled more, or sent him flowers... These are just ifs and ands,' said Grace.

Adam paused for a moment and then continued. 'I saw them, Cassells and his friends, in the driveway and I walked the long way round to the annexe. I was going to walk down the corridor from the far side but then I saw Tim. I held him from that time until I went to get help.'

'The inquest said the call was logged at 4.52. Ambulance arrived on the scene at 5.07,' said Grace.

'Adam, you couldn't have held him from midnight until nearly five in the morning,' Anna said.

Adam looked at Anna. 'I held him for as long as I could. After a while someone came, a young man. I'd seen him before around the place, a couple of times. Once in the middle of the night on the long corridor staring out of the window. I talked to him. I saw him in the garden where I found Tim. He came to help. He said he would hold Tim while I went for help.'

'There was nothing about that in the coroner's—'

Adam put his hand up. 'I never told anyone.'

'Why not?' said Anna.

'Because when I got back he was gone. There was no trace, nothing to suggest he had ever been there. I thought that I must have... imagined him.'

The women sat in silence for a moment.

'Adam, Tim was dead long before you let him go.'

Adam nodded. 'I get that. The thing is... The young bloke, the one who I thought was helping me, who in fact *was* actually probably helping me because the chances are I would still... Anyway, he said he was waiting for the dew to form. He told me I should pay more attention to the dew.'

Anna stared at him. Grace ate slowly and looked a little confused.

'What sense have you made of that?' It was Anna's turn to be gentle now.

Adam shrugged. 'I haven't. I've left it alone, treated it like a dream. I think one of the advantages of living like this is that you don't have to give a name to things that happen.' Both Anna and Grace looked at him and waited. 'It's true, I get that we can label it, I get that I was pretty messed up, I was randomly taking drugs that might change my mental state... I was probably experiencing something a bit like Post Traumatic Stress Disorder, but we didn't use those words then, so we called it not coping. Or I was unconsciously looking for a route out of something that had become very destructive...'

'When did you start believing in an unconscious?' smiled Grace.

Adam half laughed. 'Well, the boy I spoke to on three occasions—and this is the weird part and I have never said any of this out loud before by the way—when he came to help me with Tim and he took some of the weight, I felt him.'

'What do you mean?' said Anna.

'I mean the weight did get easier, he was physically present. I smelt him, we touched shoulders as we steadied ourselves... I know I am out of touch with the world of mental health and I

257

may have forgotten everything, but that is a strange psychosis, isn't it?'

Grace nodded. 'Strange maybe but...'

'What did he look like?' asked Anna.

'Good looking, light brown wavy almost curly hair, lots of it, very blue eyes, grey canvas jacket, blue jeans.'

Anna had closed her eyes. 'I suspect this makes me officially mad,' she said. 'But mine too.'

'Yours too?' said Grace.

'Yeah,' said Anna. 'He sounds a lot like mine. Let me tell you about my day.'


Tom and Laura had vowed to have sex in every bed they ever slept in together. They were believers in shared firsts. The first night they stayed there was the first time they had had sex in Margate and the sex they had just had was the first sex they had had since their parents knew they were a couple. They had sex together outside of England for the first time in 2009. Anna believed Tom was in Spain with friends. Grace believed Laura was in France. In truth they were both in Portugal, feeling like Bonnie and Clyde and having sex. Including the first sex they had outdoors.

'Have you heard your mum come in yet?' asked Laura.

'I haven't been listening,' Tom said. 'But no, I don't think she is taking us in her stride,' he said softly.

'To be fair, Tom, she has had a lot to deal with.' Laura lay with her head on his shoulder, Tom stroked her arm and played gently with her hair. 'Does it feel different to you, them knowing?'

'Not really, but then I haven't seen my mum yet. Does it feel different to you?'

'I don't think so. I think if we had started seeing each other when we were still living at home it would have been weird, like it had something to do with them... but now? I think maybe we grew up.'

She reached her hand across and gently touched his face. 'That's no bad thing.'

He kissed the top of her head. 'So, where are we going to live?'

'Where do you want to live?'

'With you,' he said quickly.

She giggled. 'OK, where?'

'Anywhere.'

'Well, you need to be in Manchester for the next year doing your MA. The best place for me to get a house job is Cambridge, so for a year or so...'

'I don't want to wait a year.'

Laura looked at him. 'Neither do I, but—'

'I don't need to do this MA. I could get a job near Cambridge.'

'Really? Doing what?'

'Bar work.'

'Yeah, that'll make you happy.'

'Don't you want me to come to Cambridge?' He sounded petulant.

'Hey, where is this coming from?' She sat up and took his face in both hands. 'What's the matter?'

'I don't know,' he said. 'I suppose... if we are noticing that we're grown ups I'd quite like to live like grown ups. Together. Looking at Adam, mum, your mum, they're all on their own, they've always been on their own. I think that's sad. I get that that's what they chose, but I don't want that.'

'You haven't got that and neither have I,' Laura had tears in her eyes. 'I love you.'

'You say that...' he laughed.

'I do love you.' Staying under the duvet she moved her leg across his body and sat astride him.

'So marry me then,' he said. 'Please.'

She moved her head to one side and smiled, asking without speaking if he was serious. He smiled and nodded. 'OK,' she said. She kissed him softly on the lips. 'And let's not keep it a secret.'

'He's aged pretty well,' said Grace.

'A lot better than might have been anticipated,' smiled Anna.

It was 1am and the two women were walking slowly back along the coast road to the Bed and Breakfast. It was a cool evening but not cold. A bright moon shone on the cloud cover and the sound of the sea lent them a peacefulness they wouldn't have constructed alone.

'Were you tempted to stay?' Grace asked.

'He didn't ask.'

'He would have if I hadn't shown up. Sorry.'

'Oh don't be silly.' It had crossed Anna's mind. Not the idea of sex, not at first anyway, but the idea of staying at Adam's. Of not having to sleep in a room next door to Tom and Laura. But then she wondered about sex, she wondered what it would be like to make love to someone she made love to a quarter of a century ago. If she would remember, or if they would simply make each other feel like shadows. But she didn't think about it in a wanting way; she may have forgotten how to want. She just thought about it and then it passed.

'So what are you going to do?'

'About Adam? Nothing.'

'No, about this meeting.'

'I'm going to go to it,' she said, surprising herself. 'I think I have to and I think I need to.'

'Would you like me to come?'

'No, but thank you. I will drive up, go to my place in the morning, head on up north tomorrow evening, book into a hotel...'

'I don't mind coming,' said Grace.

'It's OK, I need to do it on my own.'

'Don't you always,' said Grace.

The next morning, Anna went down to breakfast and explained to the landlady that a good friend had travelled down the previous night and had stayed with her. 'I will pay extra.'

'Ten pounds for breakfast,' said the landlady with a glint in her eye. 'I do not charge extra for your friend. I in the sisterhood.' And she winked.

Grace went and knocked tentatively on Tom and Laura's door.

'Just a minute,' shouted Tom.

All Anna heard when he finally opened the door was Laura shouting: 'Mum!'

Anna had finished her breakfast and was on her third cup of tea when they all came bounding down. Grace hardly noticed the landlady winking at her. 'Tell her,' Grace said. 'Tell her,' she said loudly.

'Mum.' Tom was blushing. 'Laura and I are getting married.'

Anna knew that she was allowed two or maybe three seconds of not speaking in order to eliminate all the things that are unsayable from her mind. These included 'Why?' 'Is she pregnant?' and 'Isn't that a bit sudden?' To her own amazement, she bought herself a few more seconds by starting to cry.

'That's what I did,' said Grace, who began to cry again. But Tom was staring at his mother, waiting, expecting something other than joy, expecting complaint. He didn't know where the expectation came from, he had never articulated it before, although he had a sense that he had invited it the day before by being short and irritable with her and feeling guilty about it.

Anna shook her head and stood up. She put her arms gently around her son and whispered: 'You all growed up now?'

'Wasn't that my part of the bargain?'

Anna let go and hugged Laura. 'He is very lucky,' she said, and she meant it and she was happy. But she also felt something else, and she couldn't find a name for it yet.

Adam opened the shop a little before 9.20. Not because he was expecting customers but because he could.

At 9.30 Alison came in smiling. 'How did the cooking go?'

'Needed fish but OK, thanks.'

'I enjoyed yesterday, thank you. I've never been on a boat before, not a little one like that.' She seemed relaxed, eyes wide, shoulders less taut.

'Have you come to talk basements?' he said evenly.

She raised her eyebrows. 'Sort of. Mostly I came to say thank you, though.' More formal, pulling herself gently back.

'Would you like a cup of peppermint tea? And you can tell me your plan.'

'Thank you, yes.'

Adam made tea and Alison browsed through books. 'I don't really read much fiction,' she said. 'Except on holiday that is.'

'It can slip out of life too easily, I think,' said Adam neutrally.

'I think the move here, getting settled, my brother... other things that have been going on make ordinary pleasures more disposable. Do you know what I mean?'

Adam didn't. It didn't feel like an invitation to ask questions. In truth he had nothing to say and didn't have the energy to construct something, so he nodded, waited a few moments and said: 'So, talk to me about my basement.'

Grimy Nige and Jim came in. Jim nodded. Grimy Nige simply said: 'We came in early in case you were planning on going out anywhere today.'

'No, no plans.'

Grimy Nige looked disappointed. 'Well if you change your mind...'

'Yeah, thanks fellers.'

'I was wondering if you would consider renting out your basement to me. Well, to my brother and me.' Alison was looking him directly in the eye.

'What do you want to do down there?'

'Sell records.'

'Records as in LPs?'

'Yes.'

'Is there a demand for records?' Adam asked.

'Yes. The nearest record shop is Canterbury. My brother, my brother has a mental health problem. I told you that. It is psychotic in nature. It is usually reasonably well controlled although sometimes he gets unwell. He is living almost indepen- dently and the only thing he has ever really loved is music. He plays guitar, very well, but mostly he loves records. He collects them and reads about them and remembers them.'

'I used to know someone a bit like that.' Adam said. 'He loved pots. Loved them so much he couldn't sell them.'

'My brother isn't like that. When he got ill at first he held on to himself, but as he got older and began to spend more and more time in and out hospitals he lost part of himself, his softness I think. He had to. If he'd stayed vulnerable they'd have eaten him alive on those wards. But music... He loves it and he loves sharing it. He's become a sort of record detective, online. People ask him if such and such a record is available and he loves finding it. If he had a shop, somewhere to do that from, where people came, it would be great for him.'

Adam looked at her. It had been hard for her to say all of that, she had folded her arms across her chest when she had finished speaking and her shoulders had hunched again.

'Why me and why here?' he asked.

'I like it here, this place is nice. It feels nice.'

'If it has anything to do with the fact that I used to be a nurse...'

'No. I promise. If anything, that's almost a reason not to ask. The last thing he needs is another nurse. Hell, he has me hassling him enough. He hates psychiatry, all of it.'

'How old is he?'

'Twenty-seven.'

'What does he think about this idea?'

'He thinks it is the most perfect thing he could ever imagine.'

'A perfect thing?' Adam smiled for the first time. 'OK, I'll think about it. There are logistical issues. We'd have to change the layout of the shop to allow access, we'd need to clear out downstairs and rig it up with better lighting... There will be building regs to consider. Would he sell coffee?'

Alison looked at him quizzically. 'I have no idea. I don't think so, why?'

'I just think selling coffee in here would help.' Adam looked over at Grimy Nige and Jim who were engrossed in Autobiography and Biography.

'What do you think, fellers?'

'Sounds like a great idea, Mr Sands,' said Grimy Nige.

'More things to look at. And we have a record player,' said Jim.

'Only got four records, though,' said Grimy Nige. 'And we don't like any of them.'

'I'll think about it. In the meantime, if it doesn't get his hopes up, why don't you bring him in later and we can look at the basement together and at least say hello?'

Alison tried to control her smile. 'End of the day OK? Towards four-thirty or five?'

'That's fine.'

'Thank you, Adam,' she said, looking at him evenly. 'I mean just for thinking about it, thank you.'

Later, after the veritable rush that was selling eleven books to four different people and an internet order for academic books from a student at Alison's university that came in at over £60, Anna, Grace, Tom and Laura came in. Anna was carrying two cups of coffee.

'I took a wild guess,' she said.

'You'll have got it wrong,' he smiled. 'But thank you for the thought.'

'Large soya latte?'

Adam looked surprised. 'How did you guess that?'

'You're not as unpredictable as you think,' she smiled 'And I noticed there was only soya milk in your fridge last night.'

They stood in an uncomfortable silence for a few moments. Grace was looking around the shop and smiling. 'I imagined you would run a record shop,' she said.

'Funny you should say that...'

Silence again.

'I suspect you've come to say goodbye,' Adam said, looking at Anna and then at Tom.

Anna pursed her lips. 'Sort of.'

'We've come to tell you that we're getting married,' said Tom.

Adam smiled and hugged Laura. 'Congratulations. When did he propose?'

'This morning.' Laura was blushing. Another uncomfortable silence. 'Will you come to the wedding?'

'I'd love to. Will you be doing the music yourself?' he tried to joke.

'You should get Mr Sands to play guitar for your wedding,' said Grimy Nige. 'He's the best guitarist you'll ever hear.'

Tom smiled. 'I'm not bad myself,' he said.

'Yeah,' said Jim. 'But you'd be nowhere near as good as him.'

'My agents,' said Adam. Tom was looking at him intently, desperate to ask something but not quite sure what. 'Anyway, are you heading home?'

'Yes,' said Anna and Grace.

'We thought we might stick around for a few days,' said Laura. 'Have a wander round the coastline. Maybe take you out for a drink?'

Anna looked surprised, Adam noticed and asked her: 'And what are you going to do when you get home?'

'I have a meeting to go to, remember? I'm heading north.'

Adam sipped his coffee. Too hot. He blew into the hole in the plastic cup and looked at Anna. He could probably count the amount of times he had been in the company of this woman on the fingers of both hands and still be able to pick up a book. It was always fleeting, never planned and they had managed to design a relationship based on never having to waste time getting to know each other. He blew on the coffee again, looked at Grimy Nige and Jim and nodded. 'I'd like to come with you. Not been north for a while.' He stared at her as evenly as he could and noticed, as she held his gaze, that she swallowed hard, nodded once and said: 'Yeah, OK.'

# 16. The Turns We Took

David Cassells had done well for himself, although he was haunted by the perpetual sense that he could and indeed still might do better. He had tired of the face-to-face clinical work very early in his career. Frankly, most of the mad bored him rigid and he came to realize that the post-industrial dualism of psychiatry and psychology did not exist to seek out anything interesting or different. Its narrative, indeed its very purpose, was to explain how each personal presentation of insanity was essentially the same as the last one; that all phenomena could be explained, diagnosed and treated according to the existing model, language and tablets. Modern psychiatry was a celebration of its own brilliance and its often earnest, occasionally convoluted, whimsically interpretative and increasingly expensive discussions always resulted in a diagnosis and some medicine from a scientifically limited if economically expansive drug pool.

Of course, he had come across one or two interesting patients, mostly through his trainees because he himself had limited his own caseload to a bare minimum at the earliest opportunity. There had been the old dear without a body: she was interesting in the sense that she appeared to have so definitely chosen a delusion that would offer her solace. But you couldn't talk to her, or at least not so she would ever talk back. And on the same ward a woman who thought she was a man, same thing really, a delusion that actually relieved her of her own sense of unhappiness, which must, to Cassells way of thinking, have been sexual but was unbreachable. This was what he had found frustrating. Interesting cases were rarely susceptible to the skills of psychology. He tended to get the over-articulate worried well banging on about the 'fundamental disappointment of it all' and they reminded him of his mother.

Later in his career he met the three hundred and fiftieth person to tell him they were psychic, only to find that she was. She predicted a plane crash, the weather, several football results and the fact that Cassells was not to be trusted. He envisaged a government-sponsored laboratory where he and a team he personally selected would work with Edna Bristle to discover how they might harness her power for good, or better still, profit. As a child he had been a fan of the X-Men comics and Edna was the bridge between his professional world and his youthful fantasies, or at least she was before they crammed her full of haloperidol to the extent that she could barely predict which of her legs was going to move in front of the other first when she set off on the long walk to the toilet.

He had done a bit of television work. Most psychologists had, and he had found he rather liked it. However, he knew he would only ever get the call if they were looking for gravitas and they rarely were, and when they did there were plenty of other lively middle-aged men wrapped in earnestness and Boden to provide it. He was a plump man confused by clothes. He had grown a straggly beard, hoping it would make him look interesting but it simply made people think he liked folk music. No, most television work required pretty female psychologists with long hair and strong jaws to look profound and answer questions like 'But why do people behave like this?' with: 'It often goes back to their childhood, Lorraine. Although sometimes it doesn't.'

He had published widely and written about how 'taking the mickey out of mad people is actually a good way of integrating them back into mainstream society' and 'the mad are the last brutalized and stigmatized social group on Channel 4 comedy programmes' for The Daily Mail and The Guardian respectively, and managed to survive the potential embarrassment of those two articles coming out in the same week.

In short he had cast his net wide, motored by a restlessness and a genuine and deeply-held sense that he should have his own institute by now, and never quite caught what he wanted.

Despite his quiet sense of disappointment, he was not an unsuccessful man. A visiting professor at a former polytechnic in the Midlands, the author or co-author of seven books, four of which marked him out as a leading figure in the unfashionable but crucial field of therapeutic alliance. It was all very nice, he would argue recurrently over anything up to 650 pages, for people to draw warmth and comfort from the pact between therapist and patient, 'but the true alliance exists away from the point of contact: it rests instead between the medical practitioner and the psychological expert.' He was covered in eggs and flour at a large mental health conference for having written the line: 'Patients are not the experts. If you crash your car you seek the expertise of a mechanic, not someone else who is good at crashing cars.' He claimed he had been quoted out of context and later that he may have been drunk or suffering from a mental health problem himself, which confused people enough to leave him alone.

Cassells had been married four times and divorced three. His second wife had died in a diving accident in the Seychelles. He wrote a paper about the Psychology of Love and Loss that was published eight months later. He read an extract from it at the reception of his third wedding. Each of his wives had been a trainee of his; three of them had divorced him and married people they were sleeping with while still married to him. Cassells, being a trained psychologist, could easily detect a pattern. He was attracted to, indeed sought to rescue, unhappy women who could never be satisfied psychologically or sexually, although they all seemed quite happy now.

He was also still a consultant clinical psychologist but he had another consultant clinical psychologist who did most of his clinical work for him. And of course he was head of CREAK. 'What exactly is that, dear?' his mother had asked him.

'Think of it as an MBE waiting room,' he had replied.

'While you are in there waiting, might you miss the knighthood?' she had said, tapping the side of his face and leaving a faint smell of lavender.

As for CREAK, at its inception it promised much. Set up in the late 1990s, it was nearly as ambitious as he was. An independent, government-backed research hub designed to forge partnerships with private industry and fund, support and disseminate cutting-edge research across the health and social care world. It gave government the formal means—and Cassells thought this constituted political genius—to determine the research agenda, to choose what questions needed to be asked and who got to ask them. To decide what to release loudly and what to ignore. And actually to take credit for what emerged. Cassells was not in charge when it started. He was brought on board by his old Professor, a very clever eccentric who always wore shorts and drank his own urine. The Professor believed that psychology, thanks to the remarkable work of neuro-psychologists, was on the cusp of being heralded as the truth finder of the modern age. He had no doubts about his science, nor of the expertise around him, but he was an academic, not a strategist, and he felt that while Cassells was intellectually mediocre his relentless hunger would serve CREAK in terms of profile and politics. He was half right. Cassells brought strategy and hunger and—thanks to a series of well positioned press releases, in-depth interviews in the Sunday magazines and a well timed piece of research into the relationship between poor nutrition and misery—sold the nation the illusion that CREAK was the personification of New Labour progressiveness and the idea that Cassells was in charge. His Professor slipped from leader to non-executive president to retired academic inside nine months and Cassells prepared to rule the world.

By 2004 he had come to believe that the small successes that he and CREAK had accumulated were as good as it was going to get. Evidence that supported the licensing of 64 new drugs, a wonderful piece of Breakfast TV-friendly research suggesting that liquorice tea increases the success rate of smoking cessation by 76% and, timed for the new year, the discovery that the older you were when you stopped believing in Father Christmas the more likely you were to believe that Princess Diana was still alive and working in a care home in Bury.

Government funding had been drastically reduced. Where initially CREAK could wait for research funding agencies to come to them for money and blessing, now CREAK went to them for money and maybe a name check. Cassells inevitably found this demeaning. It wasn't so much that he was overseeing the fading of what was almost a flagship of progressive partnership—and that was going to look bad on anyone's CV—it was more the fact that people had stopped asking him questions. Cassells believed the world was divided into two sorts of people: those who ask questions and those who answer them. He answered them, even if he had to make up the answer off the top of his head.

And so he had changed CREAK, subtly, from being a hub of research enquiry to a filter for research findings. It wasn't knowledge that needed wrangling, it was information that needed controlling. Everyone knew that, it was the cornerstone of modern politics and it would become, thanks to him, the fount of social scientific knowledge.

When he made this proposal to central office, they behaved almost as if they liked him. He led with the savings he could make. A much reduced research budget, a slashed staff budget, cheaper—albeit significantly nicer—offices in the North of England and the unspoken promise that his version of science would not simply align itself to the political needs of government but also to the economic needs of private industry.

'Haven't we always done that anyway?' asked a veteran and impossible-to-impress Civil Servant.

'Not this efficiently,' Cassells answered without looking at him. And in using the 'efficiency' word he was given their blessing.

It had been something of a rebirth. The new CREAK lacked the breadth and grandeur of the original. It didn't get to choose what truths to construct, it no longer had the power to play kingmaker or oversee the nation's research agenda, which Cassells felt offered him the chance to straddle scientific enquiry the way he once saw his third wife straddle one of his PhD students. But Cassells knew that you had to sway with the wind. These were more austere times but they would pass and, when they did, the service he now provided would serve as illustration of his potential for greater things.

In the meantime, Cassells actually enjoyed his work more now than he ever had. The consequences of his power may have been less impressive but the mechanics of it were in fact so much more exciting. CREAK didn't bring much of substance to the table any more and, off the record, the large funding organizations considered it little more than a press office. However it was still attached to government, still had the power to generate attention, to ensure licensing for endlessly profitable drugs and to sustain a share price with a well chosen pat on the back. CREAK offered something and Cassells was very skilled in ensuring it got something back. It oversaw research contracts for example, when and how findings would be released and most importantly it vetted research teams, helped select research staff and retained the power of recommendation for future projects.

It is said that all people gravitate to a place in the world where their particular strengths can sustain them. Cassells was living proof of that. He was a gloriously unconscionable manipulator, well practiced, highly skilled. He was also a fantastic record keeper. He had the CV and accompanying psychological profile—with any useful stories or frailties that may or may not be real, attached—of everyone he had ever worked with, known someone who had worked with or even heard of. He longed for control, not simply because of his naked ambition but because it excited him. He also hoped that ultimately, if he could get enough of it, it might shut his mother up.

The pleasure he derived from making people make choices that they would otherwise have not considered was visceral. It was also intellectually affirming. He was in essence applying the science of psychology in an undiluted and specific way to the world around him. He didn't always plan the outcome, psychology was an inexact science after all, but he certainly built the ballpark the outcome would land in. He didn't plan his predecessor's retirement but he certainly designed a CREAK where retirement sat beside sudden death, petulant resignation or wholesale personal reinvention as the only options available. Under the circumstances, and given his vague sense of loyalty to all the old man had taught him years before, he was pleased retirement was the result. Even if Cassells was not invited to the Professor's leaving dinner.

Cassells, of course, did not have anything to do with the fire at Meena Ahmeds flat, nor did he slur Paul Stern. To be close enough to organize that level of detail, or sordid enough to design it, would be demeaning: indeed, it would make him little more than a mechanic. But he knew what and who were involved in the project from the start and he felt eternally in control.

*

It was like someone in heaven had gathered together their birthdays with Christmas and come up with the perfect present. Grimy Nige and Jim had a list of rules that Adam had written in capital letters and pinned to the counter.

1. Do not give things away for free.

2. Sell books when people want to buy them, even if they are books you like.

3. Show Alison and her brother the basement and explain I will be back late tomorrow. 4. Phone me whenever you are unsure about something.

'We promise we won't let you down Mr Sands.' Grimy Nige was almost tearful with earnestness.

'I know you won't, fellers. I trust you.'

'And if it goes well, Mr Sands?'

'Who knows, Jim?'

'Who is Alison?' Anna asked when they were on the road.

'A woman who wants to rent my basement.'

'Kinky sex?'

'Don't know, haven't slept with her.'

'I meant the basement.'

'It's a bit dusty down there, but thanks for the offer.'

Anna laughed, turning her laugh into an exaggerated sigh. 'Oh, those were the days. I think. I'm not sure, I can't remember. You?'

Adam paused. 'I can barely remember to buy tea bags.'

They drove on in silence, joining the old dual carriageway that passed through Herne Bay and Whistable, finally turning into the motorway.

'So,' said Adam finally. 'How has your life been?'

'Been good thanks. Yours?'

'Not bad. Thanks.' There was a pause before Adam added: 'Mostly I just sell books.'

Anna smiled. 'Yeah, I stayed with the nursing thing, then became a researcher, better hours.' She paused and, with a change of tone, said more quietly. 'Was I wrong?'

Adam didn't turn to look at her. 'About what?'

'About Tom.'

'He seems a great kid to me.'

'I meant about the father thing. When I look back on my life, and I have done it more lately, with Tom not being around, all I think of are the things that I might have got wrong. The small misjudgements or mischosen words and the larger choices that... that were perhaps selfish or wrong or downright mad.'

'Maybe when we look back we can only see the decision, we can't feel the context. It occurred to me more than once that in some odd way you might have done me a favour.'

'Really? By tricking you into maybe being the father of my child and never speaking to you again?'

Adam laughed. 'Well, if you put it like that... No, my sense was, and I am aware that we rewrite our pasts all the time and I may have done that, so be gentle with me here, but my sense was that I was really—'

'Fucked up?' interjected Anna.

'Yeah, is that the technical term now? I'm a bit out of touch. Yes, fucked up. And ridiculous as it sounds now but I had lost my sense of purpose. I honestly remember believing, don't laugh, that I could do some good. After Graham's suicide I lost any sense of that, and any sense that I was even capable of doing good if I had the opportunity. I suspect I didn't have either the nerve or the clarity of thought to simply leave, so I set about sabotaging...'

'Have you had therapy?'

'Of course not.'

'You sound like you have.'

'I swim a lot.'

'OK. Sorry.'

'Where was I?'

'Sabotaging,' she said helpfully.

'Yeah well, floating around the hospital corridors at night visiting psychotic old people.'

'Well, just the one psychotic old person, to be fair,' offered Anna. 'She did OK, you know.'

'Who?'

'Libby. In the house she moved to. I think she was happy. Lived until she was ninety-nine. The house had a cat which would sit on Libby's lap.'

'She didn't have a lap.'

'Indeed. She would say that. If anyone ever said "Libby, that cat loves sitting on your lap", she'd grin and say "I don't have a lap" and stroke the cat. And apparently she used to get up in the mornings and stand at the window and watch the kids going past the house on their way to school. No idea why. She seemed happy.'

'Do you know why she was admitted?' Adam asked.

'No, someone said melancholia. 1920s-speak for being sad sometimes.'

'She got pregnant. Out of wedlock. Kid got taken away when it was born; she probably never saw it. She got committed.'

'How do you know?' Anna asked.

'I read through her old notes once.'

They were passing the only service station on the M2. It hadn't occurred to either of them to stop. They would, they reasoned, have time for a coffee at Anna's place.

'How do you know?' Adam asked.

'What?'

'What happened to her after she moved to the house.'

'I kept an eye on her.'

'Good,' he said quietly. 'Anyway,' he said, louder again, seemingly needing to finish. 'The irony was that, when I left, the nearest thing to meaning I could see was the vague possibility that I'd, sort of, well, helped you out.'

'Is that how it felt at the time?' Anna said awkwardly.

Adam smiled. 'I can no more remember how it felt at the time than you can, Anna.' It was the first time he had said her name. She nodded. 'OK,' he said. 'That's a bit crass. I mean that if I had made you pregnant I was at least leaving something tangible behind, some mark of a positive presence. And if I hadn't, well, that just sort of emphasized the whole ridiculousness that I felt about trying to do good somehow, a symbol of the fact that one's actions are at best irrelevant and at worst destructive.'

Anna stared ahead at the curling grey road and the pale green backdrop of Kent. She had never once imagined that her pursuit of Tom was about her doing anything with anyone else. She had come to acknowledge that she had done something to a couple of people but not imagined they had done anything with that experience beyond resent her.

'That's a bit nihilistic,' she said.

Adam smiled. 'Well I didn't skip down the road to the airport singing hi-bloody-ho. I felt pretty nihilistic.'

'And what do you feel now?'

Nobody had asked Adam that in a long while. His instinct was to shrug, as ever, and say 'Dunno.' But that would have felt petulant, impolite. 'I'm not sure I feel very much at all. I think that I imagine I don't have the right. I don't know why I think that.'

'You mean about Tom?'

'I suppose so.'

'Because of me?' Anna asked, leaning forward very slightly towards the steering wheel. Adam looked at her for the first time. She had a good profile and nice skin; she was biting her lip and he could see the crow's feet dancing beside her left eye.

'No. Because of Tom.'

Anna's flat smelt musty. She put her bag down in the middle of the living room as a gesture of reclamation and set about walking briskly around the small flat, looking behind curtains and in cupboards. Finally she arrived at the fridge, opened it, said 'Empty' very quietly and turned to look at Adam, who seemed large and out of place. 'Are you checking for really small spies?' he asked.

Anna took a bath. Adam went out and bought coffees and a cream cheese bagel each. 'I could buy a house in Margate for the price of these bagels,' he said. And they sat together not talking, perhaps remembering that the only other time they had ever been alone together they went to bed.

'Do you have a plan for this meeting?' Adam asked.

Anna thought for a moment. 'I have an attitude. I'm expecting that to turn into something that might look like a plan.' Adding: 'Do you have much sex?'

'Not as much as I used to have. You?'

'Hardly ever. I never anticipated a life without sex.'

'It is odd. It sort of occupies a different place now, doesn't it?'

'Hardly occupies any space at all,' she mumbled.

Later, Adam asked if she had ever heard from 'the advertising guy.'

'No. I heard about him a couple of times. He went into PR, worked on some anti-stigma stuff.'

'Around madness?'

'Yeah.'

'Well, you must have left an impression.'

'No, I think he got a bit paranoid after smoking too much dope and turned that into a career opportunity.'

'Does Tom…?'

'Well, Tom knows that either you or Black are his father. In these days of sperm donors and surrogacy it is a little easier for him to accept than it might have been at the time.'

'Has he never wanted to meet us?'

'He's never spoken about it but it's clear he has inherited his mother's bloody annoying capacity for big secrets, so maybe he has. He was pretty quick to come and see you when something resembling a reason arose.'

Adam thought she sounded cross. 'You sound cross.'

'Do I?' she sighed. 'I am cross. I have no justification for that, so please don't reason with me.'

'Take the lead.'

'What?'

'Take the lead.' Adam was staring at her impassively, inviting her to tell him to mind his own business.

'I don't even know what that means.'

'It means that maybe he wants to know more, maybe you modelled a way of being with him that involved not telling, not even knowing stuff that might be important. So maybe you have to take the lead on showing him or offering him another way.'

Anna thought for a moment. 'You mean ask him if he wants to know who his dad is?' Adam shook his head. 'No, I mean ask him what he needs, what would help, what he wants. Let him identify the questions, Anna. Stop drip feeding the boy.'

Anna felt a thin wave of resentment quelled by him saying her name. It was so rare that anyone ever said her name, she thought. 'Maybe you would just like to know if he is your son, Adam?' Adam shrugged. 'Are you telling me you don't want to know?'

'I've seen the way he plays guitar,' Adam said very quietly. 'Anything beyond that feels... It makes me feel something I can't give a name to.'

'Because anything beyond that can only tell you he isn't your son, and because he likes music you think he is?' Anna sounded more impatient than she had meant to. Adam gave her a look of gentle disdain. 'Sorry,' she said immediately. 'I'm being defensive.' She paused. 'He is a good guitarist, isn't he?'


The drive to Manchester took five and a half hours. Anna said it was because of the English motorway system. Adam felt that driving a car with the engine of a vacuum cleaner didn't help. Their hotel room, with twin beds and a shared reading lamp, was bland and smelt of carpet freshener. They could hear the traffic from the M62. The room was too hot. They were tired, irritable and unfamiliar with spending this much time with another person. For both of them, the most good manners they could muster in such circumstances was silence, so they had driven from Oxford to Manchester with no sound except the radio.

'Who are you seeing tomorrow?' Adam asked.

Anna thought: Kofi Annan, Richard Nixon, three of the Spice Girls, someone called Billy, Noel Edmonds... What does it matter who I say, you won't bloody know them. And thus noticed that she had run out of people energy. 'Why?'

'I was wondering, if it was someone senior that might reflect they thought you required special time, if it wasn't...' He shrugged.

It was a fair point. 'The letter didn't say.'

'Who did you talk to at CREAK when you talked to them?'

'I didn't, Paul did.'

'What do you know about them?'

'A quango. Never gave them a thought, just the people who oversee stuff. The health service is full of them. I never took them seriously.'

Adam nodded. 'But might they not be the people responsible for hurting your friend?'

Anna gave him a look that suggested she didn't think he was quite keeping up. 'I rather suspect that is the drug company.'

Adam screwed up his nose. 'Well firstly, that's just because you don't like drug companies more than you don't like government quangos, and secondly that assumes they are not working together and surely nothing has happened to suggest that is the case?'

'I'm finding you annoying,' she said with a smile.

'Of course you are,' he replied. 'I am annoying. If it's any consolation I am finding you annoying too, but I think that is mainly because my back hurts, I hate driving, I'm too hot and I haven't spent this much time with one other person since the 1990s. Although it is equally possible that you are actually just annoying.'

'I think...' She stopped. Actually she hadn't thought. The overwhelming point of the meeting for her was that she could stop running. Yes, she would demand to know what happened to Meena, yes she would defend Paul, but mostly, deep down, she expected to be told that the research findings were on hold, she would be forbidden to disclose any of the data, that Meena's accident, like the accusations made against Paul, was in the hands of the police. Mostly, she expected to be relieved of the burden of responsibility, of this gaze. And then, she thought,

280

*then* she would decide what to do to help. 'I think,' she said quietly, 'I got scared.'

Adam let it go. He was here to watch, or watch over. He was here because he wasn't quite ready to not be part of whatever the hell was going on. He was here because it felt like the right place to be. He had a shower. Anna flicked through the television channels, came across the news and left it on without paying much attention. When Adam came back he was wearing shorts and a t-shirt.

'Where did you get the tattoos done?'

'All over. The flowers were done in Thailand, the sea in Scotland, the smaller lines between the leaves by a wonderful artist in Greece...'

'Do they mean anything?'

Adam smiled. 'Do you not have any?'

'No. If it's not a silly question, why do you?'

Adam shrugged. 'Stuff happens, we collect the years, we get a few scars... I thought I might as well choose some of them and even colour one or two of them in. It's kind of like therapy, I think.'

Anna showered and washed her hair; she put on shorts and a t-shirt too. When she went into the bedroom Adam was in bed, eyes closed. The flickering TV was making no impression. She got quietly into her bed and picked up the remote control.

'You can carry on watching that if you like,' he said quietly. 'It doesn't bother me.'

'It's OK,' she said, turning it off. 'Goodnight.'

'Goodnight.'

They lay in the dark for nearly a minute. The cars outside were louder and she could hear some lads shouting.

'Adam?'

'Yes?'

'Thank you.'

'What for?'

'Well, for coming, I suppose.'

They both lay still and it occurred to Anna that he would fall asleep before her and so she climbed out of bed, stepped across the small space that separated them, pulled back his sheet and said 'Move over.' Adam moved over and put out his arm without opening his eyes. She climbed in and let him put his arm around her, resting her head on his chest. He smelt of hotel soap. Up close she could see that the tattoo on his arm was very intricate. She wondered how they did the shading, she wondered if it hurt, she wondered if you could really get a dahlia in that colour, and then she fell asleep.

# 17. Lemonworld

The building currently housing CREAK had been designed by a man raised on 1970s sci-fi programmes: a man drawn to buildings with the sleek straight lines and pale artifice once imagined as a moon base or a secret home where a rich person kept their Thunderbirds. Its address was a lie, implying it needed distinguishing from other buildings, whereas in fact it had its own postcode. Indeed, the white, cold, glass-walled building stood alone at the end of a private drive and was surrounded by well-cut grass.

Cassells took great comfort from the well-cut grass. The government had announced, albeit at around the same time that they announced a load of things that nobody took seriously, that it would be cutting the excessive number of quangos it funded just as soon as it found out where they all were. He knew very well that government tended to tire of looking for expenditure after it crossed London's North Circular; to be secreted away up here, in leafy, quiet Cheshire was a fantastic career move. He also reasoned that if someone at a different quango, the one charged with working out where the money was going, decided that CREAK Towers, as he liked to think of it, was costing too much, one of the first things to go would be the gardener.

Cassells did not feel anything special about the coming day. There had been a time, maybe twenty years ago, where he would have got some kind of thrill from putting Black Portier and Anna Newton in the same room and watching them blink like babies in the rain. He would have considered it research to watch people realise just how illusory their own sense of autonomy is. But even then it would have been an observation of strangers. He was not remotely interested in the idea of meeting people he had known a couple of decades previously. He had worked with Anna Newton for a while and considered her pretty, efficient and seemingly uninterested in him. She had only become interesting when his trainee, Carla Tandy, had done a routine assessment on advertising director and unusually well dressed admission Black Portier and noted that he said he knew Ms Newton. David Cassells offered out-patient follow up to a gratefully gushing Black Portier for nearly four months. Anna Newton became one more for the files.

Anyway, Cassells was not what the organizational psychologists called a completer finisher. He didn't care much for the completion of a project; as far as he was concerned the research findings were already buried. This meeting was simply to ensure that nobody ever considered digging them up. He was already moving on to the next project, one involving discrediting CCT via a rumoured suicide attempt by the allegedly recovered rock star and a Panorama investigation into the sexual activities of so-called patients and so-called staff. This would be followed by the launch of a new anti-psychotic drug from Leichter and Wallace that not only had fewer side effects and treated depression but might even help with baldness. A drug that, as part of its licensing agreement, saw CREAK benefit financially from all overseas agreements. The integrity, standards and diligence of British research was, on the open market, worth around £20 million to CREAK. And, given that in America alone people spend over $200 billion a year on prescriptions, it was worth a whole lot more to Leichter and Wallace. Cassells loved the beginning of a project but the end felt like cleaning up after a party.

For Anna Newton, however, her meeting marked the end of something significant. Two weeks ago her life crisis involved an impending menopause and the fact that her son had gone and grown up. These were significant things but they were scripted. The worries that so filled her then—was her son lonely? Had she failed as a mother? What if the aloneness she had chosen when

284

she felt strong and single minded melted into loneliness as she became more invisible to the world and less useful to her son— were all distinctly personal yet shared by millions. Now, after the fear had filled her in a way it hadn't for almost twenty-five years, the residue it left asked harder questions. How much of what she did was pointless? Was the bone-hard resilience she was convinced ran through her just an illusion? And more practically, what was she going to do to make a living now? Because being a researcher in a world where finding things out is banned is too ridiculous for words. She could go back to clinical nursing but she felt too old and impatient, and anyway she didn't really understand the language they seemed to use these days or why there were so many earnest, chest-thumping, managers. And of course she was too old to dance.

Anna knew she had to identify something she wanted to leave with, given the fact that she had felt the need to abandon her home and run away to Eastbourne. The main thing she wanted was to come away feeling safe. Deep down that was enough. And that made her feel ashamed. What about Meena and Paul? She had taken so many steps backwards, in defence of herself, she had forgotten how to consider stepping forward, in defence of others. When she had been a nurse it was that quality that defined her. Now it seemed that she was no longer a nurse. And she had no plan: the nearest thing she came to intent as she and Adam drove to CREAK was a sense that her instinct, whatever the hell that was, would act when the time came. Less a plan, more the vague hope of a child hoping that the bogey man, or the dance instructor, will choose to leave her alone and hurt someone else instead.

Adam had woken early and lay still for as long as he could before needing to pee. He felt little about the day ahead. He was here because he was curious, not about the modern industry that was psychiatry and how it sustained itself. He had always simply assumed that it would flourish, no matter what. The mechanics of that relentlessness didn't interest him. He was curious about this new past that was emerging and it seemed to be emerging through Anna. He was also increasingly curious about Tom. He had managed to limit his interest in the boy at first, partly because Tom gave him the impression that he didn't want to be interesting, he just wanted a little help. But he had noticed Tom soften a little, talk more, direct conversation at him rather than others: these were the hallmarks of enquiry. And then he had noticed him playing guitar, the way he held it, the way he moved his head when he played, gazing at the floor beneath the guitar neck, and it occurred to him that perhaps he was more curious than he thought. Once that had taken hold, it had begun to flow around his body like water in a stream.

The grass is a different shade of green here, he thought. Not darker nor brighter, just different. And it was a tiny bit colder, even though he was used to being beside the sea. However, he didn't feel far from home and he expected to be back before the sun went down and he hoped that Tom would still be there. So they could talk. Properly. He didn't know where Anna would be by then.

They were early, a habit established as nurses and never lost. They sat outside in the car on the gravelled and relatively spacious car park looking at the surrounding acres of open grassland and perimeter of trees and then at the incongruously modern, flat building that Adam thought looked like a small block of Spanish holiday lets.

'What's the time?'

'9.42.'

'Early.'

'Always,' Anna said quietly.

'You nervous?'

Anna shook her head, then thought: Who am I kidding? 'Yeah.'

'How can I help?' Adam spoke very softly.

That was something that hadn't changed, she thought. He always managed to slow down the things that were going on around him by being quiet near them. 'You could come in with me. Not to the meeting but the building, wait downstairs. If I'm not out within an hour, set off the fire alarms or something?'

'OK. Shall we go now?'

'Bit early... but yes... why not.'

They got out of the car. Anna looked smart and businesslike in a black jacket tapered to the waist over a grey scoop neck shirt. With a black knee-length skirt and flat shoes, she looked a bit like a lawyer. Adam was in jeans, plimsolls and a beaten-up leather flying jacket with a rusty zip and his old hat: he looked like her client.

'They can't hurt you, you know,' he smiled. 'Too many witnesses.'

'There speaks a man who has never seen *The Wicker Man*,' she said.

The building was glass-fronted; the revolving doors were over ten feet high and made completely of glass.

'Nice building,' she said as they entered a large spacious reception room, with a circular glass desk in the middle and a pretty, already smiling woman sitting behind it. 'Like something out of the X-Men,' Adam said, looking around him. And, before Anna could find her special 'talking to receptionists in slightly intimidating buildings' voice, Adam said: 'Must get hot in here in the summer, no?' He was smiling more broadly than Anna had ever seen.

The receptionist laughed. 'Architects hate people,' she said. 'They had to buy massive curtains to block out the sun because people kept fainting, and then they had to buy new lights because nobody could see anything when the curtains were drawn. Then the lights system didn't tally with the internal generator or summat and so that had to be replaced. Cost a fortune.'

'Still,' Adam grinned, 'I bet he still won some award.'

'He did!' she said loudly. 'And no offence meant, but it's telling that you assumed it was a man because I don't think many women would build a multi-million-pound building and think: Let's point it toward the sun, that'll look nice looking down from the hillside.'

'No offence taken,' said Adam. 'I think you're probably right.'

The receptionist and Adam were looking at each other, nodding, and Anna took the opportunity to remind them both she was present. 'I have an appointment at 10am,' she said, unfolding her letter and offering it to the woman. 'Unfortunately the letter didn't tell me who with...'

'Don't worry,' the woman said cheerfully. 'What's your name, please?'

'Anna Newton.'

The woman smiled even more broadly. 'Oh yes, I was told you would be early. Dr Cassells is waiting for you in Room 102, first floor, either one flight up the stairs or you can get the lift.' She turned to Adam. 'I don't have your name on the list.'

'Ah,' said Adam, 'I never made it on to the list. I'm not here for the meeting, I'm just the driver.'

'Cassells?' Anna turned to Adam.

'Can't be.'

Adam turned back to the receptionist. 'Dr David Cassells? Shortish, poor dresser, psychologist used to work in London, about my age but probably looks older?'

The receptionist looked embarrassed and glanced upward and to her right. 'His name is David and I believe he did work in London and I have no way of knowing how old you are, sir.' The lightness had left her.

Adam winked. 'Right. When they put in the lights they put in some cameras, eh?' She almost smiled. 'It's OK,' he said as lightly as he could. 'If it's the David Cassells we think it is we both used to work with him.' The receptionist just nodded and Adam and Anna took a few steps away from the desk.

'Bit of a coincidence. Will he remember you?' Adam asked.

'I would have thought so. We worked together for over a year after you left.'

'Did you get on with him?'

'I thought he was smarmy and self serving.'

'Well, yeah, but did you get on with him?'

'When I had to. At arms length. I wonder why he didn't sign the letter?'

'Maybe he's carrying a torch?' Adam winked.

'I hope so,' Anna said. 'I could use it to set fire to him.'

'Good luck.' Adam touched her arm gently and wandered over to sit in one of two wholly absurd transparent plastic chairs near the revolving door.

Anna took the stairs and tried to remember the last time she had seen Cassells. He left, got a job up north, big job, regional something-or-other, and she didn't go to his leaving do because Tom would have been about 6 months old and because it would have been full of psychologists. Did she bother saying goodbye? She couldn't remember. Did she ever let her disdain leak out? Probably, but he never struck her as a perceptive man. He was typical of his type, only ever seeing things when he had been told they were there. But she could see him now, as she emerged from the stairwell onto a floor that was essentially two enormous rooms with a corridor between them, both rooms visible to each other because they had long glass walls. He'd put on weight and looked shorter because of it; he had grown his hair so it nearly reached his shoulders and he had a floppy thin fringe and a beard. He looked like the sort of man who fancied a go at Question Time and who took The Rolling Stones seriously. He stood up when he saw her and smiled, walking toward the door as quickly as his pudgy little legs would let him. Any fear she had was gone. There was some disdain sweeping in and... what's that carrying it? Oh yes, that's anger.

'Anna! How lovely to see you, you look wonderful, even better than before. How do you do that?' He actually kissed her on the cheek. His beard was soft and he smelt of something expensive. He held both of her arms just above the elbow, too close to her breasts.

'David. What a surprise. Why didn't you sign the letter?'

'It wasn't signed? Oh Anna, how unprofessional, I will have a word with my PA. I don't actually send the letters but I do apologize.' He looked at her wide-eyed. 'Well. It's a small world, eh?'

Downstairs Adam was, much to his surprise, thinking about Alison. There was something about her that drew his attention. He had always been attracted to women who hid something. He had, as a younger man, worried about what that made him. A man who needed to feel like he was rescuing people? A voyeur? But he knew that that standard issue self-loathing was fundamentally lazy. He wasn't attracted to them because they hid something that he wanted to uncover, he didn't want to know what secret they had or join the internal battle they waged. He just liked the fact that they had corners. Women who had struggled with themselves had resources, surprises, insights and sometimes, although not always, a humanity that made them better to be around. He had a sense of Alison as being just a little bit dark. He didn't care where it came from: he just liked what it produced.

Someone else came through the revolving door. Expensive suit, looked like a salesman. Looked vaguely familiar, but Adam thought that was the point of salesmen. He announced himself to the receptionist but Adam couldn't hear him as the man had his back to him. The receptionist smiled briefly, the way people do when their smile is not reciprocated and asked him to take a seat for a moment. The man looked round and eyed Adam suspiciously. The only seats available were next to Adam or on the other side of the revolving door. The man had to choose to sit next to the scruffy man who didn't seem to be wearing socks, or appear rude and go and sit some distance away. He opted for rude and looked self-conscious about it.

At precisely ten o'clock the receptionist said 'Mr Portier. Dr Cassells will see you now. First floor, room eleven.' She didn't look at Portier as he stood up and didn't so much as glance over at Adam either. Black did though, briefly, quizzically, and then he headed for the lift.

'Well, David, I assume I am here to talk about the CCT research project?'

'Ah, CCT: Cuddle Camp Therapy we call it,' he smiled.

'I'm sure you do, but the research seems to suggest it works.'

'Does it Anna? Really? If we unpack the numbers, is it saying it works?'

'Yes.'

Cassells was sitting now, in a large chair that made him look smaller. He was nodding to himself, looking at the large oak table that dominated the room and occasionally glancing toward the corridor. When the knock on the door came he leapt to his feet with the relish of a fat schoolboy being excused from double PE.

'Come in,' he shouted, bounding over to the door to shake Black Portier by the hand and then turning to Anna and saying: 'Do you know Mr Portier? I think you might. Yes?'

Downstairs Adam sidled up to the receptionist. 'Quiet morning?' he said, smiling.

'Every morning is a quiet morning.' She was relaxed again. 'We don't normally have someone on reception, Cass— Dr Cassells wanted me down here this morning.'

Adam nodded. 'Forgive me,' he said 'But that man who just came in, I know him from somewhere and I can't place it. Portier? First name a colour, I believe, not mauve.'

'Black. I thought it was an unusual name too,' she laughed.

'He doesn't work here then?'

'No, up from London to see Cass— Dr Cassells.'

'We've just come from the south, if we'd known we could have shared petrol,' Adam said. 'Or, better still, Cassells could have come down to see us.'

The woman raised her eyebrows. 'He's not really the sort, to be honest.'

Adam smiled. 'Is there a toilet I can use, please?'

'Not on this floor, I'm afraid. If you go up to the second floor—yes I know, whoever designed this place should be made to work here—but second floor, take the lift, turn left out the door. You need a code 4536 to get in.'

'Thanks,' Adam said and wandered over to the lift.

'What are you doing, David?' Anna was shaking slightly, thrown completely by the pale figure of Black Portier.

Cassells exaggerated a look of shock. 'What am I doing? I am being the Director of CREAK, Ms Newton, hosting a meeting with the only available member of a research team that appears to have struggled to maintain its professional standards and the funding co-ordinator, Mr Portier here.'

'Hello Anna,' Black said quietly. 'How are you?'

Anna looked at him and nodded before turning back to Cassells. 'Funding co-ordinator? What does that mean?'

'Mr Portier was responsible for gathering together the interested parties prepared to underwrite your research. The government cannot fund every question everybody wants to ask but we can sometimes help, as we did with your project, both financially and in terms of co-ordination. Mr Portier is, I think you know, a seller of ideas by trade. Advertising, PR, marketing, whatever you want to call it. He sells the question to funding groups and then sells whatever answer you researchers come up with to a waiting nation.' It occurred to Anna that she had never seen anyone look as smug as Cassells. Particularly when he added: 'He also helps with recruitment.'

That stung. 'Did you recruit me?' Anna asked, looking at Black and holding his gaze for the first time since he had come into the room.

Black nodded. 'It wasn't difficult. If I hadn't chosen you for the job I could have been accused of discrimination.'

'The fact that you had any sort of say at all means you could be accused of discrimination.'

'Why?' asked Black. 'We had a brief, pleasant but not terribly meaningful relationship nearly twenty-five years ago. It was another lifetime. Why would that matter? Unless of course you'd got pregnant with my child and never told me.'

'Coffee, anyone?' asked Cassells.

Anna felt the coldness, a coldness that had protected her all her adult life, rush through her, starting from her heart and pushing outward until she could actually feel the tips of her fingers push the fear out through her skin and leave only cold blood.

'Well, Black,' she said evenly. 'If you are hoping to pay some child support I should tell you that you are but one of the candidates.' She turned to Cassells. 'So, I assume the research findings on our little project have unnerved enough people and I am here to be told that I cannot publish the findings. Is that right?'

Cassells smiled. 'Anna, don't be so dramatic.' Cassells had poured her black coffee and put it in front of her.

'David, it is my belief that Paul Stern has been disgracefully discredited and Meena Ahmed was seriously injured.'

'Those sound like questionable beliefs, Anna,' said Cassells, mimicking his own clinical voice.

Anna ignored the tone and words. 'So am I here to receive your support in publishing the findings to this really rather interesting research? That would be great, David, and it would go some way to re-establishing my belief that people like us came into this work to do something helpful.'

'Anna.' Cassells leaned forward crossing his hands in front of him, fixed his gaze just above her eyes and said in what he had clearly decided was his Director's voice: 'Firstly, I am not convinced the research is good. Some of the data don't corroborate the findings and some of the interviews are poorly annotated. I found the conclusions a little sweeping, not scientific, and frankly the risks are too great to put out sloppy work.'

'It wasn't sloppy, David. Call me what you like but Paul Stern is ten times the researcher you will ever be. He was bordering on autistic in how meticulous he was and we have copies of everything, so if you or anyone else have changed the work...'

'Anna, you sound paranoid,' he said loudly. He paused, giving the impression of regaining his composure.

Anna didn't believe him. Didn't believe his body language, his presentation. He was acting. He was acting like a director and nothing about him scared her.

'Anna, let me spell it out for you. The last time a piece of research suggested an anti-psychotic drug did not do what it said on the tin, the drug company concerned lost £34 million in world wide sales over the first year, £48 million from its share price and moved its tax base from the UK to Germany. It then threatened to sue the British Government for allegedly falsifying research results and sabotaging the legitimate business of what was one of the only companies to demonstrate year on year growth right through the recession.'

Anna shrugged. 'So?'

Cassells sighed. 'Three other companies including Leichter and Wallace made it known that they were considering their tax arrangements, which was one of the reasons my predecessors hired Mr Portier here, and others, to forge helpful partnerships in research with the companies who not only fund so much research and do so much good right across the medical spectrum but also generate wealth in this country.'

Anna shook her head and laughed. 'So why even bother commissioning this research?' Cassells nodded at Black. 'Mr Portier?'

Black hadn't moved since he had entered the room. Now he stepped forward and started nodding. 'Well,' he said earnestly, 'you don't measure freedom according to the range of answers available to a question, you measure it according to the range of questions people are allowed to ask.'

'What?' said Anna impatiently.

'Open mindededness, academic freedom, progressive thinking... These slightly fatuous ideas oil the economic wheels,

Anna.' Cassells spoke with a flourish, waving his hand in the air as if he was conducting music only he could hear.

Black said: 'The research profile overseen by CREAK, and indeed right across the board, needs to demonstrate a willingness to ask questions that service all political perspectives. Nobody really believed that you would come up with findings that suggest there are better ways than drugs of treating psychosis.'

'Yes but we have, so what's the problem?'

'Well, for one thing the problem is, as Dr Cassells has explained, one of simple economics. We don't turn our back on our friends in times of trouble.'

'Whose trouble?' asked Anna.

'Our trouble, Ms Newton,' said Cassells. 'Industry is not so buoyant that we can undermine one of our most effective and consistent exports: pharmaceuticals.'

'Furthermore,' said Black, trying to sound like a government official, 'quite frankly, drugs are cheaper than the holiday camps that CCT provide. It's all well and good for a handful of celebrities to fund a handful of centres, but if that responsibility fell to the NHS you could kiss goodbye to just about everything else. Cancer care, dementia care, chronic health problems: they cost money. We need affordable solutions and we need them presented in such a way as to ensure people don't believe they are being given the cheap option.'

Anna shook her head. 'Isn't the point of research to simply put the findings out there and let the world manage what they mean?'

'Now you're just taking the piss,' said Cassells.

'Who set up Paul Stern?' Anna asked.

Cassells shrugged. 'Who says he was set up?'

'I do,' said Anna.

'If that is the case I have no doubt the police will exonerate him.'

'Yes,' said Anna sarcastically. 'Because if the last fifteen minutes have shown me anything it is that the authorities are to be trusted in all things.'

Cassells was getting bored. 'Anna, you are contractually obliged not to publish, comment, present or even hint at findings until CREAK says you can.'

Black spoke quietly: 'And as Leichter and Wallace have enjoyed pointing out, we are contracted to not release data without agreeing a timetable with them. If we breach that contract they will claim we are going off half-cocked and sue us.'

'I think that this transcends contracts,' said Anna.

'Do you? Hannah?' said Cassells quietly before saying more loudly: 'Look, this research amounts to whimsy. It doesn't offer anything scientific, progressive or constructive. It amounts to a single study that suggests offering luxury, attention and unlimited patience to the mad might offer a better clinical outcome than antipsychotics. Think of what taking that seriously means, Anna, economically and politically. Hell, if people were paying attention it would challenge the underpinning knowledge base for the whole of psychiatry. Do you know how many jobs that could affect?'

'Firstly,' Anna spoke quietly, 'Don't call me Hannah. Secondly, you are interested in sustaining an industry for ideological and economic reasons. I am not so stupid as to imagine that the CCT research is going to bring your house tumbling down, but I do think it might help cleverer people than me ask more questions and maybe get to a point where the money being pumped into your precious drug companies goes somewhere else, somewhere more helpful.'

'My precious drug companies use the money they get from psychiatry to develop drugs to combat all sorts of things Anna: cancer, arthritis, Alzheimer's. I understand your father developed Alzheimer's. I understand he used to go out looking for you, long after you had gone. That had to hurt your mother and your brother. CCT wouldn't have been much use for him, would it?'

'How do you know anything about my family?' Anna said. The coldness had left her and she could feel something else rising up from the base of her spine: not fear, more likely rage.

'Mr Portier, you may recall, had a brief admission some years ago. I was his psychologist. He told me he knew you and over the course of many sessions he told me the same things you had told him: your story. After he selected you for this piece of work, a romantic gesture as far as I can tell, he was curious about your son. So many secrets, Ms Newton! Anyway, after he had selected you and Dr Stern had submitted his interim report, I found my curiosity running away with me and I looked into what had happened to your family. Should I tell you?'

Adam had wandered past the toilet and was walking down the central corridor of the second floor. It was the antithesis of the celebration of reinforced glass downstairs, a conventional floor of offices. He had his phone at his ear, ready to pretend to talk earnestly into it should anyone with a badge eye him and his plimsolls suspiciously. But nobody did. The second floor appeared as quiet as the reception area. Walking deeper into the building, past the toilets, there was an office with two voices chatting quietly about a restaurant but nobody in the office opposite. Further along there were two doors facing each other. One had a silver nameplate that read 'Dr Carla Tandy' on it, the other—an incongruous large oak door more suited to a 1930s mansion—had the name 'Dr David Cassells' in gold lettering. Adam opened the door confidently. He knew Cassells wouldn't be there, and if there was a secretary he would smile and say that he and Davie used to work together and it felt ridiculous being in the same building and not coming to say hello and to find out which of them had aged the best. But there was nobody, just a very large oval shaped office with a stunning panoramic view of the countryside. In the middle of the office, in front of a leather chair facing away from the view, was a very large round desk. Adam walked over and sat down. He touched the space bar of the computer in front of him. The screen sprang into life asking for a password. He typed in the word 'password' but it was rejected. He stared at the screen for a moment and shook his head. He spun round in the chair and looked at the view. It was all cultivated land but beautiful nonetheless. Adam wondered how often Cassells looked at that landscape, and wondered why you would have your back to it all day but be facing the door in a building where, as far as Adam could tell, about seven people worked.

None of the drawers were locked but there was nothing immediately interesting in any of them. Not that Adam was looking for anything in particular. He was just looking, mostly because he shouldn't. Adam looked at his phone, sighed and phoned Freaky Bob.

Freaky Bob believed that nobody had been to the moon and Michael Jackson was alive and well and living in Malta. He could talk for months about Roswell, the JFK cover up and the fact that the internet was essentially a very efficient CCTV system that could, if an increasingly tired and unfocused government wanted it to, find out everything about anyone who used it. Freaky Bob thought they were out to get you, and after a few pints he behaved as though Star Wars was a documentary, but he knew more about computers than Bill Gates and had once hacked into the American FBI database from a pub in Herne Bay on a borrowed laptop for a bet. He won five pints of 'Badgers Golden Champion' and a signed photograph of Fidel Castro. The owner of the laptop, a mouthy out-of-towner, is still facing extradition charges. Freaky Bob could have done anything in the world he had wanted. Mostly he wanted to read obscure political analysis, mend phones and computers for money and wait for aliens.

'Freaky Bob? Adam Sands. How do you break into a computer? No, it's not a personal computer. No, I'm in an office. Not really broken in, no, but... yeah... no... no... I'm not meant to be... its sort of a government office. Not really central government, no... well I don't know if they do the dirty work, mate, I can't get into their computer to find out... you can do that? But I don't have the password... Stop laughing, I thought that was important. What, everything? Are you sure? Oh, OK. Well... yeah OK... No, I'd like everything if you can do that please. Yeah? Cool. Hey, when I get back you get to pick whatever books you want for free. No, not all of them, five of them... Cool... So what do I have to do?'

Anna knew that there were a handful of fundamental principles that became embodied as you lived your life. There was one that she had carried around in her liver since she had left home as a furious sixteen year old: she would not be bullied by a man. No matter what.

'What's in this for you, Black?'

'Mostly I am doing my job, Anna. I liked to think I was doing you a favour when I, shall I say, helped you get the job. Frankly, there were about thirty researchers who could do it: those things tend to be a bit random. And if it wasn't for me the research would not have been funded. It was me who went to Leichter and Wallace to negotiate funding.'

'And now?

'I'm here because Dr Cassells asked me to be here. I assumed I was coming to a debriefing.' He looked mildly uncomfortable.

'Black is here because he has played a key role in co-ordinating not only the establishment of this project but the information management that has followed,' said Cassells. 'And anyway, I thought it might be a nice opportunity for you two to catch up.'

'What the fuck has it got to do with you?' spat Anna.

Cassells put his hands up and gave an exaggerated shrug.

'Actually, Anna, it isn't really fair that you didn't tell me about Tom. I had the right to know,' said Black.

Anna dropped her head to her chest and put both her hands to her face. Black looked anxiously at Cassells, who smiled reassuringly: he had expected tears, he was used to them. But when Anna lifted her head she was laughing.

Adam had retained one or two skills from his long distant nursing days. One was never to give the impression of rushing. Rushing unnerved people, it made them imagine there may be a fire they should worry about. The other was to never appear surprised, and so when Carla Tandy walked into Cassells office to find Adam sitting at the desk tapping the computer keyboard, while she was shocked he simply nodded and said 'Hello.'

She was as thin as she had been nearly twenty five years earlier but now that showed mostly around her eyes, making her look gaunt and surprised.

'What the fuck are you doing here? You can't be in here. I'm calling security.' But she didn't move.

'There's security?' Adam said with surprise. 'Looks to me as though you have to send out to get your photocopying done.'

'Get out.'

'But I thought it would be good to say hello to Dave. I bumped into him downstairs and he said to wait in here.' Tandy looked uncertain for a moment. 'So how are you? Still obnoxious?'

Tandy sneered at him. 'You dress like a tramp. I assume you never got over the drug problems?'

Adam smiled. 'I can certainly see why you got out of clinical work. Have you been a secretary long?'

'I earn more in a month than you do in a year.'

'But you can't afford the occasional pizza? Maybe a Mars bar? No?'

Tandy reddened. 'Why are you here?'

Adam stood up. 'I came with Anna Newton. I didn't know Dave worked here until I got here. Small world, I thought. Until three days ago I hadn't seen Anna for twenty-three years. I'm half expecting Maureen Marley to walk in next.'

'Who?'

'The patient you were so desperate to interview.' Tandy pursed her lips. 'Under the circumstances, if you find yourself in the same building as someone you used to work with twenty five years ago and he was talking with someone else you used to work with at the same time it would have felt odd, rude, a bit bizarre, not to say hello. A very charming young woman downstairs said the best way to catch him would be to come up here—'

'You said David had told you—'

'I think of it all as a hall really...' Adam muttered.

'Did David tell you to wait in here?'

Adam walked away from the desk, to the window. Turning his back on Carla Tandy and staring out at the trees. 'He hasn't aged well has he? Lovely view. He ought to try hiking.'

Tandy stared at him. 'I think you should go. I will tell David that you are here and you can wait downstairs.'

Adam didn't turn to face her; instead he stretched his arms over his head and nodded.

'Yeah, OK. I'll wait downstairs. Tell Dave won't you?' Tandy nodded and Adam turned and walked out of the room without looking at her. She followed him and closed the door behind her.

'Why don't you get gold lettering, Carla?' Adam said, staring at her door. She said nothing and so he walked, quite slowly, toward the lift.

'OK,' said Anna. 'Bored now. Black, my son is twenty-three. He is getting married. He is a grown-up. Who knows, you may get an invite to the wedding but I wouldn't hold your breath if I were you. David, you appear to harbour the illusion that you are a good psychologist because you can gather things which look like insight into other people and use them in a way that other people don't. That doesn't actually make you a good psychologist: it means you are a psychopath. I will not be manipulated by you or anyone like you. I don't know if you were behind the fire at Meena's or if that was Black here, or even the drug company. I don't know which of you set up Paul or who hired the two men who came to my home. I do know that I will not be bullied by inadequate tossers like you.' Anna stood up and offered Cassells all the contempt she could cram into one parting glance. She didn't look at Black as she walked toward the door but something occurred to her before she touched the handle: she had done a little too much running lately. So she stopped still, took a deep breath and turned round. Cassells stared at her. She looked him in the eyes and could see nothing. She nodded to herself and said quietly: 'The night Tim Leith died. You were there.' Cassells looked impassively at her but he swallowed and that, for Anna was enough. 'You'd arranged that silly talk, you left. You went to ward 6 and you were with Tim.' Cassells laughed quietly and went to shake his head. 'I saw you, David. I went back to the ward and I saw you, talking in the office. What did you talk about?'

Cassells folded his arms across his body and pursed his lips. He opened his mouth but nothing came out. Anna nodded. 'What did you say to him David? You'd been stirring things up, trying to get underneath people's skin, playing silly games... You said something to Tim. Come on David, it was twenty-four years ago and he was dying anyway.' Cassells didn't change expression. 'Did you know that? You couldn't have known that. How could you know that? So, what did you say?'

'I didn't say anything really. I asked him about his judgement. I was interested in what he would say, if he reflected much on what he did... It appears that he did. He reflected a great deal, too much maybe. I asked him about the Marley woman, and about the schizophrenic on all the drugs, the one who had taken his teeth out. I asked him if there might be anything affecting his judgement because he seemed uncertain, like he kept changing his mind. I talked about what a lack of clear thinking could do when directed at vulnerable people. It really surprised me how upset he was. Positively unprofessional really.'

Anna stared at him. She could see no remorse, no sense of sadness or regret. He looked like a child explaining how many legs he had collected from a family of spiders. She shook her head. She tried to sneer but realized she might cry. Not through fury or powerlessness but for Tim. 'You unutterable piece of shit,' she said quietly. She glanced at Black with contempt, turned around and left, walking along the long corridor with both men watching her from behind the glass.

When Anna got out of the lift Adam was sitting where she had left him.

'Let's go please,' she said as she approached.

'Good idea.' He waved at the receptionist, who waved back.

In the car Anna stared straight ahead, not talking until they were half way down the drive. 'Do you know who was in there?'

'Tom's other dad.'

'Don't call him that,' she snapped. 'And how did you know?'

'Well, he came in the front door and the receptionist called his name. I'm not Sherlock Holmes but...'

'Cassells is a slime ball,' she spat. 'He thinks he can intimidate me into supporting his cover-up.'

'Can he?' Adam asked.

'Can he fuck,' she said.

'Good. So what are we going to do?'

'We?' Anna asked.

'Guess who else works in there?'

'Who?'

'You remember that stick-thin trainee of his? The one who didn't like patients, nurses or Kit Kats?'

'Carla Tandy?'

'Yep.'

'How do you know?'

'I went for a wander round.'

Anna drove on for a while.

'He knew about my family: he had been snooping around. He wanted to intimidate me and he does... in a way. Not because of what he says but because of what happened to Meena and is happening to Paul. It makes you doubt everything, going to the police, speaking out. He doesn't have any boundaries.'

Adam just nodded. 'I think it is what people like Cassells do, Anna, make you believe that he has all the knowledge and the power, that he is the one establishing all the rules and you, or whoever else he is messing with, has to abide by them.'

'So how do I, we, fight that?'

'We change the rules.'

She looked at him.

'Come back down to Margate. I'd like you to meet Freaky Bob.'

# 18. Strangers When We Meet

Anna and Adam covered half the M6 in near silence. They stopped for coffee just past Birmingham and Adam took over the driving.

'You can sleep if you like,' he said as they rejoined the motorway but Anna wasn't sleepy. They drove on quietly until she said: 'I'd hate to think he was the father of my son.'

Adam let out a short laugh and said: 'You don't get to choose.'

'I suppose you can see a certain irony in that.'

'For what it's worth I think you got him this far without any help. He is talented, engaged, in love, secure, bright... I'm not sure anything else matters, does it?'

Anna didn't say anything for a few moments. 'So you don't care if he is yours or not?'

'That's not what I said. I said, in the scheme of things, it doesn't much matter. He is who he is, you and he did that. Everything else... well, that becomes someone else's story doesn't it?'

'Well, no not really. It's his story too, isn't it? Tom's. My going missing was almost the excuse he was looking for to come and find you, and he could just as easily have gone looking for Black first.'

'I'm not sure Grace would have known how to help him find Portier.'

'You know what I mean.' Anna was speaking softly. 'I think he wants to know who his biological father is.'

'And that upsets you?'

Anna thought for a few moments. 'I don't know. I think I tried to be everything and it feels like it wasn't enough, but I know that that feeling isn't reasonable...'

'Feelings aren't.'

'Yeah, thanks Professor. What if he is angry with me for not knowing? What if I got it wrong?'

Adam drove on in silence. Past Oxford, toward the M25.

'Look,' he said. "I know nothing about being a parent but I still visit my difficult, confused, loveable, annoying, demanding relic of a mother every week and I have learned only this: there is no right. No matter what you do, someone, a mother or a son, can see parenting as anything from beautiful wisdom to an assault. If Tom wants to know, he is welcome to my DNA to test against. If that simply eliminates me, then you and he can write a story where his dad is a git. If it doesn't... hell, I'll teach him to play guitar properly.'

'Oi, he got to Grade Seven by the time he was fifteen. He is a very good guitarist!'

Adam laughed: 'Could be so much better.'

They were quiet going round the M25. The conversation was limited to Adam complaining about the traffic—'too many cars for a small island,' 'This is why I don't like driving' and 'This motorway is the biggest car park in Europe'—and Anna asking random questions like: 'What do you like to read?'; 'Are you finished with the tattoos now?' and 'Shall I drive?' It was as they approached the M2 and began to head toward the sea that she said: 'What are you thinking about?'

And he said: 'I'm thinking of a woman I met the same time I met Tom.'

'Pretty?' asked Anna.

'Yeah,' said Adam.

'Young?'

'Bit younger than us,' he said distractedly.

'Interesting?'

'Well she must be, I'm thinking about her.'

'What are you thinking?'

'I'm wondering, given everything that has happened in the last few days if her appearing when she did is a coincidence.'

'What do you mean?'

'Well, she is a psychologist and she came into the shop the same time as Tom. She is friendly and flirtatious but odd too. She wants to rent the basement of my shop for her brother who sounds as if he is schizophrenic.'

'Is a person with schizophrenia.'

'Pardon?'

'That's what we say now: the person is not defined by their diagnosis, they are a person who happens to have something called schizophrenia.'

'Oh.'

'Anyway, carry on. You sound as though you have a bit of a crush.'

Adam smiled. 'Well, it's been a while but I'm not sure that's why I'm thinking about her.'

'You think she has something to do with all of this?'

Adam shrugged. 'No idea. I suppose I think that the last week or so has been an exercise in trying to figure out the space between paranoia and coincidence.'

They drove on, slowing slightly as the M2 became the A2 and the landscape began to fill with houses.

'What are you thinking about?' Adam asked.

'Sounds absurd given everything that has happened, but I'm thinking of the boy I met in Eastbourne.'

Adam nodded. 'I don't think that is ridiculous. After Tim died I didn't think of Tim, or Libby, Catherine, Stephen, Grace or you.'

'Break it to me gently...'

'I thought of the boy who I talked to. He was so real, and yet the only explanation I have now is that he wasn't.'

'Are you suggesting that my meeting wasn't real?'

'No. I am suggesting that we don't always think about the obvious things. That some stuff leaves an impression and maybe when it does we better take notice.'

'What did you do?' Anna wanted him to drive more slowly now. She had become so comfortable with the noise of the traffic and the easy company that she had stopped feeling in a hurry to get to where they were going.

'I turned it into a sign, I suppose. Isn't that what people do when they can't do anything else?'

'If I tell you something weird, will you promise not to call me mad?'

'I am no longer on the nursing register, Anna; I don't believe I have the power to call anyone mad.'

'I want to try it. I want to make tea from freshly collected dew and give it to mad people. That is mad isn't it?'

Adam nodded his head. 'Probably.'

'So why do I want to do it?'

Adam shrugged. 'Because it can't do any harm and sometimes whimsy makes us feel human.'

'Is that a polite way of telling me I am naïve?'

'Nah.' He smiled and glanced over at her. 'Hope lets the light in.'

When they got to Margate, Tom and Laura were in the shop, waiting. Anna filled them in on everything that had happened including Black's presence. Adam listened as Grimy Nige and Jim outlined every book sale, near sale and strange browsing non-buying customer they had logged in his absence. Alison had been round. She and her quiet brother had spent ages in the basement. When they emerged she was smiling and had cobwebs in her hair. Her brother spent some time looking at the books. He had asked Grimy Nige and Jim if they had any recommendations and bought a book of short stories by Raymond Carver on their advice. They liked him. Alison had asked them to tell Adam to call her when he got back please. They finished speaking and waited to see if there were any follow-up questions they needed to answer, any detail they had failed to feed back or any tests they might need to pass in order to be allowed to run the bookshop again. There were no questions, but Adam didn't know how much to pay them and said as much. They said they didn't want payment, but Adam insisted he split the day's income, £86, between them. They were very happy, Jim looked like he might cry, and subsequently they spent £23.50 on five books.

'How about,' Adam said loudly, 'Tomorrow night I make a fish curry and we eat it and come up with a plan. Anna, you bring the wine; Grimy Nige and Jim you just bring yourselves; Laura, you bring your lovely self; Tom, you can play guitar.'

'We can't come,' said Grimy Nige and Jim as one. 'We have French class.' Adam stared at them both. 'French on Fridays, Choir on Thursdays, Book Group every fourth Tuesday and Life Drawing on Mondays.'

'What do you do Wednesdays?' asked Tom.

'Pilates, but it's more a drop-in sort of thing,' said Jim.

'Are you going to try to catch the fish?' asked Anna. Adam nodded. 'Can I come with you?'

Adam smiled. 'I'd like that, and if you can stay around for a few days I would love to take you out on the boat, but first I think there is someone I need to have a chat with and the sea feels like the best place for it.'

Anna smiled. 'It's because I haven't brought my swimming things, isn't it?'

Adam laughed. 'We'd be so far out you wouldn't need them,' he said. 'Although it has turned a bit cold the last couple of weeks.'

'Invite her to dinner?' said Anna.

'I may invite them both.' He looked at her intently. 'You could make your special tea?'

'Ohh, so I better get up early and gather some dew.'

Adam turned to Tom. 'Your mother may be going a tiny bit mad.'

Tom nodded. 'It was always going to be just a matter of time.'

A little later, Adam called Alison. 'How was your trip?' she asked.

'Confusing,' he said. 'And it involved psychology. I wonder if you might lend me your expertise in return for a serious conversation about my basement.'

'I'd love to. When?'

'How about tomorrow morning? We go fishing, this time we need to catch fish.'

'I'll bring hot tea,' she said.

'Good decision. See you by the boat at ten thirty.'

He closed the shop early. He was tired, unused to driving, to being with other people who required something like engagement. He went upstairs and lay on the sofa looking at the off-white clouds passing the corner of the window and fell asleep, a wistful sleep where he dreamt he was swimming toward his boat and his boat was getting further away. He woke with a start, just after something dark and unimaginably fast had taken him from below the water line.

It was after seven and dark outside. He was thirsty and stiff. He hadn't swum in three days and he hadn't done anything physical beyond sit in a car for two. In the years that followed nursing he had travelled, read and stretched as often as he could. He had played guitar for money in a range of ridiculous circumstances including an all-Indian (except him) Clash tribute band and a hotel lobby jazz ensemble. He had learnt that without physical movement he shrank in every sense. He knew he still had things to do before giving up on the day and so he lay on the floor and breathed as deeply as he could. He could feel a soreness beneath the ribs on his left hand side and he noticed that he couldn't expand his chest as fully as he should. Shallow breathing made him think too quickly and made him tense, a tension he picked up first in his hands and wrists, making them feel as though he were wearing heavy gloves. He could feel the thickness slide down his arms to his body and gather around his spine, running to his neck, which he stretched. He thought about going to the swimming pool, but swimming pools were usually frantic smelly places, so he twisted his body from one side to the other, pushed his arms up behind his head and reached out for the wall. He steadied his breathing, closed his eyes for a moment to settle himself again and got up to go and see Freaky Bob.

Freaky Bob lived above his very small computer and phone repair shop on the same old town street that Adam's bookshop was on. The shop itself was tiny and managed to look like it had closed down long ago. Freaky Bob was not remotely interested in attracting customers. Everyone knew or would come to find out that he was the best repairer of computers in the south of England and he was more likely to turn people away if he didn't like their attitude, politics or, on at least two occasions, haircut. He liked to exchange his skills for the skills of others, believing that a reliance on money was at heart a surrender to the capitalist system. Freaky Bob could do anything with computers, indeed the view of the world they offered him was so acute they had simply convinced him that his worst teenage fears were true: the planet was full of self-interested, money grabbing, small-minded capitalists who would sell body parts of family members on ebay if they thought their username could not be tracked back to them. And, when they weren't using the World Wide Web to screw someone they can't see, they were using it to watch other people having sex they are not enjoying with people they don't like, or arguing with strangers about absolute bollocks. In short, Freaky Bob's genius was also his curse and he had one of those plastic cards above his shop counter that said that very thing.

Even though it was seven-thirty, Adam knew that Freaky Bob would be sitting in his shop messing around with the back of a phone or computer. Adam believed he did this to test the resolve of his customers. Freaky Bob rarely opened during what people might consider ordinary opening times, reasoning that if people really wanted him they would come often enough to find him open. Anyway, given his range of interests and the many time zones they occurred in, he kept unusual hours.

Adam walked into the shop wearing his pork pie hat and carrying a small shoulder bag. Freaky Bob didn't look up. Neither man spoke but Adam placed a book on the counter: *Essays on Marx's Theory of Value* by Isaac Rubin. 'Thanks, Freaky Bob.'

'You're welcome Adam. I was curious mate, what did you get yourself into?'

'I'll be honest, I was hoping you'd ask.' Adam took two bottles of beer from his bag. 'In short, I'd really like your help.'

Freaky Bob stopped what he was doing and looked up. 'Simple hacking?'

'No,' said Adam.

'Important?' Freaky Bob was a large man with a thick bushy beard that made his eyes appear darker and more intense than an uncovered puffy face would.

'Yeah,' Adam nodded. 'Wouldn't ask otherwise.'

'Tell me. Not what you need me to do, tell me why it needs to happen.'

'Needs to stay between us, mate,' said Adam. Freaky Bob nodded and Adam filled him on pretty much everything, saving his own analysis of David Cassells until last.

'I don't know if he was responsible for the fire that hurt the woman Anna worked with or for running the stories about Stern. I personally doubt it: I don't think he has the balls. I do know he is responsible for covering up what he, and maybe others, will consider an insignificant and annoying piece of research that could, if it were in the world, affect millions of people. It is the smallness of his world that gives him power in a way, that and the fact that he can hide behind something that is supposed to be trusted.'

Freaky Bob took a swig of beer and pulled his laptop toward him. 'It's not just the money that moves these people, Adam, it's the power. As long as everyone assumes that psychiatry or medicine or whatever it is that is being sold and the industry that provides it is humanity at its best, the industry and all who sail in her can rest easy. Usually, the only thing we have that suggests drugs are not the best thing for everything is ridiculous hippy nonsense like crystal healing or that magic water bollocks.'

'Funny you should say that...'

'Oh Adam, you're not going to tell me you buy into homeopathy?'

'Good god, no. Anna met this boy when she was on the run and he told her something, something that someone told me—well, they didn't tell me as such but they hinted—a very long time ago and it's ludicrous and absurd. He said that he was a former patient and he helped current patients now by giving them tea made from fresh dew, and that it... cured people.' Freaky Bob stared at him and Adam laughed. 'Look, I cannot abide all that alternative therapy nonsense. I think it's just cottage industries that thrive on people's desperation in nice-smelling rooms, but this... this dew nonsense feels different.'

'Why?'

Adam shook his head. Because of the coincidence that stretched across a quarter of a century? Because both he and Anna had been bound by it?

'I think...' he said hesitantly. 'I think it is because nobody is selling it. It's a couple of patients saying 'Look, you have never heard of this, you people didn't think of it, you are not bringing it to us in a syringe or a bottle or in the form of a shiatsu massage or steeped in ylang ylang. This is ours. We do it in spite of you.'

Freaky Bob had been tapping away on his laptop as he listened. He raised his considerable eyebrows and said: 'Sorry Adam, sounds as though you are reaching a bit there, mate.'

Adam nodded. 'Yeah, I can see that, but I think the thing is...' he hesitated, swigging from his bottle and staring at the wall. 'It's the fact that I feel the need to reach... because there is something there making me want to make sense of nonsense, even after all the things I have seen.'

'What's that then?'

'Possibility? Resistance? I don't know. I think maybe it's just the possibility of doing something in spite of reason, outside of the rules.'

Freaky Bob shrugged. 'Maybe you ought to just try it, then.'

'We're going to, I think, tomorrow evening on a young man, if he's willing. But it's only tea...'

'Do you know that your Dr Cassells counts three senior policemen, two MP's and three journalists on national newspapers among his 'ex-patients'?'

'How do you know that?'

'He has a file called ex-patients on his computer. And another called 'ex-coll'. I assume colleagues. He has little biographies and contact details on all of them.'

'How do you know that?'

Freaky Bob turned his laptop round to face Adam. 'This is his desktop, these are his files. This is like having his computer in front of us.'

'You can do that?'

Answering the question was beneath him. Instead, he said: 'My mother believes she's the Duchess of Windsor.'

'I didn't know that, mate. I'm sorry.'

Freaky Bob shrugged again. 'S'alright in itself, she isn't unhappy. Unless she goes out, then she thinks everyone is watching her and someone might attack her on behalf of the Queen Mother.'

Adam nodded and tried not to smile.

Freaky Bob glanced up at him and grinned. 'Stigma,' he said, and Adam smiled. Freaky Bob paused for a moment. 'How about I help you hang this self-important tosser out to dry and you make my mum a nice cup of tea?'

The next morning Adam opened the shop early, aware of the fact he would close again at 10.15. However, at 9.45, when Grimy Nige and Jim arrived and he told them he had to close up in half an hour, Jim said, with Grimy Nige standing beside him nodding earnestly: 'Mr Sands, we both know that we spend an awful lot of time in here not spending very much money. You have never made us feel anything other than welcome and we like being here. Near the books. Doing something helpful. How about we look after the shop? Please?'

So Adam went to meet Alison wearing warmer clothes and carrying a short wet suit and two fishing rods. Alison was waiting for him by the boat. She nodded and smiled but she seemed more distant, her movements smaller, her body pulling in on itself. Or, thought Adam, perhaps that is my eyes.

What cloud there was was in the distance and the sun offered a beautiful autumnal light. The tide was close to turning and the sea looked flat, although the boat could feel some movement. As Adam rowed Alison put on sunglasses and looked over his shoulder and out to sea.

'What did your brother think of the basement?'

'He liked it. He thought he could stock two thousand LPs down there and maybe another two thousand CD's.'

'And he could get that sort of stock?'

'He already has most of it. He collects, not as a collector collects, you know, in order to own. He collects because so many people don't want old records and even CD's. He thinks he can look after them until someone comes along who wants them.'

'Pretty good premise for a shop,' smiled Adam.

'Look, I'm not trying to rush you or anything.' Alison took off her sunglasses. 'But I know you would have to make some changes to the shop, to make it possible for people to go downstairs. I'm willing to pay for those and we'll pay rent.'

'OK,' said Adam.

'How much rent do you want?' she asked.

'£25 a week plus a share of the bills ought to do it.'

'That doesn't seem very much.'

'We'll start there, let the boy settle, take it from there. How well do you know David Cassells?'

Anna meanwhile had risen early: it was still dark when she crept down the stairs in the small B and B and found her son waiting for her by the door. 'What are you doing up?'

'I'm coming to help. Laura is asleep and I thought it might be a chance for a bit of quality mum-and-son time.' And he smiled, a bit like the smile he had on his face when he had overtaken her in height and hugged her for the first time, alluding to being the protector, to being grown up.

'You don't think this is a tiny bit ridiculous?' she asked, smiling back and opening the door.

'Oh it's completely ridiculous, but I like it when you're ridiculous.'

It was cold outside and Anna slipped her arm through her son's as they walked away from the seaside and toward where Adam had told them there was a large park.

'I thought you were staying in Manchester because you didn't want to come home,' said Anna.

'Funny the fears we keep to ourselves, Mum. I thought my biological father might be a raging psychopath.'

'Well, to be fair the jury is still out, Tom.'

Tom laughed. 'I suppose in some ways it doesn't matter, does it? Not in the way it would have mattered when I was a kid. If I had known who he was when I was eight, or if I knew what his story was, I would look for me in him before I was even me. I would look for the bits that demonstrate the genetic link and maybe even shape myself around them... Do you know what I mean?'

'I think so. Adam said something similar.' Tom nodded. 'Are you very angry with me?' she asked. 'That you don't know, didn't know, were robbed of knowing...?'

'I don't think so. I think you could have trusted me more, I suppose.'

"And is Laura your revenge for that?'

'No mum, Laura is my fiancée, that's a whole other thing.'

'I didn't mean—'

'I know, but I love her. The secret... Maybe that was revenge, although I think we both needed to have something that was ours, and maybe you made me feel secrets are just normal.' He squeezed his mothers arm to his ribs as they walked. 'I don't think you realize what doing your job cost you, mum.'

'I ran away from home, Tom. When I was sixteen. My brother was abused by a bloke and my parents—I loved my parents very much, especially my dad, I suppose—they sort of ignored it, they didn't act and I couldn't bear that. It made me sick and angry, so I left and I never ever went back. I told you they were dead because they were to me. They probably are now, but to me they were the moment I left and I think that was my secret, so everything that related to it became a secret.'

'What about your brother?'

'I heard, I met someone in a pub once who used to know Ian, he said he'd become unwell. Nervous breakdown, he said. I never had a clue what that meant. That was a long time ago.'

'Is that why you became a nurse?'

Anna shrugged.

When they got to the park the mix of the rising sun and the low buzzing street lamp made the dew on the grass sing with light. Anna had never seen the dew so clearly, or simply never looked.

'You know this is stupid, right?' she said to Tom as they walked through a small metal gate in the iron railings into an undulating expanse of green that could, if it were flatter and more engaged, have offered six or seven football pitches. As it was, it simply sloped down toward some trees and what looked like an old chalk pit.

'Yes, I know.'

'It's actually mad.'

'Well I don't know about that, mum.' Tom said. 'But I think that sometimes it doesn't do any harm to do something mad. To be honest, if you hadn't been prepared to do that when you were around my age I wouldn't be here, would I?'

They got down on their hands and knees and started to gather dew from the grass and the fallen leaves and Anna began to laugh.

After a while Tom said: 'Mum?'

'Yes, Tom?'

'Do you think he is a better guitarist than me?'

Anna laughed louder. 'I don't know, Tom, but he did say, coming back in the car, that if you two got on he might teach you to play guitar properly.'

'Cheeky sod,' said Tom. He paused, then added: 'Unless he's really good. Do you think he might be really good?'

'Who is David Cassells?' Alison was looking quizzically at Adam as he slowed his rowing and stared at her.

'Really?' he said, frowning.

'Yes, really. Who is he?'

'He's a psychologist.'

'Well, we don't all live in a big house like The Monkees,' she said.

'He is a corrupt, sadistic, manipulative man who re-entered my life at the exact moment you came into my shop. Coincidences make me uncomfortable, so I thought I'd better ask.'

'Where does he work?'

'He works for someone called CREAK.'

'They are like a research committee, aren't they?'

Adam shrugged. 'Alison, I don't quite get you and partly that troubles me and partly it interests me. Now, given that you want to rent my basement, which would require some ongoing contact between us, I'd kind of like us to be as open as we can be with each other.' She looked uncomfortable. Adam put the anchor down and began to bait the fishing lines. 'You look uncomfortable,' he said.

'Do you think I've been flirting?' She sounded defensive, almost afraid.

He shrugged. 'Not indecently. Not in any way that need matter.' He felt as if he were reassuring a Victorian woman who might faint at any moment.

Alison was looking at the water. 'I suppose you might think I was only after your basement,' she smiled, slipping from embarrassed to self-aware. 'Which is probably better than you thinking the basement became a reason to...' She shrugged and nodded toward the sea.

'To come fishing?' Adam laughed.

'Yes Mr Sands, to bob around on a boat in a fleece not catching fish and wondering if you are going to leap into the sea like Marine Boy again.'

'How about...' Adam began to take off his fleece and the shirt underneath. 'I go for a swim, and when I come back I tell you a story.' He took off his trousers and pulled his shortie wet suit over his trunks. He put some neoprene shoes on, slipped on his goggles, nodded to Alison and slid into the water. It was cold and it made him catch his breath as the water leaked into the zip and began to settle against his skin. He put his face into the water and began to swim. The coldness stung his cheeks but he stretched out his stroke slowly and felt his back lengthen in the water. He turned and floated on his back. The air was cold on his face, the sky a light blue. He had his breath now and he felt his fingers relax.

Sometimes, he thought, it's OK to just take a chance. If your instinct tells you someone is good, then let them be good until they stop being. He would fish for a while and he would tell Alison, the cute but odd psychologist—traditionally at least two of his least favourite things—about the boy who told Anna about the dew, about the boy he saw as he held a dead man who was hanging from a tree and ask her... No, not ask her: see if she asks if her brother could have some tea. He turned again, looking first out to sea toward the horizon and then spinning slowly round toward the boat, only to see Alison swimming breast-stroke toward him. She was grinning and breathing heavily.

'It's not that cold,' she said. 'And I'm not even wearing a wetsuit.'

Adam, Anna, Tom and Laura were ready. They all had wine. Laura and Tom had commandeered the piece of floor next to the record player and Tom kept looking at the guitar on its stand and trying not to pick it up. When the doorbell to the shop rang, Adam looked at Anna, who nodded. She went downstairs and he went to the kitchen to continue to cook and to create the illusion of more space. Anna returned and said 'It's, er, Freaky Bob and his mum.' Freaky Bob nodded at everyone and stood in the middle of the floor being enormous, with his tall, thin-faced and wide-eyed mother standing just behind him.

'It's not grand, is it?' she said smiling.

Adam took the five steps from the open plan kitchen to where Freaky Bob stood. 'Sit down mate, you make the place look small.' And then, to his mother: 'What do I call you?'

'Mrs Simpson is fine,' she said waving regally.

'I'm Adam,' he said.

'Of course you are, dear.'

Freaky Bob sat down on the three-person sofa, leaving space for one other person. 'I suggest a sweepstake, Adam,' he called out. 'BBC News. We all draw a number from one to six.'

'What do you mean?' asked Anna.

Freaky Bob smiled. 'Just pick a number, we all put a fiver in, winner takes the pot.'

Anna looked at Adam, who smiled and nodded. 'OK,' she said 'I'm in.'

'I'm in too,' said Mrs Simpson. 'Freaky Bob, cover my stake please. You know I don't carry money on my person.'

'OK, mum.'

The doorbell went again and Tom jumped up. 'I'll go.'

'What exactly is the sweepstake for, er, Freaky Bob?' asked Anna.

Freaky Bob folded his enormous arms and smiled, which made his eyes disappear. 'There will be a story about your Dr Cassells, and the bet is to see if it will be the first, second, third, or if it will trail in last after the funny one and the football results.'

Tom reappeared with Alison.

'Jonathan will be along later. He says please eat without him,' she said. 'Believe it or not, he's gone to a record fair in Whitstable.'

'Hello.' Anna stepped forward and put her hand out. 'I'm Anna.' Alison smiled and shook her hand and Laura poured wine.

'I told him about your tea... idea.' Alison was looking from Adam to Anna and back again. 'He said he would love to try a cup, please,' she said quietly.

'You know what's silly?' said Anna. 'We have no idea what we are doing, do we? I mean I'm not knocking it, it's just that, well... supposing tea made from fresh dew works, right?' She paused waiting for someone to say 'Oh for goodness sake we're all fucking insane!' but nobody did so she continued: 'Suppose it works, or it could work but it doesn't if the person drinking it is on medication, or...' she pointed at the wine, 'has drunk alcohol or—'

'Has grey hair or blue eyes or too many vowels in their name,' said Adam, nodding. 'I know, but this isn't a randomized controlled trial is it?' He was talking quietly and staring at the floor. 'At best it's whimsy, at worst it's despair. It's mad, we're mad, we know that. I don't think it matters.'

They were quiet until Anna said: 'Jonathan? Your brother?'

'My father's name,' said Alison.

'Apparently I'm named after my grandfather,' said Tom. Anna reddened.

'I think that's kind of cool,' said Laura.

'Did you name me after dad, mum?' Freaky Bob said loudly.

'No dear, his name was Reginald. You know that, you met him that time.'

'I know mum, I was just joking.'

Mrs Simpson turned to Adam and smiled and said: 'As if I would take up with anyone called Freaky Bob. Will you be making tea, dear?'

'Tea a little later, Mrs Simpson, when Jonathan gets here. Now we eat. We caught this fish earlier.' Adam smiled at Alison.

'Is it a big boat?' Anna winked conspiratorially at Alison. 'Does it have staff and sails?'

Alison laughed. 'I wondered that. It has two oars. I'm not convinced they match.'

They ate. Freaky Bob told them what the Roswell files said and who had killed JFK. They believed him. Alison talked about her work as an educational psychologist and how she was still adjusting to living in a corner of Kent. Tom and Laura talked about how they had hidden their relationship from their respective mothers for the best part of five years and how they had had sex in Anna's kitchen three years ago. Anna didn't smile but took some small comfort from the fact that she had changed her worktops since then. Adam talked about Greece and Tom asked him how much money he had made from the songs he had sold. Adam shrugged. 'I get a cheque each year,' he said. 'It gets smaller, I get older.'

'Have you heard him play guitar?' Freaky Bob asked Tom. Tom shook his head. 'Plays like an angel,' Freaky Bob muttered. 'But anyway it's nearly time for the news. Have you got a piece of paper?' Adam gave him a sheet of paper from a notebook beside the records and Freaky Bob tore it into strips and wrote a number on each piece of paper. He folded them up and Adam handed him his hat to put the paper in. 'Everyone put your fiver in.' Everyone obediently put £5 on the table and Adam collected it together and put it under the near-empty wine bottle. Then Freaky Bob passed the hat round and everyone took a number out.

'I got 0,' said Mrs Simpson.

'Still in with a chance mum, the story might not have made it to the BBC yet,' said Freaky Bob.

'I have six,' said Tom.

'Four,' said Laura.'

'I have one,' smiled Adam.

They put the small television on and waited.

'Can I just say,' said Anna, 'that I have no idea who you are, or why you are called Freaky Bob, but you have got me so that I am completely believing the fact that there is going to be a story about David Cassells on the news.'

Freaky Bob looked hurt. 'It's my name,' he said.

The dramatic rush-to-attention news music began and the newsreader narrowed her eyes even further and said something about an explosion at sea on an American cruise liner and then something very serious about the Chancellor of the Exchequer and the still-failing economy and then: 'A leading government advisor on mental health care is suspected of leaking research findings in an apparent act of contrition following his own attempts to bury the results and smear the lead researcher responsible for them.'

'Oh my, we have a winner.'

'Ohh,' said Alison. 'Is that the one we were waiting for? I have that. I have number three.'

Freaky Bob bathed in the afterglow as they waited for the full report. Adam was smiling and nodding. Anna was just staring at him. 'How did you...?'

'Let's hear the story, then I'll explain,' he said.

'He's very clever,' said Mrs Simpson. 'He can mend anything. I wish he'd get himself a girlfriend.'

When the news expanded its headline it did so with a picture of Cassells and one or two raised eyebrows from the newsreader. It seems that Dr David Cassells—Chief Operating Officer of CREAK, a government quango, yes they called it that— responsible for co-ordinating and disseminating key medical research, had tried to cover up a piece of research that seriously draws into question the effectiveness of anti-psychotic drugs and raises the possibility that other, less invasive treatments might be more effective. Cue a picture of heroic rock star and the initials CCT on the screen. The newsreader dropped her eyebrow and said that while a spokesperson for the pharmaceutical industry welcomed the findings they expressed concern at the statement issued by Dr Cassells. 'Unconfirmed reports tonight suggest that another member of the research team was injured recently in a house fire that the police are treating as suspicious. Dr Cassells was not available for comment but police this evening said they would like to talk to him urgently.'

'How the bloody hell did you do that?' asked Anna.

'It was quite easy really,' said Freaky Bob. 'Once Adam had connected me to the computer when he was in his office I never logged off of it. I had access to everything and I could send anything I wanted from his hard drive. He had the report. All I had to do was send it to the BBC and one or two newspapers. I chose the Sunday Times and the Morning Star, with a letter.

'Did you write the letter?' asked Anna.

'No, Adam did.'

'What will happen to him, I wonder?' Anna said. But she didn't care.

What she couldn't know was that at that moment former lover and advertising director Black Portier was tidying up. If Black was in bed with someone and they asked him to tell them a story, it would no longer be a story of wistful romance. It wouldn't be set in Greece and tell of young if vaguely tragic lovers. It wouldn't be a story about people reaching for themselves, but rather a story about problem solving.

Someone had called him once, when he was in the middle of a project, and they had asked him what he was doing. 'I'm doing the ironing,' he had said, without thinking. The other person had laughed, but it had felt accurate. It was what he did: he ironed over the little catches and creases and he made things smooth. Smoothness made him feel warm and safe.

'Do you have him? No, you can't hurt him. Yes, I know he is annoying, think how I feel. OK yes, just the once, but don't leave a mark. So what did he say? Well of course he is denying it but I'm sure you can get past that. Look, before he vanishes it would be helpful if you could find out why he did it, who paid him, that kind of thing? If not, do what you do. Well no, I think in principle a fire would be fine but I can't help thinking it's a bit samey. Yes, the river would be better. No, leave Stern, he is going to be untouchable now. And the woman, leave her too. The story is out there now, we can't change that. We might be able to change its impact though. I'll start that tomorrow.'

Adam didn't feel very much at all. Not at first. He had a sense of something feeling better in some way, freer even, but he also had a sense that his small contact with the world was passing now. These people would be returning to their lives and he returning to the stillness, changed but remaining. If he was honest with himself, he hadn't acted in defence of or solidarity with Anna. He had acted instinctively in order to stay beside people who offered his past back to him without venom. When he found out it was Cassells involved, it pleased him. Whatever Cassells did to Anna or to anyone else couldn't make Adam dislike him more than he had the moment he had walked into the ward round twenty-four years earlier and simply existed. That instinctive distaste had been visceral, the sense that this man, who Adam had originally greeted like an assault, made everything they all did appear more respectable than it was and brought a legitimacy to the things they did to Michael, Maureen, Libby and Graham. And the things they let happen to each other as a consequence.

And it wasn't that Adam thought about those days or those people or what he had seen, been or done. He didn't. He never thought about them. Not even when he woke in the night with a sore back and a sense of his own creeping mortality. Because he didn't need to think of them, they were there: in his skin, along with every lover and every mistake he had ever experienced. He had in these last few days gently accepted the opportunity to live with those experiences closer to his conscious mind, not hidden near his spleen, and he had the good grace not to call it redemption or indeed anything much at all.

'You OK?' Adam said to Anna.

'Yeah, I'm going to call Paul's son, Simon. Can I use your bedroom?'

'Of course,' he said.

The doorbell sounded as Anna left the room and Alison stood up immediately. She looked at Adam, who nodded and smiled, and she went downstairs.

He could hear Alison coming up the stairs and the muffled sound of conversation and then they emerged from the hallway, all self-conscious and—in the young man's case, at least—cold. He was a tall, good-looking, thin young man with bright blue eyes wearing blue jeans and a grey canvas jacket zipped up tight to the neck. His hair was curly and light brown and he was more alert than shy.

'Everyone, this is Jonathan. He is my brother.'

'Hello, sorry I am late. The train service around here is not always reliable.' He was well spoken and he moved his attention in a slightly conscious way from person to person as he spoke. Learned social skills, mannered and awkward but polite and touching. Finally he rested his gaze on Adam. Adam stared at him. Jonathan nodded. 'Hello.'

Adam nodded too. 'Hello.' He swallowed hard and felt a stinging behind his eyes, unfamiliar, like swimming without goggles. Like staring into the rain.

It was the sense of familiarity that filled him. Adam found himself breathing in deeply through his nose, trying unconsciously to smell his presence, It was his body that spoke first, fumbling for a foothold in the past, buzzing with a sense of recognition. His breathing followed, becoming faster, working

326

harder, straining slightly as if he were holding a heavy weight. It wasn't the same young man, it couldn't be, but he was similar: same height, same eyes, same hair. He wasn't as healthy, Adam could see that in his movements and hear it in his voice but if his body was less sedated, less restricted, he could be, almost.

Anna came back into the room and she was smiling. 'Paul's home, he is so relieved—' She stopped when she saw Jonathan and stared at him.

'Hello,' he said quietly. 'My name is Jonathan.'

Anna nodded and paused for a moment. 'I'm Anna,' she said and coughed nervously. 'I'm sorry for staring. For a moment I thought I recognized you. Have we met before?'

'I don't think so,' said Jonathan, blushing slightly.

'Would you like something to eat?' said Adam, not moving.

Jonathan smiled. 'No thank you. How are you? It's good to meet you. Alison likes you.' Still quiet, a man practicing social skills with a self-consciousness he could hear in himself but not hide. He spoke rhythmically and more like an old man than a young brother.

'I'm OK,' Adam said. 'How are you?'

Jonathan nodded as if he was thinking about the question. Adam waited. 'I am having a good day so far.'

'Me too,' said Adam. 'Shall I put the kettle on?'

Jonathan nodded again. He looked as if he was going to say something but the words wouldn't form. Alison looked at him, wondering how to hold the moment for him the way carers do. 'I wanted to say...' He was looking at the floor but his body was facing Adam. 'That if it doesn't work... I mean I don't want you to get upset or anything.'

It was the first time the reason why they were here had been made explicit. Tom and Laura looked at each other. Freaky Bob shuffled a tiny bit closer to Mrs Simpson and Alison opened her mouth to speak, but Anna spoke first. 'Thank you,' she said softly.

Jonathan lifted his head to face her and nodded. 'No,' he said. 'Thank you.'

Adam bit his lip. He closed his eyes and let a little more of the past in. How long had he stood there? How long had he held Tim, hoping life back into him, too afraid to be that close to death again, that close to failure again? He felt his eyes burn, he opened and closed them quickly and felt the dampness seep slowly on to his face. He felt the tightness in his chest ease and his lungs open, as if he were swimming. He wanted to move, he wanted to make tea but he just stood still, facing the boy, unknown but familiar nonetheless.

Someone had come eventually, if only to give him permission to let go, to leave. Something like kindness had appeared in the darkness and saved him. Maybe this moment, this absurd fairy-dust-and-dew moment, was a chance to give it back, not as a constructed act of charity—a well cooked meal, a business arrangement whereby he rent out his basement—but as something more permanent, more sustaining: possibility.

'They say it's the hope that kills you,' he said.

'They're wrong,' Jonathan whispered.

Adam nodded and opened his eyes.

# Footnote

Michael Wells lives in a large house in Oxfordshire run by a mental health charity. He is sixty, overweight and quiet but his voices are well controlled on a relatively low dose of a new anti-psychotic. The house he shares with six other people with a similar diagnosis has a large garden where they grow vegetables and keep chickens. Michael likes to feed the chickens. He always wears a beanie hat. He likes Emmerdale and smokes heavily. Every Christmas he and Grace exchange cards. Grace always tells him something about her life or the year just past. She has enclosed photographs of herself and Laura and once sent a picture of their pet tortoise. Michael's is simply signed 'Michael Alan Wells.'

Nobody has called Maureen Marley anything but George since the mid 1990s. Not because of any gender reassignment but because they simply don't have to. George works for London Transport driving a tube train. He lives alone in a small flat near Kings Cross. He is a season ticket holder at Chelsea, plays cards with work friends most Thursdays and goes to church on Sunday to talk to his God. Nobody knows what he prays for. It isn't really anybody's business but his.

Libby Hoffman died peacefully in her sleep four weeks short of her hundredth birthday. She was cremated, even though she didn't have a body.

# The Soundtrack

1.  *The Damage Is Done*   Paul Quinn and The Independent Group
2.  *This Woman's Work*   Kate Bush
3.  *Stranger Than Kindness*   Nick Cave and the Bad Seeds
4.  *In The Wee Small Hours...*   Frank Sinatra
5.  *Parade*   White and Torch
6.  *In My Secret Life*   Leonard Cohen
7.  *Pour A Little Poison*   David Ford
8.  *Strange Fruit*   Billie Holliday
9.  *Who Knows Where The Time Goes*   Sandy Denny
10. *A Prisoner Of The Past*   Prefab Sprout
11. *Seascape*   Tracy Thorn
12. *After Dark*   Paul Buchanan
13. *Where Are We Now*   David Bowie
14. *Alone Apart*   Glen Hansard and Marketa Irglova
15. *You Could Be Forgiven*   Horse
16. *The Turns We Take*   Tindersticks
17. *Lemonworld*   The National
18. *Strangers When We Meet*   David Bowie

# Acknowledgements

I'd like to thank Kate, in part for watching such rubbish TV that I was forced from the living room to a place where I might write but mostly of course for just getting it. I'd also like to thank Celia Hunt, Jamie Auld, Jess Moriarty, Kate Mason, Leonora Rustamova, Bonnie A. Powell and Tilly Bones for their helpful reading and insights. Lin Webb for her editorial diligence and care. Kevin and Hetha at Bluemoose for doing what they do so well. And last but not least I need to thank my daughter Maia who came up with the Dew idea on a long and funny walk beside the sea in the days before she was embarrassed to hold my hand.

# GABRIEL'S ANGEL

## by Mark A Radcliffe

Gabriel Bell is a grumpy 44-year-old web journalist irritated by the accumulating disappointments of life. He and his girlfriend Ellie want to start a family but Gabriel has so few sperm he can name them and knit them flippers. So it's IVF, which is expensive. If losing his job was bad enough getting run over and waking up to find himself in a therapy group run by Angels just beneath heaven really annoys him. And it doesn't do much for Ellie either. Gabriel is joined therapy by Kevin a professional killer, Yvonne, Kevin's last victim, a rarely sober but successful businesswoman and Julie, an art teacher who was driving the car that put Gabriel in a coma. In a rural therapeutic community set in an eternal September the group struggles with the therapy. If they do well they may be allowed to go back to earth to finish their lives, or pass into heaven. If they don't it's Hell or worse: lots more therapy.

'You might think you'd rather die than go through group therapy, but what if death was no escape? Gabriel's Angel is the perfect antidote to the glib platitudes of emotional quick-fix culture: tender, astute and very, very funny.'

Christopher Brookmyre

£7.99

## Also available on Kindle